## THE SUMMER OF BRO

England, 1950s: While out playing in the woods, ten-year-old Mark meets a man living in an old railway carriage. Despite his wild appearance, the stranger, who introduces himself as Aubrey Hillyard, is captivating — an irreverent outsider who is shunned by Mark's fellow villagers, and a writer to boot. Aubrey encourages Mark to tell stories about a novel he is writing — a work of ominous science fiction. As the meddling villagers plot to drive Aubrey out, Mark finds himself caught between two worlds — yet convinced that he must help Aubrey prevail at any cost . . .

## SPECIAL MESSAGE TO READERS

## THE ULVERSCROFT FOUNDATION
**(registered UK charity number 264873)**

was established in 1972 to provide funds for research, diagnosis and treatment of eye diseases. Examples of major projects funded by the Ulverscroft Foundation are:-

- The Children's Eye Unit at Moorfields Eye Hospital, London
- The Ulverscroft Children's Eye Unit at Great Ormond Street Hospital for Sick Children
- Funding research into eye diseases and treatment at the Department of Ophthalmology, University of Leicester
- The Ulverscroft Vision Research Group, Institute of Child Health
- Twin operating theatres at the Western Ophthalmic Hospital, London
- The Chair of Ophthalmology at the Royal Australian College of Ophthalmologists

You can help further the work of the Foundation by making a donation or leaving a legacy. Every contribution is gratefully received. If you would like to help support the Foundation or require further information, please contact:

# The Summer of Broken Stories

James Wilson

LARGE
PRINT

First published in Great Britain 2015
by
Alma Books Limited

First Isis Edition
published 2016
by arrangement with
Alma Books Limited



*A catalogue record for this book is available from the British Library.*

ISBN 978–1–78541–188–5 (hb)
ISBN 978–1–78541–194–6 (pb)

Published by
F. A. Thorpe (Publishing)
Anstey, Leicestershire

Set by Words & Graphics Ltd.
Anstey, Leicestershire
Printed and bound in Great Britain by
T. J. International Ltd., Padstow, Cornwall

This book is printed on acid-free paper

FOR PAULA, TOM AND KIT
AND ALL MY FAMILY

# CHAPTER ONE

It's as if for years you've had a picture on your wall. A country scene: beech trees, a smocked man with a reddish beard, two children, a dog. You know it so well that you've stopped thinking about it, or even looking at it. You could describe it blindfold: a story about the cusp between innocence and knowledge, set in a long-lost English summer. All possible questions about it were exhausted decades ago. It's just *there*, a permanent feature of your universe, fixed for all time under its crazed screed of varnish.

You get the idea? There must be an image like that in *your* life.

And then, out of the blue, something happens to you. It's only a tiny incident, but it's followed, a few weeks later, by another. And then another. To begin with, they appear quite trivial, and completely unrelated — just the irksome throwaway packaging of modern existence: an unsolicited email, suggesting an inexplicable knowledge of your private life; a stalemate encounter with the bank; the byzantine aftermath of a minor road accident. It doesn't for an instant occur to you that they might have anything to do with our pastoral scene at all. The distance between the two worlds is simply too great.

Or so, at least, you'd have imagined — until one day, you're hurrying past, and glimpse the picture out of the corner of your eye.

Bam! It's different. Something about the expressions on the figures' faces. The faint reverberations of what they've just said, or are about to say. A voice you haven't heard in half a century wells up in your head: dead phrases return suddenly to life, ringing with a startling, unsuspected meaning. You try to wrap them in their shrouds again, put everything back, restore the *status quo ante*, but it's too late. The damage has been done.

You can't resolve the problem just by tinkering, that's for sure. No good simply removing the dirty patina: all that will do is show the change in brighter colours. No, you have to find a way to re-enter the scene yourself, live it over again. Only then will you know whether the story you've always told yourself — the story, comforting in its moral simplicity, that has come to define you — is the whole truth. What's required, in fact, is something like a time machine.

So, no more trembling on the threshold: we have to go back. The globe rotating anti-clockwise. Time racing the wrong way, one of those old speeded-up films — London to Edinburgh in fifteen minutes — in reverse, the panting Mallard sucked into the maw of tunnels, hauled by the tail through embankments, skipping over points, giving you the momentary illusion that, if you ran the projector forward again, you might see the train lurch in another direction altogether, left rather than straight on, and end up somewhere entirely different. We're unravelling history, turning Barratt homes back into fields, uninventing the personal computer, mobile phones, the Internct. All those children unborn, wars unfought, songs unsung, disasters unendured. All that life unlived.

Thirty years now. Forty, forty-five. Almost there. Whoa. Slow down. Yes, yes: look. Scarcely believable. We've arrived.

Hills, trees, a village high street. Even from our vantage point, high above them, everything looks strange: half familiar and half exotic. Filling station — two upright pumps like Pez dispensers, and a cream-coloured coach poking its nose out of the garage at the back; blacksmith; post office (a woman wearing a billowy skirt is just going in, clutching her drab brown savings book). Three or four bulbous cars, parked self-importantly in front of little clapboard cottages. An old geezer in a felt hat travelling from door to door, sharpening knives and scissors. He has wispy Prince Albert whiskers and — though you can't see it from up here — is totally toothless. *He*, you think, doesn't just appear quaintly old-fashioned: he seems like a figure from a completely different age.

That's time travel for you: nothing's ever entirely what you expected. That old chestnut Class, for instance. Yes, it's a constant presence here, discernible (if you know what to look for) in clothes, haircuts, posture — above all, in the way people speak. And yes, it can be mean and ugly, stunting lives. But *lived*, rather than seen from the outside, it isn't straightforward: money despises poverty; poverty despises trade; spinsters in decayed country houses, and displaced ex-public schoolboys struggling to make ends meet in cottages, look down on well-to-do farmers and garage owners — who in turn (behind a façade of respect) look down on them, as the feckless vestiges of unearned privilege, bereft of common sense, and incapable of doing an honest day's work. From day to day, the village exists in a state of uneasy truce. And yet the endless variety of human character and experience creates odd connections across the battle lines, unforeseen moments of fraternization in No Man's Land.

Confused? Don't worry: you'll be amazed how quickly you get used to it all.

At the top of the street is a war memorial: a white cross planted on a plinth carved with names. Next to it stands the Fox and Hounds, four-square, red-brick, a kid's drawing of a house, with a little black sign over the door: *H. Doggett. Licensed to sell Beers, Wines, Spirits & Tobacco*. After three hours in suspended animation, it's just re-opened for business, and farm labourers are trickling in to the dim coolness of the public bar, snuffing at the smoky liquorice smell that means the end of the day's work.

But we're not joining them, not this evening. Instead we pan down to the end of the street, past a larger house in its own grounds (let's just quickly note the name, Hillfield, as we skim by: we'll be going there again), then off to the left, where a deep-rutted cart track runs between a wheat field — coppery now, in the evening summer light — and a wood. Halfway along it stands a boy. He's almost ten — pale, thin-faced, as if the sculptor had pinched the clay too tight — dressed in a white Aertex shirt and khaki shorts. He's not wearing a watch, but you can tell from the way he squints over his shoulder at the sun that he's worried about the time. He frowns and bites his lip, then turns back to the trees and shouts, "Barney! Barney!"

He waits, listening for a response. But all he hears is birdsong, and the far-off drone of a tractor. After a few seconds he calls again, louder this time:

"Barney! Come here, boy!"

Still nothing. He hesitates, then hunts for a stick and plunges into the trees, slashing a path through the undergrowth. After a couple of hundred yards, something stops him. Not a sound: a smell — the pungent, unseasonal rasp of woodsmoke. Who would light a fire in the woods at this time of year? A tramp? One of the gypsies Mr Montgomery warned him about? Do gypsies steal dogs? He's not sure.

He half-crouches, tightening his grip on the stick. He's never penetrated this far before — Twenty Acre is the gamekeeper's territory, tricky with traps — but he's always imagined the heart of the wood to be darker and more densely overgrown than the edges. Now, though, as he worms forward through the undergrowth, another smell hits him: the sappy sharpness of newly cut branches. A moment later, a patch of sunlit green opens out ahead. It's dotted with sapling stumps and untidy mounds of twigs and leaves, and long tangled strands of bramble like barbed wire.

He hesitates. Not a tramp — a tramp would never make a clearing like this. If it's the gypsies, they've no more right to be here than he has — but still they might attack him, and take his pocket money. If it's the gamekeeper, or one of the men from the farm, on the other hand, his one-and-ninepence will be safe, but he'll be reported for trespassing. He feels the burn of Mr Pointer's huge fingers twisting his ear, sees Dad's frown, the disappointed frisk of his head . . .

He whistles, so softly that a person wouldn't hear it, but a dog might. There's an odd sound, like someone wrestling with a sack of grain, but no sign of Barney. Still clutching his stick, he inches into the clearing on hands and knees.

This is the place. This is the moment.

A glint of glass, an unexpected flash of blue. He stops, blinks, looks again. No, he wasn't mistaken: it's a railway carriage. Even before he's fully registered his surprise at finding it there, some other area of his brain has identified it: a pre-First World War Great Northern passenger coach. The blue, which covers half of it, gives him a physical pain, like the snap of a rubber band. It's all wrong: the original livery — you can still just see it on the part that hasn't been repainted, though it's faded and lost its gleam — was a rich glossy brown.

Steps lead up to the middle door. In front of them stands a trestle table, covered in an old sheet, and cluttered with paint pots, brushes, a turps bottle, a tea mug. Smoke drifts from a thin black stovepipe poking through the roof. A little way off, close to the centre of the clearing, the boy can see the stump of an old well, its rusty arm slimy with grease.

"Barney!" he shouts. Even if whoever lives here hears him and comes out, he's far enough away to be able to vanish back into the wood before they can catch him.

"Barney!" he yells again, clapping his hands. "Where are you?"

The middle door opens. A man appears. He's older than Dad, tousle-haired, with a heavy gold-and-grey beard. Perhaps he's a hermit: a real, here-and-now hermit.

"Are you looking for a dog?"

He doesn't sound angry. And presumably he must have seen Barney, mustn't he, or he wouldn't be asking about dogs?

"Yes."

"I've got one here. Come and see if it's yours."

The boy hesitates a moment, then starts across the clearing. The man waits for him, one hand clutching the leather window strap on the door. He's wearing a blue fisherman's smock smeared with paint, and baggy cotton trousers.

"Hullo," he says, as the boy approaches.

"Hullo."

"I'm Aubrey. What's your name?"

The voice takes him by surprise. Not remotely gypsyish: well-oiled and educated, like someone you'd hear on the radio. Instantly, he feels more confident. "Mark, sir. Mark Davenant."

"How do you do, Mark?"

They shake hands.

"Come in."

Mark follows him into the carriage. There's a powerful smell of paraffin and cigarette smoke and cooked meat. The seats and partitions have been removed, and most of the space is filled with a jumble of boxes and suitcases and upturned chairs, their legs jutting out like the spikes of a giant hedgehog. Only the far end, near the stove, has been reclaimed from the chaos. It's laid out like a caravan, with a bunk bed against the wall, two tea chests for tables, a nautical-looking lamp hanging from a hook. On a kitchen chair that's lost one of its spindles is a portable typewriter, with two sheets sandwiching a piece of carbon paper jutting from the cylinder. Next to it stands Barney, his thick coat matted with burs, licking the last scraps from a sheet of greasy newspaper on the floor. He raises his head as Mark enters, then lollops over to him, wagging his tail sheepishly.

"That him?"

Mark nods. "You bad boy! Why didn't you come when I called?"

Barney cringes. Mark raises his hand to hit him.

"No, don't," says the man, grabbing his wrist. "He hasn't done anything wrong."

"Pestering you for food."

The man shakes his head. Close to, he smells strongly of paint and sweat and tobacco. His beard and fingers are stained with yellow. "Don't tell me *you've* never sneaked anything when no one was looking? Come on" — raising his arm suddenly, in a Hitler salute — "we've had enough of that, haven't we? Whatever happened to *live and let live?*"

It's like looking in the mirror and glimpsing a face he's never seen before. Him, Mark, a *tyrant?* He starts to blush.

"Anyway, I was glad of the company," says the man. "Tell you the truth, I was hoping he was a stray, and I could keep him. Never seen a brute like him. What is he? A sheepdog?"

"A mongrel."

"That's what I mean." He pokes the creamy whorls of hair along Barney's back. "Half sheep, half dog."

Mark laughs. He hooks his fingers through Barney's collar, gentler now. "Come on."

The dog shrinks back, bracing his legs, looking expectantly towards the stove.

"He's a canny one, that Barney," says the man. "Knows there's still a bit of rabbit stew left."

"Where did the rabbit come from?"

"Ah, well, that'd be telling." He takes a scuffed aluminium saucepan from the hotplate and angles it over the paper. "Here we are."

"He's had enough," says Mark. "I'll feed him when we get home."

"Never enough, eh, Barney?" He jerks a trickle of dark brown slop onto the page, obliterating a picture of Princess Margaret. "Ah, good shot, Aubrey. Come on, boy."

Barney's feet scrabble at the wooden floor. Mark resists for a moment, then lets him go. What would Dad say? *You should have controlled him better. You mustn't mustn't mustn't let him make a nuisance of himself like that . . .*

"What about you, Mark?" says the man. "Hungry work, chasing dogs. Biscuit and a cup of tea?"

"No. Thank you. We've taken too much of your time already." That, he knows, is the right thing to say. But he wishes it wasn't. He's curious. He's reached the edge of the known world. It's as if someone had prised familiar things from their separate orbits — the old railway carriage, the workman's clothes, the voice like Alvar Lidell — and mixed them together into something startlingly different.

"No, you haven't," says the man. "You haven't taken anything like enough. There's only so much paint-slapping-on a man can do before he needs a break, and a chat with a new friend." He holds up both hands, fingers spread. "Just ten minutes, all right? And then you can nip off . . . Where do you live? Round here somewhere?"

Mark points. "There. Beyond the church."

"Well, you can nip off back beyond the church. And I'll do another door before the sun goes." Without waiting for a reply, he turns and nudges a tin kettle onto the hotplate. Instantly it starts to shiver and clunk.

"Why are you painting it blue?" says Mark.

The man looks over his shoulder. "Why shouldn't I?"

"Great Northern passenger stock was always varnished teak."

"Well, it may have escaped your notice, Mark, but this isn't Great Northern passenger stock any more. It's Aubrey Hillyard's living quarters. And Aubrey's a bloody-minded old son of a so-and-so, I'm afraid, and he'll paint the thing any damned colour he pleases."

Mark flushes.

"Sorry, sorry," says Hillyard. "You're clearly a railway sort of a chap, and these things are important to you. I ought to show a bit more regard for my guest's sensibilities, oughtn't I? Specially since I used to be quite keen on trains myself when I was your age." He waves Mark to a seat on the bunk. "Got your own set-up, have you, at home?"

"Yes, I have, as a matter of fact."

"And you're a real stickler for detail, are you?" He slooshes hot water into a pot, empties it into a bucket by the stove, then bends down and takes a couple of heavy beakers from one of the chests. "Everything just the way it should be? All the colours, and the initials on the engines?"

Mark nods. "It's all old LNER stock. With an 0-6-2 tank. The station's in a little village. There are local services to the next town. Where you can pick up the London express."

"Well, you've obviously worked it all out." He scoops in tea and fills the pot from the kettle. "What's it called, this village of yours?"

Mark hesitates. He's never told anyone but his mother and Miss Murkett, and to let a complete stranger into the charmed circle feels like a betrayal, not just of himself, but of them too. But something about this man — the attentive tilt of the head, the genuine interest in his eyes, as if he's talking to an equal — suggests the secret will be safe with him.

"Peveril, sir. Peveril on the Swift."

"Not *sir*. Aubrey. I'm finished with *sirs*." He sits on the other end of the bed, fumbles in the pocket of his smock, pulls out a pouch and a packet of Rizlas. "Peveril," he says, gazing at the window, so beguiled by the word that he seems unaware his fingers have started to roll a cigarette in his lap. Mark feels a spasm of pride. "Yes, I like that. Very English. Like *Pevensey*. Or *Pippin*. And the Swift, I take it, is a river?"

"Yes. There's a weir. And a bridge."

He nods. "I can just see it. Hear the water gurgling over the stones." He lifts the cigarette to his lips, licks the gummed strip, then squeegees it shut with his thumb and forefinger. "So what happens in Peveril? Anything? Apart from the trains?"

"Well . . ." He's caught in a quicksand. He can't lie. But the idea of exposing Mr Makepeace, the Gallions, Mrs Dauntless, to the gaze of someone he's just met horrifies him. It conjures up one of those pictures he's seen of the Blitz: a house broken open like a nut shell, revealing family pictures, a rocking horse, an unmade bed . . .

"Well, I . . . I do make up stories sometimes," he says.

The man nods, drags deeply on his cigarette, then settles back in his seat and stares at him through a thin grey veil of smoke. His Glacier Mint-coloured eyes are speckled with black, like tiny birds' eggs.

"But they're not very interesting," says Mark.

Barney finally lifts his head from the paper and lumbers towards them. Grateful for the distraction,

Mark bends forward, holding out his hand. To his dismay, the dog ignores him and lies down at the man's feet.

"Well," he says finally, "I should like to see this Peveril. Sounds just my sort of thing. I make up stories too, you know."

Mark glances at the typewriter. "What, you're an author?"

The man nods. He half-closes his hands, then holds them one behind the other in front of his eye, to form a telescope. "Those kinds of stories," he says, pointing it towards the window, and peering through the makeshift lens. "About what's out there. The future."

"What, like *Journey into Space*, you mean?"

"That sort of idea, I expect." He gets up heavily and fills the two mugs. "No milk, I'm afraid," he says, handing one to Mark. "Ought to keep some of that powdered muck, I suppose. But I can't stomach it. Had more than my fill in the war. Sugar?"

*I don't drink tea*. But that would sound childish. So he nods and says:

"Yes, please."

The man offers him a teaspoon and a chipped bowl. A steep drift of sugar is stuck to the side, its surface crusted over like snow about to melt. Mark cracks it, excavates a few granules, stirs them into the marmite-brown tea.

"Is that why you're here?" he asks. "To write a book?"

"Yes."

"Why couldn't you do it where you were before?"

“Ah, too many distractions.” There’s an odd detached quality to the way he says it, as if he’s trying to distance himself from his own words. For the first time, he sounds like an adult speaking to a child. “Whereas here,” he goes on quickly, prodding Barney with his toe, “the worst I have to contend with is the occasional unannounced visit from a dog.”

“Why don’t you have your own dog, if you like them so much?”

“Ah, well, there’s a question. I do, as it happens. Or did. Trouble was, I couldn’t bring her with me.”

“Why not? Because of Mr Montgomery?”

The man smiles, shakes his head. “No, not because of Mr Montgomery. But there’s all sorts of damned nonsense, isn’t there, when you own a dog? *Excuse me, sir, but have you got a licence for that there quadruped?*”

Mark laughs. “It’s only seven and six, isn’t it? I mean, I know that’s quite a lot, but —”

“It isn’t the money. It’s the damned nonsense. I’m not much of a chap for forms and licences and what not.” He sips tea, puckering his lip to avoid scalding himself. “In my experience, the best policy is to have as little to do with the powers that be as possible.”

Mark thinks of the post office: dim and quiet and dusty-smelling, with gentle old Mrs Pledger tilting Barney’s licence towards the light and screwing up her half-blind eyes to see where to put the stamp.

“Why?” he says. “Because of what you’re writing?”

“Heavens, never at a loss for a question, are you?” He siphons another slurp from his mug, watching Mark steadily over the rim. "But since you ask — well, yes, there are certain individuals who might take an interest. Think perhaps I'm sailing a *bit* too close to the bone."

"You mean the wind."

"I do, don't I?"

Mark giggles. "Why would they think that? I mean, what's it about?"

Hillyard laughs again. "You really want to know?"

Mark nods.

"Just between ourselves?"

"Course."

"It's about a brain."

"Whose brain?"

"No one's. Its own."

"How does it exist, then?"

"Ah, well, that's the point. It's cunning. All I can do to keep up with it. *More* than I can do, if I'm honest, as things stand at the moment." He waves towards the typewriter. "Score as of oh-nine-hundred hours this morning: Brain five, Aubrey nil."

Mark laughs. "So what does the Brain do? And why are the powers that be —"

"Goodness, you never stop, do you?"

"Sorry," mumbles Mark.

Hillyard nods. He studies Mark closely, absently sucking the last wisps of smoke from the singed stump of his fag. "Tell you what," he says finally. "Are you a man for a bargain, Mark?"

"What sort of bargain?"

"A story for a story. You come back here tomorrow, and —"

"I can't tomorrow."

"The day after, then. You tell me a bit more about Peveril. And I tell you about the Brain. I'd like that. Always good to talk to a fellow professional. And might help to get the juices going." He squashes his cigarette against the side of an empty tin, then pings it to the bottom with his thumb. "What do you say?"

Mark hesitates. He's flattered, of course: he can't imagine the man talking to fat Nigel, or sporty Ben, or any of the other kids at school, like this — one yarn-spinner to another. And the idea of hearing about the Brain thrills him. But still he's uneasy. Can the man really be trusted? What if, after all, he simply laughs at Peveril on the Swift? Or yawns? Or — even worse — blabs about it to people in the Fox and Hounds or the shop?

"I'll have to think about it," Mark says. And then, before the man can try to convince him, he gets up, leaving his untasted tea, and calls, "Come on, Barney. Let's go."

To give himself time, he goes home by a roundabout route, taking the hard rutted track away from Twenty Acre Wood towards the Black Barns. After half a mile or so, where the path passes through the bottom of an old chalk pit, he scrambles up the slippery white cliff and hides in the little huddle of trees at the top. He's safe here: no one else knows about it. And, even now, it hasn't completely lost the magic it had when he was small. If he lies with his eyes half-open, he can still almost imagine, as he did then, that he might hear animals speaking to each other, or a kindly wizard bidding him welcome and asking him what the matter was.

"Down, Barney! Lie down!"

He leans back against an ash trunk and starts preparing the case for the defence. *Barney got lost in the woods. I had to go after him*. Could he get away with saying that? Or would God punish him for lying? He imagines Barney run over by a lorry, Mummy and Dad killed in a car crash. He wants to tell *someone* what happened, but not *them*. It's not just that Dad would tick him off for bothering the man in the carriage: it's also that he worries he could have been guilty of something worse. What it is, exactly, he's not sure, but he suspects it may have carried him, for the first time, beyond mere naughtiness, into the realm of grown-up misbehaviour, with its minefield of concealed dangers. At some point, he'll have to ask someone to explain the rules to him. In the meantime, he decides finally, it isn't wrong to keep quiet about it: not saying something isn't the same as telling a lie.

"Come on, boy." He edges towards the rim of the pit, then stops. A tractor's coming up the track. He presses himself to the ground, his hand on Barney's collar. Always the same feeling — a shivery, half-pleasurable pang in the guts — when he's hiding here and someone goes by. And then the tractor's gone, and he slithers down over the cold knobbles of chalk and jog-trots home.

"You were gone a long time," says his mother, as he walks in through the back door. It's not a criticism. It's not even a question: just a token acknowledgment of his presence. She's too taken up with chopping chicken livers and stirring the pan of rice to want to engage in real conversation. But that, he knows, could change at any moment. Safer to make himself scarce again.

"I'm just going out to the shed," he says.

"Can you do it afterwards? I'd like you to go and tell Daddy this'll be ready in ten minutes."

"Where is he?"

"In the darkroom."

Her eyes linger on him. He understands that expression, what it's asking of him. His muscles start to unclench. He knows what to do now, how to pick his way through the obstacle course without knocking into anything hard.

"OK," he says.

He runs upstairs. He can smell the vinegar fug of the stop bath, see a rim of faint orange light under the door. He taps lightly.

"Yes?"

"Daddy? Mummy says supper will be ready soon."

"Hang on." The click of the key in the lock. A gap appears at the edge of the door, revealing a strip of blanket. "Come in. Quickly."

He squeezes past the makeshift curtain. Dad shuts the door behind him. The air is sour with chemicals. Water gushes into the sink, sluicing the fixer from a wodge of prints. In the dim glow of the safety lamp he can see a strip of negatives drooping from the Mekon head of the enlarger. Next to it, an image is starting to form on a sheet of 10 X 8 in the developing tray. He leans forward to watch it. A patch of dark, a larger area of speckled grey, more dark — ah: leaves, a branch. Now, almost in the centre, something small and circular. An eye. A bird's eye. A thrush, head back, beak open as it sings.

"That's terrific, Dad."

Dad puts a hand on his shoulder. "Know where it is?"

"The apple tree in the back."

Dad nods. "Quarter to six in the morning. Old man thrush telling the other birds to steer clear. This is *his* territory, and his hen, and his brood."

"Quarter to six?" It's an effort to say it, like pushing his bike over a hump. But he knows it's what Dad's expecting.

Dad dabs the print with his tongs, then lifts it by one corner and lets the developer drip back into the tray. There's a lightness in his movements that tells Mark he's pleased. "Yes," he says. "I was up at four-thirty. I'd been there almost an hour when he finally deigned to show up and sing for me."

"What are the other pictures?"

"You'll see in a minute." He douses the print in the stop bath, then rinses it and drops it face down in the fixer. "You can help me hang them up."

Mark feels as if he's ebbing away, melting into the furniture, becoming part of the furniture himself, an object without a will of its own. But he knows it's the price he has to pay. To resist the flow, to re-establish himself within his own boundaries by saying he has something else to do, would instantly change Dad's mood from white to black, and send him on the attack. Once that happened, it would only be a matter of time before he'd screwdriver the truth about Aubrey Hillyard out of him.

"OK," says Mark.

Dad checks that the packets of paper are sealed, then switches on the main light. He unhooks the blanket, opens the door and gathers up the pictures from the sink. They flap and slither in his hands like a net full of fish.

"All right?"

Mark follows him to the bathroom. The clothes line is already strung across the bath. Dad gives Mark the pile of photos, then picks up the top one and pincers it to the line. Mark attaches two more pegs to the bottom to hold it flat.

"Recognize that?" says Dad.

It looks like the edge of Twenty Acre Wood. The sun is rising, making a brilliant fan of rays above the trees. A young deer is breaking cover, one foot tentatively raised, checking to see that the coast is clear. Obviously it hasn't noticed the photographer.

"I think so," Mark says.

"I'll show you." He slips the Ordnance Survey map from his jacket and half-unfolds it. It's dotted with pencil crosses. He points at one on the corner of Willetts Lane. "Just here. See?"

Mark nods. No more than a couple of hundred yards from Aubrey Hillyard's railway carriage. The thought of it makes him giddy.

"It's beautiful, Dad."

Dad returns the map to his pocket and starts hanging more prints: a blackbird feeding her young, a kingfisher peering at a facsimile of itself in a pond as smooth as a mirror. Mark follows him with a fistful of pegs.

"I think these are the best photos you've ever done."

Dad nods. He puts a hand on Mark's shoulder again and guides him downstairs. Supper is already on the table.

"You should see Daddy's pictures, Mummy," says Mark, as he pulls out his chair.

He tries to catch her eye, feel the warmth of her appreciation for a moment. But she smiles at Dad, not at him.

"Wonderful, are they?" she says.

"Yes," says Mark.

"Why don't you pop up and get one of them, old thing?" says Dad.

"Which one?"

"You choose."

Mark runs up to the bathroom, scans the line of dripping prints. Which one did Dad seem most pleased with? He unpegs the thrush and carries it carefully downstairs. When he walks in, his parents are standing in front of the stove with their backs to him, arms round each other's waist. As he lingers in the doorway, waiting for them to separate, Mummy turns to kiss Dad and catches sight of him.

"Ah, and here we are," she says.

Mark holds up the picture. She pulls away to admire it. "Oh, my goodness, yes. That's really tremendous, isn't it? I'd say it's the best thing you've ever done."

"That's what I said," says Mark.

"Did you?" She kisses Dad again. "It's super. Congratulations, darling."

"Thank you. I'm pleased with it." He turns to Mark. "Better put it back now, or it won't dry properly."

"OK," says Mark.

When he returns, they're both sitting at the table.

"It's what I always said," Dad says, warming his still-pink hands over the plate in front of him. "If you want to do a professional job, you need professional equipment."

"So that's really it, is it, you think?" says his mum. "The new camera? That's made all the difference?"

"I couldn't have got results like that with the Agfa."

"Well, I'm so glad we bought the Leica, then."

But the energy's gone from her voice, and her jaw is tight with worry. As she starts to serve the risotto, Mark remembers the conversation he half-heard a few nights ago, across the landing: not so much the fragments of phrases — *love me, trust me, of course I do, darling: it's just whether we can really afford it at the moment* — as the tone. It still troubles him: the way Dad's strength seemed run through with weakness, like an unexpected flaw in a piece of marble.

How would the man in the railway carriage have behaved? The question leaps out at him, takes him by surprise. For a moment, in place of Dad's fine small features, the sulky mouth and wounded gaze, he sees the jungle of Hillyard's face, the "think what you like" iciness of his eyes. Would someone like that have used his capacity for being hurt to get what he wanted? No:

he'd have said, *Aubrey's a bloody-minded old son of a so-and-so, and he'll have whatever damned camera he pleases*.

Mark tries to push the image away, but all through supper it keeps coming back to haunt him, leering, winking, mocking his discomfort. As soon as he's finished eating, he carries his plate to the sink and bolts for the shed. It's warm and stuffy after the heat of the day, and still smells of last year's apples. As he walks in, he can hear rats scuffling under the pile of boxes in the corner.

He flicks the light switch. The village blossoms into life. Its completeness — the castle ruins on the papier-mâché hill, the old hermitage by the painted river, the delivery van in the high street and the coal lorry in the station yard — makes him shiver with pleasure. On the platform, Mrs Dauntless and Patty Gallion are waiting for the local to Swiftbridge.

*Morning, Patty*.

*Morning, Mrs Dauntless*.

*Where are you off to today?*

*Just into town. It's Paul's birthday tomorrow, and I'm getting him a book I know he wants. The new Rosemary Sutcliff.*

*He's a lucky boy, having a sister like —*

He leaves them frozen in mid-sentence, turns on the controller and eases the 8.14 towards them, squatting down so that he can see it emerging from the tunnel at eye level. His nose fills with the oily metallic tang of the electric motor. He slows the train into the station, then edges Mr Makepeace out on the platform, spruce in his blue uniform.

*Peveril! Peveril! This is Peveril on the Swift!*

He picks up Mrs Dauntless and Patty and drops them into the old Oxo tin. The real Mrs Dauntless and Patty are on board now, in the middle carriage. He turns the knob, and the 0-6-2 jerks forward again. He watches it past the level crossing and round the bend, then pushes the station master back into the ticket office.

*Fine morning, Mr Hoskins.*

*Yes, Mr Makepeace. We're in for a beautiful day, I think.*

He stops. This, more than anywhere or anything, is *his* world. To tell Aubrey Hillyard about it would be to weaken its borders and risk exposing it to a cold blast of grown-up reality. But then Aubrey Hillyard isn't like other grown-ups. He doesn't care about neatness or tidiness, or fitting in: all he's interested in is writing about his *own* imaginary world. Sharing Peveril with a grown-up like that could make it stronger, even more alive.

Mark stares at the layout, trying to sense what *it* feels. But he senses nothing. After a couple of minutes, he turns off the controller and the lights and goes back indoors.

# CHAPTER TWO

The next day, he's due at Miss Murkett's at three. Dad's in a mood again, for some reason — sighs; frowns; scarcely a word at breakfast, until the very end, when he suddenly snaps, *Murky, eh? You'd better watch out, or you'll turn into another of her lame ducks at this rate* — and the weight of his temper squeezes the air from the house, making it impossible to breathe properly. So, although it's only a half-hour walk, Mark decides to leave immediately after lunch, and take his time. Barney follows him eagerly down the hall.

"No, sorry, boy, you can't come. C-A-T-S. Stay!"

Barney droops. Mark turns quickly, shrugging off his guilt. Next moment, he's out of the door, and free. He stands there for a moment, feeling the breeze ruffle his shirt, snuffing the heavy scent of roses and ripe wheat and hot tar, then sets off at a slow amble. As he cuts down the lane that runs behind the Fox and Hounds, he sees scrawny Harry Doggett and his plump wife Betty stacking barrels by the back door. Harry looks up and makes his usual strange salute, twirling a finger above his head as though he's dialling a telephone number in the air.

"Hullo," calls Mark, with a wave.

Smiling Betty laughs. "Lovely day for it!"

At the garage, the little man with a limp is hosing down a coach. Mark stops to admire the gleam of the cream-and-brown livery, and the picked-out gold lettering on the side: *Barrons Coaches*. As always, it leaves him feeling dissatisfied. It's beautiful, of course — but that kind of beauty doesn't belong on a bus: it's the preserve of railway engines, big and magnificent enough to wear it.

He sidles down the High Street, shoulders hunched, hands in his pockets, kicking at stones on the pavement. Out of the corner of his eye, he sees the edges of the houses soften, and walls begin to billow and shiver, like scenery in a play. A cavalcade of knights rides by, weapons jangling, armour ringing, and he raises his own invisible sword in salute. Behind them is a band of Elizabethan players, cartwheeling and singing, who beckon as they pass: *come, join us* — and then a stagecoach, with a wigged man peering through pince-nez from the window, making him bow his head. As they reach the crossroads they all start to fade, and the ungainly clutter of the present-day village suddenly becomes solid again: telephone wires; the droopy *Halt at Major Road Ahead* sign, like a falling-over scarecrow; Mrs Drake's rust-specked Wolseley, off to meet someone at the station.

It's still too early when he gets to Hillfield. He lingers by the gate, looking along Willetts Lane towards Twenty Acre Wood. As he watches, trying to imagine what Aubrey Hillyard is doing behind the thick wall of trees — painting? Crouched over his typewriter, wrestling with the alien Brain? — he spots a Land Rover, crawling towards him at barely a walking pace. As it draws alongside, Mr Montgomery tortoises his big head through the window.

"Hullo, Mark." He's bulgy-faced, half strangled by the collar and tie cutting into his beef-red neck. "Haven't seen you for a while."

Mark feels an urgent need to pee. He presses his thighs together. "No."

"No dog today?"

Mark shakes his head.

"So where are you off to?"

"Miss Murkett's. She's asked me to tea."

Mr Montgomery nods towards Hillfield, eyebrows raised.

"I'm waiting," says Mark. "I got here early."

"Ah." Slowly, half-smiling. That expression again: *You may think you're clever, but you can't fool me*. He braces his arm against the steering wheel as if he's about to drive on. "You know" — gazing straight ahead, through the windscreen — "there's a chap living there, do you?"

"Where?"

"Twenty Acre Wood."

Mark's face is burning. "Who is he?"

"Name's Hillyard. Everyone seems to know about it now. I just caught two boys spying on him." He glances up at Mark again, studies his face for a moment, then nods. "Ask Miss Murkett about him. She'll tell you. But he's an odd sort, by all accounts. Makes the devil of a noise and scares the birds. You take my advice, you'll keep well clear of him. Just thought I'd mention it." He touches the edge of his fawn cap with a forefinger. "Give my regards to Miss Murkett, will you?"

Without waiting for a reply, he revs the engine, and the Land Rover continues slowly to the end of the lane. Mark stands watching as it turns onto the High Street and starts climbing towards the war memorial, trailing chalk dust and scabs of mud. He's confused. If Miss Murkett knows about Aubrey Hillyard too, why hasn't she mentioned him before? It can only be because — here it is again, that uneasy knot-in-the-stomach feeling, as if he's strayed beyond some invisible boundary — there's something about the man that makes her reluctant to discuss him with a child. He must be careful what he tells her.

He turns and starts slowly up the moss-eaten drive. The flagged yard at the top, between the old laundry and the house, is seething with cats. At a sound from inside, they merge into a shoal and swarm into the kitchen.

The front door is ajar, but he yanks the bell pull anyway. The sound — the high trill in the echoey hugeness of the house — always intrigues him. After a few moments, he hears the clack of Miss Murkett's brogues.

"Ah, young Aurelius! Come in!" Seventyish, tall and long-faced, with heavy straight eyebrows and hair curled in grey swags over her ears, giving her the air of a Hanoverian king. She wears a floral-pattern skirt and thick brown stockings that make Mark think of the raspy feel of Elastoplast.

"Let's go in here," she says, ushering him into the sitting room. Even now, on a hot summer afternoon, it's dark and cool, and has the autumnal smell of stale wood ash. An engraving of Oliver Cromwell glowers from the wall. In the grate stands an earthenware jug of roses. Above it, on the mantelpiece, a couple of pewter plates wink rheumily in the dimness. To Mark, they're worse than Cromwell: the eyes of the house itself watching him, and finding him wanting. He turns his attention instead to the low table in front of the fireplace. It's draped with green velvet, and spread with glasses, plates, a cluster of bottles, a venerable willow-pattern bowl webbed with cracks and half-filled with biscuits.

"Sit down," says Murky.

He knows better than to take the big button-back chair: that's hers. He finds it disconcerting, anyway: ever since he can remember, he's imagined its curved legs suddenly coming to life and scuttling across the room like a giant malformed insect. And there's something dead-looking about the couple in the photograph on the table next to it: a staring woman in a wide-brimmed white hat and a moustachioed man wearing a monocle. So he settles in his usual place, on the end of the sofa. The over-stuffed arm reaches up almost to his ear. Balanced on top of it, ready for use, is *Old Possum's Book of Practical Cats*.

"So — what's it to be?" says Murky. "Flower or berry?"

"Berry, please." He doesn't really enjoy it. But at least, unlike her other wines, there's a cough-syrupy warmth about it that he finds comforting.

"I thought as much. A man after my own heart. Puts fire in your veins, doesn't it, the good old berry?" She levers the cork from the bottle with her thumb and trickles a swirl of purple into a small green glass. "Here we are." She fills a tumbler for herself. "Your very good health, young Aurelius."

"Thank you." He takes a sip. It burns his throat and sends an aftershock through his belly and legs. He mustn't have too much. The last time, he got home flushed and unsteady, and scowling Dad blamed Murky for encouraging him to make an exhibition of himself.

"So. At last. The holidays are upon us. No more traipsing off to The Hoops every day."

"Oh, The Hoops is all right."

"Well, I'm glad to hear it. I still find the idea of a school in an old pub rather odd. And calling the headmistress by her Christian name. Just a sign of my age, I suppose."

"It's not really her Christian name. More a sort of nickname."

"A nickname, then. Rather than Miss Phelps, or whatever it might be."

"I call *you* by a nickname."

"Ah, but we're friends, aren't we?" She pats her skirt with both hands, marking an end to the argument. "Anyway, you're enjoying your freedom?"

He nods.

"That's good. Not much time for Peveril, I imagine. Not in this weather. You're out beating the bounds with Barney, I expect. Seeing off the Romans. And the Normans."

"Yes."

"Quite right too. I certainly shouldn't want a Norman poking his head in here. Not wearing one of those helmets." She lays a finger on top of her nose. "No wonder poor old King Harold took fright. Must've been like fighting a lot of machines."

"I know."

"You *do* know, young Aurelius. Wise beyond your years." She takes a gulp of wine. "If Mr Barron or Mr Montgomery or Harry Doggett could hear us now, I dare say they'd think us great fools, talking about the Normans like this. But that's because they don't realize, do they?" She raises her eyebrows expectantly. "Hm?"

"Time's an old fraud."

"Ex*act*ly!" She slaps her thigh in triumph. "Time's an old fraud. But we'll just have to keep it to ourselves, won't we? How about a biscuit?"

"Thank you." Murky's digestives — kept in an old tin that's lost its paint, and only, as far as he can tell, brought out for him — disgust and fascinate him. Normally they're so soggy that he can dent them with his fingers, like plasticine. But when he squeezes this one, it breaks, showering the table with crumbs.

"I'm sorry."

"Oh, don't worry. Sign of a healthy young biscuit. In honour of the occasion, these are fresh from Mr Bennett. Have you met him yet?"

"No." Should he explain the reason: that when Dad had gone in for a packet of cigarettes they'd refused to put it on the account, and he'd vowed never to go back?

No: though he can't say why exactly, he knows Dad wouldn't want him to.

"Really? Well, I think you ought to pop in and introduce yourself. They're very unshopkeepery. He was in something hush-hush during the war. Or so his wife said. Seems a pleasant enough woman. And there's a daughter. About your age."

The wine has set up an unpleasant thrub in his ears. He wants to know why she's happy to talk about the Bennetts, but not the man in the railway carriage, but he can't think of a polite way to ask. Instead he blurts, "Mr Montgomery sends his regards."

"Does he indeed?" She looks curiously at him. "Do you know what a non sequitur is, by any chance?"

"Yes."

"Well, that, if I may say so, was a particularly fine example. When did you see Mr Montgomery?"

He gestures towards the drive. "Just now."

"Well, I'm glad he can still be civil, at least," she says, busily bulldozering the biscuit crumbs from the tablecloth with her hand. "I don't think I'm in his good books at the moment."

"Why not?"

She seems not to hear. "Has it ever occurred to you," she says, holding a crumb out for his inspection, "that every one of these might actually be a miniature world? Or a solar system? Or an entire universe? And that when we do something like this" — she gets up and brushes them out of the window — "we're changing the course of history. Hm?"

He shakes his head. It makes him feel worse — as if his skull is full of fluid, and the movement has sent it slopping from one side to the other.

"By the same token, of course, *we* may simply be a crumb, sitting in a giant hand we can't see. And that treats us just as cavalierly. Hence all the wars and natural disasters. The giant decides to do a bit of spring-cleaning, and *boom* — Germany invades Poland. What do you think?"

"I don't know, Murky."

"Well, you *should* know, young Aurelius. Or at least have an opinion on the subject. You're going to be ten soon, aren't you?"

*Tomorrow*. He almost says it, then realizes that would make her feel bad for not getting him a present. She'll remember eventually. She always does. "Yes."

"Double figures," she says. "Time to start giving these things some thought. Here" — popping the cork from the bottle again — "have another sip."

He watches the blood-coloured liquid — dark blood, from deep in the heart: he remembers that from the circulation diagram Tony showed them at school — trickle into his glass. Should he say no? No: this is the seal of their new, more grown-up relationship. She fills her own glass, then re-enthrones herself in her chair, an elbow on each arm.

"Your very good health."

"And yours, Murky." He nods and holds his glass towards her, the way he's seen adults do. "Who's Aubrey Hillyard?"

"What?"

"Who's Aubrey Hillyard?"

She stiffens, but says nothing. A procession of cats starts to file into the room. The way they move — tails arched, winding themselves round the furniture — deepens the silence, enlarges the awkwardness.

"Sorry . . ." he mumbles. "I didn't mean to be" — groping for the word his parents would use — "*tactless*."

She shakes her head. "That's all right. But why do you want to know?"

"It's just that I met him yesterday. When Barney got lost in Twenty Acre Wood. And then when I saw Mr Montgomery on my way here, he said you'd tell me about him."

She raises her eyebrows. The meaning's as clear as a signal hoisted from a ship: *Did he indeed?*

"And what did Mr — what did *Aubrey* — did he tell you to call him Aubrey?"

"Yes."

"What did *he* tell you?"

"Just that he's writing a book."

She nods. "Nothing else?"

*It's about a Brain*. But no, that was a secret. "Not much. We talked about Peveril on the Swift a bit. And Barney."

"Ah, yes. I'm sure he'd like Peveril on the Swift. But that was all, was it?"

"More or less."

"Hm. Well." She puts down her glass, then presses her fingertips together as if she's praying. "Years ago, my aunt let a chap live in Twenty Acre Wood. He'd been in the *Great* War, as we used to call it. He had a bit of shell embedded in his head. Afterwards, he found it difficult to settle to anything. So he had an old carriage moved in there, and grew carrots, and kept chicken, and paid Aunt Mag with eggs. He didn't last long, poor man. After that, she let the wood to Mr Montgomery's father."

"But it's still yours?"

She nods. "Mr Montgomery still rents it, of course. For the shooting. He'd like me to sell, but I won't. I've always had the feeling that it might just come in useful again some day. So when my niece in London told me about Aubrey Hillyard, said he was looking for somewhere quiet to write a book, I thought: well, why not? Why shouldn't *he* have the wood? It's a similar story, you see. He had a bad time of it in the war. And he's never really got over it."

*Another of Murky's lame ducks*. "What happened?"

"Oh, Heavens." Her eyes are bright. She blinks heavily and gives a quick exasperated shake of the head, like a horse refusing the bridle. "Sometimes, people see things that the rest of us . . . that you and I couldn't really imagine. And afterwards, it's impossible for them just to go quietly back to" — waving a hand, drawing into her realm the room, the house, the village beyond. "Poor Aubrey tried, evidently, but it was too much for him. He just couldn't cope, you know, with rents, and taxes, and hire-purchase agreements, and —"

"All that damned nonsense," says Mark.

She frowns slightly. "There's a wife somewhere, I believe," she goes on, her voice so quiet now he can barely hear her. "Dreadful for her too, of course. And I dare say Mr Montgomery is slyly suggesting to everyone he meets . . ." She taps one nostril, watching Mark's face for a response.

"Finger on nose," he says.

She smiles and nods. "Finger on nose. Precisely. Slyly suggesting, finger on nose, that Miss Murkett is helping a man who's abandoned his family. Is that what he told you?"

Mark shakes his head.

"Well, that's something, I suppose. But the point is — just remember this, in case anyone ever *does* say it — Aubrey Hillyard *hasn't* abandoned his poor wife. He simply needs some time to himself. But of course, if people are determined to get the wrong end of the stick, they will." She pauses, then holds up her hands, fingers fanned. "Anyway . . ."

The door is suddenly closing. In a desperate attempt to keep it open, Mark says:

"How does your niece know him, Murky? Is she a friend of his?"

"No, no, not a *friend*. An acquaintance. She works for a literary agent. Aubrey approached them a few months ago. Hoping they'd take him on. Jane would like to have done, evidently: she thinks he's very talented. But —"

"But the powers that be?"

She laughs. "Oh, I don't know about the powers that be. The crotchety old chap in charge. Who apparently thinks his ideas are a bit far-fetched."

"What ideas?"

He holds his breath, waiting for her to mention the Brain. But she just laughs again. "There you have me, young Aurelius. No one's told me. And if they don't want to volunteer the information, I'm certainly not going to ask. All I'm trying to do is be a good neighbour." She looks down. A lanky ginger cat is calculating the distance between the floor and her lap. She pats her knee, and it jumps up. "And Mr Montgomery doesn't approve, does he, Bertha?" she says, scratching its head. "No, not one bit. And I've a nasty feeling he's making up stories. To try to scare people and put them off him." She hesitates. "What else *did* he tell you?"

"Just that Aubrey's an *odd sort*. And that, if he was me, he'd keep well clear of him."

"Hm," says Murky. "Well, I suspect Mr Montgomery might be a bit of an odd sort himself, if he'd seen what Aubrey Hillyard did. Being in the Home Guard's not quite the same thing."

"But it isn't true? Aubrey's not really a bad man?"

She thinks about it for a moment, then shakes her head slowly. "No worse than the rest of us."

*What did Aubrey Hillyard see in the war?* But Mark knows he's at the limit of what Murky is prepared to tell him. And, if nothing else, he's established one vital fact: Hillyard is there with her blessing.

"How's the voice?" she says, derailing his train of thought. "Well-lubricated? Ready for action?"

Mark nods. "Yes, I think so."

She waggles a finger at *Old Possum*. "Bertha and I would be glad of some diversion. Wouldn't we?"

He opens the book.

"What shall I do first?"

"*Mr Mistoffelees*, please."

He finds the page and begins to read.

He leaves just after five. He ought to go home and take Barney for a walk. But he doesn't want to face his parents — not feeling like this. His head's thudding, his legs weighted with lead. And he's still puzzling over Aubrey Hillyard. What Murky revealed about him — the hint that he'd done something dangerous and heroic in the war — makes him even more fascinating. But Mark can't forget her slight hesitation before she said he was "No worse than the rest of us".

Still two hours to supper time. What can he do? The answer suddenly caterpillars up his bare arms, making him tremble. The trouble is, he's already told the man he couldn't come today. And if he *did* go, Hillyard would expect an immediate answer: would he tell him about Peveril or not? Still . . .

At the bottom of the drive, he hesitates. Then — battling a violent gust of nerves that almost halts him in his tracks — he turns right along Willetts Lane. Just because you're going this way, he tells himself, that doesn't mean you have to do it. You can just walk straight past, if you want to.

But as he reaches the wood, his eyes automatically start searching for the place where Barney disappeared yesterday. Yes, there it is: the tunnel he hacked through the grass and brambles. It would be easy enough to follow the same path today. And it still wouldn't commit him to anything — not irrevocably. He could be completely noiseless this time. The man wouldn't need to know he was there at all. Mark could watch from the safety of the bushes, and only make up his mind what to do then.

He glances back towards the village to make sure he's not been seen, and slips through the gap into the wood. Half crawling, ducking to avoid overhanging branches, he inches towards the clearing. After a couple of minutes he pauses again, listening for footsteps or a voice. Nothing. He edges forward.

He feels it first: a sudden yielding under his hand. He tries to whip back, but it's too late: the ground is collapsing, in a din of snapping twigs and crumbling soil. To his over-alert ears, it sounds like an earthquake. He's fallen no more than a foot or so, and it's easy enough to scramble out, but Aubrey Hillyard must have heard him. Hurriedly, he starts to retrace his steps. The hole wasn't there yesterday, so — though Mark can't imagine why — it's obvious that Hillyard has changed his mind and decided that, after all, he doesn't want visitors.

As he retreats towards the lane, Mark sees a stick — no, more than a stick: a whole branch, still green with young leaves — barring his way. Where did it come from? It can't have blown down: there's no wind. Has Hillyard somehow managed to get round behind him and put it there? On its own, it doesn't look like much of an obstacle, but climbing over it might set off another trap.

*He's an odd sort, by all accounts. You take my advice, you'll keep well clear of him.*

Mark's heart is pistoning in his throat. Why would Hillyard want to imprison him in the wood? Because he's a kidnapper, and plans to demand a ransom from his parents? Or for some other reason that Mark can't quite identify — though its elusive, half-formed shape makes the skin on the inside of his legs tingle?

He searches for another way out. There: a tiny slit in the undergrowth, barely wide enough to wriggle through. Holding his breath, he drops to his knees and gingerly parts the curtain of leaves. Somehow, their lemony scent, the way they finger his face like half-blind Mrs Pledger in the post office, make him feel safer.

"What are you doing?" A child's voice. He snakes out from the bush and looks up. A girl stands a few feet away, watching him. On one side of her belt hangs a holster: on the other, a coil of rope. She's wearing a Lone Ranger mask, ink-blotting out the area round her hazel eyes, and a loosely knotted red snuff handkerchief that shadows her chin. But from what he can make out — the straight line of her nose, the dark hair cut short over the ears — he's pretty sure he's never seen her before.

"I'm trying to get out," he says. "There's traps everywhere."

She pulls a toy revolver from the holster. "Why are you in the wood?"

*That's none of your business*. But he doesn't say it. Something in the way she holds herself — tense and jittery, like a horse nerving itself to take grass from your hand — makes him wary of scaring her off. Maybe this is a game, and she expects him to play along with it.

"Indians," he says.

She brandishes her gun. "Where?"

"There's a camp" — gesturing towards the clearing — "over there."

"That belongs to a good chief," she says. "He only wants to live in peace. But some of the cowboys are trying to drive him away. So I'm here to protect him."

"Do you know him, then?"

"No. But he isn't doing anyone any harm."

*I've* met *him. He and I are friends*. He'd like to tell her, to establish his prior claim on Aubrey Hillyard, their plan to swap stories. But to say it would break the spell.

"I know," he says. "I was going to see him. To smoke the pipe with him."

"Honestly?"

He nods.

"Swear?"

"Swear. But then I fell in that pit."

His ears are hot. He braces himself, expecting her to laugh. But her mouth doesn't even twitch.

"I did that. It was meant for the other boys."

"What other boys?" But he's pretty sure he can guess: Stan Green, the milkman's son, and toothless Ernie (no one knows who *his* father is), with one blank eye, like a pickled onion.

"I don't know their names," she says. "But I saw them spying. Throwing things at him."

"Who are *you?*"

"I'm the Lone —"

"No, I mean *really?*"

She hesitates, then loops her thumbs through the elastic and pushes the mask onto her forehead. Her face is what his mother would call *elfin:* small, lightly freckled, with high cheekbones tapering to a sharp chin.

"I'm Lou Bennett," she says. "I live at the shop. What's your name?"

"Mark."

"Mark what?"

His mouth's dry. "Davenant."

He steels himself again: *Did your father come in to buy some cigarettes the other day?* But it's all right: the name obviously means nothing to her.

"What do you like playing?" she says.

"Lots of things."

"Such as?"

"Knights. Romans. Highwaymen. And I've got a model railway."

Her gaze narrows, as if she's trying to stare him out. Finally she nods and says, "Shall we play together sometimes?"

What should he say? Dad wouldn't approve, of course. But his mother might. He imagines telling her, the next time she says "You need someone to play with", and watching the anxiety melt from her eyes.

"I don't have to be the Lone Ranger. I can be knights or highwaymen. As long as we give what we take to the poor."

"Like Robin Hood?"

She nods. He's suddenly aware that the winey muzz has cleared from his head, and he can see the girl quite clearly, in sharp relief. She's not like Ben, or fat Nigel, or pigtailed Peggy Akers: she actually *understands* about imagination games.

"I've got a dog," he says.

She glances round. "A *real* one?"

He nods. "I left him at home today. But he usually comes with me."

"What's he called?"

"Barney."

"Well, that's all right. He can be *our* dog. We can tie the booty round his neck and send him to our hideout, while we fight off the excisemen."

"Not excisemen. That's smugglers."

"Soldiers, then. Bow Street Runners."

"I don't mind," he says.

"OK."

She tosses her head and begins to move away. He feels a sudden coldness on the skin, as if the sun's just gone in. He trails after her, trying to stop her slipping from his orbit.

"Shall we go and see him now?" he says.

"Who?"

He points towards the clearing.

"You know him?"

He nods.

"*Really?*"

"Really."

She hesitates.

"He's an author. He's writing a story about a giant Brain. He said he'd tell it to me. You can listen too, if you like."

For a moment, he thinks he has her. Then she says:

"Tomorrow. I've got to go home now."

"Tomorrow's my birthday."

"So? You can play on your birthday, can't you?"

He calculates. He'll need to be back for tea. But the morning should be all right, after he's opened his presents. Dad, he's pretty sure, would be glad to get him out of the house. Mark will just have to tread carefully, think how to explain where he's going.

"Ten?" he says.

She nods. "Here?"

"All right."

"And bring Barney." She hesitates. "And we need a sign."

She holds up her hand, folding the thumb and forefinger together. Mark mimics her.

"And a secret word," he says. "That only we know."

"What word?"

He thinks for a moment. "Dauntless."

She shakes her head. "Too much like *doubtless*."

"Gallion, then."

"Gallion. OK."

He watches her turn and dressage her way through the foliage, spinning the revolver on her finger. When she's finally gone, he crawls back through the tunnel and sets a cross made of two twigs by the entrance, so he'll know the place tomorrow.

# CHAPTER THREE

He wakes in the dawn half-light. His room's hot and airless, full of the acid smell of his own body. He gets up and opens the window. A bank of coolness rises from the garden, scented with tobacco plants and sodden grass. He leans out, feeling it against his cheeks like a damp flannel. A thrush is singing in the apple tree behind the house, and from beyond the churchyard he can hear the soft yodel of a wood pigeon. Should he rouse snuffling Barney and go for an early morning walk, like Dad? It's tempting. But it would be an intrusion. The world isn't ready for him yet. For another hour or two — despite the birdsong — it will still belong to the owls and the foxes.

Leaving the window open, he goes back to bed and lies down with only the sheet over him. That's better. But even so, he can't sleep. It's not just the heat, or the familiar birthday excitement: have they got him the Horn by 4-6-0, or will he have to settle for a signal box and a new set of points? Something else — something new — is troubling him. He feels it in his stomach, and the front of his thighs: a sense of dissatisfaction, of incompleteness. He tries to work out what it is by imagining himself in different situations: eating an ice cream, swimming in the sea, running barefoot along the beach. Nothing helps.

He forces his thoughts onto the day ahead. Hillyard's expecting him to come alone. Will he mind if Lou's there, too? And what will they do afterwards? Should he take a mask, and the plastic flintlock pistol that doesn't work any more, so that they can play highwaymen?

And suddenly, in his mind, he sees her, sees both of them, in the hideout at the chalk pit. As they slither forward, side by side — *Someone's coming! Let's see who it is!* — the cramped space squeezes them together. And there the story stops. There's no action, no *Stand and deliver: your money or your life*: they just lie there, Siamese twins, arms and legs and shoulders joined.

A wave starts to build at the edge of his consciousness, turning the light to darkness, carrying him into sleep.

"Happy birthday, Mark," says his mother. He'd hoped for bacon and eggs, but apart from the little bag of packages by his place and the newspaper next to Dad's there's nothing on the table except three bowls, three cups and a packet of cornflakes. That means that breakfast shouldn't take long, at least. He'll have time to play with his presents before he has to leave.

"How does it feel to be ten?" Not looking at him, but at the grill pan.

He shrugs, eyeing the bag on the table, trying to work out what's inside from its contours. In one corner he can see the sharp angle made by a box. His heart breaks into a gallop. "Where's Dad?"

Her face softens. "There's a change already: *Dad* now, not *Daddy*. He's outside."

"Shall I call him?"

She shakes her head. "He shouldn't be too long." She pulls out the grill pan from the stove, then picks up the breadknife and starts sawing at the remains of a loaf.

"What's he doing?"

"Oh, just mending the mower."

Mark squirms.

"I know," she says. "You want to open your presents. But —"

"No, I'm going out."

"Where?"

"I'm going to play with somebody."

"You mean Nigel?"

"No. Someone else."

"Who?"

"Someone I met."

She stops cutting, leaving the knife halfway through the rump of the loaf. "You're being very mysterious."

He hadn't expected her to be so inquisitive. "I'll be back for tea," he says.

"Well, I should hope so." She smiles coaxingly. When he doesn't respond, she says: "Look, I'm sorry, lovey, but we can't let you go unless we know who it is. There are some strange people about."

Does she mean Aubrey Hillyard? "It's just a girl," he says.

"What's her name?"

"Lou."

"Lou what?"

"Bennett."

"*Bennett?* They're the new people at the shop, aren't they?"

"Yes."

She looks startled — frightened, even. She glances towards the back door, distractedly twisting a loop of hair round her finger.

"She's nice," says Mark.

"Is she?"

"She likes imagination games. And she doesn't like bullies."

She nods. "Where did you meet her?"

"Twenty Acre Wood."

"What? . . ."

"When I was coming back from Murky."

"Ah." She sounds breathless. The mood of her face changes from one moment to the next, like a field shadowed by clouds. "Well, I don't like you playing with children we don't know."

"I could ask her to tea."

"Yes. No. I don't think that'd be a very good idea. Maybe another day. When Daddy's out."

"Because Mr Bennett was rude to him?"

She shakes her head. "It would just be better, I think."

"Well, can I still play with her today?"

She nods. "Only don't mention it" — another glance at the door — "when . . . Let me pick the right moment. To talk to him about it. All right?"

"OK."

"Right." She stares round, as if for a moment she can't remember what she's meant to be doing. Then she spots the stranded knife and starts hacking at the loaf again. When she has four slices, she arranges them carefully on the grill pan, like the squares of a Battenberg cake. As she looks up, she asks, "What time did you say you'd meet her?"

"Ten. Can I take some sandwiches, please?"

"Hm." She hesitates, then walks to the door and opens it. "Darling!" No response. "Jeremy!" Still nothing. She goes outside. After a moment, Mark hears a clatter of tools, then his parents' murmuring voices. He moves quickly to his place, slips his hand into the bag, finds the box. Just feeling the weight of it, the way whatever's inside thuds against the cardboard, excites him. It has to be an engine! The only puzzle is that it seems too long to be the 4-6-0 . . .

Footsteps. He backs away.

"Here we are," says Mummy. She hurries to the sink and turns on the tap. A few seconds later, Dad appears, wiping his fingers on a rag. His neck's shrunk, his head jutted forward, like a man battling a stiff wind. He leaves the door open, as if he's going to be there for such a short time that it isn't worth closing it.

"Come on," says Mummy. It's the tone she used to Mark when he was small: *Just one last spoonful . . . Eat up . . . Good boy*.

"I don't think you understand," says Dad. "If I don't get this done, it's going to be a jungle out there."

"I know. But you have to have breakfast. And it's Mark's birthday."

"Happy birthday." As mechanical as a cuckoo clock registering the hour. "It would be lovely if the grass recognized the occasion and stopped growing for the day. But unfortunately . . ." For a second, Mark thinks he's going to turn round and go out again. But then he walks over to the sink, and lets Mummy sploosh water over his hands.

"There," she says, patting them dry again. "Go and sit down, and I'll bring things through."

"Any post yet?"

She shakes her head. Dad settles himself at the head of the table and scans the announcements on the front page of *The Times*.

"What's wrong with the mower?" says Mark.

"I somehow don't think you'd be terribly interested," says Dad, without looking up.

*I might be*. But he knows it's true: he wouldn't. He tries to find another approach, a gap through the castle walls. Finally he says: "Have you got any more pictures?"

"I haven't had time. I was going to try to do some today. But . . ."

"Well, you still can, can't you?" says Mummy, carrying in the tea tray.

He shakes his head.

"Oh, come on! It won't take *that* long to fix the mower, will it?"

Dad squints through the window at the sunlit garden. "The morning's gone."

"It's only just after eight!"

"And where am I going to find badgers and deer now?"

She starts to pour. “Well, there are still birds, aren’t there? Listen to —”

He holds up his hands to silence her.

“But —”

“Please!”

She winces, as if she’s been hit. Then she picks up the cereal packet and slowly trickles cornflakes into Dad’s bowl.

“Thank you.” His face is as stiff as a ventriloquist’s.

“Oh, won’t you have a bit more than that?”

He shakes his head.

“Not hungry?”

“No.”

She sighs softly, and hands the packet to Mark. He piles a mound of cornflakes in his bowl, hoping that his enthusiasm will make up for Dad’s sulkiness.

“Leave some for your mother,” says Dad.

“Sorry.” Mark peers into the box. It’s still half full.

“There’s more than enough for me,” says his mother, smiling. “Let the birthday boy have as much as he wants.”

“Of course.” Hunched forward, hands on the table, lips barely moving, Dad looks as if he’s in the last stages of being turned into stone. The power of his disapproval is frightening. It’s as if — even though he said he doesn’t want more himself — he feels Mark is somehow stealing the cereal from *him*.

“I can put some back.”

“No, you don’t!” says Mummy. “You’re still growing. And you need the energy, if you’re going to —” She stops, flushing.

“What’s he going to do?”

"Well . . ."

"I'm going out. With Barney." He avoids meeting his mother's eye. But again, it's not exactly a lie, is it? And she can't blame him: she told him not to mention Lou.

"What do you think of that, boy?" says Mummy quickly. Barney starts to thump his tail. "Yes, you like that idea, don't you? Now . . ."

She dribbles milk into Dad's bowl. He stops her with a curt nod. She passes the bottle to Mark. "Here we are. Tuck in."

They eat in silence. With every mouthful, Mark waits for the tension to break and a full-scale storm to erupt. The inside of his stomach throbs and tingles, as if someone's been at the lining with a cheese grater. He wants to finish his breakfast, open his presents, escape into the shed, put together a train with the 4-6-0 and run it into Peveril on the Swift. *Gracious! Is that a new engine, Mister Makepeace? Yes, Mrs Dauntless. New driver, too. Chap called Ted Bennett*. But he's worried about appearing greedy. And he can't help feeling that the atmosphere is in some way his fault. If it hadn't been his birthday, if he hadn't asked for presents and a special meal, then Dad would have been chatting about thrushes and starlings, or reading aloud some amusing story from the newspaper.

"Right," says Mummy, gathering up the bowls. "Why don't you have a look in there" — nodding at the bag — "while I get the toast?"

"What shall I start with?"

"The littlest one."

He gropes for it. It's only a few inches long, but mysteriously heavy. He unpeels the paper, taking care not to tear it, so that it can be used again. Inside is a box. He thumbs open the lid.

"Oh, thank you! This is super!"

A penknife. A ridged bone handle, making it easy to grip. Two blades. A tin opener. A bottle opener. And something else: a short, slightly curved spike, so powerfully sprung that it's hard to move. As he struggles to pull it out, he's aware of Mummy looking back over her shoulder at him.

"You know what that is?" she says.

"No."

"A thing for getting stones out of horses' hooves."

"No, it isn't," says Dad.

"That's what Gramper used to call it."

"Here," says Dad, holding his hand out. "I'll show you."

Mark wants to go on playing with it himself. But this is his chance. He daren't pass it up, and risk seeing the drawbridge raised again. Reluctantly he drops the knife into Dad's palm.

"It's a kind of bradawl," says Dad. He folds *The Times* into four, then rams the spike into one corner, twisting it backwards and forwards until the point appears on the other side. "See?"

"What do I do with it?"

Dad almost smiles. "Apart from boring through newspapers, you mean?"

Behind them, Mummy laughs: a wonderful sound, like the first gurgle of water in a thawing stream.

"Well," says Dad. "You can use it to get a screw going. Or make a hole in a bit of wood."

"Only remember," says Mummy, returning with a tray, "it's not a toy. It's a proper grown-up knife."

Dad nods. "Don't do what a boy I knew did once, and stick it in your pocket with the blade open."

"Oooh!"

Mark laughs. "I won't."

His mother sits down, begins spreading a slice of toast. "But it'll be handy to have it when you're out and about," she says. "It's good always to be prepared."

For a moment, the room seems to melt into a kind of tapestry: him and Lou together in the woods, cutting branches to make a camp.

"Here we are, darling," says Mummy, giving Dad the marmaladed toast. Then she leans across and pats the bag. "Why don't you see what else you've got?"

Mark pulls out a flat rectangular package.

"Yes, open that one."

He unwraps it. The sweet bookshop smell: the smoothness of the dust jacket. An eerie drawing of two children standing in front of a house. Above it — the looping letters stark in a patch of moonlight — the title: *Tom's Midnight Garden*.

"Have you heard of it?"

He shakes his head.

"Mr Drake thought it'd be just up your street."

He opens it and starts to read. It isn't hard: he's hooked from the first line. But he's conscious, too, that he's giving a performance, acting out how much he likes it.

"Don't get too caught up in it," says his mother, laughing. "You should ration yourself, or you'll have finished it by lunchtime." She gives Dad a conspiratorial glance. "I think you'll find there's something else in there."

He closes the book and reaches for the last present. It clunks enticingly in his hand. It *must* be an engine. He'll be able to run a long-distance service — maybe even a slow to London.

"Can you guess what it is?" says his mother.

He nods. He scrabbles free the sellotape at the end and slides off the sleeve of wrapping paper. Yes, the picture on the emerging box is the right colour: apple-green. And there's the gold LNER on the tender. But something about it is wrong. It's the line: too streamlined, too sleek.

And then he sees the name: *The Flying Scotsman*.

"There," says Mummy. "What do you think of that? Come on. Why don't you open it up?"

His fingers feel frozen. Clumsily, he forces them to lift the lid. Inside, the locomotive lies on its side, gleaming like a chrysalis. Everything's perfect: the valve gear, the driving rods, the buffers, as bright and delicately shaped as a piece of jewellery. His eyes fill with tears. It's unbearable: all that power and intricacy, and he's barred from it.

"What's the matter?" murmurs his mother. "Don't you like it?"

"It's beautiful," he says.

"So? . . ."

"It's a 'top link' locomotive. It's only used for expresses. They'd never put it on a branch line."

"Is Peveril on a branch line?"

How could she have forgotten? "Yes! The junction's at Swiftbridge. That's why I wanted the 4-6-0!"

Dad sighs. Mummy glances at him, twining hair round her finger. "Oh dear," she says. "Well, maybe we could change it?"

"No," says Dad. "He's opened the box. They won't take it back now." His face has set solid, like a mask. "I'm sorry I seem to have got things wrong again."

"Oh, Mark didn't say that! He said it was beautiful!"

"Anyway," says Dad. He jolts his chair back. It gives a chalk-on-blackboard shriek.

Mummy touches his arm. "Oh, don't leave us, darling."

Dad twitches free of her and stands up.

"Finish your toast," says Mummy. "Just to please me!"

He shakes his head. "I have to get on."

He walks out, shutting the door behind him. Mummy stares after him for a few seconds, as if she half-expects him to change his mind and come back in. Only when they hear the distant clang and thud of his tools does she turn away, pincering her forehead with her fingers.

"Oh dear, oh dear."

Mark squeezes his eyes to slits, trying not to cry. She probably thinks he should say sorry. But he's *not* sorry: he's angry.

"We thought it was what you wanted," she says.

"I wanted the 4-6-0. I *said* that's what I wanted."

"Well, I can't really see it makes much difference. It's still an engine, isn't it? I'm sure Patty Gallion would love to go on a train hauled by *The Flying Scotsman*."

"It'd be *wrong*."

She sighs. "Daddy said, when he was a boy, that's what *he* wanted. More than anything in the world. A model of *The Flying Scotsman*. And Gramps and Grannie never got him one. They never got him *anything* he asked for. And that's why he was determined that *you* were going to have one."

He's too miserable to reply.

"Ah well," she says, after a moment. She gets up and starts clearing the table.

Mark puts his presents back into the bag. "Thanks for the knife," he says. "And the book."

Up in his room, he stows *The Flying Scotsman* on top of the cupboard, where he won't be able to see it. Then he opens *Tom's Midnight Garden* again, and writes on the inside cover:

Mark Davenant
Perry Cottage
Church End
Oatley
England
Europe
The World
The Solar System
The Universe

There: it's really his now. He lies on his bed and abandons himself to the story. *Chapter II: The Clock Strikes Thirteen*. He's so engrossed in it that, when he hears the church clock strike the half-hour, a current arcs across the gap between his world and Tom's, and for a split second he doesn't know where he is. Reluctantly, he gets up, slips the knife into his pocket, then searches out the broken pistol and the old handkerchief he uses as a face mask and puts them in his knapsack.

"I'm going!" he calls from the bottom of the stairs.

His mother appears at the end of the hall, clutching two bottles and a cracked pudding bowl and a package wrapped in greaseproof paper. She's smiling, as if she's already forgotten about breakfast. "Here are the sandwiches, sweetie. And some lemon squash. And water for Barney. Have a lovely time."

"Thanks. Come on, boy."

They leave by the front door, to avoid having to pass Dad.

When he gets to the wood, the cross is still there. He dismantles it and throws the twigs into the bushes. He doesn't want anyone else to come upon it and realize that it's a sign.

"In there, boy! Go on! Through there!"

But Barney refuses to go. Normally, Mark would let him off his lead and leave him to find his own way. But he's worried that, if he does, the dog will simply make a bolt for the railway carriage, in hope of getting more stew. So he slips the loop of the leash round his wrist and crawls in himself, dragging mulish Barney after him. They're halfway through when Barney suddenly stops altogether, whimpering and driving his paws into the soft soil.

"Come on! Come *on*, Barns!"

Barney doesn't budge. Mark reaches back and clutches a handful of collar and fur, but there's not enough space to get any leverage. He peers out into the clearing. No sign of Lou. That's something, at least: if he's quick, she won't see him caught in this humiliating battle of wills with his own dog.

"Come on!" He tightens his grip, braces his feet against the trunk of a bush, and pulls with all his might. Suddenly, Barney stops fighting — not reluctantly, but so eagerly that the release of tension sends Mark sprawling on his back. Barney scrambles across his chest and stomach, scraping his bare skin, spattering him with earth. The leash flies free, burning Mark's wrist.

Blasted dog. He must suddenly have remembered where he was. Or seen something: a rabbit, a squirrel.

"Barney! Come back!"

Mark twists over, scrambling to his feet, ready to give chase. But there's no need: Barney has stopped no more than twenty yards away and is noisily scoffing something from Lou's hand.

"Gallion," she says, as he emerges. She makes the sign with her fingers.

"Gallion. Where did you come from?"

She glances up and behind her, at a heavy beech branch crowded with leaves.

"In that tree?"

She nods. She's still carrying the gun, but the mask has gone. She's wearing a long green blouse, belted at the waist like a tunic, and a handkerchief wound into a bandana round her hair. On her back is a battered khaki knapsack, stained with rust under the buckles.

"Were you there all the time?"

She nods again. But no smile — nothing to suggest she'd seen his struggle with Barney, or thought it funny. "I was keeping a lookout. Making sure the coast was clear."

He waits, wondering if she'll remember and wish him a happy birthday. But instead she bends forward and rubs her forehead against Barney's head. "He's a nice dog," she says. "Aren't you, boy? Just right for a gang of highwaymen."

Barney's tail paddles the air. Mark pulls out the broken flintlock and takes aim along the barrel at an invisible traveller.

"Is that what you want to be?" he says — hoping, suddenly, that she'll have forgotten about Aubrey Hillyard too, and say *yes*.

"Not yet. You said we were going to see the good chief."

He sighs. It's inescapable. "All right."

"But we can afterwards. I brought some sandwiches. Barney's had half of one of them, but there's still some left."

"I brought some, too." He clips on Barney's leash. "Let's go, then."

He expects Lou to lead the way. Instead, she waits patiently for him, and then follows a few paces behind. This was *his* idea. If it goes wrong, it'll be his fault.

For a moment, as they come out into the clearing, he thinks he's safe. Hillyard has obviously been busy — the carriage is now three-quarters blue, and the trestle table has been moved to the other side of the steps, but the man himself is nowhere to be seen. Not only that, but the door is closed. Surely, on a morning like this, it would be open, if he was there? Perhaps he's gone out for the day.

"What a funny place," says Lou.

He looks back. She's stopped at the edge of the trees, as if she's undecided whether to go on. "Haven't you seen it before?"

"Not close up like this." She wrinkles her nose.

"I know," he says. "It's a bit pongy." It is: worse than he remembered: a mixture of wood smoke and lavatory and a sharp smell that he can't put a name to. "We can go back if you want. I don't think he's in, anyway."

She starts to turn, then stops abruptly, her eyes focused on something behind him. At the same instant, Barney suddenly yanks the lead from his grip again. Mark swings round. Hillyard is standing in the doorway, one hand on the handle, the other holding a pair of binoculars. In his paint-spattered smock, and with the sun glittering on the gold threads in his beard, he looks like a picture of Odin.

"Oi!" he calls. "What do you think you're doing?"

"Nothing."

Barney launches himself at the steps and spreadeagles at Hillyard's feet. Without shifting his gaze, Hillyard bends down to greet him. "What do you mean, nothing? You were sneaking off. I saw you."

"We'd come to see you," says Mark. "But we thought you weren't here."

"Did you now?" He starts heavily down the steps, Barney at his heels. "And why was that?"

"The door was shut."

"Perhaps you're not familiar with that fine old tradition known as knocking?"

Mark senses Lou fidgeting at his side. He blushes.

"It didn't occur to you that the door might be shut for a reason?" says Hillyard.

Mark shakes his head.

"No, evidently not." He moves ponderously towards them. "Well, the fact is, I've had some unwelcome visitors lately. And I didn't particularly relish the thought of finding yet another broken beer bottle on the floor." He stops in front of them, eyeing Lou. "I suppose *you* wouldn't happen to know anything about that, would you?"

"I've seen a couple of boys," says Lou. "Throwing things. But I don't know their names."

"Ah" — his voice heavy with disbelief — "you don't know their names."

"No!" says Mark. "She couldn't! She's only just moved here! And she doesn't know anyone yet, except me. She was trying to protect you, if you must know. She made some traps, just over there. I fell in one yesterday. That's how I met her. So you're being very unfair!"

Hillyard scrutinizes her for a moment longer. Then the corner of his mouth puckers.

"Traps, eh? All right. Show me."

They lead him along the path to the pit. Hillyard crouches down, touches the freshly dug earth, riffles through the broken twigs.

"Neat," he says. "Clearly an apology is in order —" He raises his eyebrows, inviting her to fill in her name.

"Lou," she says.

"Lou. Right." He stands up. "Are you ready?"

Mark and Lou watch fascinated as he rubs the crumbs of dirt from his fingers, then suddenly lunges out and snatches wildly at the air.

"There," he says, opening his empty hand in front of Lou. "One apology. Don't often see such a fine specimen as that. Mint condition. One lady owner."

Lou giggles.

"Come on. It's yours."

She hesitates, then mimes taking something from his palm.

"That's it," says Hillyard. "Now — all square, are we?"

Lou nods.

"Friends?"

She nods again.

"Splendid. How'd you do, Lou?"

He holds out his hand. She gives it a tentative little shake.

"I'm Aubrey Hillyard," he says. "As Mark here has doubtless told you. What he may *not* have mentioned is that the only part of that name I answer to is *Aubrey*. No *Mr Hillyard*, if you please." He turns to Mark. "So you've had a chance to think over my proposal, have you?"

"Yes."

"And have come to give me your decision?"

He still hasn't really made up his mind. But yesterday he more or less promised Lou that Hillyard would tell them about the Brain. If he backs out now, she'll think he was just boasting.

"What's it to be?" says Hillyard. "Yes or no?"

"Yes. As long as Lou can listen as well."

Hillyard glances at her. "All right," he says, after a moment. "We have a bargain. But only on one condition. We must all swear ourselves to secrecy. Not a dickey bird, not a *whisper*, to anyone else. Careless talk costs lives. So I shan't breathe a word about Peveril on the Swift. And you must promise to keep mum about" — looking round quickly, then dropping his voice — "the Brain. Agreed?"

Mark hesitates. Hearing Hillyard say "Peveril on the Swift" out loud suddenly makes him feel naked. He glances at Lou. He's been treating her like an old friend, but the truth is he hardly knows her. What if she laughs at Peveril? On the other hand, if he says no, she'll think he's not just a show-off, but a sissy too.

"Lou?"

She looks at Mark. "I don't know what you're talking about."

"Ah. You haven't told her yet? About our arrangement?"

Mark shakes his head.

"All will be revealed," says Hillyard. "As long as you promise not to tell."

She looks at Mark again. "All right."

"Right."

They troop back to the carriage in Indian file.

"You will observe," says Hillyard to Lou, as they climb the steps, "that it lacks the woman's touch. You'll just have to avert your gaze, I'm afraid."

Inside, it's even more chaotic that it was before. The light coming through the windows is hazy with dust and marbled with cigarette smoke. The saucer next to the typewriter is piled with fag ends. More or less every other flat surface is crowded with dirty crockery. Hillyard quickly sweeps it into a noisy armful and clatters it into the sink, then lifts the kettle to feel how full it is.

"You find a seat for our guest," he says to Mark. "And I'll make the tea."

Mark wrestles a chair from the pile at the other end of the carriage and manoeuvres it into position by the tea chest. Lou sits down stiffly, hands crossed, one on each knee. Mark takes the seat next to her. When he catches her eye, she looks away sharply.

"Right," says Hillyard, laying out mugs and teapot, sugar bowl and a brand new tin of powdered milk. "The meeting is convened." He settles himself opposite them and turns to face Lou. "How much do *you* know about Peveril on the Swift?"

She shakes her head.

"Ah, so we're in the same boat. Well, that's good. This will be as much of a treat for you as it is for me." He pours the tea, pings the powdered milk with his fingernail. "Help yourselves to muck. Now, Mark."

"What?"

"You first."

"Why?"

"That's the agreement, remember? Peveril first, and then the Brain."

"Well . . ." He's not ready for this: for some reason, he'd always imagined that Hillyard would go first. He feels horribly inadequate. What if they're bored? What if Hillyard decides, after listening to him, that he's being asked to swap a shiny half-crown for a dull threepenny bit and calls the whole thing off?

"Well what?" says Hillyard.

"What do you want to know?"

"Everything."

"There isn't much. Honestly. It's only a made-up village. To go with my model railway."

"Yes, you told me. But no difficulty there. I'm just the man for a made-up village. And — unless I've entirely lost my power to judge character — I'd say Lou here is just the woman for one too."

Mark glances at Lou. She looks as tense as an overdrawn bow.

"Well," he says, "it's a bit like here, I suppose. Like Oatley. Only more hilly. And with a river. The Swift. That's why people settled there. Stone Age hunters. Then Iron Age farmers. Then the Romans. You can't see anything now, of course. But Mr Gallion, he's an archaeologist, and he found some remains in a big field."

"Excellent!" says Hillyard. "You've equipped the place with a proper history. That's what I call doing a thorough job."

"And then in the Middle Ages, there were monks there." His voice is easier now, the words coming more freely. "You can see where *they* were. The abbey ruins. And an old hermitage."

"How did you make the ruins?" asks Lou.

"Wire. And Polyfilla. And then paint. Grey, and a bit of green for the moss."

"Admirably practical," says Hillyard. He screws up his eyes. "I'm a visitor. Just off the train. Set the scene for me. Where do I go, if I want to see this abbey?"

"Through the station yard, and into the High Street —"

"The High Street." His eyes are still closed. "Some fine old buildings there, I imagine. Half-timbered pub? A shop with a bow window? Something Georgian, in handsome red brick?"

"Yes. Dr Dauntless's house. With an orchard behind."

"Oh yes, an orchard. Naturally. And then?"

"And then you turn left up the footpath. And there are the ruins."

"Yes, yes, I can see them. Very romantic." He flicks his ear lobe. "And I think — correct me if I'm wrong — that from where I'm standing I can just make out the sound of the Swift?"

Mark nods. "You can hear it everywhere in the village. It's a fast-moving river. In the old days, there used to be a watermill."

"Of course there did."

"The mill house is still there. Mr Gallion lives there now."

Hillyard opens his eyes. "What, on his own?"

Mark laughs. "No, with his family. Mrs Gallion. And their children. Patty and Paul."

"Ah." He fumbles in his pocket, pulls out a pouch of Golden Virginia and a packet of cigarette papers. "And how old are Patty and Paul?"

"Patty's thirteen. She's the eldest. But they still have adventures together. In their boat."

"Ah, their *boat*." He worries out a strand of tobacco and lays it on an open Rizla. "What, like in *Swallows and Amazons*, you mean? Or Rat and Mole?"

Mark nods.

"Does it have a name, this boat?"

"*Pintail*."

He rolls the cigarette shut and licks the edge of the paper. "And they keep it on the river, do they? The Swift?"

"Yes."

Hillyard nods. He lights up, inhales deeply, presses his lips together and sends a fine jet of smoke across the tea chest, stinging Mark's eyes. "Very good adventures too, I dare say. Finding the gold plate of the ancient de Peveril family, buried on an island during the Civil War? That kind of thing, eh?"

"Yes." But he's embarrassed. Patty and Paul taking care of a stray dog, or rescuing a little girl lost in the abbey ruins and returning her to her grateful parents, sounds childishly simple. And some of their adventures aren't even as definite as that. They're more just the *idea* of being together and doing something exciting. "And then there are the people who work on the railway," he goes on quickly. "Mr Makepeace, the station master. And Percy Strong, the engine driver."

"Yes, we mustn't forget them." Hillyard takes an unhurried pull on his cigarette. "Well," he says finally, "I think it sounds first-rate, this Peveril of yours. I should like to go there and pop into the pub, and . . . What's its name, by the way?"

"The Waggon and Horses. But everyone calls it the Waggon."

"The Waggon. Yes, of course they do. Well, I'd like to pop into the Waggon one day and buy Mr Makepeace a drink, and then saunter on down to the mill, and see what Patty and Paul are up to. But I can't, can I? So I'm just going to have to rely on you instead."

"On me? For —"

"To be my eyes and ears. Give me the low-down, as the Americans say. On everything that's going on there." He takes a swig of tea and grimaces, as if he doesn't like the taste. "A weekly bulletin, say?"

*But it isn't a real place. It's only made-up*. But to say that would be a defeat. Lou must have noticed the respectful way Hillyard treats him, as one storyteller to another. If he refuses the challenge, he'll just make himself seem an ordinary boy again.

"All right," he says.

Hillyard puts his hand out. Mark shakes it.

"There," says Hillyard. "Done and dusted. He licks the tip of his finger, waggles it at Lou. "And you're our witness?"

Lou nods, then picks up her mug and sips from it, just like a grown-up. Gingerly, Mark tastes his own tea. The bitter, coppery taste makes him pull a face.

"Excellent."

"Will you tell us about the Brain now?" says Mark.

Hillyard says nothing.

"Come on. You *said* you would."

"Yes, I did, didn't I?" He gets up and peers out of the window, slowly scanning the clearing from left to right.

"All right," he says, returning to his seat. "A bargain's a bargain. But remember . . ." He draws a circle in the air, looping them together.

"Why is it a secret?" asks Lou.

"Official answer: someone might steal the idea and write the thing before I do."

"What's the unofficial answer?" says Mark.

"Ah, well." He sucks in a last lungful of smoke, then screws the cigarette butt into the ashtray, crushing it with his thumb as if he were killing an insect. "You never know who's listening. Someone — or some*thing* — might think it was about them. And decide to take appropriate action."

"Who?" says Lou.

"Or what?"

Hillyard pinches his nose. "Let's play a game. Inventions. The last hundred years."

"What inventions?" says Mark.

"Any inventions."

"Cars," says Lou.

"Aeroplanes," says Mark. "Helicopters. The jet engine."

"Radio. Television."

"The telephone."

"Good," starts Hillyard. "So —"

"Records," says Lou. "Tape recorders."

"Films —"

Hillyard holds up a hand. "Well, that's a good crop to be going on with. Any pattern you can see emerging?"

What's the link between planes and films and cars? Mark's desperate to find the answer first, show how quick he is. But try as he may, his mind's a blank.

"They're all — well, most of them . . ." starts Lou, hesitantly.

"Yes?" says Hillyard.

"Most of them are ways of getting about, aren't they? Or — what do you call it? Communicating?"

"Yes! Precisely! That's *exactly* what they are!" He leans forward confidentially, as if — even here — he's worried about being overheard. "And this is my question for you," he says, in a stage whisper. "What if it's not an accident? What if there's something *behind* the whole strange business?"

"What business?" says Mark.

"All this moving around at breakneck speed. Sending messages, images, words, more and more of them, into every corner of the globe. Hm?"

Mark's stumped again. He looks at Lou, to see if she understands any better. She's hunched forward, hands gripping the front of her seat. Her small, sharply outlined face is puzzled but alert, like an animal trying to make sense of a far-off sound.

"First you had cinema," says Hillyard. "But that wasn't very efficient, because people had to *go* to picture houses to see it. So then they brought in the radio. That was better: you heard that in your own home. But it was easy to turn off. So now there's television."

"You can still switch it off," says Lou.

He shifts noisily. "You have one of the infernal things, I take it?"

"Yes."

He turns to Mark. "And you?"

Mark shakes his head. "My father won't get one."

"Wise man. So what do you watch, Lou?"

"*The Lone Ranger. Champion the Wonder Horse*."

"And how often do you say" — clapping his hands together — "*Right! That's it!*, and walk out in the middle?"

Lou hesitates. "Not very often."

"It has you, doesn't it? Under its spell?" The way he says it — deep in his throat, as if he's suddenly been taken over by an alien intelligence — makes the back of Mark's neck tingle.

Lou says nothing. Still watching her, Hillyard gropes blindly for the Golden Virginia and starts to roll himself another cigarette.

"So is it like *Journey into Space?*" says Mark. "The Brain uses television to hypnotize people?"

Hillyard smiles. "That's what happens in *Journey into Space*, is it?"

"Yes. Didn't you hear it?"

Hillyard shakes his head. "Like to keep this" — touching his temple — "as clear as I can. No, in my story, the Brain doesn't just *use* television. It *is* television. And radio. And all the rest."

"But how?" says Lou. "A brain can't be a television. It can't be anything, can it? Except a brain?"

"It's made up of cells. A television is a kind of cell. And the more of them there are, the bigger the Brain gets. The more aware of itself. The craftier."

Lou stares at him.

"But there's got to be a main bit," says Mark. "Where the *thing* is. Whatever it is."

Hillyard shakes his head. "That's the point. You ask a scientist where *we* are, and he'll say in here." He taps his temple again. "But if you say *which bit?* — in the cerebellum, or the amygdala, or the hippocampus? — he won't be able to tell you. My Brain — the Brain in my story — is the same. It's nowhere and it's everywhere. The way it grows is by duping poor old *us* into building it." He lights his roll-up, then leaves it drooping from his lips as he stretches out his hands, splaying the thick yellow-stained fingers into tentacles. "We think we're doing all these things for our own good. But actually we're just the Brain's slaves. Doing its bidding without realizing it. And, if we're not careful, eventually we'll just be reduced to so many *components*. Like bees in a giant hive."

"Are you just making this up?" says Lou, her voice sluggish with apprehension.

Hillyard laughs. "What do you think?"

Lou stares at him, saying nothing. To break the silence, Mark says:

"But how does the Brain do it? Persuade people, I mean? *I* wouldn't be persuaded."

"Wouldn't you now? Don't be so sure. Chances are, you wouldn't even be aware of it."

"Yes I would. If it told me to do something."

"Ah, but that's the cunning of the thing. Little by little, it chips away at who *you* are. Slowly turns you into someone else entirely. Or some*thing* else."

"Brainwashing, you mean," says Lou.

Hillyard nods. "So you start to forget the story of Lou, or Mark. And gradually become part of *its* story instead. Until eventually . . ."

Lou makes a hissing sound. Mark glances at her again. Her shoulders are raised, and she's straightened her arms and braced them against her thighs. He can't decipher the look on her face. Fear? Disgust? Whatever it is, she's uncomfortable. He brought her here. It's his responsibility to get her out again, back to the straightforward, adultless world where they met.

Hillyard must have noticed the change in her too. "Anyway," he says, "We can talk about that next time."

"Yes," says Mark, standing up. "We should be going."

"Oh, no hurry," says Hillyard. "Finish your tea. I should have got biscuits. I will. When you come again. That's a promise."

"We have to be somewhere," says Mark, gathering up Barney's leash. Even to himself, he sounds younger and less convincing: no longer the creator of Peveril on the Swift, just a boy making up excuses.

"All right," says Hillyard. "How about Friday, then? About the same time?"

"Maybe. Thank you for the tea." Mark touches Lou's shoulder. "Come on. Let's go."

He drags Barney down the steps and — with Lou close behind — races across the clearing and into the wood. Only when he's reached the track does he stop. As Lou emerges, batting leaves away from her face, he studies her, searching for some clue to how she's feeling. Already he seems to hear her voice in his head: *Why did you take me to see him? He's horrible*.

"Do your parents know?" he says. "What you're doing?"

She shakes her head.

"Better not to tell them."

"All right."

"So what do you want to do now?" he says quickly.

She hesitates. "Let's be highwaymen."

The relief makes him laugh. "Righto." He hesitates, then goes on, "I know a super place for a hideout."

"Where?"

"By the chalk pit."

She pulls a blade of grass, tickles her lip with the stem. "I don't know where that is."

"I'll show you."

# CHAPTER FOUR

They trudge back through the clumpy tussocks of Willetts Lane, their feet making a steady *swish swish swish*. The rising heat of the day seems to have thickened the air, so that it weighs on their shoulders and snatches at their clothes and sticks to their skin. Even Barney feels it: instead of running on ahead, he stops every ten paces, huffing like a tank engine taking a gradient, to wait for them to catch up. When they reach the end and turn right up the flinty track to the chalk pit, he lingers for a few seconds before following them, as if he'd rather have gone home.

"Here," says Mark. He points to the chalk cliff. "Can you climb that?"

She stands back, assessing the height and angle. Then she takes a run at it, gets halfway, loses momentum and starts to slip again.

"Hang on!" He scrambles up the easy route, using the bumps and cracks as footholds. His plan is to lean over and give her a hand. But by the time he's got there, she's managed to grab a root and haul herself up on her own. Panting, they lie side by side on the rim of grass between the wheat field and the edge of the pit.

"Yes," she says. "This is a good place. Do you come here a lot?"

He nods. "When I was young, I used to think it was magic."

"How?"

"Oh, you know. Silly stuff. I thought there was a wizard here. He had a big pointy hat and a long beard, and a wand. And he'd put a spell on the animals, so they could talk."

"I don't think that's silly."

He pushes himself onto his elbows, twisting towards the little group of stunted trees. "That's the hideout. Over there. You want to see?"

She gets up. "OK."

He leads her round to the far side and shows her the entrance. She squats down to peer inside.

"Oh, this is good," she says, working her thumb into a hollow in the thickest trunk. "We can leave each other messages here, can't we? And no one will know."

"OK." He's suddenly hit with a longing, so powerful that it makes his skin tingle: she'll crawl in and he'll follow her, and it will be like his odd — what? not a dream: he can't think of a word for it — this morning.

"Want to go in?" he says.

She wrinkles her nose. "Oh, not today. It's too small. We'd just swelter. Let's have lunch out here. And then play a game."

"All right." He's disappointed. But maybe later, when they've eaten . . .

"Where's Barney?"

"He'll be here in a minute. He's lazy. He'll have gone the long way round. Through the field." He raises his voice. "Barns! Barns! Here, boy!"

She laughs. "Why do you call him Barns?"

Mark shrugs. There's a noise behind them. The wall of wheat starts to sway like a bead curtain.

"See?" he says.

Barney limps out, panting and shaking dust from his coat. His muzzle's dark and slimy with saliva.

"Oh, he's thirsty!" says Lou as he flops down next to Mark. "Aren't you, boy? You want something to drink."

Mark takes the picnic things from his bag, fills the cracked bowl with water and offers it to Barney. Lou giggles as Barney slavers at it, spraying Mark's shirt and shorts.

"No more now," Mark tells him. "Or there won't be any left for later."

Barney sighs and collapses again. His nostrils twitch as they unwrap their lunches, but he's too tired to get up and demand food.

"What have you got?" says Lou. "I brought corned beef."

"Cheese."

She holds out half a sandwich. "Want one? There's enough."

"Swap?"

"All right."

They munch in silence, concentrating on what they're doing, taking perfect round bites to make their sandwiches look like the ones the characters eat in comics, holding them up for each other's approval. Lou saves her last couple of mouthfuls for Barney. As he gratefully gobbles them down, she reaches into her bag and pulls something out. Mark recognizes the red-and-cream striped colour scheme even before he sees the big curvy lettering: *Nestlé Milkybar*.

"Here. Happy Birthday."

"Thanks." He wonders how you get sweets if your parents are shopkeepers. Do you just help yourself? Or do you have to buy them, like everyone else? "You want a bit?"

She nods. He snaps off the first two squares and gives one to her. She licks it gingerly, as if it were a lolly.

"What presents did you get?" she says.

"A new engine."

"For Peveril on the Swift?"

"Yes." He wants her to share his disappointment, to sympathize. But if he tells her it was the wrong *sort* of engine, she won't understand: she'll just think he's a crybaby. "And this," he says, hoisting the knife from his pocket.

She holds her hand out. He gives her the knife. She weighs it in her palm, then opens the long blade and runs a fingertip along the edge.

"Good," she says. She crawls to the bush and carves a cross into the nearest branch. "That can be our signal. To show when we've been somewhere. OK?"

He nods. But he feels left out: it's *his* knife, and she's taken it and used it for the first time.

"You shouldn't carry it like that," he says, as she snakes back. "You could have a nasty accident. My dad knew someone who —"

"All right." She closes the knife and returns it to him. "Did you believe all that?"

"What my dad told me?"

She shakes her head. "All that stuff about the Brain?"

"The *Brain?* How it's taking over the world, you mean?"

"Yes."

"Course not. It's a story."

"I don't think *he* thinks it is. Mr Hillyard."

"Aubrey."

"All right. Aubrey."

Mark scoffs. "And of course he does! He's writing it. He's an author."

"Why's it such a big secret, then?"

"He said. He's worried someone'll pinch the idea."

"He said that was the *official* reason. And did you notice the way he whispered? And kept looking round? As if the Brain might be listening? Or watching?"

"You're imagining things." He almost laughs with the pleasure of saying it to someone else rather than having it said to him. "That's just — what do you call it — dramatic effect? You know, like" — leaning forward and lowering his voice — *"It was a dark winter's night. Clouds scudded across the moon."* He clasps his hands together and blows into them. "*Whoo-whoo-whoo-whoo-whoo.*"

Barney stumbles to his feet, tail wagging, ears half-pricked.

"Oh, look!" says Lou, laughing. "Poor Barney! He thought that was real!"

Mark shakes his head. "No, he didn't. Did you, boy?" He clutches the slack ruff of hair round Barney's neck and gently kneads it. "You knew it was just a —"

Barney suddenly stiffens, yanks himself free and runs to the edge of the chalk pit.

"What is it?" says Lou.

"Blast! Someone must be coming. Here, boy!"

Barney doesn't move. His hackles rise. He starts to growl. Mark crawls next to him and peers over. At first he can't see what's caught Barney's attention. Then, halfway down the hill, he notices a girl coming slowly towards them, stopping every few seconds to pick flowers from the bank.

"Can you see anything?" says Lou.

He turns and mouths, "Peggy Akers."

"Who's Peggy Akers?" She crab-scuttles over to join him, keeping her head down to avoid being seen. "Oh, *her*. She comes into the shop sometimes. Shall we ambush her?"

"Mm —"

"Why shouldn't we?"

"It seems a bit unfair, doesn't it? Two against one."

"Oh, come on, it's only a game."

But would Peggy Akers realize that? He's seen her at school making patterns with gummed paper, or — her small eyes red and teary with concentration — sewing little felt angels and snowmen to give people as Christmas-tree decorations. He's never seen her playing an imagination game or reading a book she didn't have to.

"Not much point being highwaymen if we don't hold people up," says Lou.

"It's just her. I don't know — I don't think —"

"We won't *really* rob her. We'll give everything back."

Half-crouching, she starts along the edge of the field, shielded by the hedge. Mark hesitates for a few seconds, then clips on Barney's lead and hurries after her. As she reaches the gap where the tractors go in and out, he puts his hands together and bellows in a stage whisper:

"Lou!"

But it's too late. By the time he and Barney get there, she's already in the lane, with her mask pulled down and her hand reaching for her holster. He sees Peggy Akers clasping her little posy to her chest, watching open-mouthed as the Lone Ranger descends on her brandishing a revolver.

"Stand!" yells Lou. "Let's see the colour of your money!"

Peggy Akers blinks through her round glasses and peers round frantically, presumably in the hope of spotting someone she can call for help.

"Resistance is useless! There's none here but you, and our gallant band of footpads!"

As she turns back, Peggy Akers catches sight of Mark. Her face squishes, like a rubber ball being squeezed.

"Come, madam. No call for tears!" says Lou. "Just give us your purse and your jewels, and you may leave with your honour and your life!"

Peggy Akers continues staring at Mark for a moment. Then, with a wail, she turns and starts running down the track.

"Quick!" shouts Lou. "She mustn't escape! Let loose the hunting dogs!"

She sets off in pursuit. Mark follows, Barney tugging at his leash. As they close on her, Peggy Akers suddenly cries out, stumbles, then collapses onto the bank, strewing the ground with buttercups and daisies. Grimacing with pain, she clutches at her ankle — revealing a pair of lumpy green knickers. To Mark's horror, they're stained with darker patches, and the top of her thigh is wet.

"Sorry, Peggy, we didn't mean to —"

She stops him with a shriek so loud that it hurts his ears.

"What's the matter?" he says. "What have you done?"

Still screaming, she screws up her eyes and shakes her head.

"Must have twisted her ankle," says Lou. "Or sprained it." She pushes up her mask, wipes her sleeve across her forehead. Despite the heat and the running, she's very pale.

"You want a hand?" says Mark.

Peggy shakes her head again. "You're horrible! You're a bully! And you" — squinting up at Lou — "You are too!"

"Sorry," she says. "We were only playing —"

Peggy Akers lets out another howl.

"You want us to help you? We could give you piggybacks. Take it in turns . . ."

"No!" She kicks out wildly. Mark and Lou back away. Peggy Akers rolls over, gingerly pushes herself to her feet.

"Do you want your flowers?" says Lou, starting to gather them up.

Peggy Akers shakes her head. "They're all spoilt now." She sniffs and begins hobbling down the track. After twenty yards or so, she turns back and calls:

"I hate you!"

Mark and Lou look at each other, then plod back to where they left their knapsacks. *There: what did I tell you?* He can't say it: she looks miserable enough already, and might burst into tears like Peggy Akers. But he hopes she'll realize and say sorry.

But she doesn't. Instead, as she finishes buckling her bag, she looks up and asks:

"Can you show me Peveril on the Swift?"

It's completely unexpected: a jab in the stomach, which knocks the wind out of him.

"Well . . ." How can he explain?

"Don't you want to?"

"It isn't that. It's just that . . . Well, we ought to be outside, oughtn't we? On a day like this?"

She laughs. "Is that what your mother says?"

He shrugs.

"Well, we can't be highwaymen, can we? We tried that, and it didn't work. So —"

"All right. Come on, Barney."

"I've never seen a model railway before. Not a proper one."

He shoulders his knapsack and starts off down the hill, trying to keep ahead of her. He doesn't want to talk: he needs to think. He mustn't let her see that he's scared of his parents — but he knows that if they find out what he's doing, there'll be hell to pay: Dad in a days-long sulk, Mummy shaking her head, saying, *I told you not to bring her here, didn't I?* There's always a chance, of course, that they'll have gone out. If not, he'll just have to come up with some way of getting her into the shed without their noticing.

"Why don't you want to show me?" says Lou, catching him up.

"It's all right."

"Why are you so grumpy, then?"

"I'm not grumpy."

"Yes, you are."

"Not."

"Are."

"Is it because of Peggy what's-her-name?"

"I just told you, didn't I? It isn't because of anything!"

He quickens his pace. But she hurries after him.

"Does she go to your school?"

He nods.

"Where's that?"

"The Hoops."

"Oh, that's where *I'm* going to be going. At least, I think I am. What's it like?"

"All right."

"My dad's not sure about it. He says the headmistress —"

"Tony."

"Tony's not a woman's name."

"She's probably called Antonia or something."

"But that's what *you* call her? Tony?"

He nods. She frowns, thinking about it.

"Well, anyway," she says, after a moment. "He says she's got too many ideas. And she's more or less a Communist. But still, it's probably better than the village school. What do you think?"

He shrugs. They're at Horseshoe Farm now, and the noise of the farmyard makes it seem more natural not to speak. As he reaches the road, he's suddenly aware that Lou is no longer with him. He turns and sees her staring into the pig pen. A portly Large White sow, surrounded by squealing piglets, looks back at her, ramming its snout against the bars, grunting and snoring. He waits. After a moment, Lou looks up at him and calls:

"Is it all right?"

He nods.

"But it sounds hurt."

"She's just hungry," he shouts.

Lou lightly touches the pig's nose, then breaks away and half-runs towards him.

"Haven't you ever seen a pig before?" says Mark.

"Not like that."

He eyes her curiously. She must be more or less the same age he is. How could you get to ten years old and have never been to a farm?

"There weren't any where I used to live," she says.

"Where was that? On Venus? With the Treens?"

"In a town, stupid. They don't have pigs in towns."

*I'm not stupid*. But he doesn't want to start a fight with her now, when they're so close to home.

"Well, you don't need to worry about her," he says. "She's just a greedy guts. She gets plenty to eat. Potato peelings. Swill. Yum yum." He clutches his belly, screws up his face, makes a honking, spluttering noise. But when he glances at Lou, she isn't laughing.

They walk along the pavement in single file, keeping clear of the traffic: the doctor's black Super Snipe, sly and purry as a cat; toothless Ernie on his bicycle; a tractor wagging a heavy rake that almost bounces up onto the kerb as it passes. When they get to Church End, he stops by the flint wall of the graveyard.

"Can you wait here?"

"Why?"

"I just need to check something."

Without waiting for a reply, he hurries on. There's a powerful smell of petrol fumes and freshly cut grass, but he can't hear the mower. He peers in at the gate. Yes, that's something: Dad's finished. But the car's still there — which means they must be somewhere in the house. The question is *where* exactly? Once he knows that, he'll be able to plan a safe route to the shed.

Mark glances back at Lou. She's sucking on a grass stem and watching him curiously. He holds up a finger — *just a sec* — and pushes open the garden gate. He moves quietly, peeking at the windows every couple of seconds to make sure he hasn't been spotted. When he reaches the back door, he ties Barney to the boot scraper and murmurs: "Stay." Then he lifts the latch and sneaks inside.

The kitchen's warm and full of the salty reek of boiling bacon. On the stove, a big pan rattles and throbs, its lid lifting every few seconds to let out steam. But there's no sign of Mummy, and her apron's hanging on the hook.

He edges into the hall. The study door's open, and he can see that both the chairs are empty. Perhaps his parents are up in the darkroom. That would be perfect: the window's blacked out, and they wouldn't be able to hear anything from the garden.

As he moves to the bottom of the stairs, a sound stops him. He can't tell what it is — a person? An animal? — but something about it makes the hairs stir on his arms and neck. Steadying himself on the banister, he creeps up, and looks through the balusters on the landing. It's his parents all right: it's coming from their bedroom. What are they doing? Fighting? No, people yell at one another when they fight — and Mummy and Dad aren't yelling exactly.

A tiger, that's what he's reminded of: a tiger they saw last year at the zoo, so absorbed in clawing and tearing at a bleeding hunk of goat that it was impervious to the line of faces pressed to the bars of its cage. It would be the same if he walked in now: they wouldn't be able to stop themselves. He half-imagines them: clearly sees the bare arms and legs. But what about the rest? When he thinks about it, it just blurs into a grey fuzz.

He feels faint. He grasps the banister more tightly, drops his head forward. The blood floods back into his brain, thudding in his ears. He waits until he's got his balance, then tiptoes away again, holding his breath.

He collects Barney, to stop him barking, then hurries to the gate and beckons Lou. She runs to join him. He puts a finger to his lips.

"What's the matter?"

He shakes his head. "We have to be quiet, that's all."

He doesn't want to look at her. He doesn't want her near. If she gets too close, some boundary will be breached, some vital part of what it is to be Mark will be lost. Not looking behind him, he hurries up the path and round the back of the house.

"Here we are."

He lifts the latch and opens the door to the shed. Lou hesitates, then walks in, hugging herself and wrinkling her nose. Even today, the place is chilly and smells of damp cardboard and rats and coal dust. Mark prods Barney inside with his leg, checks again that they're not being watched, then quickly shuts the door again behind them.

"What are you doing that for?" says Lou. "I can't see anything now."

"There's a light. Hang on."

He gropes for the switch. A haze of dirty yellow spills from the overhead bulb, so muted by grime that it only half-dissolves the darkness. Peveril on the Swift emerges into a winter dusk, the papier-mâché hills a dim grey green, the tracks just an indistinct tyre mark skidding across the board. Beyond the layout, they can see the lawnmower handles jutting out like antlers, but the pile of old boxes and the jumble of tents, tarpaulins, old croquet mallets in the corner are still bat-winged with shadow.

"Is this really where you live?" says Lou. "Well, not *here*, I mean." She nods towards the house.

"Course it is."

"Why are you behaving like this, then? As if you're a burglar or something?"

"My dad works at home. He doesn't like to be disturbed, that's all."

"But we're not disturbing him, are we? Not if we're out here, playing with your railway?"

Mark shrugs. He can feel himself starting to blush.

"What does he do?" she says.

"He just gets a bit —"

"No, silly! I mean, what's his job?"

"Oh, he writes things. And —"

"What, like Aubrey?"

He shakes his head. "Not books. Articles. And he takes pictures. And gives lectures to people."

"That is a *bit* like Aubrey, isn't it?"

He shrugs. "I suppose." He finds it hard to keep Dad and Aubrey Hillyard in his mind at the same time — particularly now, for some reason, after hearing the sounds from his parents' room.

"I'd like to do something like that when I'm older," she says.

He nods and turns towards the layout. "That's it, anyway. Peveril on the Swift. What do you think?"

She bends close to study it, her gaze panning slowly past the church and the rectory, the Dauntlesses' house and the half-timbered Waggon and Horses, the red-brick façades of the high street. When she reaches the station yard, she pauses a moment to read the miniature advertisements on the hoardings.

"Is it a circuit?" she says, looking up. "Does the train just go round and round?"

"Yes." He traces the route with his finger: out of the Sheepfold Tunnel, through the station, past the main-line points, then looping back behind the village and into the Abbey Tunnel.

"So where is it? The train, I mean?"

"Here." He takes the torch from its hook and angles the beam along the track. "See?"

Lou crouches down to squint into the Sheepfold Tunnel. "Oh, yes, I can! Can you move it?"

"Course."

He switches on the controller, gradually increases the power. The tank whines into the open, hauling its three coaches. Lou stiffens with excitement.

"Can I have a go?"

"All right," he says, stopping the train in the station. "But be careful."

"What do I do?"

"Just turn it."

She twists the knob abruptly. The engine jerks forward, the coaches rattling in its wake.

"Not like that!" He brushes her out of the way, snatches the knob, reduces the power. The tank slows, just in time to take the first curve without derailing. "See?"

"All right, then. Let me have another go."

"OK. But gently, all right?"

She nods.

"All right."

She stops the train, leaving it stranded on the other side of the layout, under the abbey ruins. Then she takes a deep breath and cautiously starts increasing the power again. The engine inches ahead and enters the tunnel at a stately pace. She waits for it to reappear on the other side, then slows it to a halt in the station.

"There!" Her face is beaming.

"Yes, that's a bit better."

She bends down to peer at the figures on the platform. "Who are those people?"

He starts picking them up, one by one. "Well, this is Mr Makepeace, the station master."

"Yes, yes, I can see that. Cos of his uniform. But what —"

"And this is Mrs Dauntless."

"Did you paint her?"

"My mother helped."

"She looks very smart. All dressed up like that, with her hat and a coat and skirt."

"She goes up to town a lot."

"How can she?" She runs her fingers along the plastic side of the carriage. "The doors don't open, do they?"

"Like this." He drops the figure in the Oxo box. "Now the real Mrs Dauntless is on the train."

Lou nods. "And is that Patty and Paul?"

"Yes."

"Can I see?"

He drops them into her palm. She weighs them for a moment, then sets them down on the board, looking from one tiny face to the other.

"I like them," she says finally. "Where's the *Pintail*?"

He retrieves the boat from the mill-house jetty and slides it round the blue-green ribbon of the Swift.

"Hm," says Lou. "They can't really go in it, can they? Their stands are too big. And they can't sit down."

"You have to imagine that bit."

She nods again, still staring at the boat. Then she picks up Patty and waddles her across the painted meadow towards the river.

" 'Hey! Paul! Quick! The *Pintail's* drifting away!' "

" 'OK! Don't worry!' " He snatches Paul, skips him over the Swift, hooks the edge of the boat with the base and drags it towards the bank.

" 'Phew!' " says Lou, laughing. " 'That was close!' "

" 'All in a day's work!' "

She catches his eye and smiles. After a moment she says, "Are we going back?"

"Where?"

"To see Aubrey? On Friday?"

"Oh, I see. I don't know. Do you want to?"

She hesitates a moment. "I think so. Don't you?"

"All right."

She smiles. "And *I* can tell him a bit about Peveril on the Swift this time, can't I?"

He nods distractedly. A thought has suddenly struck him. "Did you say anything to your parents about me? Or Aubrey?"

"Not really, no."

"What do you mean, *not really*?"

"Well, just that I was playing with a boy I'd met."

"And they didn't mind?"

She shakes her head. "They're glad. They're always saying I need to make friends here."

He nods. "Well, don't tell them any more, OK?"

"Why not?"

"It's our secret, all right? Just between us."

# CHAPTER FIVE

When he wakes, the world looks subtly different. The *shape* of everything's the same — the pile of books, his old stuffed lollopy-eared rabbit, the table with the broken leaf — but there's a new quality to the light coming through the curtains, as if during the night someone replaced the sun with a not quite identical replica. It's a few moments before he can remember just *what* has changed, the patchwork of good and bad things that happened yesterday. He's ten now, first of all. Then there's the disaster of the *Flying Scotsman*, and his sloping off to see Hillyard and Lou without telling anyone, and the attack on Peggy Akers, and bringing Lou here, like a sneak, and hearing sounds he shouldn't have done from his parents' bedroom. And, above all, finally having a friend: a friend with whom he can share Peveril on the Swift.

He gets up, brushes his teeth, goes downstairs. His mother's in the kitchen, standing in front of the stove. She looks quickly over her shoulder, eyebrows raised, her pale un-made-up face not quite managing a smile.

"Hullo, Mummy. Shall I lay the table?"

She nods. "All right. But just for two of us. Daddy's not feeling well, I'm afraid."

"What's wrong with him?"

"Oh, he sent some pictures in for a competition. In the *Amateur Photographer*. And he hasn't heard anything. So he's very cast down, poor love."

Is that it? Or is the real reason that Dad's still angry with him?

"Is it bad?"

"What?"

"Whatever's wrong with him?"

"Well, you know."

*Well, you know*. The way she says it makes him think of a pair of heavy dice, shaken together, then carefully spilled onto the table. Double six: *Of course it's bad. You know how sensitive he is. How could it be anything else, after the way you've been behaving?*

"I'm —" But he can't come out and say *sorry*, just like that. "Anything I can do?"

"Well . . ." She gives him an appraising glance. "I'm just making him a bit of toast. And a cup of tea."

*Oh, no*, he prays. *Please don't ask me to take it to him*.

"And I was just wondering, when I go up with it, whether you'd mind running down to the shop for me?"

He nods.

"Don't forget, will you?" — finally forcing her mouth into a smile — "And start being Normans and Saxons or whatever it is you play with that new friend of yours?"

"Lou?"

She nods.

"I won't."

"And then we can have breakfast when you get back, all right?"

"All right."

"Thank you, poppet: you're an angel." He wonders if she can see how relieved he is. But she's already turning away, wrapping a tea towel round her fingers.

"What do we need?"

"Twenty Players for Daddy. And some Summer County." She bends down, slides out the grill pan. "Ask them to put it on our account."

"You sure that'll be OK?"

"Yes, it's fine now." But he notices she doesn't look at him as she says it: she's searching for something in the cupboard, her face screened by the door. "There was just a bit of a misunderstanding, that's all. It's all sorted out."

"But they've never met me," he says. "They won't know who I am."

"Just tell them you're Mrs Davenant's son. Ah . . ." She takes down a jar of Marmite, twists off the lid and peers inside. "And you might pick up more of this, while you're at it. We're getting a bit low."

He grabs a shopping bag from the hook on the door. "OK. Come on, Barney. Walk!"

"You will be careful, though, won't you?"

Her tone surprises him. What does she think's going to happen between here and the shop?

"Course."

"It's just that Mr Green knocked when he brought the milk. There's a strange man living in Twenty Acre

Wood, apparently. And he was really horrible to Stan. Threatened him with all kinds of things. So Mr Green said I should tell you to watch out. I know you've got Barney, but —"

He starts towards the door. "OK."

"Honestly, Mark. He sounds perfectly dreadful, this man. Said he'd do something really unspeakable. I don't want you talking to people like that."

"Don't worry, Mum." *His name's Aubrey Hillyard. He's a friend of Murky's. And you shouldn't believe what Stan Green says about him*. But that would only lead to more questions and a serious ticking-off: *Why didn't you tell us? You're not to go and see him again*.

"And now, ladies and gentlemen," he says, lifting the latch. "You will observe the dog and the boy *disappear*. Before your very eyes. Da-dah!"

At the gate, he pulls up a squeaky grass stem and sucks the sweetness from it. Letting it dangle from his lips, the way he's seen Hillyard do with a rumpled roll-your-own, he starts down the road at a gentle amble, hands in his pockets — looking, he hopes, like a boy who's going about his own business and doesn't care what anyone thinks of him. He mustn't be too long, of course, but he wants to stretch the moment of freedom — the interval between home and shop, when he's answerable to no one — as far as he can. And anyway, he needs time to figure out what to do if Lou's there. She might forget what he'd told her and introduce him — in which case, her parents, after Dad's scene in the shop, could decide to stop them playing together. He practises their secret sign with his fingers. If he made it the instant he saw her, would she understand that it meant *say nothing*?

As he turns into the High Street, he notices a woman in the pub yard, talking to Harry Doggett. She stands with her back to him, but from the black stripe in her grey hair and her odd stance — one shoulder higher than the other — he can tell that it's Ernie's mother, Winnie. Barney strains towards them, tail wagging.

"Here, boy! Heel!"

The sound of his voice makes Winnie jump. She and Harry stop talking. As he saunters by, with a quick wave, they both smile craftily at him, like kids caught doing something naughty.

He ties Barney's lead to the ring in front of the shop and walks in, screwing up his eyes to adjust to the dimness. It's OK: he's entirely alone. He stands there, enjoying the cool on his cheeks, absorbing the eerie buzz of the deep freeze and the salt-sweet smell of cheese and sliced ham. As the tinkle of the door bell fades, a woman appears from the back.

"Good morning."

She's about his mother's age, wearing a rust-coloured summer frock. He studies her face, looking for Lou. There are only a couple of echoes: the line of the nose, the watchful hazel eyes.

"Can I have twenty Players, please?"

She pulls a packet from the rack of cigarettes behind her. As she twists back and puts it on the counter, her big lipstick mouth breaks into a smile. "Not for you, I hope?"

"No. For my father."

"Well, that's good. Anything else?" Murky was right: she doesn't seem like a shopkeeper at all. To hear her speak, you'd think she was a lady.

"Some Summer County, please. And a jar of Marmite."

As he waits for her to get them, he tries to stop his gaze drifting towards the deep freeze. It's no good: the old queasy fascination is too strong. Those odd shapes — blocks of ice cream; dimpled bags of peas — jutting out of the whiteness, crusted with frost like the remains of a mammoth, or the debris of a plane crash in the mountains.

"Here we are. Anything else?"

He shakes his head.

"Right." She scribbles the prices on a corner of paper and quickly tots them up. "That'll be —"

"Can you put it on our account, please? Mrs Davenant?"

"Mrs Davenant?"

"Yes."

He steels himself. *Ah: that means you must be Mark, then*. But instead, she lays down her pencil, opens a drawer and takes out a little notebook. She picks up the pencil again, then stops suddenly, frowning at him.

"Just a moment." She turns and pokes her head through the doorway into the back of the shop. "Jack!"

"Yes?" A bored drawl.

"Can I ask you something?"

A sigh, and the creak of a chair. The top half of a man's profile appears: thin, dark-skinned, furrowed with creases. His eyes are masked by the glint from a pair of tortoise-shell frame glasses.

"What?"

Their voices shrink to a murmur. Mark covers his burning cheeks with his hands, trying to draw the heat into his fingertips. The injustice of it! How *can* they not trust him, or his parents? Should he say, *All right, leave it, then?* That's what Dad would do. The thought of returning home empty-handed makes him want to cry, but at the same time, for some reason he can't understand, it seems to promise a kind of guilty satisfaction.

The door bell rings behind him. He swivels round.

"Ah, young Aurelius!"

"Hullo, Murky."

She's wearing a shapeless skirt and an old straw hat nibbled around the edge of the brim, as if a family of rabbits have been at it. Slung over her arm is a spiky basket. Silhouetted against the light from outside, she looks like a scarecrow.

"I thought when I saw Barney out there that you couldn't be far behind," she says. "How are you?"

Out of the corner of his eye, he can see Lou's mother watching them. This'll show her. "All right, thanks."

"How was the birthday?" She leans towards him, raising a finger to delay his reply. "See? I remembered. The very instant you left. But by then it was too late, of course. You know what they're going to put on my gravestone? *Mark's birthday is the 11th, not the 15th.*"

"Morning, Miss Murkett," says Mrs Bennett.

"Morning. I was just apologizing to Mark. For forgetting his birthday."

Mrs Bennett folds her elbows on the counter, smiles down at him. "Oh, when was that? Yesterday?"

"Yes," says Murky. "Shows what a rotten friend I am, doesn't it? But don't worry, I shall make amends. I've got something for you. If I'd known I was going to bump into you, I'd have brought it with me. Can you come back with me, and I'll give it to you now?"

"Well —"

"It won't take two ticks. If Mrs Bennett will just let me have some cat food . . ."

Mrs Bennett's throat colours. "Well, I just need to put this down for Mrs Davenant," she says, with a smile that doesn't match her voice. "And then I'll be with you."

He watches intently while she writes in the book. It's like seeing your defeated enemy signing the peace treaty. Only when she's finished does he load everything into the carrier.

"And how is young Lou?" says Murky, as Mrs Bennett nudges a tin of Kit-e-Kat from the shelf.

"Oh, yes, she's fine, thank you."

"Not here this morning?"

Mrs Bennett shakes her head. "No, she'll be out and about somewhere. Chivvying outlaws and Indians, I expect."

"Outlaws and Indians, eh?" says Murky.

She glances at Mark, raising one eyebrow. He nods, then bends down to pull up his ruckled socks. She turns back to Mrs Bennett.

"And a good job, too. Mark, let me tell you, knows all about chivvying. Don't you, Mark? Normans and Romans, in his case. But perhaps they could make common cause. And then, if the Normans and the Romans and the outlaws and the Indians ever decide to join forces, we'll be well protected, won't we?"

Mrs Bennett is loading tins into the basket. She smiles, but doesn't reply.

"The trouble is, most people are blind, aren't they?" says Murky. "They're not even aware there *are* Normans and outlaws prowling about the place, seeking whom they may devour. So I, for one, would sleep a good deal more soundly in my bed, knowing that Lou and Mark were about their business, keeping us safe."

Mrs Bennett laughs. "I'll put this on the account, shall I?"

"Well," says Murky, as they emerge blinking into the sunlight. "It sounds as if you really *should* meet young Lou, doesn't it?"

He sucks his lips between his teeth and busies himself with untying Barney. He doesn't want to lie. But if he admits that he's met Lou already, she'll wonder why he didn't mention it in the shop. And as soon as *she* knows, it'll only be a matter of time before their parents do, and start to interfere.

"So," says Murky. "Are you coming back with me? To get your present?"

"OK. But I mustn't be too long."

"You won't be. Promise." She starts off at a brisk pace, her stick legs moving stiffly. "Ah, this is nice.

Walking down the High Street, with a young man at my side."

"And a dog," says Mark. "Don't forget Barney."

"Perfectly right. One man and his dog. Went to mow —"

The sound of a car stops her. It's very close, slowing as it draws alongside. They both turn to look. A green Morris Oxford, curvy and smooth-shelled like a turtle.

"Who's this?" says Murky.

"I don't know. Harry Doggett?"

She narrows her eyes. "Yes, I think you're right."

The car sidles to a halt. The driver's door opens. Doggett gets out, unpacking himself one spindly limb at a time. He dials a number in the air with his finger.

"Morning." A big yellow-toothed grin. But there's something awkward and shame-faced about it.

"Good morning, Mr Doggett."

"Glad to have a chance . . ." he mumbles, then breaks off to nod at Mark. "Hullo again, young man."

"Hullo."

Doggett scratches his head and looks enquiringly at Murky.

"I can't believe," she says, "there's anything you might wish to say to me that Mark shouldn't hear."

"Well, it's just a bit . . ."

"What is?"

Mark can't remember ever hearing Murky talk like this before. He wonders how she and Harry Doggett know each other. As far as he's aware, she's never set foot in the Fox and Hounds.

"Well, it's just this chap of yours . . ."

"Which chap?"

"Fellow in Twenty Acre Wood."

"Mr Hillyard?"

He nods. "There's a lot of people starting to . . ." He hesitates, splays his fingers on the roof of his car. "You know."

She shakes her head. "No, I don't, I'm afraid."

"Well, I hear it in the pub. All the time. Who is he — why is he there? And so forth."

"He's there because he wanted a quiet place to work, and I told him he could use the old railway carriage."

Doggett nods. But he's not satisfied: he sighs and pinches the end of his nose.

"I really don't see how his being there can inconvenience anyone," says Murky. "He doesn't come into the Fox and Hounds, does he, and cause trouble?"

"He's been in a couple of times. But I've got no complaints on that score. Keeps himself to himself. Half of bitter. Off he goes. It's —"

"Well, then."

"It's just folks don't like it. They think he's up to something."

"*Up* to something?"

"I mean, you hear a lot about spies and that, these days, don't you?"

"Well, all I can say is, things must have come to a pretty pass in Moscow, if they're reduced to relying on Mr Hillyard in Twenty Acre Wood. What secrets is he going to tell them, for Heaven's sake?"

Doggett juts his chin, avoiding her eye.

"Fat sow at Horseshoe Farm," says Mark.

Murky laughs. "Just so."

Doggett's smile has gone. He looks sulky and obstinate, digging in for a fight. "I was talking to Winnie Ostler this morning," he says. "She told me he said something unmentionable. To her boy Ernie. And Jimmy Green's lad, Stan."

"In what circumstances?"

"What do you mean?"

"What were Stan and Ernie doing?"

He hesitates, scratches his head again. "They'd gone in Twenty Acre."

"Why?"

Doggett knows he's on thin ice. "Point is, they saw this Mr Hillyard of yours. And he told them to clear off, in no uncertain terms."

"Well, that can easily be remedied, can't it? If they stay away from him, he won't. They've no business being in the wood in the first place, as Winnie very well knows."

She nods, then turns and starts walking again.

"Even so," says Doggett, "he'd no call speaking to them like that."

She stops and looks back at him. "Tell me, Mr Doggett: what would you do if you found two boys you'd never seen before peering in at your window?"

"I'd phone the police."

"And if, like Mr Hillyard, you didn't have a telephone? Wouldn't *you* tell them to clear off, in no uncertain terms?"

Harry Doggett's stumped. His jaw moves, but he says nothing.

"I bet you would," says Murky. "And I'm sure that Ernie and Stan have heard far worse than whatever it is Mr Hillyard's supposed to have said to them. But please tell them that all they have to do, if they want to spare their maidenly blushes in future, is leave him alone. All right?"

She nods sharply again and — without waiting for a reply — continues down the street, leaving Doggett leaning on his car. After a few seconds, they hear the door slamming behind them, then the clunky judder of the engine and the whine of reverse gear.

"Hm," says Murky.

He expects her to go on — to acknowledge his joke or make a comment about Winnie's failure to keep her son under control — but she doesn't. He glances up at her and taps the side of his nose. She doesn't even respond. Her head's bowed, as if she's deliberately trying to shut out what's going on around her, so as to concentrate on her own thoughts.

*She's wondering if she did the right thing*.

He can't immediately get a grip on the idea. *Murky* and *doubt* belong to different worlds. He wants to help her. But it's like seeing a fortress that you'd always thought was impregnable suddenly give way and start to crumble. How do you begin to prop it up?

"It was their fault, I expect," he says.

"Hm?"

"Ernie and Stan Green. They were throwing things at him. Well, *someone* was."

"How do you know that?"

"And I bet it was them." He pauses, forces himself to meet her gaze. "He told me."

"What, Aubrey Hillyard, you mean? When you met him?"

He nods. "And he didn't tell *me* to clear off. He was —" What? *Nice*? No. He runs through every word he can think of — *polite, decent, kind* — but it's like trying to dress someone in the wrong clothes.

"Friendly?" suggests Murky.

"Yes." He hesitates. "So don't worry, Murky. You were right to stand up for him."

"Thank you, Mark." They're at the Hillfield gate now. She waves at the sagging post. "Now tie Barney up, and we'll go in search of this present, shall we?"

"OK." He loops Barney's lead over the old hinge. "Just one thing."

"Hm?"

"Can it be between us?"

"What?"

"What I told you. About me meeting Aubrey Hillyard?"

She stares at him for a moment. "All right, young Aurelius. If you like. Mum's the word."

Ten and sixpence. As he jog-trots home, he feels it in his pocket with his free hand, holds it against his thigh to keep it from getting creased, runs his finger along the saw-tooth edge of the paper, where it was torn out of the book in the post office. Ten and six is a lot. If he saves up his weekly ninepences as well, by the end of the summer he should have enough to buy the 4-6-0.

Turning into Church End, he sees a man walking down the road towards him. Blast: Peggy Akers's dad, wearing a dark jacket stretched smooth by the bulk of his shoulders. His fists are clenched and he stares straight ahead. When they're twenty feet from each other, Mark calls tentatively:

"Morning."

Mr Akers lifts his head, scowling. When he sees who it is, he nods, then turns away again, saying nothing. Blast, blast, blast. Peggy must have told him what happened yesterday. Soon it'll be all over the village.

As he opens the gate, Mark glimpses a pale blur behind the garden reflection in the sitting-room window. Mum, presumably, wondering where he'd got to.

She's at the back door, waiting. "You've been gone a long time. Oh, down, Barney!"

"Sorry." The word sticks to his lips.

"Was there a problem?"

He shakes his head. "I met Murky. She wanted me to go home with her. She'd got me a birthday present."

"That was nice of her."

It's so quick, so automatic, he's not sure she's really taken in what he said.

"Here," he says, pulling out the postal order.

She nods. But she isn't listening: she's glancing towards the hall. He slips past her, puts the carrier on the table.

"There you are."

"Thank you."

He rummages for the packet of Players.

"Shall I take these up to him?"

"He's actually come down now. He's in the study."

"Is he feeling better, then?"

She fidgets with her hair. "He . . . He'd like to see you, I think."

About what? The *Flying Scotsman*? It's only when he's actually in the hall, about to knock, that he realizes how stupid he's been. He should have made the connection the instant he saw Mr Akers coming along Church End.

"Come in."

Dad's sitting in the big chair, eyes closed, fingers spread on each arm. The curtains are half drawn, making a band of dusty light. It cuts the desk in two, catches the dial of Dad's wristwatch, burns a rusty track across the threadbare remains of the old Turkish rug. The room smells like an ashtray.

"Here are your fags, Dad."

Dad reaches out a hand, without opening his eyes.

"Are you feeling better?"

"A bit."

"Mum said you wanted to see me."

Dad nods. Unhurriedly, he fumbles open the packet of Players and lifts off the silver-foil cover. He taps out a cigarette and pats his pockets in turn.

"Can you hand me the matches on the mantelpiece?"

He opens his eyes, then blinks, as if even the dimness of the study is too much. Mark gives him the box. He lights up, fills his lungs and releases a grey vapour trail into the hazy air. "Sit down."

Mark perches on the upright chair.

"Ten," murmurs Dad. "Your second decade. Have you started to notice any difference yet?"

Mark shrugs. "I don't know."

"You're always off somewhere these days, Mummy says. Out and about with Barney."

"I suppose."

He takes a deep breath. Here it comes.

"I hear you had a bit of set-to yesterday. With the Akers girl."

But it's not what Mark expected. He sounds interested. Kind, even.

"Who told you that?"

"Her father. He was here just a minute ago. He said you and Barney chased after her and made her fall over."

"We were just playing. But she got the wrong end of the stick, and thought we were being serious."

Dad lets out a clot of smoke, and watches it gradually dissolve into shreds. "What was the game?"

"Highwaymen." Should he say it was Lou's idea, that he'd tried to stop her? No, that would be sneaking. And anyway, if he didn't know she was there, Mark doesn't want to risk souring his mood by telling him now.

"But you didn't mean to hurt her?"

"No, course not! I wouldn't!"

Dad nods. "That's what I said. I told him you weren't a bully. And that he should think twice before going round accusing people of things."

Mark's tongue is a lump: all he can do is nod back.

"When I was ten," says Dad, so quietly that Mark has to lean forward to hear him, "my aunt Eleanor told your grandfather I was a thief. She said I'd gone into her room and taken some change from her dressing table. And he believed her." His eyes flicker open. "That won't happen to you. Not if I've anything to do with it."

This time, Mark manages to mumble, "Thanks, Dad."

"Only from now on, try to be a bit more careful. Ten's a funny age. Remember when we first got Barney? How he used to chew things and bite your fingers? And you didn't mind, because he was just a puppy, and it didn't really hurt? And then one day it *did* hurt, and you smacked him?"

Mark laughs. "Yes."

"Well, ten's a bit like that. People start thinking of you less as a child and more like a grown-up. So just keep that in mind."

"All right, Dad." He swallows painfully. "Thanks."

"OK, old thing. And ask Mummy to come in, will you?"

She raises her eyebrows as he walks back into the kitchen. He manages a smile.

"Oh, good," she says, holding a hand above her heart.

"He wants to see you now."

After she's gone, he sits down at the table again. The end of *The Hound of the Baskervilles*, when Stapleton misses his footing in the Great Grimpen Mire and gets sucked under. That, *that* — as he admits it to himself, his skin suddenly erupts into goose pimples — is how he feels. Not just now. Always. You take a step, expecting solid ground, and find a quagmire. Or you expect a quagmire and find solid ground.

But out there, beyond the garden, is a different world: sharp lines, clear-cut distinctions, the metallic brightness of a day washed clean by the rain. On one side, him and Barney and Lou and Murky and Aubrey Hillyard. On the other, Mr Montgomery and Harry Doggett and Stan Green and onion-eyed Ernie.

He takes out the postal order and smooths it on the table. No, he won't save up for the 4-6-0. He'll keep it for the time being. Who knows when it could come in handy for something else?

# CHAPTER SIX

"Gallion!"

He waits, holding his breath. But all he can hear is Barney's panting, and the thud of his own heart.

"Gallion!" Louder, now. But still no reply.

He imagines himself back into the fusty darkness of the shed, recovers a few fragments of conversation. *Do you want to go on Friday? Yes, I think so. And* I *can tell him a bit about Peveril on the Swift this time, can't I?* No mention of a time. But that just meant, surely, that they both assumed it would be the same as before?

Barney stiffens. A rustling sound, from the direction of the railway carriage. Perhaps she's decided to go ahead on her own.

Half crawling, he reaches the edge of the clearing in a couple of minutes and hides himself under a bush. The carriage is entirely blue now. The trestle table's still there, though, strewn with paint pots, old mugs, a half-carved block of wood. There's no sign of Lou.

After a few seconds, Hillyard appears at the top of the steps, holding a teapot. He looks round, head back, eyes half-closed in the brightness, wrinkling his nose like a dog sniffing for rabbits. Then he clatters down — heavy black boots, Mark notices: the kind soldiers wear — and starts filling one of the chipped white mugs.

There's another rustling sound, close to Mark's hiding place. He turns towards it. The neighbouring bush — no more than twenty feet away — is quaking, as if a rattle of wind had caught it. But there is no wind today. Lou wouldn't be hiding too, would she? A fox, perhaps? A pheasant?

Aubrey Hillyard seems to have heard it as well. He puts down his mug and — without taking his eyes from the bush — moves gingerly towards it, craning his head. For a few seconds, he stands there, studying it. Then, unhurriedly, he starts to unbutton his trousers.

Mark blinks. He isn't . . . He can't be . . . He is. Hillyard hoists his underpants and pulls out his . . . His willy. His old man. Mark knows he shouldn't watch, but it's impossible to look away. The size of it . . . The pink-grey colour, like a newborn puppy. The feeling that, even as Hillyard holds it, directing it like a fireman's hose, it isn't entirely a part of him, but has a sleepy life of its own.

The man's peeing. A waterfall gush, thick as a strand of rope, drenching the leaves, turning them a glossy darker green. Suddenly the bush explodes again, a tumult of whipping branches. Two boys scramble out and run darting and leaping towards Willetts Lane. Their hands are over their heads, so Mark can't see them clearly, but he just catches a quick flash of orangey hair. Yes: Stan Green.

Hillyard straightens himself, flexing his shoulders. For a moment Mark thinks he's about to set off in pursuit. Instead, he bellows:

"I'm open for business if you want to introduce yourselves — but I won't stand spying!"

Then he laughs and ambles back to the railway carriage, fastening his flies.

Mark clamps Barney's muzzle shut and burrows himself into the powdery earth. What if Hillyard discovers him there and thinks *he's* been spying too?

"Gallion!"

It's some way off. Even so, Barney recognizes her voice, and wriggles violently. Mark tightens his grip. He waits until Hillyard has picked up the teapot again and started noisily refilling his mug. Then he backs out and tiptoes away.

"Gallion!"

"Gallion!"

As he approaches the meeting place, she drops lightly from her tree. She's the Lone Ranger again today. She spins the six-shooter on her finger, then squats down to greet Barney.

"Where were you?" says Mark.

"I got held up."

Have her parents decided, after all — despite Murky putting in a good word for him — that they don't want Lou to play with him? He's desperate to know, but can't think of a way to ask.

"I've been here ages," he says.

She presses her face into Barney's ruff, then levers herself onto her heels and stands up. "Come on, then. Let's go."

He barges past her and takes the lead. After what he's just seen, he wants to make sure he gets there first, in case the man's doing something rude again. But it's OK: when they reach the clearing, they find Hillyard removing the clutter from the table. All that's left is the block of wood, surrounded by shavings, and a rumpled white cloth lying in an untidy heap.

"Hullo!" calls Mark.

Hillyard straightens up, narrowing his eyes against the brightness, then raises a hand in salute.

"Faith rewarded," he says.

What does that mean? Mark glances at Lou. She's frowning: she doesn't know either. To hide his confusion, he nods at the half-carved lump of wood.

"Are you making something?"

"Trying to," says Hillyard, quickly gathering it up, as if he's ashamed of his handiwork. He reaches under his smock and — with a wriggle of his waist — produces a sheath-knife, its edge wavery and notched with overuse. "Trouble is, this blighter isn't really up to the job."

"Mark's got a knife," says Lou.

"I dare say he has."

"You want to see?" says Mark. He yanks the penknife from his pocket and pulls it open.

"Ah, yes, very nice," says Hillyard. He holds out his hand. "May I?"

Mark gives it to him. He runs his finger along the blade. "Yes, this would do it."

"You can borrow it, if you like," says Mark.

"Really? That's very decent of you."

"I can collect it next time."

"All right. A generous offer, and I accept." He closes the knife and slips it into his smock. "Thank you. Now, I thought, in view of the weather, we should be out of doors today. Would that suit you?"

Mark nods.

"Chairs, then," says Hillyard. "Chairs, for the love of God." He nods at Mark. "Go on, in you go. And Barney and Lou and I, the while, will don our pinnies and magic up some tea." He brushes off the wood shavings and spreads out the tablecloth. "Come on, Barney. You come with us."

Inside, the carriage is suffocatingly hot. Mark wrestles three old kitchen chairs from the muddle of furniture and escapes into the fresh air again, banging them down the steps. Behind him, he can hear the *pish* of the kettle, the clink of teaspoons, Lou giggling at something Hillyard has said or done.

He manhandles the seats into place round the trestle, then lowers himself onto one of them to make sure it doesn't wobble. A brilliant needle of light suddenly jabs the corner of his eye. It's coming from the grass at the rim of the clearing. He walks over and finds a half-buried milk bottle broken off at the shoulder. He picks it up. The edge is so sharp that it roughens his fingertip when he touches it.

"Ah, inspecting the defences, eh?"

He turns. Hillyard's standing by the table, unloading a tray. Lou hovers next to him, clutching an open Peek

Frean tin to her chest, to keep it from prick-eared Barney's nose.

"Look at this," says Mark, holding the bottle in front of him. "Good job I spotted it, isn't it? Barney might have cut his paw."

"Hm," says Hillyard. "So he might." But his eyes are wide, as though it's the first time the idea has struck him. "Better be careful. There's probably a few other things out there he'd be well advised to steer clear of."

"Shall we go and look?" says Mark.

Hillyard shakes his head. "Just keep him on his leash. It's not a bad policy to have the occasional deterrent lying around."

Mark lays the broken bottle on the table. "Did *you* put this there, then?"

"Only after they'd thrown it in the first place. But it'll serve the blighters right, won't it, if they're hoist with their own damned petard? Anyway . . ."

He nods at Lou and bows comically, making a flourishing gesture with his hand. She slides the tin onto the table.

"See?" he says. "As promised. Biscuits. And non-muck milk." He rearranges the chairs, so that they all have their backs to the carriage. "Sit down."

"What's wrong with the way *I* had them?" says Mark.

Hillyard holds a finger to his temple. "Always face the enemy," he says. "There were a couple of them here just a few minutes ago. One of them a carrot-haired little swine I've seen before. Who would that have been? Any idea?"

"Stan Green," says Mark. "From the dairy."

Hillyard nods. "I'll remember that. Well, I gave them something they won't forget in a hurry, but they'll be back again, I expect. He hesitates. "You didn't by any chance happen to say something to him, did you? About me? And the Brain?"

"No, of course not. I haven't spoken to him all holiday."

"Or anyone else?"

"No!"

Hillyard turns to Lou, eyebrows raised. "You?"

She shakes her head. "We promised, didn't we?"

He nods. "Well, we mustn't let them spoil the occasion, must we?" He picks up the heavy brown pot, steadies it with a finger under the spout. "I'll do the tea. You help yourselves to everything else. And then I want all the latest intelligence from Peveril on the Swift. All right?"

Lou reaches for a sandwich cream. "I've seen it now. Did you know?"

"What, Peveril on the Swift?"

She nods.

"Excellent. And what's the verdict?"

She bites the end from the biscuit, then chews it meditatively for a moment, as if she's been asked to pronounce on that instead. "Yes, it's good," she say finally.

"Except you nearly caused an accident," says Mark.

She sticks out a crumby tongue at him. "Well, I'd never done it before. I was all right when I got the hang of it, wasn't I?"

Mark juts his lower lip: *I suppose so*.

"Trains all up to scratch, were they?" says Hillyard. "Boilers nice and shiny? Everything a credit to the old London North Eastern? Which of course you don't remember and I do?"

Lou glances at Mark. "I think so. It all looks just like the real thing. When you get close. There's a shop, like the one we used to have. And lorries and cars. Even miniature advertisements."

"*Guinness is Good for You*?" says Hillyard. "*Drink Ovaltine for Health*?"

She nods. "And the tiny little people. I really like them. You should see Mrs Dauntless. She's terribly smart. You know."

She draws herself up, head to one side, arms stiff, hands turned out, like a picture in a magazine. Hillyard and Mark laugh.

"Waiting on the platform, was she?" says Hillyard. "For the train you nearly crashed?"

Lou flushes. Her eyes are bright, her fists clenched. For a fraction of a second, Mark has the odd sensation that he's looking at her through a telescope, and seeing what she'll be like ten years from now. Murky's right: time really *is* an old fraud.

"I said, didn't I?" says Lou. "I'd never done it before!"

Hillyard laughs. "Yes, I know. I'm only teasing. And Mr Makepeace?"

She says nothing. She's still flexing and unflexing her fingers.

"*Peveril!*" calls Mark, in his Mr Makepeace voice. "*This is Peveril on the Swift!*"

That does it: Hillyard laughs again, and Lou's face relaxes into a smile.

"Yes," she says. "He was there. And Patty and Paul Gallion."

"You introduced yourself, I take it?" says Hillyard.

"Well, we played with them a bit, if that's what you mean. The *Pintail* broke free of its mooring, and they had to get it back."

"*Paul* got it back," says Mark.

She sticks out her tongue again.

"How did he do that?" asks Hillyard.

"Waded out and grabbed it," says Lou. "Then threw the rope to Patty, who was standing on the bank."

"Well, that shows character," says Hillyard. "Clearly the kind of kids it's good to have on your side in a tight spot. If they ever feel like a change of scene, do please give them my address. I bet they'd be more than a match for Stan Green and his chums."

Lou shifts in her chair. Mark catches her eye. Her hands are pressed flat underneath her thighs. She looks as uncomfortable, as unsure how to respond, as he is.

"Yes, bring the whole lot of them here!" says Hillyard, opening his arms. "The Gallions! The Dauntlesses! The Makepeaces! And together we'll make a final, glorious stand for old England!"

Is he joking? Yes, there: he's smiling. Or, at least, the line of his mouth has buckled into an uneven curve.

"Why are they so horrible?" says Lou. "Stan Green and those other boys?"

"Ah, well, that's the question, isn't it?" says Hillyard. "The natural tendency of children to torture cats and pull the wings off flies? Or something more particular to the case? What do you think, Mark?"

*Well, you did swear at them. And now you've piddled on them too*. "I don't know," he mumbles, looking at his feet.

"No more do I. But I am starting to wonder." He squints past them, scanning the trees fringing the clearing.

"What?" says Mark.

"Well, I do seem to have created a bit of a stir. Would that be a fair assessment, do you think?"

Mark hesitates, then nods.

"So perhaps someone doesn't like what I'm doing. Or —"

"But you're not doing *any*thing, are you?" says Lou. "Just living here, writing a book. So —"

"Precisely." He pats the pocket of his smock, pulls out an almost-empty Golden Virginia pouch. "Someone, I suspect, may have let slip what the book's *about*. I fully accept your assurances that it wasn't you. But —"

"Well, I can't see why anyone should mind anyway," says Lou. "It's only a story. Most people like stories, don't they?"

Hillyard breathes in slowly, filling his lungs. "I know it's annoying," he says. "When you're whatever age you are, and someone who's whatever age I am pulls rank. Says, *There, there, you'll see things differently when you're older*. But the fact is, sometimes people *don't* like stories. Not just that: they think they're downright dangerous."

"But who'd think that about the Brain?" says Lou.

"The people who're working for it, obviously!" says Mark. "Honestly, you're such a baby sometimes!"

"You're the baby!" says Lou. "You're the one who didn't think it was real, remember?"

"Imagine you're a cow," says Hillyard. "Three square meals a day, bijou cowshed, all mod cons. Then someone sets up shop in the next-door field and starts telling you you're being fooled. That nice fellow the farmer isn't nice at all. You'd be better off making a break for it and taking your chances in the big bad world. What would you do?"

"But cows can't talk, can they?" says Lou. "So they wouldn't be able to understand."

Hillyard laughs again. "All right. But let's just say, for the sake of argument, they can." He teases a long straggle of tobacco into a Rizla and adds the last dust from the packet.

"Don't your thumbs get tired doing that?" says Lou.

He shakes his head. "Natural talent. According to the midwife, I was born with a fag paper in my pink little baby hands. And I've been doing it ever since." He licks the gummed strip, folds it down. "So anyway: there you are. You're a talking cow. And the surly old bull on the other side of the hedge starts telling you the farmer's a bad lot. What do you do?"

Lou shrugs. "Well, I'd try to escape, I suppose."

He nods. "I'd expect no less. But that's because you're a very superior kind of cow. Most of the rest are simply run-of-the-mill Ethels and Daisies. So how are *they* going to react, when someone tells them that their comfortable life is a snare and a delusion? Hm? They're going to get into the chap's field, aren't they, and go" — he lowers his head and butts Mark's shoulder, laughing — "*Mooo! Mooooo!*"

Lou starts to laugh too. Mark can't help joining in, even though he has no idea what the man's talking about.

"Appropriate enough, isn't it," says Hillyard, "that the ringleader should turn out to be the milkman's son?" His shoulders heave. He dabs his eyes with a paint-stained cuff, then slaps the back of his own hand. "Damn it! See? I said I wouldn't. And now I am. Discussing the enemy. Instead of hearing the latest news from Peveril on the Swift."

"We've told you about Peveril on the Swift," says Lou.

"Yes, it's your turn," says Mark. "Come on! The Brain!"

Hillyard shakes his head. Lou and Mark look at each other. In unison, stamping their feet, they chant:

"Brain! Brain! Brain!"

Hillyard holds his hands up. "All right, all right," he says, peering into the trees. "Not so much noise." He lights his flimsy cigarette and sucks in smoke. "The Brain," he says, so quietly they can barely hear him, "is up to its usual tricks. The stronger it gets, the wider it casts its net, the cleverer it becomes." He stretches out his hands and mimes typing. "I keep hoping to find its weak spot, but the damned thing's too quick for me. Now it's decided to put its plan for world domination into action. Starting with a small village in England."

Lou shivers.

"Yesterday, when I settled down to write, I thought I had it licked. Finally had a young couple capable of standing up to it. Plucky. Resourceful. Unflappable."

Lou presses her hands together. "What are their names?"

"Ah well." He clears his throat. "That's something I still haven't quite decided yet. Let's call them Mr and Mrs X for the time being. Anyway, they're recently married, and just back from their honeymoon. They've had no radio, no television, while they were away, so they're completely unaffected. And obviously, the very first thing they notice is that everyone else has changed. Staring eyes. All talking like this: *Good-morning-it's-a-lovely-day-isn't-it*."

"Oh, yes, that's good," says Lou.

"Ah, but wait. They think maybe it's just their village, do you see? So the chap drives to the next town to see if he can get help. The girl, meanwhile, thinks maybe there'll be something about what's happened on the news, so she switches on the television —"

Lou slaps her hands over her ears. "Oh, no!"

"Yes," says Hillyard. "And the Brain's so powerful now, it can sense there's someone there it doesn't control yet. So it immediately sets to work. By the time the husband gets back, she's —" He drops his head on one side, eyes staring, jaw slack.

"Well, what about the people he asked to come and help him?" says Mark. "Surely they ought to be able to do something?"

"Yes, that's what I thought. Until I actually got to that bit. And then I realized: no one's going to believe him. This is England, after all. So when he tells them what's happened, they're going to be terribly English about it, aren't they? Just say, *Hm, sounds like a case of an overactive imagination*."

"But what *has* happened?" says Lou. "I mean, what is it the Brain actually *does* to people?"

"Makes them forget who they are."

"How?"

Hillyard reaches into the tin, takes out a jam sandwich ring. "Here," he says, holding it up. "A prize for anyone who can tell me something about Henry Ford."

Lou and Mark exchange glances, both searching for a sign that this is a joke, and the right response would be to laugh.

"Any suggestions?" asks Hillyard.

"You mean the car chap?" says Mark.

Hillyard nods. "As in Ford Prefect. Ford Popular."

"Ford Anglia."

"Yes. Ford Consul. Et cetera. OK, that'll do." He hands Mark the biscuit. "Founder of the Ford Motor Company. And the man who introduced mass production to the world. What's mass production?"

Mark looks at Lou again. She shrugs.

"Making lots and lots of stuff?" he says.

Hillyard nods. "But the point is: how, exactly?"

Neither of them says anything.

"Well, I'll tell you. In the old days, if you were building a car, you'd see the whole thing through, start to finish: chassis, wheels, suspension, engine, seats, bodywork. Rolls Royce still do it like that, I'm told. But not good old Henry. He came up with the brilliant idea of the *assembly line*. Thousands of people, all of them doing just one thing. You're chassis, Lou. Mark, you're suspension. I'm doors." He sticks his cigarette in his mouth and mimes screwing, fitting, tightening. "One, two, three. One, two, three. My entire life, day in and day out, for forty years: nothing but doors, doors, doors. Can you imagine? Then, in short order, there's the gold watch, if you're lucky, and the one-way ticket to the crematorium."

His roll-up's gone out. He relights it, inhales, releases a fine thread of smoke, watches it slowly dissipate in the air.

"So there's no development," he says. "No growth. People aren't part of a living process any more: they're part of a machine. How the devil do you make them put up with that?"

"You make them forget," says Lou.

"Yes!" He bangs his knee with the heel of his big hand, then leans forward, takes another jam ring from the box, dangles it in front of her. "Here. You should have one of these as well."

She colours with pleasure. "Thank you."

"Yes," he says, dropping it into her palm. "That's the point: they're in an endless present moment, unconnected to anything there's been before and anything that'll come after. So if you want to make people like that, what do you tell them?"

Lou shakes her head. Mark longs to shine, to say something that will impress Hillyard with *his* cleverness, but he can't think of anything.

"Well, here's Henry Ford's prescription," says Hillyard. He tilts his head back, shuts his eyes. In the sun, the golden strands in his beard flare into a brilliant red. "*History is bunk. It's tradition. We don't want tradition. We want to live in the present and the only history that is worth a tinker's dam is the history we made today*."

"Is that what he said?" says Lou.

Hillyard opens his eyes. "That's what he said. Make enough people believe that, and you can do what you like with them. It may not come as much of a surprise to learn that Henry counted among his many admirers a certain Mr A. Hitler. Who spiritedly set out to take his ideas to their logical conclusion." He hesitates. "As I can testify."

*As I can testify*. Mark shivers. This, finally, must be a clue to what Hillyard did in the war. But before he can nerve himself to say, *How?*, Lou asks:

"And the Brain?"

"Yes," says Hillyard. "The Brain's an admirer, too. In fact, you could say what it's doing is just picking up where Messrs F. and H. left off. The trick, as Dr Goebbels so astutely realized, is *propaganda*. But of course, Dr Goebbels only had radio at his disposal."

"So what's going to happen?" says Lou. "In the story, I mean? Can anyone? . . ."

"We'll have to see, won't we? Can our chap manage to organize a resistance movement in time? Or is it all up for the human race?"

"*I'd* be a resister," says Lou.

"Course you would. But the question is, would there be enough like you?"

"Well, will you tell us next week?" says Mark.

Hillyard nods. "As long as they don't get me first."

"Who?"

"The Brain's minions."

No one says anything. In the silence, Barney whimpers and prods Hillyard's hand with his nose, hungry for reassurance. Out of the corner of his eye, Mark sees Lou shifting again — stealthily, like an animal trying not to attract attention to itself. He glances at her. She's drawn her legs up to her chest, and hugs them close, her chin on her knees, staring at Hillyard open-mouthed.

Hillyard stiffens. At the same moment, Barney jumps up and stands quivering, ears pricked, dog-frowning at the wood. Lou turns, trying to see what's alerted them.

"What is it?" says Mark.

Hillyard shakes his head: *Listen*. Mark holds his breath. After a moment, he hears, some way off, the squawk of a pheasant. Hillyard hooks a hand through Barney's collar.

"What about your parents?" he says, scanning the trees.

"What?"

"Have . . ." — darting him a sidelong look — "have they said anything?"

"About the Brain?"

"About me?"

Mark swallows. His throat hurts. "No, not really."

"Not *really?*"

"I mean, I think maybe they've *heard* things."

"Who from?"

"Stan Green. Well, Stan Green's dad."

"Friends, are they?"

"What, with Stan Green's dad?"

Hillyard nods.

"No!"

He nods again, still squinting into the wood. Another pheasant thrashes noisily into flight, no more than a couple of hundred yards away this time.

"What do they do?"

"My parents?"

"Yes. You never told me. Father's not the vicar, is he?"

Mark laughs. "No. He's a freelance."

"Freelance what?"

"Well . . ." Why does he feel embarrassed talking about it? Dad's no odder than Hillyard himself. He's less odd, in fact. At least he lives in a house . . . "It's hard to explain."

"No, it isn't!" says Lou. "He gives lectures. And he writes things. Like you."

"Ah, a ducker and a weaver," says Hillyard. "A just-getter-by. That's all right, then. I'd like to shake his hand." He turns to Lou. "And what about yours?"

"They own the —"

"No, I know what they do. I mean, have they heard things?"

"A bit, I think. From people when they come into the shop."

Hillyard nods. “Hm. I’ve a feeling we’re going to have to rethink our strategy, then,” he says, getting up. “Probably not a good idea for you to be found here.”

“But surely,” says Lou. “If they’re going to attack . . . Wouldn’t you like us to help?”

Hillyard shakes his head. “I’m touched. But the fact is, it’d just stick an almighty spanner in the works. Put an end to your visits here once and for all. Stop our . . . collaborating. And I shouldn’t like that.”

“No,” says Lou. “I wouldn’t, either.”

“If you want to help, keep your mouths shut. And your ears open. Let me know if you hear anything. People muttering. Asking questions. All right?”

“OK.” says Lou.

“And now,” he says, “I suggest you head sharpish for the exit. And we re-convene” — screwing up his eyes and looking at the horizon, as if he’s working out the time from the position of the sun — “the day after tomorrow, say?”

They both nod.

“Only check first, all right? That the coast is clear?”

“How?” says Lou.

“Look at the window. That one there. The kitchen. If you see a tea towel hanging in it, it means stay away —”

Barney growls and tries to break free of his grip. They can hear footsteps now: a regular, surreptitious whoosh-and-crunch through the undergrowth.

“Go on: scoot! Scoot!” says Hillyard.

Lou pulls down her mask. Mark clips on Barney’s lead.

"But we're going to run into them, aren't we?" he says.

"There's a back way," says Hillyard. He flaps his hand at the fringe of trees behind the carriage. "Brings you out in the field below the farm. Just follow the line of the hedge. It'll take you to the lane."

"Come on, boy," says Mark. But Lou still hesitates.

"*Go!*"

She bites her lip, then nods. "'Bye, then."

They find the path, but it's half overgrown, and they keep tripping over brambles and having to swerve and duck to dodge branches. Neither of them speaks until they reach the hedge. Then Mark raises a hand and says:

"OK, stop for a sec. I'm going to take a dekko. Make sure Mr Montgomery isn't about."

"Why? Are we trespassing?"

Mark shrugs. "He might ask questions, that's all. Here, hold Barney, will you?"

He tunnels through the hedge. A knot of bullocks huddles in the far corner. Otherwise, the field looks empty.

"OK. All clear."

Lou sends Barney ahead, then wriggles after them. They start off towards the lane, walking half on tiptoe, even though there's no one to hear them. After they've gone a hundred yards or so, the herd of cattle suddenly twitches into motion and streams into the centre of the field in two jostling groups. A second later, Mr Montgomery's Land Rover appears in the gap between them.

"Blast!" says Mark.

It's too late to go back: that would just make him more suspicious. They keep moving at the same pace, trying to look like people who believe they have every right to be where they are. Mark monitors the approach of the Land Rover out of the corner of his eye, determined not to turn his head until the last moment.

"Morning."

"Oh, hullo."

Mr Montgomery peers out of the window, touching his cap. "Glad to see the forces of law and order at work," he says, nodding at Lou, with his can't-fool-me smile. "But this is private property, I'm afraid."

Mark signals frantically at her: *Don't tell him anything!* But either she doesn't see, or she doesn't understand. "We were in Twenty Acre Wood," she says. "And we got —"

"Well, you shouldn't have been," says Mr Montgomery. "You're new here, aren't you, so maybe you didn't know any better. But" — turning to Mark — "*you* should have done. I told you, didn't I, the chap living there's a menace?" He nods sharply, his jaw quivering like a bull's dewlap. "Keep away from him."

Lou starts to speak. But this time, she notices Mark shaking his head and stops herself.

"So," says Mr Montgomery, "if I see either of you round here again, I shall tell your parents. Make a complaint. All right?" He wags a finger, first at Lou, then at Mark. "That clear?"

Neither of them replies. He nods and touches his cap again. They watch as he drives the Land Rover back up the field, veering like a pie-eyed character in a cartoon, then stops and gets out to open the gate.

"Does he have a television?" says Lou.

"I don't know. I expect so. Why?"

"Instead of highwaymen, I vote we're resisters," she says. "Fighting against the Brain's minions."

Mark thinks about it. It sounds like a good game. They wouldn't be picking on defenceless little kids like Peggy Akers: their enemies would be Hillyard's enemies, Stan Green, Ernie, Mr Montgomery — the people trying to stop him writing his book. But he can't imagine how you'd actually play it.

"What would we do?"

"He told us, didn't he? We're to keep our ears open. And our eyes. And tell him if we see or hear anything."

Mark nods.

"So that's what we'll do. We'll use the special place in the hideout to leave messages for each other. Saying what we've found out."

She looks questioningly at him. He thinks for a moment, then nods again.

"Right." She takes her six-shooter from its holster and squints along the barrel, aiming it at the retreating Land Rover. "*Bang!*"

# CHAPTER SEVEN

A day later? Two? Three, at the outside. When he clumps downstairs for breakfast (bleary, tousled, trying to imprison the obstinate edge of his shirt inside his shorts), he can immediately sense a change. The atmosphere in the kitchen seems thinner and less heavy: dust motes fizz in the light from the window; his mother's face, when she turns from the open cupboard to greet him, is unexpectedly flushed.

"Good morning, sleepyhead." But it's not a criticism: she's smiling. And he can smell scent, as if it's a special occasion.

"Hullo."

What's going on? Mark glances towards the table, searching for a clue. His father is already sitting down, but *The Times* is still folded next to his plate. On top of it is a letter, with a glossy embossed address. He's flushed, too, but there's a tightness about his mouth, as if excitement is fighting it out with some other emotion that Mark can't put a name to.

"Morning, Dad."

Dad raises a hand.

"Are you going to tell him?" says Mummy.

"Tell me what?" says Mark.

"Daddy's had some wonderful news. Oh, come on, darling. Show him the letter."

Dad gives it to him without a word. At the top, Mark sees *Amateur Photographer*. The raised letters are so appealing that he can't help running his fingertips over them: they're like a feature on a relief map, the contours of a range of hills in a world even tinier than Peveril on the Swift. Then he scans his eye down until he reads: *We are pleased to inform you that your print* Song Thrush at Dawn *has been selected as a runner-up in the Wildlife Category*.

"Oh, that's great, Dad! Well done!"

Dad nods, but still says nothing. Is he pleased or not? Mark's aware of Mum watching them from the kitchen, her uncertain gaze travelling from Dad to him and back again. She must be wondering the same thing. Maybe Dad feels *runner-up* isn't enough. He should have got a prize. Or been the overall winner . . .

"It *is* great, isn't it?" says Mum. She's there suddenly, standing behind Dad, leaning over him, fingers on his shoulders, an escaped strand of hair tickling his cheek. "Just think of all the people who are going to see it! That marvellous picture!"

Dad closes his eyes.

"What are we going to do to celebrate?" says Mum. "What would you *like* to do, darling?"

Dad shakes his head, then immediately *oohs*, pincering his temples between thumb and forefinger.

"What is it?" says Mum. "Oh, no, not another beastly migraine!"

Dad nods.

"Oh, what a thing to happen! Shall I get you some codeine?"

"I'm going upstairs." He gets up slowly, clutching the edge of the table, visoring his eyes with his hand.

"Here, let me help you, then."

She guides him towards the hall. As they reach the door, she turns for a second to look at Mark, eyebrows raised, lips pinched together. Is she cross with him? Does she think this is somehow his fault? He glares back, feeling his own face setting in a sulky frown.

He could just have breakfast on his own, of course, but his stomach's too fluttery. Instead, he waits until he hears the click of his parents' door, and then — blocking his ears with his fingers — tiptoes upstairs to his own room. He can't make his getaway yet, but at least he'll be all prepared when the time comes.

Notebook, pencil, telescope. The telescope's only a toy, really, and there's a nasty grey crack in the plastic which might split open at any moment, but it's better than nothing. He holds it to his eye and looks through the window at the Robinsons' garden. Something fuzzy is moving on the overgrown crazy-paving path. When he screws up his eye he can see it's a robin, poking in the weeds for food. Yes, the telescope might come in handy. He drops it in his knapsack with the other things.

Camera. He gets the old Halina down from the top of the cupboard and wipes off the dust on his shorts. Somewhere, he knows, there's a film. It takes him a few minutes to find it: an FP3. How on earth did it end up there, in his sock drawer? He unpeels the crinkly wrapping, slots the spool into the camera, then feeds the tongue into the take-up slit. There's something exciting about the warm chemical smell, the promise that with *this* film, finally, he'll manage to take a picture as good as one of Dad's.

He slings the knapsack over his shoulder and creeps back down to the kitchen. There's still no sign of his parents. He sits down, tries squeezing the bag under his chair, gives up and balances it on his knees instead. It's no good: wherever he puts it, they're bound to notice and ask him where he's going. He gets up and carries it out to the shed. He can stow it inside the door and pick it up again when he's leaving.

He flicks on the light. Peveril is in suspended animation, exactly as he left it. The black nose of the 0-6-2 is just emerging from the Sheepfold Tunnel. Behind it, still hidden under the hill, are the three coaches of the stopping train to Swiftbridge. On the platform, Mr Makepeace and Mrs Dauntless are awaiting its arrival, while Patty and Paul Gallion are in the High Street, chatting to the driver of the delivery van.

Mark hesitates, then turns on the power and puts his hand over the humming controller. One twitch of the knob, a couple of nudges with his finger, and the whole place will miraculously return to life — a world where *he* is in total command.

But what then? A week ago, Mrs Dauntless would have exchanged some pleasantry about the weather with Mr Makepeace, and Patty and Paul would have made a dash for the train and got there just in time.

*Gosh, you look puffed out, Patty! Yes, Mrs Dauntless, it was a close-run thing*. Now, suddenly, it no longer feels enough. There needs to be a story. A *real* story: something he can tell Aubrey Hillyard and Lou.

He holds the Oxo box under the light and shakes it like a kaleidoscope. The mass of little figures erupts into a wild rattly dance. Some he hasn't used for ages: the man in the brown suit, the woman carrying a suitcase. A few, like the two soldiers and the little boy in the school cap, haven't even been painted yet. Surely, given such a big cast, he ought to be able to come up with a really exciting adventure?

He takes out half a dozen likely characters and lines them up. First is an old man with a hat. Maybe he's a tramp. Or he turns up in the village out of the blue and people *think* he's a tramp. Mark puts him in the ruins of the old hermitage. One day, when they're out walking, Patty and Paul find him hiding there. Yes, that's a good idea.

He moves them to the top of the hermitage path.

*What's that, Paul?*

*It's an old man. Hullo, there! Are you all right?*

*What's that to you? Can't a fellow have forty winks any more, is that it?*

*It's just we've never seen you before.*

*No surprise in that. I ain't never* been *here before, see?*

*Where are you from, then?*

*Ah, that'd be telling, wouldn't —*

The latch clicks behind him. He drops the figure back inside the hermitage ruins.

"Mark?" His mother. She leans in, peering round. "What are you doing out here?"

"Playing."

"I thought I heard voices."

"That was just me."

"What, pretending to be all the different characters?"

Mark nods.

She tries to smile, but it's too much of an effort. "Can you come inside a moment, please?"

He switches off the power and follows her into the kitchen. As they sit down at the table, she notices his unused bowl.

"Haven't you had any breakfast?"

He shakes his head.

"Don't you want anything?"

"No."

She sighs. "No, I'm not very hungry, either."

"How's Dad?"

She grimaces.

"Still the same?"

She sniffs and pushes a handkerchief against her nose. Her eyes, he notices, are red-rimmed. He can't remember ever having seen her cry before.

"He's very upset, sweetie."

"About the competition?"

She nods.

"Why? Did he think he was going to win it?"

"No," she says, "it isn't that, I don't think. It's us, I'm afraid. He feels we weren't pleased enough for him."

"But we were! I said 'well done', didn't I?"

"Yes, of course you did, poppet. But when he showed you the letter, he thought you seemed more interested in the letterhead than in what it actually said."

Mark clenches his eyes shut. But it's no good: the tears force their way through anyhow.

"I know," says Mum. Mark feels her hand on his. He half-opens his eyes again and peeps out past the blur. She's breathing noisily through her mouth and slowly shaking her head. The comparison's so unexpected that it takes him an instant to think what she reminds him of: fat Nigel, after Ben had beaten him in a fight in the Barley Field.

"That's not true," says Mark.

"No, I know that. It's just a silly misunderstanding, that's all. But we must try to make it up to him."

"How?" *Please don't ask me to say I'm sorry. I couldn't. I just couldn't do it.*

"I've told him I need to pop down to get a few things at the shop. And I thought maybe you could come with me, and we could choose him a present."

"OK." He can hear the grumpiness in his own voice. But at least it means he won't have to apologize. "I'll use some of my pocket money."

"Oh, that would be lovely, sweetie. A very nice gesture. I'm sure he'd appreciate it. And we'll take Barney, shall we?"

"I was going to take him out later."

"Well, it doesn't matter, does it, if he gets two walks? The more the merrier, eh, boy? And I don't want him disturbing Dad. So . . ."

"Can we go down Willetts Lane, then?" Even without his equipment, he can still keep his eyes open.

"We mustn't be too long —"

"It's not much further."

Perhaps, he thinks, they'll see Mr Montgomery again. He hopes they do. He can imagine the scene so vividly that for a moment it blots out the kitchen: they turn the corner at the bottom of the farm track and catch beet-faced Montgomery red-handed, snooping on Aubrey Hillyard at the edge of the wood. Montgomery would be embarrassed, of course, but he couldn't very well be rude, could he — not if Mark was with his mother? The thought of it briefly dissolves the tension in his stomach. It fits perfectly, like a key slipping into a lock: not only would he be getting his own back, but he'd have something to report to Lou and Hillyard as well.

But they don't meet Mr Montgomery. They see no one at all, in fact, until — Mark striding slightly on ahead, to avoid having to make conversation — they reach the end of the lane. Then, as they turn into the High Street, Mark notices a huddle of people talking in front of the shop. He's still too far away to identify them, but — from the solid dark blue of his uniform — he guesses that one of them must be PC Pointer. After a few seconds, the group suddenly freezes. A man emerges from inside and starts down the pavement towards them.

"Who's that?" says Mum.

Mark says nothing. Even though he can't see the face, he knows it's Hillyard: no one else moves with that strange rolling baboon lope, heavy and springy at the same time. Mum narrows her eyes.

"I don't recognize him," she says. "You don't think it might be that horrible man who lives in Twenty Acre, do you?"

Mark shrugs. Hillyard, of all people. It had never occurred to him they might bump into *him* in the High Street: Hillyard is a creature of the woods, unimaginable outside his own habitat. Though, of course, now he thinks about it, he can see he's been stupid: even Hillyard must have to go shopping sometimes.

"Shall we cross over to the other side?" he says.

Mum hesitates a moment. "No, we don't want to make him think we're frightened of him, do we?"

What should he do? Pretend he's forgotten his pocket money and turn back? No, Mum would just say she'd pay, and he could give her his share when the got home. He'll simply have to hope that Hillyard realizes the situation and passes them without saying anything.

It seems to be OK: they're no more than fifty yards away now, and Hillyard hasn't given any sign of recognition. He's shabbier than ever, still wearing his paint-spattered smock, his hair a knotty mat of grey and gold. He's carrying a bag in one hand and appears to be completely absorbed in rolling a cigarette with the other.

Thirty yards. Twenty. And then, suddenly, Barney — tail thrashing, whimpering with pleasure — breaks free and hurls himself at Hillyard, jerking the unfinished roll-up from his fingers.

"Barney!" yells Mum. "Mark! Why didn't you hold on to him?" She grabs the trailing end of the leash. "I'm so sorry."

"Oh, please, it doesn't matter," says Hillyard. "No harm done." He bends down to play with Barney's ears. "Barney and I are old friends, aren't we, boy? And one should always greet an old friend in the approved manner. By knocking him off his feet."

Mum looks quickly at Mark.

"He ran away," mumbles Mark. He can't meet her gaze. "Into the woods."

"He did indeed," says Hillyard, straightening up. "Caught a whiff of my cooking and made a beeline for it. I regaled him with rabbit stew, served on a picture of Princess Margaret. Result: pals for life."

Mum looks as if she's going to giggle, but coughs instead.

"And you, I deduce, from the family resemblance, are Mark's mother?"

"Yes."

Hillyard pinches his fingers together on top of his head, then lifts them a couple of inches. "Raises invisible hat. Executes bow. Difficult manoeuvre in a smock, but there you are." He holds his hand out. "How do you do?"

She laughs. "Hello." She gives the leash back to Mark, then stoops down to retrieve a tuft of tobacco from the pavement. "I really am terribly sorry."

"Just leave it, please," says Hillyard. He opens his bag. "Look. See how well provided I am."

Inside, there are boxes of tea, pouches of Golden Virginia, five packets of rolling paper held together with a rubber band. Mum examines them for a few seconds, then looks up at Hillyard with an odd expression — half frowning, half smiling — that Mark has never seen before.

"Yes, yes, the essentials of life," says Hillyard. "There are fakirs in India, I believe, who have subsisted on nothing else for ten years. Although it's a moot point, apparently, whether for best effect you should use Golden Virginia or Old Holborn."

Mum laughs again.

"Anyway," says Hillyard. "Think no more about it. Goodbye, Barney. Goodbye, Mark." He looks steadily at Mark's mother and lifts his invisible hat again. "Goodbye, Mrs . . . Mrs . . ."

*He knows*, thinks Mark. *I told him*.

"Davenant," says Mum.

"Goodbye, Mrs Davenant."

They watch him set off again on down the street, big-shouldered, his free arm swinging loosely at his side, apparently impervious to the impression he's creating. Mark clenches his fists, preparing himself for a ticking-off. But after Hillyard has finally disappeared into Willetts Lane, pink-cheeked Mum turns round and continues on her way in silence.

The group in front of the shop is still there. Mark can see them all quite clearly now: Mr Pointer, and Harry Doggett, and Mr Barron from the garage. They stop talking and wait, solemn-faced, as Mark and his mother approach. Only at the last moment does Harry

Doggett give a tight little smile, as if he's just eaten all his teeth, and Mr Pointer touch a finger to his forehead.

"Morning," says Mum. She walks straight in, leaving Mark to deal with Barney. As he's tying the lead to the ring on the wall, he notices a tiny scuffling sound from somewhere above his head. Barney must have heard it too, because he stiffens and pricks his ears. But when he glances up, all Mark can see is the parapet round the flat roof of the shopfront. Perhaps there's a cat up there. Or a bird.

Mum is already scanning the shelves of confectionery.

"What" — her hand butterflying over first one thing, then another — "do you think Daddy would like?"

"Turkish Delight?"

He braces himself for *You mean that's what* you'd *like*. But she doesn't say it. She's too distracted, for some reason.

"I don't think they've got any," she murmurs. "Not *proper* Turkish Delight. That's just at Christmas time." She runs her eye along the shelf. How about" — reaching for a box of Newberry Fruits — "these?"

"All right." He gives her one-and-six from his pocket, then lingers by the deep freeze as she goes to the counter. He doesn't want to risk another embarrassing encounter with Lou's mother. He watches surreptitiously as she emerges from the back of the shop. It seems to be all right: she nods at him and smiles at Mum.

"Morning, Mrs Davenant."

"Morning."

"Just these, is it?"

He starts to look away, then something behind her catches his eye: a furtive movement at the edge of the door frame. He waits. After a moment, Lou appears. She checks to see he's watching, then quickly holds up a piece of paper. On it, she's written: *Hideout later?*

He nods. She vanishes. His heart's thumping. He glances round. No one else seems to have noticed.

"Right," says Mum. "Let's be off, shall we?"

When they get outside, Harry Doggett and Mr Barron have gone, but Mr Pointer is still there. He appears to be waiting for them. As Mark is untying Barney, he nods at Mum and says:

"Couldn't help noticing. A few minutes ago. You were talking to that chap."

Mum flushes. "What chap?"

"Mr Hillyard. Friend of yours, is he?"

"No. Today's the first time I ever met him."

"Seemed like you knew each other."

She shakes her head. "He'd seen Barney before, that's all."

Mr Pointer clears his throat. "Well, just be careful, all right? He's a funny customer, that one."

"So everyone says. But he seemed pleasant enough to me. A bit eccentric — but perfectly harmless, I'd have thought. I hope we haven't got to the point where eccentricity's a crime." She takes Mark's arm. "Anyway, we must be getting back. Goodbye, Mr Pointer."

She barely speaks on the way home. Mark says nothing either: one comment, one question, he knows, would be enough to break the seal of her silence, and then he wouldn't have time to think about what's just happened. Amazingly, Mum seems to like Hillyard. More than that, she's even prepared to defend him. Does that change anything — mean that he can take her into his confidence? Or would that still be a betrayal of his promise to Hillyard? By the time they reach the house, he's decided it would. He mustn't do anything until he's asked Hillyard about it, and been released from his word.

Mum goes straight upstairs with the Newberry Fruits. Mark sits down to wait for her, tap-dancing his fingertips across the table, praying, *Please be quick*. What did Lou mean by *later?* An hour? Two hours? This afternoon? He's no idea, but he's terrified he'll miss her.

"Mark?" Mum's voice, from the landing. "I shan't be down for a bit, poppet, so go ahead and eat something."

He hurries into the hall, calls up:

"That's OK. I'm going out with Barney again, all right?"

"All right."

He whistles Barney, then goes into to the shed to collect his bag.

"Gallion." He takes the chalk cliff at a run, then stands at the top, grass tickling his legs, listening. Barney starts to whimper.

"Gallion," he says again.

He holds his breath. After a moment, from deep inside the hideout, he hears:

"Gallion."

He slips off his knapsack, squats down at the entrance.

"Hands up!"

He peers in. He can see the pale blob of her hand, and the glint of her revolver.

"Why?"

"You might be an impostor."

"An impostor wouldn't know the password."

"They could have tied you up, and not let you go till you said it."

"Well, they didn't. So let me in."

She wriggles backwards. He unclips Barney's lead, then crawls in after her. She's cleared the twigs out of the way and raked the earth smooth with her fingers. Her bag is open, and he can see sandwiches and a bottle of ginger beer. On the ground next to it are a book and an open copy of *Girl*, which she quickly folds up and balances on top of the sandwich box.

"You brought a lot of stuff," he says.

"I didn't know how long you'd be, did I?"

It's their own little camp. They could stay there, spend the night, even. He wishes *he'd* brought things now . . .

"Did you find something out?" he says. He didn't mean it to sound grumpy, but somehow it does.

She nods. "I was up on the roof. When those men were out in front of the shop. There were talking about *him*."

"Aubrey?"

She nods again. "I didn't hear all of it. They'd already started by the time I got there. And they were speaking so fast I couldn't keep up." She unlatches the back pocket of her knapsack and pulls out a notebook. "But I did write some things down. Things that seemed important. You want to see?"

He holds his hand out. The notebook's brand-new, the watered-silk sheen of the blue cover uncreased and spotless. He opens the first page. She's written in pencil, the words set out like lines in a play. Mark feels a sudden spasm of — what? He doesn't know the word for it. But Lou has done this — and all *he's* done is stop himself blurting out Hillyard's secret to his mother. It doesn't seem fair. Hillyard was *his* friend first.

"Who's pub man?"

"The man from the pub, stupid."

"You're the stupid one. His name's Harry Doggett."

"Well, I didn't know that, did I? So I called him pub man."

"Why didn't you call Mr Barron *garage man*, then?"

"Cos I know his name. He's friends with my parents. Honestly . . ."

Mark starts to read:

Mr Barron What do have in mind

Pub man Indecent expo something

Policeman Laughing stock. Couple of bad lads in the witness box. Miss Murkett will pay for a brief. Client relieving himself on his own property. Boys trespassing.

Pub man Must be something else then.

Policeman He lives there with Miss Mu permiss doesn't he? Not illegal to need haircut bath

Pub man Not as the law stands. Law needs to be changed

Mr Barron Agree but till it is have to think. Why don't we discuss over sherry Not tomorrow got a trip going out Maybe Friday Pub man All right

He goes through it all again, trying to fill in the missing words. Most of it seems pretty clear, but he doesn't understand *Miss Murkett will pay for a brief*. He could ask Lou, but he doesn't want to admit his own ignorance.

"What do you think? Should we show him?"

*We*, not *I*. "Yes," he says, slapping it back in her hand. His throat's dry. "Good work," he adds, not looking at her.

"Thanks." She slips the notebook into its pocket. "You want to go now?"

He doesn't want to. Or, at least, the skin on his arms and legs doesn't want him to: it wants him to stay here, close enough to Lou to feel the warmth of her body. But he can't put that hunger into words, even to himself. He yawns, stretches full-length on the ground.

"We could do it tomorrow," he says.

She shakes her head. "Well, not in the morning, anyway. Mummy's taking me to get some new shoes. Look" — she lifts her knee and waggles a white plimsoll at him. The sole's worn almost smooth, and the upper is starting to pull away along the seam. "Feel how tight they are."

He clamps his fingers over the stretched canvas. Under it, her foot feels hot. The bony curve of the instep, the tiny pulse, make him think of a small animal's back.

"Stop it! That tickles!" she giggles, snatching it away again. "Anyway, we'll be back by lunch, I expect. So we could go after that."

"Can't," he says.

She rests on one elbow, pillowing her head in the cup of her hand. "Why not?"

"I'm going to see Miss Murkett. At Hillfield."

Lou nods.

"Murky. That's what I call her."

She laughs. "Murky!"

"Yes." He hadn't meant to tell her all this, but now it's just tumbling out. "She likes me to read to her. *Old Possum's Book of Practical Cats*."

She laughs again. But she's not mocking him: she's sharing his amusement. "Well, not tomorrow afternoon, then," she says, sitting up.

"Day after?"

"That'll be too late. I think we should go now."

"All right. I don't mind."

They scrabble out, heave their bags on to their backs and call Barney from the wheat field.

"Here," says Mark. "Give me the notebook."

"Why?"

"Case we meet Mr Montgomery. I'm going to hide it."

"Where?"

"In my shorts."

She shakes her head. "*I'll* hide it." She takes the notebook from her knapsack again and slips it down the front of her shirt. "There. He won't look there, will he?"

They *left-right, left-right* for a few paces, then catch each other's eye and break into a jog-trot. The quicker they are, the less chance there is that they'll bump into anyone. Only when they're in the wood and out of sight of the track do they finally stop to get their breath.

"Have to make sure it's safe," says Lou. "You keep Barney on the lead. I'll go and see if the towel's hanging up."

She creeps forward, hunched below the level of the leaves, swivelling her hips to place one foot directly in front of the other.

"OK! It's all clear!"

Mark lets Barney go, then hurries after her. By the time he reaches the clearing, Barney's already at the top of the carriage steps, whining and scraping at the door. Mark glimpses Hillyard peering from the kitchen window, his face moony and featureless, like a still-developing image on a print. Then the door opens and he cranes out.

"No one saw you?" he calls, squinting at the wood behind them.

"No," says Lou. "We were careful."

"In here, then. The pair of you. Double-quick time!"

He stands aside and beckons them through the entrance, still watching the trees. The heavy air, the smell of tobacco and sweat and dirty clothes make Mark feel faint. He steadies himself against the wall, trying to stave off a rising surge of nausea by taking in his surroundings. The portable typewriter is on the tea chest, with two three-quarter used pages, separated by a sheet of carbon paper, sticking out. In the clutter around it are a half-empty mug, a saucer dotted with fag ends, Mark's knife and the block of wood — which now, unmistakably, has started to take on the shape of a boat. Hillyard pockets the knife and the wood, then shoves the typewriter on the floor and drops the cover on it, as carelessly as if he was putting the lid on a saucepan.

Mark wants to know when he's going to get his knife back. But Hillyard is obviously still using it, and he doesn't want to seem stingy. So, instead of asking for it, he says:

"How's it going? The book?"

"A struggle," he says abruptly. "You want to know the truth, I've pretty much had to go back to the drawing board with it."

"Start again, you mean?"

"More or less. Right, you two. You know the drill."

Lou lifts down a couple of mugs from the rack next to the little sink. Mark collects two chairs from the pile.

"Inside or outside?" he asks.

"Most definitely inside today, I think." He glances at the window, then hurriedly closes the curtains. Mark slides the chairs next to the tea chest.

"Grab a seat," says Hillyard, turning back and batting the kettle onto the gas ring with the flat of his hand. "Preferably one apiece." Hunching his big shoulders, he squats down and rummages in the tin cupboard. "Now then, let's see if we can liberate some biscuits, shall we? Poor devils have been stuck in here so long they've forgotten what the light of day looks like. Ah, there we are." He plucks out the remains of the Peek Frean assortment and — lumbering round on his haunches — slaps them onto the tea chest. "So, what's the news? No ill effects from our chance encounter in the High Street, I hope, Mark?"

"No." He's on the point of adding *I think my mother liked you*. But when he runs the words through in his head, they sound wrong.

"Well, that's good." He levers himself to his feet, then straddles his chair. "She didn't ask any more questions, then?"

"No."

He nods. "Still, we should be careful." He looks down at Barney. "You don't realize, do you, boy? Just how close you came to precipitating a disaster?"

Barney whines. Hillyard snaps off a piece of biscuit and gives it to him.

"What happened?" mouths Lou.

"Oh, nothing," says Mark. "We bumped into Aubrey, that's all. When we were on our way to the shop. Just before I saw you. And Barney gave the game away." He sticks his tongue out, licks the air furiously.

"But quick thinking saved the day, Lord be praised," says Hillyard.

"Something important *has* happened, though," says Mark. He wishes it was his secret, his story to tell. But this is the closest he can come to claiming credit for it.

"What?" says Hillyard.

"Ask Lou."

Hillyard turns towards her, eyebrows raised. She slides a hand down her shirt front and takes out the notebook.

"Da-*dah*!" says Mark.

"What is this?" asks Hillyard.

"Some men were talking," she says. "In front of the shop. And you said to keep our ears open. So I wrote down what they said. Well, everything I could."

"Which men?"

"PC Pointer. And Mr Barron from the garage."

"And Harry Doggett," says Mark.

"Ah, yes. The chap at the pub. And they were talking about me, were they?"

"Yes."

He holds his hand out. "May I see?"

She gives him the notebook. The kettle suddenly shivers and hisses. Hillyard glances at it.

"You be mother, can you?"

Lou gets up and adds water to the already half-full pot. Hillyard starts to read, frowning slightly, combing his beard with his fingers. Sometimes his lips move, as if he's saying the words to himself.

"Well, Miss Bennett," he says finally. "You make an excellent spy, I must say." But his eyes aren't part of the joke: they're wide open, and keep straying past Mark and Lou towards the door.

Lou fills the three mugs. "Is it useful?"

Hillyard nods. "Just the sort of the thing I had in mind, thank you kindly." He flaps the notebook on the edge of the tea chest. "Am I allowed to keep this?"

"Well . . ."

"Ah, yes, I see. That'd be wasteful. Well, how about if I just tear out the relevant bit, then, and keep *that?*"

Lou nods. Hillyard seizes the edge of the first couple of pages and pulls them free with three violent tugs.

"Why are they? . . . I mean, is it something to do with the Brain?" says Lou.

"Remember those cows I was telling you about?" says Hillyard. "The ones that like their comfortable field?"

"Yes."

"Well, there you have it." He opens his hand above the notebook. "A whole lot of damned mooing." He half-closes his eyes. "And it does rather make you wonder."

"What?" says Lou.

"Who might be putting them up to it."

"Who do *you* think's doing it, then?" says Mark. Will he actually say, "The Brain?"

"Well," says Hillyard. He shifts in his seat and settles his huge hands, fingers splayed, on his thighs. "I'm sure if you suggested to them that they were in the grip of some sinister force, they'd think you were stark raving mad. But that's hardly conclusive." He takes a noisy sip of tea, wrinkles his nose, sniffs. "Mr Barron, I take it," he says, glancing at the two sheets again, "gave no indication as to where this summit conference of his might take place?"

"No," says Lou.

"*Chez* Barron, presumably. And if sherry is in the offing, probably — what? Six? Six-thirty? I wish I could be — not a fly on the wall, too easily swatted. A mouse under the sofa, say. Or a blob of damp on the ceiling. A witch could have done it. Sent her familiar, or gone herself in disguise. But my witchy powers are sadly diminished, I'm afraid."

"Why isn't it conclusive?" says Mark.

Hillyard blinks at him.

"You said it wasn't conclusive," says Mark. "That they'd think we were mad. But surely, if they were really in the grip of a sinister force, they'd know we *weren't* mad to say it."

"Not if they've been brainwashed," says Lou.

"*Exactly*," says Hillyard. He points a big finger at her, a teacher acknowledging his cleverest pupil.

"But they haven't been brainwashed, have they?" says Mark. He's cornered himself. He wants to be persuaded that Hillyard's right, but he can't admit that goody-goody Lou has guessed the answer. "That isn't real life, silly!" he blurts. "That's just the story. How could they *really* be brainwashed?"

Lou looks at Hillyard, searching for guidance. "Television," she says, as if she can read it in his face.

Hillyard nods. "Permit me," he says, waving the two sheets of paper, "to go through this again, underlining a word or two." He scrabbles in the muddle on the tea chest and picks up a pencil. He clacks it absently between his teeth for a moment, then nods and says, "Right."

Mark and Lou watch in silence as he reads, stopping every now and then to make a neat little horizontal stroke.

"There," he says finally. "What does that suggest to you?"

He hands the pages to Lou. Mark squeezes himself into his chair, clutching the seat with his fingers. When she's finished, she passes the sheets on to him without a word.

Mr Barron What do have in mind

Pub man Indecent expo something

Policeman Laughing stock. Couple of bad lads in the witness box. Miss Murkett will pay for a brief. Client relieving himself on his own property. Boys trespassing.

Pub man *Must be something else* then.

Policeman He lives there with Miss Mu permiss doesn't he? *Not illegal* to need haircut bath

Pub man *Not as the law stands. Law needs to be changed*

Mr Barron *Agree but till it is have to think*. Why don't we discuss over sherry Not tomorrow got a trip going out Maybe Friday

Pub man All right

"Well?" says Hillyard.

Mark looks at Lou. She seems puzzled too. "I don't know," he says.

"Observe, if you will, the references to the law," says Hillyard. "As it stands, as they freely admit, it provides no penalties for the crime of being Aubrey Hillyard. But it's clear, isn't it, that they anticipate a change? *Till* it happens, they say. Not *if* it happens. Someone — or something — must have begun to prepare them. For the morning when there'll be a knock on the door at dawn" — rapping his knuckles on the tea chest — "And . . ."

"And what?" says Lou.

"And no more Aubrey Hillyard."

"And you think it's the Brain doing it?" says Mark.

"You're bright kids. I leave you to draw your own conclusions."

Lou glances desperately at Mark. "Oh, it's not fair!"

Hillyard shakes his head. "As you get older, I'm afraid," he says slowly, all the playfulness squeezed from his voice, "you'll realize that fairness is the last thing you should expect from life. Doesn't mean you shouldn't fight for it, of course, whenever you get the chance. But in my experience, it's generally a losing battle."

"We'll fight!" says Lou, looking at Mark again. "Won't we?"

"Course we will."

"As always, I'm touched," says Hillyard. "But I have to warn you, if you stick by me, it won't be easy. I mean, you've seen already, haven't you" — tapping the pages with his finger — "people are prepared to say all kinds of things about me to shut me up, stop me writing the book. And that'll only get worse, in all probability. There'll come a time when admitting you're a friend of Aubrey Hillyard is going to be damned tough."

He speaks in a slow, featureless monotone, every word forced out as if saying it causes him physical pain. Mark is shocked: it's the first time he's ever heard him like this. And Lou's noticed the change too: her eyes are shiny, and she reaches out and touches Hillyard's hand.

"I don't care!"

Hillyard sighs. "Thank you. I appreciate it. But *I* care. Wouldn't want either of you to come to grief on my account. So if you decide to back out now, I'll quite understand. And no hard feelings, eh?"

"We *don't* want to, do we, Mark?" says Lou.

"No. You just tell us what to do and —"

"Well, you're a couple of young heroes. And I count myself damned lucky to know you." His voice is suddenly more animated again. He nudges the Peek Frean box towards them. "Here. Tuck in. Put the poor beasties out of their misery. Being stuck in that damned cupboard is a living death to them."

Lou and Mark take a biscuit each.

"Right," says Hillyard. "I'm just going to check the lie of the land."

Clutching his mug, he manoeuvres his way to the window and stealthily parts the curtains with one finger. "Seems all clear for the time being," he reports. "But I've a funny feeling. Bit of electricity in the air. Something could happen at any moment. So less time you're here, the better, I'm afraid. Sorry to be inhospitable, and rush you. But —"

"That's all right," says Lou, getting up. "We're going."

"But I shan't forget this," says Hillyard, fanning the air with the two pages. "And any other snippets of intelligence will be gratefully received."

"Leave it to us," says Mark. "Here, Barney!"

"Oh," says Hillyard suddenly, as they start towards the door. "We haven't talked about Peveril on the Swift, have we?"

Mark shrugs. "There wasn't time."

"No. Still, any news on that front? Just give me the headlines."

Mark thinks for a moment. Lou's done her bit. This is *his* chance. "*Paul and Patty Gallion find strange man hiding in the hermitage*."

For the first time since they got here, Hillyard laughs. "Sounds intriguing. Nothing too sinister, I hope?"

"Have to see."

"Well, I look forward to hearing the whole story."

Mark nods. Lou opens the door. As he follows her out, Hillyard bear-walks up behind him and touches his shoulder.

"Do you think," he mutters quietly, "there might be a chance of my seeing it at some point?"

"What?"

"Peveril on the Swift. I know it would have to be a clandestine operation. But I can keep myself out of sight as well as the next man. Better, probably, unless the next man's Houdini."

How could it be done? Mark can't imagine. But he doesn't just want to say no. "I'll have to think about it."

"All right. But *do* think about it, will you? Being able to get a dekko at the place would be a real shot in the arm. Somewhere wholesome. Brain-free."

"OK." Mark launches himself down the steps. At the bottom, he looks up and calls:

"See you later!"

Hillyard raises one hand.

They avoid the path and circle through Twenty Acre in a spiral, not speaking, listening for voices. They hear nothing but birdsong and the tramp of their own feet, and the swish of Barney's tail feathering the leaves. Only when they reach the lane does Lou finally say:

"Did he remind you of anything?"

"Who?"

"Aubrey just now."

He shrugs. "Don't think so."

"He seemed different today. He made *me* think of poor Aslan. In *The Lion, the Witch and the Wardrobe*. Before he's killed by the White Witch."

Mark shrugs again. But it's true, if he thinks about it: Hillyard *was* like that.

"Anyway," he says. "Let's split up here. You go that way" — pointing down Willetts Lane. "And I'll nip back through the farm. If Mr Montgomery sees us together, he'll think we're up to something."

"All right." She loops her thumbs through the straps of her knapsack and — without looking back — starts running towards the High Street.

# CHAPTER EIGHT

"We're going into town."

"Why?"

"There's a few things we need to get. Will you be OK on your own?"

He nods. "When will you be back?"

"Lunchtime."

"OK."

Blast. If only they'd told him sooner, he'd have been able to arrange for Hillyard to come and see Peveril on the Swift. But there wouldn't be time now. And, anyway, it would be too dangerous in broad daylight.

He watches from the window as Mum and Dad walk down the path, their voices fading until he's just looking at a dumbshow. What's going on? Is it good or bad? He can't tell. Dad doesn't seem sulky: he's talking animatedly and sweeps open the gate to let Mum go through first. But she's clearly jittery, for some reason, her movements nervy as a bird's, her smiles coming and going too quickly. Then they disappear, and he hears the slam of the doors and sees the car roof start to skim the top of the hedge.

He turns away, shivering. It always makes him feel funny being here alone, even when he's got Barney with him. It's not that he's scared of ghosts, exactly: more that the house itself seems suddenly alien, as if it's changed from a living organism to something strange and dead. All that *stuff* — books, furniture, the picture of the horse over the fireplace, the pad on the kitchen table where Mum makes notes for herself — without his parents to give it life, it all becomes inert and meaningless. He wishes Lou were here. But of course Lou's in town as well. She's there now, probably, sitting in the shoe shop, while the thin man with Brylcreemed hair kneels in front of her, measuring her foot . . .

Oh, blast: there it is again. Why does it keep coming back to him like this, the memory of his fingers clamped over her plimsoll? He doesn't want to go on thinking about it — it makes him feel jumpy and slightly sick — but it seems to have lodged itself in some part of his brain beyond his control. It even troubled him in the night, wriggling its way into a dream about Barney biting his hand, and prodding him awake with a jolt.

"Come on, boy! We're going out!"

He clips on the lead, locks the door and slips the key under the mat. The weather's changed: it's still bright, but there's a cool east breeze, and a procession of starchy white clouds takes the edge off the heat of the sun. A perfect morning for a longer ramble. It'll be a relief to walk somewhere else for a change: going back to Twenty Acre Wood and the chalk pit without Lou would feel odd and unsatisfactory — a bit like staying in the empty house.

He hasn't forgotten his duties, of course. He takes Church End at a slow amble, holding eager Barney back, craning to look up the footpath by the graveyard, peering into gardens, windows, open doorways. Nothing. When he reaches the top of the High Street, he lingers in front of the war memorial, pretending to read the names carved into the stone. It's still early, but Harry Doggett might have decided to convene a meeting with his fellow conspirators; so he ties Barney to the railing and bends down to rebuckle his sandal, squinting between his legs at the Fox and Hounds. There's no sign of life at all: the yard's empty, apart from the usual clutter of barrels, and the curtains in the pub windows are still closed. Nothing requiring his attention.

The garage is more interesting. One of the coaches is drawn up in the forecourt, its flanks already pulsing with the drub of the engine. Mr Barron stands by the open door, laughing and chatting as twenty or so old people file on board at a snail's pace. He's just greeting batty Mrs Slater, who wears brogues and a heavy winter coat and carries a large bag, as if she's going away for a week. She frowns at him suspiciously and fumbles for something in her pocket. Mr Barron shakes his head, smiling. Mark edges closer and tries to hear what they're saying, but the noise of the motor drowns it out. It doesn't matter, he decides, backing away again: whatever they're discussing, it won't be Aubrey Hillyard.

"Hullo, there!" Mr Barron has seen him. He raises a hand, pausing his conversation with Mrs Slater, and strides over. For a second, Mark considers turning and bolting — but of course that would only make Mr Barron think he was up to no good. "What are you looking at?"

He's sort of smiling, but his heavy face is flushed. As he approaches, Barney starts to squirm and whimper. Mark tugs on the lead, holds him close. Why can't his own blasted dog tell the difference between a friend and an enemy?

"Where are they going?" He flaps the back of his hand towards the bus.

"Clacton," says Mr Barron. "Day out by the sea. How about you? Where are you off to this fine morning?"

Mark shrugs. "Just a walk."

"Anywhere in particular?"

"Tunnels, probably."

Mr Barron nods. The smile flickers off, then on again. "Sounds like a good plan. Won't come to much harm at the tunnels." He laughs. "Unless you let your dog go after one of Mr Montgomery's pheasants. That *wouldn't* be a clever idea."

He turns and walks back to the coach. Mrs Slater is just at the door. She stops and says something to Mr Barron, scowling at him through her round glasses. Mark just catches the response:

"It's all right, Mrs Slater. You don't need your Identity Card. They've done away with them."

*Won't come to much harm at the tunnels*. So where does Mr Barron think he *might* come to harm? The answer, presumably, is Twenty Acre Wood. Mr

Montgomery must have been talking to him, telling him about his meeting with Mark and Lou.

"Come on, Barney."

All the way up the Burdon Road he has the sense that he's being watched. He can *feel* it, in a small triangle between his shoulder blades and the base of his neck. He tells himself he's being stupid, that no one's remotely interested in him and Barney. As he reaches the old Wool Pack, he tries — as he's always done — to imagine it in its heyday fifty years ago, sprucely painted and presided over by Florrie Poulter in a long dress. But it's no good: the blank windows and peeling woodwork don't just appear neglected any more: they look sinister. Who knows what's really behind them? A gang of coiners at work? No, that's a childish idea. Something worse, half-hidden by shadows, impossible to put a name to.

It's only when he finally turns off onto the Tunnels Lane that the sensation leaves him. After a hundred yards or so he stops and looks about him. Yes, the familiar landscape: he can breathe again. Nothing but a sea of wheat and the flinty shine of the track, and on the other side of the valley a bright field of mustard, fringed by dark-green trees. From here, you can just make out the faint lines of the medieval terraces wrinkling the opposite slope, like coils of clay on a pot. Below them, next to the nearly dried-up stream, is the site of the Roman villa. Three years ago, when the archaeologists were here, it was a maze of square chalk-sided pits, interspersed with piles of earth. Now it's vanished beneath the swelling tide of corn. But still, if he half-closes his eyes, he can almost imagine he sees the tunicked labourers coaxing their vines into fruit, the lady of the house fanning herself with a peacock feather in the garden, her skin gleaming with oil from a wobbly amphora . . .

"Down!" he whispers. "Down, boy!"

Barney drops heavily to the ground, panting. Mark squats beside him, weighting him down with an arm across the neck. Somewhere over there, just beyond the hedge, are the enemy. Of course, there are far more of *them* than there are of *us*. The only hope is to creep up stealthily and take them by surprise.

He inches forward. Barney tries to get to his feet, but Mark stops him, so he's reduced to slithering along the ground, huffing and whining. In Mark's other hand is a weapon. He pauses, readies it for the attack.

But what is it? A sword? A spear? A gun? He suddenly realizes he's not sure. Who *are* the enemy? Who is *he*? A Briton fighting the Romans? A Roman fighting the Saxons? A Saxon fighting the Normans? An Englishman fighting the Germans?

He crawls towards the hedge. He'll know when he sees what's on the other side. Cautiously, he peers through. A dance of brown figures, too indistinct, and swirling about too quickly, for him to be able to identify them, or even tell what they're doing. As he's watching, waiting for them to slow down, thicken out, start to come into focus, they're gathered up like chaff in a whirlwind and whisked into nothingness.

Something's pressing against his hand. He looks down: Barney's nose. He glances quickly behind him:

no, there's still no one spying on him. But, for a moment, he sees what *they* would see if there were: a boy in shorts and an Aertex shirt, forcing his dog to play a game he can't understand. There's not a Norman or a Saxon in sight: just an ordinary patchwork of crops and woods, formed by nothing more mysterious than wind and rain, and the coming and going of the seasons. He bends down and pats Barney's shoulder.

"OK, boy."

Barney pricks his ears hopefully, beats a cloud of dust from the ground with his tail. Mark gets up.

"All right. Off you go."

Barney races ahead along the track. Mark saunters after him. He's at a loss. Why can't he do it any more? Why doesn't it work? Is he just too old now, or has the real-life adventure of Aubrey Hillyard made the made-up kind seem silly and unsatisfying? His tummy tingles with unease. Maybe *that's* the problem: he really shouldn't be here at all. It was OK before, when he had only himself to think of, but now he's part of a gang, a *team*. What would Hillyard and Lou expect him to be doing? Patrolling the High Street, looking for clues? Or . . .

*Do you think there might be a chance of my seeing it at some point? Being able to get a dekko at the place would be a real shot in the arm. Somewhere wholesome. Brain-free.*

Yes, that's what he *ought* to be concentrating his mind on: how to get Hillyard in to see Peveril on the Swift without his parents knowing. It must be possible.

All it requires is enough advance warning of their movements.

"Barney!" But it's too late: Barney's spotted something and chases it into the cornfield. Mark can hear the click and thrash of parting stalks, but all he can see is an advancing furrow rippling along the golden surface.

"Barney!"

No response. And now Mark notices something else: Mr Montgomery's Land Rover at the bottom of the hill. It's just turned and is crawling up the track towards him. He remembers Mr Barron's warning, every sly syllable of it: *Unless you let your dog go after one of Mr Montgomery's pheasants. That* wouldn't *be a clever idea*. Blast. Blast, blast, blast.

"Barney. Come here!" But the crease through the ears of wheat continues. Perhaps it would be better just to leave Barney and hope he doesn't reappear until after Mr Montgomery has passed.

"Morning, Mark."

"Morning."

"Didn't expect to see you here. Long way from home."

Mark shrugs.

"I was starting to think you always went down Willetts Lane?"

Mark shrugs again. "Not today."

"Well, that's good. Between you and me, it might not be the best place to be just at the moment. Things are afoot."

For a second, Mark can feel the warm throb of Lou's arch in his hand. He quickly closes his fingers, squeezing it out.

"What do you mean?"

"I mean concerning your friend."

"Lou?"

Mr Montgomery tugs his mouth into an ugly smile.

"No, not Lou," he says. "The other one. Mr Hillyard."

"What's going to happen to him?"

Mr Montgomery shakes his head. "Can't tell you any more than that. Just thought I'd mention it." He revs the engine, shifts the long gear stick into first, then suddenly looks out again. "Where's the dog?"

"He's over there."

"Where?"

"In the field."

"Well, it shouldn't be."

"He isn't doing anything wrong."

"It is if it's trampling down wheat. Or going after a pheasant. You get it back and" — nodding at the leash — "put it on that when you're on my land, all right? Wouldn't want it to get shot."

He touches his cap and lets in the clutch. As he passes Mark, a cock pheasant rises squawking from the corn, feathers ragged. A split second later, Barney dolphins up after it, snapping at the bird's feet. Mark holds his breath. But the Land Rover continues its slow climb. Thank goodness: Mr Montgomery can't have noticed.

"Barney! Come here, you bad boy! Grrr!"

Barney breaks cover and stands uncertainly in front of the wall of wheat. He knows he's in trouble: his tail's drooping and his ears are flat. Mark leans over and snaps on the lead.

"No more of that, you hear?"

He tries to walk on, but for a moment he can't: his legs seem to lack the power to take him either down to the tunnels or back the way he came. What to do? He must, of course, warn Hillyard. But if he tries to go there now, it sounds, from what Mr Montgomery said, as if someone — maybe Montgomery himself — will see, and stop him entering the wood. Better to wait till this afternoon, when he'll have the excuse of visiting Murky. And, of course, no Barney to worry about.

He watches till the Land Rover is out of sight, then trudges up the hill in its wake. Still a couple of hours to go before lunch. He'll spend the time till his parents get home in the shed, sprucing up Peveril on the Swift.

He half expects the atmosphere of the village to feel different. He walks slowly, looking for signs of the impending move against Aubrey Hillyard, but it all feels absolutely normal. At the garage, the coach has gone, and the little limping man is at the pumps, filling up a curvy white sports car. On the other side of the High Street, the pub has woken up finally, and is open for business. Harry Doggett stands in the yard, talking to the driver of a green-and-gold dray lorry stacked with barrels. As Mark passes, he dials a number in the air, and shouts out:

"Morning, boy and dog!"

He and the drayman laugh.

But there *is* something strange. Mark notices it as soon as he starts along Church End and catches a glimpse of his own house: there's a ladder leaning up against the wall. The car isn't there, so his parents aren't back. It couldn't be a burglar, could it? No: burglars work at night, when no one can see them.

As he gets nearer, he can hear whistling. He peers up and sees a man silhouetted on the ridge of the roof, next to the chimney. After a moment, the man senses his stare and half-turns his head to look down. Mark recognizes him: the young chap with the comedian's face who works in the electrical shop in town.

"How do," he calls.

"What are you doing?" asks Mark.

"Oh, you know, I just thought I'd climb up and take a look at the view."

"No, honestly!"

The man picks something up and holds it above his head. It's a straight metal bar, a yard or so long, with spikes sticking out at regular intervals on either side.

"Ever seen one of these before?"

Mark has: it's a television aerial.

He's out of his depth, all of a sudden. A television aerial on a house without a television. Is this what Mr Montgomery meant when he said *Things are afoot?* There must be a connection. But it's hidden from him, like the secret network of veins under the skin. He's too young to see it.

He shuts Barney inside, then goes into the shed and switches on the light. That, at least, looks just as it did when he last saw it. He's so relieved he says out loud:

"Thank you."

He should be preparing for Hillyard's visit: dusting off the houses; touching up the backdrop — hills so faint they're barely visible, trees in need of a fresh covering of leaves. That's what he *told* himself he'd do. But Hillyard — for the moment, at least — has been displaced from the map of the known world and become part of the baffling terrain beyond the door. And Mark's only refuge from *that* is Peveril — Peveril as it used to be.

He returns the figure of the old man to the Oxo box and moves the Gallions from the hermitage to the High Street. Then he turns on the power and edges the train out of the Sheepfold Tunnel. As it draws up next to the platform, he snatches Patty and Paul and drops them down between Mrs Dauntless and Mr Makepeace.

*Gosh, you look puffed out, Patty!*

*Yes, Mrs Dauntless, it was a close-run thing.*

*Peveril! This is Peveril on the Swift!*

He puts everyone except Mr Makepeace in the Oxo Box, then moves the train forward, watching it carry Patty and Paul and Mrs Dauntless into the Abbey Tunnel. And beyond that, he thinks, closing his eyes, on to a day of shopping and cream teas in Swiftbridge, followed by a slow journey back along the valley, watching the windy ribbon of the river glow red in the setting sun.

Just after twelve, there's the sound of car doors closing and the groan of the gate. He waits, holding his breath. It must be Mum and Dad, but they seem to be taking a long time. He resists the urge to go out and look. If he stays here, Mum will eventually come out to find him, and he can ask her what's going on.

"No, no, no!" Dad's voice, irritable, out of breath. "Please! Be careful!"

"All right, all right! I know!" She sounds snappish too. He's never heard her talk to Dad like that.

Shoes shuffling along the paving stones, a collision between soft and hard, a gasp. Barney yelps, breaks into a long yodelling bark.

"Let's put it down here for a minute." Dad again, just outside now. "Where's Mark?"

"In his room, I expect. I'll call him. In just a minute."

Dad says something else, but Barney's barking so furiously that Mark can't hear it.

He waits till they're inside, then starts the train again. This time he leaves it going, round and round, engine whining, wheels rattling over the joins in the rails. Perhaps if he seems absorbed enough, they'll think he just didn't notice them coming home.

"Mark?" She unlatches the door, cranes her head round inside. "Ah, there you are. What are you doing?"

"Just playing. I'm running the one o'clock local."

"Well, don't be long. It's lunchtime. And we've got a surprise."

She starts to retreat towards the house.

"Mum —"

She stops. "What?"

"I took Barney for a walk. And when we got back, there was a man putting a television aerial up on the roof."

"Yes, I saw he'd been. We weren't expecting him till this afternoon." She feels for a strand of hair, can't find one, strokes her cheek instead. "Well, that's the surprise.

Only don't say, will you? That I said? Dad wants to tell you."

"You bought a television?"

"Yes."

"Why?"

"Well . . . We thought . . . I mean . . ." She frowns. "We thought you'd be pleased. Don't you *want* a television?"

"No."

"What?" She puts a hand on her forehead, as if she's wondering if she has a fever. "Why ever not? It'll be fun, won't it?"

He says nothing.

"Well don't, whatever you do, tell Dad *that*. Can you just pretend? Please?"

She stares at him. He looks away, towards the open door.

"Please?"

There's no way out. He nods.

"Thank you." She sighs. Then, more brightly, she says, "I mean, think of all the things you'll be able to see. *The Lone Ranger*. Isn't that what the girl at the shop likes? And Charlie Drake, or whatever his name is. He's supposed to be very funny, isn't he? There's tons and tons."

"But Dad said he was never going to get one."

She pulls her mouth into a rueful pout. "I know. But I think that was just, well, making a virtue of necessity. Televisions are expensive."

"That's all right! We don't need one!"

She shakes her head. "The thing is, yesterday, while you were out, we had a long chat. And, bit by bit, it all came out. He was still feeling hurt. About the competition. Felt we hadn't made enough of it."

"We did!"

"I know, I know, poppet. But you just have to remember. What a rotten childhood he had." But her voice is lacklustre, as if she's repeating the words by rote. And her eyes, instead of looking away, find his and convey a startlingly different message: *Yes, he is impossible, isn't he?*

"Anyway," she says. "I asked him what we could do to celebrate. And finally, he said what he'd *really* like was a television."

"Why?"

"Well, he thinks it'll be useful. Keep him informed about things. Give him ideas for pictures and articles." She hesitates, tries to smile. "But to be honest, as much as anything, I suspect it's Mr Barron."

Mark's scalp tightens. "Mr Barron? What did he say?"

"Oh, it's just that he's always boasting about what he's seen. And I think Daddy was a bit tired of going to the garage, and hearing him say, you know, 'Did you watch that programme last night about the — oh, sorry, I forgot, you haven't got one, have you?' "

She pauses, waiting for him to laugh, but he can't.

"What is it, Mark? What's wrong with you? Tell me."

He hesitates. Forcing himself to look at her, he says: "You know Aubrey Hillyard?"

She nods. "What about him?"

"Well, he thinks . . . He says . . ." No, he can't do it. She likes Hillyard, that's obvious, but that doesn't necessarily mean she can be trusted with his secret. Maybe Mr Barron has started to get at her, too. And anyway, Mark promised, didn't he?

"He says what?"

"It doesn't matter."

"Yes, it does. Please, lovey."

He shakes his head, pushes past her, runs into the house. Dad's in the sitting room standing in front of a large box. He's slit open the lid and pulled out the packing. Now he's just staring at what he's uncovered: a flat expanse of honeycomb-coloured wood.

"Hello, Dad."

"Ah, there you are, old thing." He nods at the box. "Come and have a look at this. Know what it is?"

Mark takes a couple of steps towards it. "Gosh, is it a television?"

"I thought you were going to say a donkey. Or a fire engine. But no, you're right, it's a television." He gropes inside the box. "What's this gubbins? Ah, yes, the plug. Right. Seems all present and correct, then."

He turns, takes the Newberry Fruits from the table and offers them to Mark. "Would you care for one of these? They were a present. Given to me by two very important people. And then perhaps you'd lend me a hand" — nodding at the box again — "getting this out."

"OK," Mark says, picking out the lemon fruit.

"Right," says Dad. "You take that side. One, two, three."

The weight of it, the awkwardness, takes them by surprise. They only manage to raise it a couple of inches before it breaks free and settles back again with a sigh, pinching their fingers against the cardboard walls.

"Bloody-minded so-and-so, isn't it?" says Dad. "All right, we'll tip the whole thing over. And get it out that way. Careful! Careful!"

Together they tilt the box on its side, then gingerly invert it.

"Right. Let's see what you look like."

A helmet: that's what Mark thinks of. And under it, a head. He trembles slightly as they lift off the box. Yes, that's it: the huge curved eye; the gold mesh of the mouth, with *His Master's Voice* scrolled across the bottom.

"What do you think?" says Dad, running his fingertips over the polished surface. "Not bad, is it?" He laughs. "*You'll be the envy of your friends*, or whatever it is they say in the advertisements."

"Are you going to switch it on?" He half wants Dad to say *Yes*, so that he can see the effect for himself. But what if *he* falls under the spell, too, and doesn't even notice?

Dad shakes his head. "Chap's coming tomorrow to set it up. He said he'd bring it with him. But I said, no, I want my son to see it *today*."

It's inescapable. "Thanks, Dad."

Dad frowns. But Mark's saved by Mum calling from the hall: "Lunch!"

She pushes open the door. “Oh, you’ve got it out already. Doesn’t that look nice? It could have been made for this room, couldn’t it?”

# CHAPTER NINE

He gets to Hillfield on the dot of four. As he approaches the gate, he again has the sense that he's being watched. He looks round. The field next to the house is empty, except for something scuffling in the jungle of cow parsley along the edge, and there's no one in the High Street at all. He tells himself to stop imagining things.

There's a car he doesn't recognize in the drive: a fawn Morris Minor with a fold-down roof. It's parked at an odd angle, one wheel on the lawn, as if the driver was in a hurry to get into the house. He hopes whoever it is will be leaving soon. It's all right reading to Murky, but he doesn't want anyone else to hear.

The door is shut. That's unusual: at this time of year, she usually leaves it open when she's expecting him. He tugs on the bell pull and listens to the thin querulous tinkle in the kitchen. He waits. There's no response. He tries again. Still nothing.

He steps back and scans the windows. A couple of them are open, but the only sign of life is a cat stretched on one of the sills. From somewhere, though, he can just hear a droning voice. She and her visitor must be in the garden.

He walks round through the stable yard. Yes, there they are: Murky and a younger woman Mark's never seen before, sitting on the bench under the overgrown rose pergola. Murky, ramrod-straight as ever, has her back to him. The other woman leans close to her, elbows on knees. She's slight and dark, with a small-featured face his mother would call pretty. She's talking energetically, making quick movements with her hands for emphasis, but keeping her voice low, as if — even here — she's frightened of being overheard.

"You'd be within your rights."

"Rights fiddlesticks!" says Murky.

"Well —"

"If we all stayed within our rights, it'd be a pretty dull world, wouldn't it? And a pretty heartless world too, more to the point."

The other woman sits back, shaking her head. Mark stops dead. Neither of them seems to have noticed him yet.

"Honestly, stop being so hard on yourself," says Murky. "You couldn't have known."

The woman shakes her head again. "I can't help it. I feel awful."

"Well, don't. Aunt's orders."

*Aunt*. This must be her niece. In which case they can only be talking about Hillyard.

"But your neighbours —"

"Oh, I'm not bothered about my neighbours," says Murky. "They're a lot of humbugs. It's this other thing. I'll have to give it some thought. But if it comes to it, I'll tell him myself."

"You're a brick," says the other woman. She half-turns, resting her arm on the back of the seat. Mark tries to retreat, but she catches the movement out of the corner of her eye and looks sharply towards him. For a couple of seconds they stare at each other in silence. Then she bends forward and taps Murky's knee.

"What?"

She nods towards Mark. Murky grabs the arm of the seat and hauls herself round. Her eyes widen. She frowns and smiles at the same time.

"Oh, young Aurelius!"

"Hullo, Murky."

"You startled us. What are you doing here?"

"You asked me. To tea."

She hits her temple with the heel of her hand. "Did I? Oh yes, of course I did, didn't I? Oh, dash it!"

"That's all right. I can come back another day, if you like."

"No, no." She glances at the other woman. "Well, maybe. If you wouldn't mind. That actually might be best. I'm sorry. You're probably thinking, *Murky's gone completely gaga*, aren't you?"

He shakes his head.

"But just come and meet my niece first. Jane. Miss Saunders. Who's popped down from London for the day."

*There*, he thinks. *Good detective work, Mark*.

"Jane, this is Mark Davenant," says Murky. "A very good friend of mine."

Miss Saunders's face softens into a smile. "Ah, yes. You're the boy who reads *Old Possum's Book of Practical Cats*, aren't you?"

Mark nods.

"My aunt talks a lot about you. How do you do?"

"How do you do?"

"See?" says Murky. "Your reputation precedes you."

"Which is your favourite?" says Miss Saunders.

"The Rum Tum Tugger," says Mark.

"Mine too. I'll tell Mr Eliot the next time I see him."

"There now," says Murky. She glances at her niece again. "Why don't you get the book and give us a quick rendering before you go? Then Jane can hear for herself. And report to Mr Eliot how well you do it."

He shakes his head. "I should be going."

"What do you say, Jane? Wouldn't you like to hear?"

"I'd love to. But I've a feeling Mark isn't too keen on the idea." She smiles up at him. "Hm?"

He says nothing. His face is uncomfortably hot.

"And why should he be?" says Miss Saunders, still looking at Mark. "He wasn't expecting to have to read to a complete stranger, was he? Maybe another time? If my aunt lets you know when I shall be here?"

Mark nods.

"All right, young Aurelius," says Murky. "I know I'm in no position to insist. But please: do come back next week, will you? And if you don't find me ready and waiting with a tea tray then, you can have me straitjacketed and shipped off to Bedlam on the spot."

Miss Saunders laughs.

"OK," says Mark. He takes a couple of steps back, bobs his head, then turns and runs. As he reaches the stable yard, a mob of cats leaps out of his way and scatters. He only stops when he's at the bottom of the drive and out of sight of the house. He doesn't think they'll come after him, but he has to be sure. No, it's all right: no voices — no footsteps on the gravel.

Pressing himself close against the wonky gatepost, he peers out. A couple of people stand talking in front of the post office, but they're too far away to notice him. Willetts Lane seems deserted. There may be someone waiting further along, of course, at the place where he usually goes into Twenty Acre. But this time he'll take a different route: under the barbed-wire fence on the corner, then diagonally through the wood to the old railway carriage. Best not to run, though: if someone *did* spot him, they'd immediately realize he was up to something. And Willetts Lane is a right of way, after all. He prepares a little speech, just in case: *I hope we haven't got to the point where walking on a public footpath is a crime*.

He does a final check and darts out.

"Wooooh!"

His neck clenches. It came from behind him, he's certain, but when he spins round, there's nothing there. A machine of some kind, like radar, that goes off when anybody passes?

"Boo!"

A masked figure rises from the cow parsley, pointing a gun at him. *Snap snap snap*.

He jumps back, nearly loses his balance. She laughs.

"Golly, that scared you!"

"No it didn't."

"Yes it did."

He shakes his head. The air is laced with the firework smell of spent caps. He starts to blush. "Why are you being such a baby?"

"You're the baby!" She laughs again. "You almost fell over!"

"I was surprised, stupid. That's all. Anyone would have been. What are you doing there, anyway?"

She shrugs. "I was bored after we got back from town. And you said you were going to see Miss Murkett. So I thought I'd wait for you."

"You must have been there ages!"

She shrugs again. "I was all right." She bends down, picks up her bag and holds it out. "I had my book. And a comic." She giggles. "And my new shoes."

"You can't do anything with shoes."

"Yes you can. You can look at them." She tramples her way out of the weeds. "Here." She balances on one leg, stretches the other towards him, waggling a brand-new plimsoll. It's dazzling white, streaked here and there with smears of green. "You want to feel?"

"All right."

He kneels down. It's looser than the old shoe and smells powerfully of cow parsley and fresh rubber. But still there's the squeamish thrill of the foot inside, the sense that he's plunged his hand deep into a nest or a burrow and touched something that isn't yet ready for the outside world.

"Why do you always do that? Tickle me?" she says, pulling it away again. "Anyway, they're good, aren't they?"

"They're all right, I suppose."

"I bet I can run faster than you in them. You want a race?"

"No."

"What do you want to play, then?"

"Nothing. I've got to see Aubrey."

"Why, what's happened?"

"Tons. Lots of gubbins to tell him."

That's got her. She stares at him.

"Don't you know what gubbins is?"

She shakes her head.

"You will when you're older. Lots of *stuff*. Know what *that* means?"

"Course I do. What stuff? Tell *me*."

"There isn't time."

"All right. I'll come with you, then."

"OK." He glances round. The coast is still clear. "But we'll have to watch out. They may try to stop us."

"Who?"

"Mr Montgomery. Mr Barron. Could be any of them. They're all in it together, aren't they?"

She thinks for a moment, then nods.

"They could be keeping watch at the usual place, so we'll go a different way."

He leads her to the corner of the wood and holds the wire up so she can wriggle underneath. Once she's through, she turns back and does the same for him. They stand there for a few seconds, holding their breath, listening. They hear nothing but birdsong and the lazy sound of a small plane, closing up the sky above them like a zip.

"Right." He's so buoyant that he only just manages to stop himself from whistling. He's evaded the combined forces of Mr Montgomery and Mr Barron, and the information he's carrying will, he knows — he can see the reaction now, more vividly than the trees in front of him — reduce Lou and Hillyard to awed silence and admiring glances.

They pick their way through the undergrowth, avoiding paths, stopping every twenty paces or so to make sure they're not being trailed. Neither of them says anything until they're almost at the clearing. Then Lou taps his shoulder and whispers:

"This is a good way."

They pause at the edge of the trees. The clearing's deserted, but the carriage door is open. He must be at home.

"It's no go," says Lou.

"Why not?

"Look." She points. The tea towel is hanging in the kitchen window.

"But it's really important," says Mark. "Maybe I should go and tell him anyway."

He crouches, hands splayed on the ground, ready to sprint. She hooks a finger through his belt.

"No!"

"Let go!" he snarls over his shoulder. "Why shouldn't I? There's no one there! You can see!"

"There might be someone inside," she says. "And anyway, he told us, didn't he? That's the signal. And we promised. So . . ."

Did they promise? He can't remember. But he knows she's right.

"OK!" He tries grumpily to shrug her off. She tightens her grip.

"You won't do it?"

"I said, didn't I?"

"*Swear* you won't do it."

He nods.

"All right. Let's go, then."

They return the way they came, saying nothing, pausing regularly to listen. They've gone no more than a couple of hundred yards or so when Mark thinks he hears something behind them: a stealthy tread, so perfectly synchronized with his it might be an echo. Except, of course, you don't get an echo like that in the woods.

"Ssh!" He touches Lou's arm. She stops, spins towards him.

"What?"

He cups his hand over his ear. They both look round, holding their breath. Nothing but the background chatter of the wood. Maybe he imagined it.

They set off again. Almost immediately he hears the same sound. He glances at Lou. This time, she nods.

"Keep going," he says. He can only guess who might be following them: Mr Montgomery, probably, or one of his men. Presumably, he's planning to wait till they've reached the fence and catch them as they're crawling under it. But if they plod on at the same rate, pretending they haven't heard, and then make a dash for it at the last minute, they may have enough of a lead to escape him.

"When I say the word, run, OK?" says Mark.

She nods again.

"And when we get there, take your bag off and chuck it over first."

"OK."

"Right. Now."

"Stop!" A man's voice, closer than he expected.

"Run!" yells Mark.

He dodges to the left, Lou to the right.

"Don't be a couple of young asses! They could be watching the lane!"

Mark slithers to a halt so quickly that he misses his footing and falls over. Out of the corner of his eye he sees Lou, hopping on one leg, clutching the other with both hands.

"Who'd you think was after you, for Heaven's sake?" says Hillyard. He leans against a tree, dabbing his forehead with a red handkerchief.

"We didn't know," says Lou. "We saw the towel in the window, so we thought maybe they'd got you or something."

"Ah, no, that was simply a precaution. Your comings and goings have been observed, I'm afraid. So it seemed wiser for our next rendezvous to be somewhere else."

"Where?" says Mark.

Hillyard waves towards a patch of grass between two thick-trunked beeches. "That'll serve as well as anywhere. For the time being, anyway."

He lopes over, settles himself heavily on the ground, stretches out his feet. He's wearing odd socks, Mark notices, and both his boots are split along the seams.

"Here we are," he says, beckoning them to join him. "Robin Hood and his merry kids, all together under the greenwood tree."

Mark glances in the direction of the railway carriage. "Are you sure they didn't follow you here?"

Hillyard nods. "Eyes in the back of my head. Come on. Sit down." He looks past them, points at his lips. "And not too loud, all right?"

They arrange themselves in a small circle. From the pocket of his smock Hillyard pulls a brown paper bag, rumpled and dark with grease stains. He tears it open and spreads it out to form a makeshift plate. Inside is a little archipelago of broken biscuits.

"Help yourselves," he says. "Iron rations. What you really want's a flank of venison. But we'll just have to make do with what we've got, won't we?" He takes half a custard cream and bites it in two. "So, to what do I owe the honour, etc. etc.?"

"Mark's got something to tell you," says Lou.

Hillyard raises an eyebrow. "Has he, indeed?"

"Lots of things," says Mark.

"Concerning?"

"Mr Barron. And Mr Montgomery. And my parents. You know what they've done? They've —"

Hillyard holds his hand up. "*Adagio*. One step at a time. Mr Barron."

"Mr Barron warned me. Not to come here. Said it'd be dangerous."

Hillyard shrugs. "Probably talking about me. You know, *Don't have anything to do with that Hillyard chap. He's a thoroughly undependable fellow*."

Mark shakes his head. "It's not just that. I saw Mr Montgomery afterwards. And he told me more or less the same thing. Said they were planning something."

"Planning what?"

"He just said that things are afoot."

"Five toes and an ankle, you mean?"

Lou laughs. Why won't Hillyard take him seriously? He didn't treat Lou like this when she told him about the conversation outside the shop.

"Well, if you're just going to make a joke of it . . ."

"Best thing you can do, in my view, with Mr Montgomery's pearls of wisdom."

"I thought you'd want to know."

"I *do* want to know, Mark. But *things are afoot* can scarcely be said to amount to a threat, can it? It strikes me as just another inept attempt to follow Dr Goebbels's advice. *Propaganda should be used as a weapon to demoralize the enemy*. Montgomery told you because he knew you'd tell me. And thought it would have me quaking in my boots."

"I suppose," says Mark.

"Just as well I'm not," says Hillyard. He nods at his feet. "Because one quake in these, and the pair of them would be goners, wouldn't they?"

Lou laughs again. Mark's face is scorching.

"You mentioned something about your parents," Hillyard adds, casually

"Yes," he says. "I'm afraid they've fallen under the influence of Mr Barron."

Hillyard laughs. "Heaven forfend! Not Mr Barron, that notorious womanizer and cheater at cards? What has he done?"

"He's made them buy a television."

Hillyard frowns. "*Made*?"

Mark nods.

"How do you make someone buy a television?"

"By telling them how good it is. And making them feel stupid for not having one."

Hillyard darts a glance at Lou, eyes wide, mouth slack.

"I mean, that *must* be the way it happens, mustn't it?" Mark goes on. "When you're brainwashed, it makes you want to brainwash somebody else. It's like a kind of infection. Mumps or something. That's how you have it in the story, isn't it? When Mr and Mrs — have they got names yet?"

Hillyard shakes his head. "Not yet."

"Well, Mr and Mrs X, then," says Mark. "When they get back from their honeymoon. *He* goes to the next town. And *she* stays in and turns on the television. And by the time he comes home, it's got her, hasn't it? So she goes to work to get *him*."

Hillyard nods. "Well, yes, I take your point. But I think we can reasonably assume that in your parents' case the effect won't be immediate. So probably no need to panic just yet. Is that it?"

Lou laughs.

"Just the television?" Hillyard goes on. "They didn't *say* anything at all? About me? Or? . . ."

Mark shakes his head.

"Right." Hillyard leans forward, takes another pinch of crumbs. "Am I the only one availing himself of the iron rations? You'd better dig in pronto, or they'll all be gone."

"There is something else," says Mark. "I went to see Murky this afternoon. Miss Murkett. And there was someone with her."

"Ah, yes, well, rather the *grande dame*, isn't she, Miss Murkett? So if you answer a summons to the big house, I imagine you're always likely to find a pensioner in attendance."

What's a *grande dame*? And why would she have pensioners with her? But the tone, at least, is unmistakable.

"Don't you like her?" says Mark. "I thought she let you live here?"

"I jest, dear boy," says Hillyard. "Admit me to the secret. Who was with Miss Murkett when you called at her house today?"

"A woman. Called Miss Saunders."

Hillyard's head and shoulders become rigid.

"Who is she?" says Lou.

"Miss Murkett's niece," says Mark.

"*Jane* Saunders?" asks Hillyard. "Small? Dark hair" — making a helmet with his hands — "like this?"

"Yes."

Hillyard shrinks, letting out a *pish* of air. "So what *were* they saying?" His throat sounds dry.

"Miss Saunders . . ." He hesitates. Is he being a sneak? "Miss Saunders was apologizing. For doing something."

"For doing what?" His lips barely move.

"Something that upset her neighbours. Miss Murkett's, I mean."

"And what did Miss Murkett say?"

"She said, 'I'm not bothered about my neighbours. They're a lot of humbugs. It's this other thing.' "

"This — other — thing."

Mark nods.

"But she didn't say what the other thing was?"

"No."

They stare at each other.

"Do *you* have any idea what it might be?"

"No."

Hillyard sighs. "You know what she does, do you? Jane Saunders? For a living?"

"She works for a what-you-ma-call-it, doesn't she?"

"A literary agent."

"Yes, that's it. That's what Murky said."

"And what does a literary agent do?"

Mark shakes his head.

"Lou?"

"I don't know."

"A literary agent reads an author's work. And then tries to sell it to a publisher."

"Ah!" says Lou. "And she — this woman — is *your* literary agent!"

"Alas, no. She wanted to take me on. But —"

"But the chap she works for thought his ideas were a bit far-fetched," says Mark.

It was a mistake. He hoped to impress them both with how much he knows. Instead, he's just made Hillyard suspicious.

"And where, may I ask, did you hear that?" he says.

"Murky told me."

"Well, far be it from me to contradict the sainted Miss Murkett. But 'far-fetched' is something of a euphemism." He gropes in his pocket for the makings of a cigarette. "A better word" — peering past them into the trees, and lowering his voice — "would be *dangerous*."

"The Brain!" says Lou.

"Very astute, Miss Bennett." He slips a Rizla paper from its slot and lays it open on his thigh. "The Brain has evidently been up to its tricks again. Persuading her that she was mistaken about me. And that her employer is right, after all."

"You mean she's been brainwashed?"

Hillyard nods.

"She didn't *seem* brainwashed."

"Ah, well, no, she wouldn't. That's the devilish cunning of the thing, you see. Proceeds by stealth." He makes his hand into a giant spider, advances it surreptitiously along his leg, leaving the cigarette paper undisturbed. "You can't see it coming. Don't know who's been got and who hasn't. Until all at once" — pouncing suddenly on his own knee — "*Bam!*"

Lou, sitting closer to him, shrinks back.

"And by then it's too late," says Hillyard. "Another name ticked off, another little square on the chart blocked in." He hatches the air with an invisible pencil. "One more cell for the Brain."

Lou starts to giggle.

"No laughing matter, I'm afraid," says Hillyard. He pinches a thick tuft of Golden Virginia from the pouch and worries it into a string. "Heavens! If even *she's* not to be trusted now. Jane Saunders, of all people . . ." He shakes his head slowly, a man mourning the loss of his last illusion.

"You can still trust us!" says Lou. "Can't he?"

Mark nods. "Course."

"We haven't changed," says Lou. "And we're not going to. Ever. Are we?"

There's a strange movement in Hillyard's throat, as if something's dislodged his Adam's apple, and he can't work it back into place. He blinks, then leans over to lick the cigarette paper.

"I can't tell you what it means," he says, looking up again. "When you've lived the sort of life I have. And then, finally, you find a couple of pals like you two." He shakes his head. "But still, for the love of God, be careful."

"We will," says Lou.

"Promise?"

"All right."

He nods. "Problem is, there are some battles even friendship can't win."

Mark glances at Lou. She drops her gaze again: she doesn't understand either.

"With the necessary consequence . . ." He seems to finish the sentence in his own head, his lips moving silently, his eyes staring past them towards Willetts Lane, but seeing something — or so Mark imagines — completely different. Then he shakes himself and turns to Mark:

"Had any thoughts, have you?"

"What?"

"About getting me in?" He lights his roll-up. It's the spindliest cigarette Mark has ever seen: no thicker than a match. "To take a dekko at Peveril on the Swift?"

Mark shrugs. "It'll have to be one evening, I think. When my parents are watching television."

Hillyard touches a finger to his temple, saluting his canniness.

"How about tomorr —"

He catches a movement out of the corner of his eye. Lou is shaking her head.

"Or maybe the day after?" he adds, looking not at Hillyard, but Lou. She nods.

"OK," says Hillyard. "Whenever you can manage. But please: sooner rather than later." He half-turns, puts his fists on the ground like an ape, pushes himself to his feet. "Time, I very much fear," he says, slapping the earth from his clothes, "may be shorter than we thought."

Lou starts towards the fence, but Mark lays a hand on her arm and whispers:

"Wait."

They watch Hillyard lumber back into the trees, heavy and delicate at the same time, brushing the leaves from his path with a gentle sweep of the hand. When they can no longer hear him, Lou says:

"What?"

"Why couldn't I show him Peveril tomorrow?"

"Cos of Mr Barron. That's when he's having his sherry thing, isn't it?"

"So? . . ."

"Well, that'll be our chance, won't it? To find out what he's up to."

"How?"

"By spying on them."

"You can't spy on him in his own house!"

"There's a place we can go."

"What place?"

"There's a back way in. And a pile of tyres. Behind his house. Next to the sitting room."

"How d'you know that?"

"Cos I've been there, silly. I told you, didn't I? He's friends with my parents."

"Well, what good's a lot of tyres, anyway?" says Mark. "We won't be able to hear what they're saying inside, will we?"

"We will if the window's open." She spreads her arms. "It's this close."

Mark says nothing. His imagination swarms with angry grown-up faces: Mr Barron, Mr Pointer, Dad.

But he can't back out, seem less keen than she is. Getting caught would be awful — but it'd be even worse for Lou to think him a coward.

"All right."

"You know that path opposite the old Wool Pack? We'll meet there at six o'clock."

He nods.

"Right." She turns towards the fence. "You want me to hold this for you?"

He shakes his head. "That's OK. You go first."

He lifts the wire, and she scrambles out onto the lane. Only when she's reached the corner and disappeared from view does he crawl through himself and run after her.

# CHAPTER TEN

"Look," says Dad. "You know who that is?"

He nods at the television. A man in a large checked suit is walking onto a stage. His sleek black hair and square face gleam, as if they're wet. Perched on top of his head is a pork-pie hat that's too small for him. Dad gets up and jerks the volume knob. Mark hears, *How do, everybody? How's the boys and girls?* — followed by a roar from the unseen audience.

"Who is it?"

Dad scowls. "You don't know?"

"How could he?" says Mum. "He's too young to remember, isn't he?"

Dad shakes his head. The whole world's his enemy: everyone but this man in the flashy clothes, whom his son has somehow heedlessly slighted. "That's Dicky Pringle," says Mum. "Dicky P. Used to be on the wireless a lot during the war. *Little Bothering in the Vale*. You must have heard of that, haven't you?"

"I don't think so."

"Oh dear." She catches his eye, recognizes the thought in it. "I know," she says, smiling. "It sounds a bit like Peveril on the Swift, doesn't it? But it wasn't the same sort of thing at all. Lots of catch phrases. And funny characters."

Dad shakes his head again, sighing. Why? Because she mentioned Peveril?

"You've no idea," she goes on, changing tack, "what it was like." She's looking at Dad as she says it, monitoring his response. "You know, sitting there in the dark. Listening for the drone of a plane. And, when you heard it, wondering if it was one of theirs or one of ours. And then you'd turn on the wireless, and there'd be the signature tune for *Little Bothering*, and you'd feel everything would be all right, at least for half an hour."

Dad's neck stiffens. He glowers at the screen. Obviously that was wrong too, for some reason. What *should* she have said, then?

"So I said," Pringle is saying, over a building wave of laughter, "is that yours, madam, or did the tiddlypom tiddlypom it?"

"He really kept us going, Dicky P.," she says, still watching Dad. "Didn't he? Brought everyone together. Because you knew there'd be millions of people, all over the country, tuning in at the same time. And the next day, you'd go into the shop and somebody'd say, *mine's a tuppenny one, thank you very kindly*, and everyone would simply burst out laughing."

Dad says nothing. He's staring at the television grim-faced, untouched by the hilarity washing out of the golden mouth. Pringle has moved to the front of the stage, tipping his hat so far forward that it looks as if it's about to slither off.

"Your poodle had three puppies and a kitten?" he's saying, scratching his head. "I said, that's unusual, isn't it? She says, well, you see, the last week, there wasn't any dog food to be had. So we ended up giving her a popular brand of cat food . . ."

Mum titters, looking nervously at Dad. Dad's mouth twitches, but he doesn't laugh. Maybe he's starting to be brainwashed already.

Mark gets up. This, he knows, is going to be difficult; but if he doesn't make a move soon, he'll be late for Lou.

"Where are you going?" says Mum. Her eyes are pleading: *Don't leave. Please*.

"Lavatory," says Mark. It'll be easier to do it in two stages: break the thread first, and then, when they've got used to his not being there, tell them he's going out.

He runs up to his bedroom, takes his knapsack from its hook, assembles notebook, camera, telescope. Then he waits a couple of minutes before tiptoeing into the bathroom and flushing the lavatory. When he goes downstairs again, Mum is waiting for him in the hall, one hand on the sitting-room door handle. As he reaches the bottom, she pulls it gently towards her.

"Are you all right?"

He nods.

"Haven't got an upset tummy or anything?"

"No."

"Well, that's good. I know" — glancing at the sitting room and lowering her voice to a stage whisper — "it's a bit difficult in there. Dad feels . . . I think he feels . . ." She trails off, shaking her head, the effort to justify her husband suddenly too much for her.

"It's all right," he says.

She smiles, stretches out to touch his hand, notices his knapsack.

"Oh, where are you going with that?"

"Out. I've got to meet someone."

She blinks. He's startled, too. He sounded like a grown-up, suddenly: not *can I?*, but *I've got to*.

"Who? Your friend from the shop?"

"Yes."

She glances at the sitting room again, then nods, as if she's finally resolved something in her own mind.

"All right. But supper at eight, OK?"

He hurries along Church End with his head down, not wanting to meet anyone's gaze, in case they can somehow see in his face what he and Lou are planning to do. As he passes the garage, the man with the limp calls, "Evening." Mark raises a hand without turning his head, for fear he'll blush.

His stomach's a drum skin, beating with the rhythm of his heart. That might give him away too, so he pulls his shirt out and lets it flop over his belt. His best hope is that Lou won't be there. Maybe she's realized her plan is just too dangerous, and decided not to go through with it. Or else she was all ready to come, but at the last moment her parents told her she couldn't. *Yes,* he thinks, *as he climbs the stile on to the footpath, that's much more likely . . .*

"Gallion."

The tom-tomming in his stomach accelerates. The voice came from the dried-up ditch at the side of the path, but all he can see when he looks towards it is a patch of dead-nettles.

"Gallion," he says.

"Coast clear?" she whispers.

He peers back out into the road. "Think so."

She scrambles to her feet. She's wearing a pearl grey blouse that's too big for her, and a midnight blue silk scarf tied under her chin. Slung over her arm is a black handbag, closed by a criss-crossed gold clasp.

"Why on earth are you dressed up like that? You think we're going to be invited in, or something?"

She giggles and holds an invisible sherry glass in front of her, pinching the stem between thumb and forefinger.

"No, honestly," says Mark.

"Camouflage. We're going to be hiding in the tyres, remember."

"Tyres aren't grey. Or blue."

"Sometimes they are."

"No, they're not."

She glances down at the blouse, then shrugs.

"Where'd you get that stuff, anyway?"

"My mother, of course. I told her I wanted to play at grown-ups. And she said I could borrow anything I liked." She nods at his knapsack. "They're not as bad as *that*, anyway. You stand out a mile, with that on your back. You'd better leave it here."

"I can't. It's got all my stuff in."

"What stuff?"

"My spy stuff."

She flicks open the handbag. "Put it in here."

"There won't be room."

She shakes her head, rummages for something, pulls out an Aero and a Kit Kat. "Here. Iron rations. Stick them in your pocket. Now . . ." — yanking the bag wide — "See? Tons of room."

He peers into the darkness. It smells of lipstick and face powder and leather.

"There's nothing in it!" he says.

"Told you."

"Why'd you bring it, then?"

She turns it over. On the back is a separate zipped compartment. She pats it.

"Notebook. So go on. You can have all the rest for your things."

He slips off the knapsack, unbuckles the flap, takes out his own notebook, the telescope, the Halina.

"That's good," she says, dropping the telescope into her bag. "If we can't catch everything they're saying, we'll be able to lip-read. But not the camera. I think you ought to leave that behind."

"Why? We're going to need it."

She shakes her head again. "He doesn't want to know what they look like, does he? He wants to know what they're talking about. And if we're close enough to hear that, they'll be close enough" — picking up the Halina and shaking it — "to hear this, won't they?"

"Well, all right. But I'm not leaving it here."

"Then you have to promise not to use it, OK?"

He puts the camera next to the telescope, saying nothing. After a moment, she snaps the bag shut.

"Give me that," she says, reaching for the empty knapsack. He hands it to her. She folds it, then works it into the space she's made under the dead-nettles. "Right. Ready?"

She goes first. The path is so overgrown that whenever she gets more than a few paces ahead of him, he almost loses sight of her. But that's good: it means they won't be visible from the road.

After a couple of hundred yards, there's a sharp turn to the right, and the tangle of brambles and cow parsley gives way to a ribbon of tussocky grass. It stinks of dog mess, and every few steps they have to pick their way round a little brown mound crowded with flies. On one side there's a brick wall, capped by a rough layer of concrete spiked with broken glass. Hanging over it they can see a branch heavy with hard green apples. Lou points at it and mouths:

"That's their garden."

At the end of the path is a wooden gate. From a distance, it's something from a fairy story. When they get closer, though, Mark can smell the creosote and read a freshly painted sign screwed to the top: *Private Property. No Public Right of Way. Beware of the Dog*. Lou squints between the planks, then glances back and nods.

"OK?"

"OK." But his tongue's dry.

She lifts the latch. To his surprise, the gate starts to open.

"What about the dog?" he whispers.

"That's all right. He'll be in the house. The only place they ever let him out is here. But just, you know, when he needs to —" She points back along the path, wrinkling her nose.

He nods.

"Otherwise he might get run over."

She tiptoes through the gate. He follows, holding his breath, and she re-latches the gate behind them. They're in the cool oil-stained yard where the man with the limp washes the buses. It's shielded from the sun by the corrugated iron coach garage to the right and the workshop to the left. Through the gap between, they can see the little island of petrol pumps — deserted now, and locked up for the night — and then, on the far side of the road, the Fox and Hounds. Harry Doggett stands in front of the entrance, talking to a man Mark doesn't recognize: small, dark-haired, wearing a rumpled linen suit, carrying a square black case with one hand and flapping a white cotton hat against his leg with the other. As they watch, Harry turns and jabs his finger towards the garage. The meaning's obvious: *I've got to go over there in a minute*. The other man nods.

Mark and Lou edge forward, keeping close to the wall. Mark strains to catch what the men are saying, but the tattoo beating in his stomach has moved up into his throat and ears, making it impossible for him to hear properly. What do they do to you if you're caught trespassing? If you're somewhere like Twenty Acre Wood, probably nothing worse than giving you a telling-off. But here? He and Lou couldn't say that they hadn't realized, or they were lost, or they were looking for Barney, could they? The only people who break into garages are criminals.

They're at the end of the yard now. Craning out, they can see Mr Barron's house at the other end of the forecourt: square, red-brick, trailed with creeper. Behind it, parked next to Mr Barron's Riley, is a Land Rover, dull with dust.

"Mr Montgomery?" whispers Lou.

Mark nods.

The back door is half open, revealing a strip of dark, heavily patterned wallpaper. And Lou's right — next to it are two piles of tyres, neatly stacked on their sides, like giant tubes of Fruit Gums.

Lou mouths something at him. He bends his head near to hers. She whispers:

"Shall we?"

He glances towards the Fox and Hounds. "No. Better wait. Till they're out of the way."

He's so close that his lips brush her ear. She giggles, puts a hand over her mouth to silence herself, then pulls away, nodding. In the same instant, out of the corner of his eye, Mark notices another movement. He shoves Lou against the wall, then twists round and stands next to her, forcing his shoulder blades into the hollows in the corrugated iron, pinioning her back with his arm.

"What is it?"

"Ssh."

Harry Doggett is crossing the road. When he reaches the garage, he stops and glances behind him, frowning slightly. Then he turns and continues into the forecourt. In his left hand he's holding an unlit cigarette, which he seesaws between the thumb and two fingers. He's stooped forward, still frowning, and worrying his lip with his big teeth. If he raised his head even a couple of inches as he passed the yard, he'd be bound to see them. But the weight of his own thoughts keeps him staring at the ground.

He hesitates at the door, then gives three quick raps. After a moment, half of Mr Barron's face appears, blotting out the gloomy wallpaper.

"Evening, Harry."

Harry's hand feels for a hat, doesn't find one, ends up scratching his head. "Sorry if I'm a bit late. Not the last one, am I?"

Mr Barron laughs. "Afraid so. But don't worry about it."

"Well, I'll tell you," says Harry, stepping inside. "The reason is, is that I've just been talking to someone. And I think you'll be interested —"

The door shuts.

"OK!" says Mark.

They sprint across the yard and duck behind the tyres. The funnel shape formed by the two piles makes a natural hiding place, protected on three sides. At their closest point they're separated by a gap of no more than two or three inches. No one looking out from the house would even know it was there. But from where *they* are, Mark finds, if you press your face up against the rubber, you can see the edge of the open sitting-room window. As they watch, Harry Doggett edges into view, hesitates a moment, then perches on a chair with his back to them. Next to him, Mark notices, is a blue knee, covered with a fan of big fingers. Mr Pointer, presumably.

"See?" whispers Lou.

Mark inches back, turns towards her. She slaps her hand over her mouth again.

"What?" he says.

"You look like a black-and-white minstrel."

*What's a black-and-white minstrel?* But that would mean admitting she knows something he doesn't. Instead, he whispers, "No, I don't."

"Yes, you do." She licks her finger, dabs his cheek with it. His arms and neck tingle. She waggles the fingertip in front of him. It's smudged with grey.

"Oh, blast." He scrubs his face with the back of his arm.

"Better be careful," she whispers. "Afterwards, I mean."

He nods. "What are we going to do? Take it in turns?"

She shakes her head. "No need. You get down on your knees."

He hesitates.

"Go on."

He kneels down, facing the crack.

"And then I can be like this." She leans over him, her legs against his bum, her elbow resting lightly between his shoulder blades.

"Sweet for you, I take it, Harry?" Mr Barron is saying, out of sight, but close to the window.

"Yes, please, uh," mutters Harry.

"Here we are, then." A hand appears, holding a knobbly little glass.

Harry takes it. "Oh, ah, thank you."

"Right. We're all here." They still can't see Mr Barron, but they hear the comfortable sigh he makes as he settles himself in a chair. "So. You've got something to report, have you, Harry?"

"Yes." Harry can't seem to keep the glass steady, for some reason. Swaying dangerously, it starts the jerky journey towards his face, then vanishes from their sight. "Yes," he says again after a couple of seconds, smacking his lips. "I was just getting ready to come over here when a chap I never seen before walks in the public. 'Evening, landlord,' he says, polite as you like. 'A half-pint of your very best bitter, if you please.' "

Someone, they can't see who, starts to laugh.

"So I draw him his half," Harry continues, more quickly. "And he says, 'Thanks you. Now what, speaking . . . speaking hypercethet —"

"Hypothetically?" says Mr Barron.

The back of Harry's neck reddens. "That's the one. 'What, speaking hyper-whatever-it-is, would you say if I was to mention the name Aubrey Hillyard?' "

He pauses. No one laughs now. Even from his hiding place, Mark can sense the tension in the room.

"And you say you'd no idea who he was?" That must be Mr Montgomery: the words sound as if he's fighting for breath.

Harry shakes his head. "Drove down from London, he said."

"So what did you say?" Mr Barron.

"Well, I says, 'That all depends who's asking. And why.' And he looks round the public, cos of course everyone's staring at him, and he says, 'An interested party. Who'd be happy to buy you a drink. And any of these other gentlemen too, if they've got anything to contribute.' "

The blue knee shifts slightly. "Not police, was he?"

For some reason, the others all laugh.

"No," says Harry. "But he was *something* all right. I tell him, I says, 'Look, I've got to take my hook in a couple of jiffs. But you want to come back later, maybe I can tell you something then. And maybe not. We'll just have to see, won't we?' "

"Yes," murmurs Mr Barron. "Well done, Harry. That's quite right."

" 'And now I'm off,' I says. But he follows me outside. 'Listen,' he says. 'Here's how the thing stands. I couldn't say anything in front of all those other chaps. But I can see I can trust you. Knew that straight off. Got the eye for it. Never wrong.' "

"Wasn't Irish, was he?" Mr Montgomery says. "Sounds to me as if he'd got more than a touch of the Blarney Stone."

He and PC Pointer laugh. Harry's neck turns the colour of rare beef.

"No, come on," says Mr Barron. "What did he say?"

" 'And between you and me,' he says, 'there's people in high places that have taken quite an interest in our friend Mr H. And exactly what it is he's doing here.' "

"What?" Mr Montgomery says.

Harry nods. " 'Oh, yes? What *people?*' I says. He says, 'Ah, that I'm afraid I can't tell you. But I will say this. Anything you can do to help them — well, let's just say you won't find them ungrateful.' "

There's a short silence.

"You're sure he was talking about Hillyard?" Mr Barron finally says.

Harry nods. "I told you, didn't I? That's the first thing he says to me: 'What would you say' " — lifting a finger and dialling a number in the air with it — " 'if I was to mention Aubrey Hillyard?' And then it's *Mr H. this* and *Mr H. that*."

"All right," says Mr Barron. "And what was *his* name? Did he tell you?"

"Sammy."

"Sammy what?"

Harry shakes his head. "He just gave me a number, said he'd be back on Monday, and if I had anything to tell him, I should ring, reverse charge, and ask for Sammy."

"Have you got the number?"

Harry reaches inside his jacket and draws out a sheet of paper, folded thin. "Here."

Mr Barron smooths it open. "ARC 4570."

"Where's that?" grumbles Mr Montgomery.

"London. Archway," says Mr Barron.

"Not Scotland Yard, anyway," says PC Pointer. "That'd be Whitehall."

"Mm," murmurs Mr Barron. He's still staring at the number, as if he thinks it might be in code, and he's trying to work out the key. "Did he give you this?"

"Yes, uh."

"I mean" — brandishing the sheet — "*this*. You didn't write it down yourself?"

"Couldn't, could I, cos I didn't have any paper. So he opens up his case and takes out a notebook. Blimey, you should've seen the stuff in there. Couldn't believe my eyes. There's this little camera. With extra what-d'you-ma-call-its."

"Lenses?" says PC Pointer.

"That's the one. And a pair of field glasses. And something, no bigger'n this, like a box. And I says to him, 'What's that?' And he laughs, and he says, 'Funny looking blighter, isn't it? That's a miniature tape recorder. Don't go into a shop and try to buy one, though. They're not available to the public yet.' "

Another silence. Harry slowly drains his glass, then sets it down noisily on the floor.

"Let me fill that up for you," says Mr Barron, after a moment.

"I won't say no."

A whiff of sherry escapes through the window, adding a syrupy tinge to the hot reek of the tyres. All at once, Mark's five again, sitting in the dentist's chair, struggling as grey-faced Mr Gaskell clamps the gas mask over his nose and mouth. The same rubbery smell; the same nerveless, not-quite-warm sensation on the skin; the same sudden gush of dizzy sickness.

"Hey, what you doing?" whispers Lou.

He wriggles free, slumps with his back to the tyres.

"Are you all right?"

He shakes his head. It makes him feel sicker.

"What's the —" She spins round suddenly, kicking his shin. "Oh, blast! They're coming!"

She yanks his hand. He stumbles to his feet and follows her into the forecourt. She hesitates a moment, her ear cocked towards the house. Voices swell towards them from the hall. She glances back the way they came, calculating the distance.

"We can't do it," whispers Mark.

She nods, and darts instead across the concrete and through the open entrance of the workshop. Without looking back, Mark sprints after her. They take refuge behind a thick pillar and peer out. The men are already in the forecourt, and hurrying towards the road.

"Where are they going?" whispers Mark.

"To see if he's still there."

"Sammy, you mean?"

They haven't got long, then: if Sammy *isn't* there, Mr Barron and the others will be back almost immediately. The best thing would be to wait until they'd gone inside the Fox and Hounds, and then make a dash for it. But from where they're standing, Mark and Lou can't see further than the corner of Mr Barron's house.

"How long'll it take them, d'you reckon?" he asks.

"What?"

"To get to the pub?"

She shrugs. "Two minutes? Three?" She tilts her watch into the light, so as to catch the exact moment when the second hand reaches its destination. "Ready? Five, four, three, two, one — Go!"

They sprint towards the gate. As the pub looms into view, Mark glances at the front door. It's OK: there's no sign of them. But a few seconds later, while he's fumbling with the latch, Lou suddenly prods him.

"Hurry! Quick!"

He looks back. Mr Barron is just emerging, shaking his head, blinking in the evening light. Mark eases open the gate, holds it for Lou, then slips through himself and shuts it behind him.

"Do you think he saw us?" says Lou.

"Don't know. Let's wait a sec."

They press their ears against the wood. No shouts. No footsteps. After half a minute or so, they catch each other's eye and nod.

Neither of them speaks until they've reached the burrow under the dead-nettles. Lou pulls out Mark's knapsack, clicks open her handbag and starts transferring his things from one to the other.

"So," she says. "What are we going to do?"

"Tell him, of course."

"I know *that*, stupid. I mean, *when*?"

"Tomorrow?"

"Don't you think we should go now?"

"Can't. I've got to get home."

She stares at him, nibbling her lip.

"All right," she says finally, nodding at a thought in her own head. "Tomorrow. Nine o'clock. Meet at the hideout."

"OK."

"OK. But make sure you write everything down, will you? That's what I'm going to do. Otherwise we might forget something. Something important."

They pick their way through the long grass. When they get to the end of the path, Mark cranes his head and checks both ways.

"OK," he says. "All clear."

They step out onto the road and start back in the direction of the village, arms swinging, kicking a stone back and forth, two kids with nothing to hide.

# CHAPTER ELEVEN

"Where are you going?"

"Upstairs."

"But you haven't finished your breakfast yet."

"Yes, I have."

"What about a bit of toast?"

He shakes his head. Dad's still hidden behind his newspaper, the stiff line of his arms suggesting that he's too taken up with the weighty business of world affairs to become involved in a petty family squabble. But Mark knows that, at any moment, the wall may come down with an irritable rustle. And there's something about Mum, too: an odd, overwound stillness in her face that reminds him of the carriage clock in the sitting room when it's about to chime the hour. He inches towards the door, sidestepping Barney, edging his way round a chair to avoid his father's eyeline. As he gropes for the handle, his mother makes one final attempt:

"Are you sure?"

Her eyes are pleading.

He nods. There: he's done it. He runs upstairs and shuts himself in his room. He'll wait till he hears Dad going into the study, then sneak down again and out through the back door.

He slips his hand under the mattress, pulls out his notebook, opens it. His notes on the conversation at Mr Barron's house run to five pages. He missed a bit at the end, but he thinks he's got the gist of it. From time to time, as he's skimming the surface of the words, a phrase suddenly reaches out and snatches at him. *People in high places. Afraid I can't say. Not available to the public*. His skin tingles, as it does when he's running a train and accidentally touches both the rails at the same time . . .

"Mark?"

Blast: she must have crept up without his hearing. "What?"

"Can I come in?"

He shuts the notebook, but before he's able to hide it again, she's opened the door and is peering round the edge.

"What are you up to?"

"Nothing."

Her eye strays round the room and comes to rest on the notebook. "Is that a diary?"

"No."

She reaches out a hand. "May I see?"

"It's private."

She lowers her head and stares directly into his face. He holds her gaze for a few seconds, then has to look away.

"All right," she says. "But tell me. What exactly is going on?"

"Nothing."

She sighs. "Oh, come on. *Some*thing obviously is. We hardly see you these days. You're always off somewhere. Last night you got in at Heaven knows what time, looking like a street urchin."

Mark glances at her upside-down watch. Nearly ten to nine. "I can't talk about it now."

"Why not? It's not something to do with the television, is it?"

He shrugs.

"We have noticed that you don't seem to like it," she says. "I can't imagine why. I mean, there's a play on tonight. All about spacemen and Martians. Just up your street, I'd have thought. It isn't till eight-thirty, but it won't matter if you're a bit late getting to bed. It is the holidays, after all."

She smiles, coaxing him to respond. When he doesn't, she adds:

"Well, *we're* going to watch it, anyway. And it'd be nice to have your company." She pauses. "What are you afraid the thing's going to do? Bite you?"

He gets up. "Look, I really do have to go out."

She retreats to the door and leans against it, arms folded.

"I'm *late*!"

"For what?"

"Meeting someone."

"The girl?"

"Yes. All right?"

But Mum doesn't move. She stares at him for a moment, then nods and says:

"Three things" — counting them off on her fingers — "The television. The new people at the shop. And that man living in Twenty Acre Wood, Hillyard, or whatever his name is. They're all somehow connected, aren't they?"

He says nothing.

"Sit down." She lays a finger on each shoulder and pushes gently, trolleying him back towards the bed.

"I told you! I've got —"

"Mark!"

She shakes her head, frowning. He's never seen her like this, the sternness of her expression unsweetened by even the hint of a smile.

"I met Mr Montgomery yesterday," she says. "He asked if you and the girl — Lou, is it — were still sneaking off when no one's looking to see the chap in the old railway carriage? And I told him I'd no idea what he was talking about. And he said, 'Oh, sorry, I assumed you knew. Everyone else does.'"

Mark says nothing, but he can feel the heat surging into his cheeks.

"I thought perhaps he was just making mischief for the sake of it," Mum says. "But obviously —"

"It's nothing to do with Mr Montgomery," says Mark. "It's none of his business!"

"You shouldn't talk about him like that. Or anyone else, for that matter. And anyway, it is his business if you've been trespassing on his land, isn't it?"

"It's not his land. It's Murky's!"

"Well, but he rents it from her, doesn't he? For the shooting." She hesitates. "And what about Dad and me? Don't you think *we* ought to be told who you're with and what you're up to?"

"I suppose."

"So why didn't you tell us? Or tell *me*, anyhow."

He can't think of a reply that won't give the game away. So he shrugs again and continues staring at the floor.

"When we bumped into him that day, Mr Hillyard," says Mum, "in the High Street. You told me the only time you'd ever seen him before was when Barney ran off into the woods."

"I never said that."

She goes on gazing dreamily at the window. "Well," she says after a pause, turning back, "that was the impression I got. So if you didn't lie, you didn't tell me the truth, did you?"

"You didn't ask."

She shakes her head. "I shouldn't have to ask, should I?"

"Well, I *couldn't*, anyhow. I'd promised not to tell anyone. And breaking your promise is just as bad as lying, isn't it?"

"Not to tell anyone *what*?"

"That's what I promised not to tell anyone!"

She looks quickly behind her, as if she's wondering whether to call Dad.

"Honestly, Mum, it's nothing *bad*."

"Did he *do* something to you?"

What is she talking about? "No."

She cranes closer, eyes wide. "Are you sure?"

He nods.

"Really?"

"Cross my heart and hope to die."

She draws back, moistening her lips with her tongue. "Has Daddy — has Dad — ever had a chat with you? About — you know. Things?"

"Don't think so," he mutters.

She hesitates. "Well . . . You know . . . Boys and girls . . . When they're older . . . When they grow up . . . Well, usually they get married, don't they? And that's lovely. It's absolutely normal. But . . ."

He can't bear to look at her. He longs to yell, *Stop it! Please!* — but his throat is locked shut.

"But there are a few people," she says, forcing herself to take a run at it, "a few men, who *aren't* normal. And sometimes those sorts of men try to make friends with boys. And then take advantage of them. Get them to *do* things."

He shakes his head.

"Then afterwards," she says, more gently, leaning closer to him, "they say, 'This is just between us. Our secret. You mustn't tell anyone else about it. If you do, something horrible will happen.' "

His voice breaks free. "Honestly, Mum! That isn't what the secret is. It's to do with why he's here. And why everyone's against him."

"And that's what you can't tell anybody?"

He nods.

She hesitates. "But he hasn't broken the law? It's not that?"

He shakes his head. Her eyes seem stuck to his face.

"All right," she says. "I won't ask you to break your word. But I don't think you should go on visiting him in Twenty Acre Wood."

He shakes his head. "We're the only friends he's got."

She sighs. "I know, sweetie. And I'm proud of you for being so loyal. But if he really is a decent chap, as you say —"

"He is!"

"Well, then he won't want to get you and Lou into trouble, will he?"

"No, he doesn't."

"There you are, then. You just drop him a note. Saying you're sorry, but your parents have said you mustn't come and see him any more. It's nothing personal, tell him: just that people are starting to talk, and it's making life difficult."

He bites his lip, drives his nails into the palms of his hands. He's trapped. If he doesn't agree, she'll stop him going out at all. If he does, he'll be lying.

"Look, poppet," says Mum. "Of course you don't want to let him down: that's only right and proper. And to be honest, I don't understand why everyone else is so nasty about him: I thought he seemed rather nice. Perhaps it's just the way he looks. But you've got to see it does put us in a bit of a spot."

Mark shrugs.

"I know," she says, nodding. "It's awkward for you too. And I don't want to be horrible about it. So go and see him now, if that's what you'd arranged. And tell him in person. That'd be less . . . less, you know, than sending him a note, wouldn't it? More . . ."

He turns away, feeling the full force of her gaze on his cheek.

"Only . . . If you do . . . I want you to say something," she says, lowering her voice suddenly. "Ask him something. From me."

"What?"

"It's just that . . . Well, of course I'm concerned. That you shouldn't be mixed up in anything, you know . . . But I don't want him to think that I'm just like all the other people. I'm not *against* him. Will you say that?"

Mark nods. He waits for her to get out of the way and open the door. But she just stands there, arms and shoulders slack.

"Tell him," she says, looking past him at the bed, "that I asked you what his secret was. And you wouldn't tell me. But say that . . . that if he releases you from your promise, so that you *can* tell me, well then, depending on what it is, maybe we'll think again."

"All right. But can I go now? Please?"

She steps aside and presses herself against the wall. He flings open the door and hurtles downstairs. At the bottom, Barney's waiting, his tail thumping on the floor.

"Stay, boy!"

He glances at the kitchen clock: almost nine-fifteen. Lou's probably given up on him. But he might still find her there if he runs all the way.

When he calls "Gallion" there's no reply. He kneels down and crawls inside the hideout. It's empty. Lou must have left already.

He backs out again and peers into the cleft in the tree trunk by the entrance. There's something white just inside. He works his finger into the opening and wriggles it out. It's a single sheet of lined paper torn from her notebook. On it, in thick blurry pencil, she's written: *You were late so I went on you know where*.

He sprints to the gap in the hedge and out onto the cart track. At the bottom he stops, cups his hands round his mouth and shouts:

"Lou!"

There's no answer. But as he peers down Willetts Lane, searching for some sign of her, he notices a shudder in the greenery.

"Lou!"

Still no reply. It can't be her: she'd have shown herself or shouted back. But again there's a stirring in the leaves and a flash of brilliant light. He moves towards it. After a few seconds he hears a click. He starts to run. A white-hatted man suddenly breaks cover fifty yards ahead and, without looking back, hurries off in the direction of the High Street.

"Oi!" bellows Mark. "What are you doing?"

The man quickens his pace, heeling to counterbalance the weight of the square black bag in his hand.

"I know who you are! And who you're working for!"

But Sammy has already disappeared round the bend in the lane. For a moment, Mark imagines giving chase, like Norman and Henry Bones, the boy detectives. He'd corner him by the shop, keep him there till smiling Mr Pointer arrived. *Here's your phantom photographer, Constable. Well done, Mark. Thanks to you, a particularly ugly customer will be spending a good long time behind bars*. And then the whole landscape suddenly spins, blurring the old divisions. Black is still black, but white isn't white any more. Sammy and PC Pointer are both in the pay of the powers that be.

He turns round, checks he's not being watched, then ducks under the barbed-wire fence. In less than three minutes, he's at the edge of the clearing. He hides himself behind a spindly beech and cranes out to peer at the railway carriage. The door is open, and there's no towel visible in the window.

"Who goes there? Friend or foe?"

"Friend, stupid."

"What's the password?"

She's a few trees away, sitting astride a low branch.

"I don't need a password. You can see who I am."

"You might have been brainwashed. Password."

He sighs. "All right, then. Gallion. What are you doing up there, anyway?"

"Keeping watch. Where on earth were you?"

"I saw Sammy," he says. "He was taking pictures. So I went after him."

"Did you catch him?"

He shakes his head. "Why didn't you wait for me?"

"I did. For ages. But you didn't come. So in the end I thought I'd better go on my own. Did you find my message?"

"Course."

"Well then."

"So have you told him yet?"

"Yes."

"And what did he say?"

" 'Thank you. For telling me.' " She swings a leg over the branch and drops to the ground. "He didn't seem very surprised. I think he was almost expecting it."

"Where is he now?"

She points at the carriage. "Writing a letter."

"Who to?"

"I don't know. But he doesn't want to go into the village, so he asked me to wait and post it for him. And of course I said I would."

"I'll come with you."

"You don't have to."

"You might need help."

"I know how to get to the post office."

"What if that man comes after you? Sammy, or whatever his name is?"

She hesitates a moment. "Well, all right then. If you want —"

"Lou!" They turn. Hillyard's at the top of the steps, clutching an envelope and squinting into the clearing.

"Here we are," says Lou.

She prods Mark out in front of her. Hillyard nods and raises his hand.

"Ah, Mark. The very chap." His voice seems to have lost its energy. "Lou tells me you were quite the young hero yesterday."

Mark flushes. "No more than she was. She was really brave. Honestly."

"I don't doubt it. You're a couple of young bricks."

"And I've just seen him again now," says Mark. "On my way here."

"What, the little chap with the bag of tricks?"

"Yes. He was taking pictures of me."

"Where?"

"Just there. Willetts Lane. A few minutes ago. Hiding in the bushes. I chased after him, but he ran away."

Hillyard laughs. "Obviously realized you were more than a match for him."

"But I told him: I said, 'I know who you're working for!' "

"And what did he say to that?"

"He didn't say anything. He just . . ." He hobbles a few paces, mimicking the man's lopsided walk. Lou giggles.

"Ah, Mark, Mark," says Hillyard, laying a hand on his shoulder. "Well, you did very well. As usual. But if you see the fellow again, just ignore him, all right?"

Mark nods.

"With any luck, though, you won't. None of us will. If I'm not much mistaken, this" — waving the letter — "ought to settle his hash once and for all."

"What is it?" says Mark.

Hillyard holds a finger to his mouth. Lou reaches out her hand.

"All right. We'll take it now."

"Not yet." He retracts the letter and presses it against his chest. "First I want to hear the news from Peveril on the Swift."

"There isn't much, I'm afraid," says Mark.

Hillyard pulls a disappointed face.

"I haven't had much time . . ."

Hillyard winces. "Ah, no, of course not. Been too busy risking your neck on my account. Yet another link in the heavy chain round my waist."

"I don't mean that. It's just —"

"I know you don't. You're too damned nice to reproach me." He sniffs and swallows noisily, then shakes his head.

Why is he so crestfallen? Mark tries to invent something on the spot, a snippet of a story about Patty and Paul and a stray cow on the line, but his imagination refuses to fire into life.

"My mother . . ." he starts.

"What about her?"

"She . . ." But no: he can't tell Hillyard what she wants him to. He racks his brains for something else to say. Yes, that's it, of course . . .

"She and my dad are going to be watching something tonight. On television."

Hillyard's forehead creases. "Well, that's very nice. But —"

"So if you come while it's on, I can show you Peveril then."

"Ah, I see." As he starts to absorb the idea, the weight seems to lift from him. "Yes, good thinking, Mark."

"If you wait by the church, I'll signal, all right? With my torch? When the coast is clear? Dot dash dot?"

Hillyard ponders a moment. "OK."

"It's meant to begin at half-past eight. So if you get there a few minutes before . . . And then I'll come out when I can."

"All right." He sounds almost light-hearted. "I'll lurk among the gravestones, scaring the wits out of the poor ghosts."

Lou giggles. She stretches her hand out again. "Shall I take that now?"

He nods. "Thank you. Stick it in the post, and let's hope it does the trick. And I'll see you tonight, Mark."

All the way back through the wood, Mark keeps glancing at the letter out of the corner of his eye.

"Let's have a look," he says.

"No."

"I just want to see the envelope."

"It's private."

"It's not private, stupid!"

"Is!"

"Isn't! How's the postman going to know where to take it, then?"

She says nothing, but after a moment hands him the letter. It says:

*Mrs Aubrey Hillyard*
*The Old Granary*
*Moreton Dean*
*Bucks*

# CHAPTER TWELVE

"It's about to start," says Dad.

Mum checks the kitchen clock. "OK. Well, you go and switch it on. And we'll be in in a couple of minutes."

To Mark's surprise, Dad doesn't protest. He nods, slides his packet of Players into his pocket and goes into the sitting room. After a moment they hear a click and the static hiss of the television.

"So," says Mum in an undertone, watching the door. "Did you see him?"

"Yes."

"And you told him what I said?"

"I didn't have a chance. When I got there he was writing a letter and he asked me to take it the post. And it was important, so I did."

"Who was it to?" she asks, smiling.

"What?"

"The letter."

"I don't know."

"You must have seen."

He shrugs.

"A man or a woman?"

"A woman."

"But you didn't recognize the name?"

He hesitates. "You won't tell anyone?"

She shakes her head.

"Mrs Aubrey Hillyard."

"Oh, that must be his wife, mustn't it? Silly of me. I assumed he wasn't married." She flushes. "Have you ever met her?"

"No."

"Does he talk about her?"

"No."

"Well, that's a bit of a funny situation, isn't it? His wife's in — what was the address?"

"Moreton Dean, Bucks."

"She's in Buckinghamshire. And he's here, living in an old railway carriage in the middle of a wood." She twists a loop of hair round her finger. "But then he's a funny chap, isn't he? So perhaps we —"

A wisp of music drifts in from the sitting room: spiky strings, fighting it out with a slow plaintive horn.

"It's on!" calls Dad.

"All right!" She gets up. "Coming?"

He shakes his head. She holds a hand out.

"Do. Please. Just this once."

"I can't."

"Why not?"

"I've got to go out."

"What?" She frowns at the clock. "No, you can't. Not at this hour. It's much too late. I absolutely forbid it."

"Only to the shed. There's something I have to do there. With Peveril."

She stares at him a moment, then sighs. "Well, I give up," she says, and walks into the hall. As she pushes the sitting-room door, a voice spills out from the television: "Mars Colony. Twenty-third year of the New Era."

He lifts the latch noiselessly and slips outside. The sun is low on the horizon, and a red-gold beam slices his eye, making him wince and turn his head. Obviously he's miscalculated: it's still far too light for him to signal with the torch. If he stands by the gate and waves, anybody might see him, so he'll have to sneak into the churchyard and catch Hillyard there. But he'd better wait for a minute or two, just in case one of his parents makes a last-ditch attempt to persuade him to watch the television play.

He goes into the shed, turns on the controller and starts to get the village ready for Hillyard's inspection. He puts Mr Makepeace and Mrs Dauntless on the platform, drives the delivery van back into the High Street and leaves the local to Swiftbridge just out of sight in the Sheepfold Tunnel. He takes the old man from the Oxo box and dangles him above the hermitage. Should he or shouldn't he? The idea makes him queasy for some reason, so he drops the figure in the box again and decides to station Patty and Paul on the river bank, next to the *Pintail*. As he nudges them into position, he glances at the back door. It's still shut, and there's no sound from inside. It's unlikely they'll come for him now. He's as safe as he's going to be.

He leaves the light on and the door ajar, and tiptoes down the path. At the garden gate he stops and peers along Church End. There's no sign of Hillyard — or of anyone else. He lets himself into the road, and half-runs to the churchyard. He's never been there so late before. The lychgate is deserted, and the church unlit. The graveyard, which even on a sunny morning has the feel of a foreign country, is becoming stranger and more alien by the minute. It's already criss-crossed with shadows from the wonky headstones. Soon, he knows, it will be entirely dark.

*I'll lurk among the gravestones, scaring the wits out of the poor ghosts.*

Mark shivers, then forces himself through the gate, praying, *Please just don't let him jump out at me*. To the left, as he starts up the path, is the mound of a recently dug grave, still unmarked, and with patches of earth showing through the ragged grass. That, he knows, is where they buried old Mrs Webb in the spring. He still remembers exactly what she looked like, and it's frighteningly easy to imagine her rearing up suddenly, glowing in her white shroud like the mantle of a gas lamp. He hurries past and takes refuge in the porch, putting a thick stone wall between himself and her. That's better — but not much. Ahead of him is a dense crop of older graves; behind him, just beyond the door, the echoey dimness of the church. It ought to be empty, but every now and then he can hear a tiny clicking sound from inside. Field mice, probably. But even so . . .

The simplest thing would be to call Hillyard's name. If Hillyard doesn't respond, that means he isn't there, and Mark won't have to explore any further. He makes his hands into a loud-hailer, draws air into his lungs, then stops. Someone in the village could hear. Or — the idea is so frightening that he pushes it away before it can gain a foothold in his mind — he might unknowingly summon up something else . . .

Maybe he should just go home. That would be fair enough, wouldn't it? He's done what he can. But if he gives up now, he knows he'll be left with an annoying, stone-in-the-shoe feeling about it. He has to make absolutely sure that Hillyard hasn't come.

He launches himself out of the porch and tiptoes quickly along the side of the church. At the end, there's another cluster of graves, huddled under the shade of a shaggy yew tree. He picks his way between them, and comes out in a more open expanse at the back, with a clearly marked path snaking among the headstones and vases of wilting flowers. This shouldn't take long. In a minute he'll be at the lychgate again . . .

"Evening."

He stops. He knows that voice. But even so, it's too late to stop the sudden prickle of sweat on his neck and in the small of his back. He turns slowly, fighting to keep his breathing under control. Hillyard is lying stretched out on a grave, his hands under his head.

"What are you doing there?"

"Relying on your intelligence," says Hillyard. "I knew you'd realize I'd be too conspicuous if I waited by that gate in daylight. So I thought, *If he needs me before dark, he'll come and find me*. And you did. And you *did*." He sits up, wrapping his arms round his knees. "Shall we go?"

Mark nods. At least in the deepening twilight Hillyard won't be able to see that he's shaking.

"Right." He scrambles to his feet, bends down again to pick up a battered knapsack. "You lead the way."

"OK." Mark guides Hillyard back round the church, then signals: *wait in the porch*. He creeps to the road and looks both ways. Church End is still deserted. He raises an arm and beckons. Hillyard starts towards him, moving stealthily on the balls of his feet.

*I can keep myself out of sight as well as the next man*. It's true: when Mark's in the lead, he can't hear any footsteps following him; and when he glances over his shoulder, to make sure Hillyard's still there, it's a couple of seconds before he's able to spot him in the shadows. Even so, when they reach the garden gate, he turns and holds a finger to his lips. Hillyard nods.

There's a faint blue haze behind the sitting-room curtains and a waft of eerie music. When they reach the shed, it's exactly as Mark left it. He opens the door, ushers Hillyard inside, then latches it behind them.

"Ah!" says Hillyard. It's more a sigh than a word. He leans forward, brushing his fingertips over the papier-mâché hill, the roofs of the houses, the painted ribbon of the Swift. Then he squats down to see everything at eye level. "Yes," he murmurs. "Just as I imagined. Every detail. Perfect. You going to introduce me to the cast of characters?"

"Well, there's Mrs Dauntless —"

"Ah, yes. Deep in conversation with — that must be Mr Makepeace?"

Mark nods.

"They're waiting for the train, are they?"

"Yes."

"So where is it?"

Mark flicks on the controller and eases the local out of the tunnel and into the station.

"Peveril . . ." prompts Hillyard.

"Peveril!" says Mark, in his Mr Makepeace voice. "This is Peveril on the Swift!"

"Excellent," says Hillyard. "And now how does Mrs Dauntless get on?"

Mark picks her up and drops her in the Oxo box.

"That's it?"

Mark nods. He readies himself for a derisive laugh. But instead, after a moment, Hillyard whistles under his breath and says:

"Yes. Very clever." He stands back, folding his arms. "All right, then. Come on. Off we go."

Mark coaxes the train into life, sends it round the bend and then — gathering speed on the straight — into the Abbey Tunnel. Hillyard watches, nodding approvingly.

"OK if I get a few snaps?" he says. "Just to show the lie of the land?"

"All right."

Hillyard balances his knapsack on the edge of the table. The canvas is dotted with darned holes, and there's only one strap. He unlatches it and takes out an old twin-lens reflex and a flash gun in a flimsy case.

"My dad takes pictures," says Mark. "He's got a Leica."

"Has he indeed?" He rummages in the bag and retrieves a metal bar with a shoe for the flash at one end and a bolt at the other. "Lucky chap." He screws the bar to the bottom of the camera and slides the flash gun into place. "Ready?" He opens the reflector. "If you don't want to be half blinded, I'd look away."

Mark covers his eyes with his hand. Even so, a dazzle of light spills through his fingers.

"Just a couple more," says Hillyard. "One. Two. There we are."

Mark opens his eyes. Hillyard is packing the camera away again.

"Right," he says, returning to the layout. "And these two here" — homing in on the river — "are Patty and Paul?"

"Yes."

He reaches out a big hand. "Mind if I? . . ."

Mark shakes his head. Hillyard picks the figures up and stands them on his palm, half-closing his eyes to look at them.

"Yes," he says. "Obviously a couple of splendid kids. Destined to grow up into as exemplary a pair of solid citizens as you could hope to meet. You know what I'd like to do? I'd like to crack open a bottle of *Alice in Wonderland's* shrinking potion. Get myself down to this size. And take up residence in Peveril on the Swift. Can't think of anything better." He scans the High Street. "Where would you recommend?"

Mark shrugs. "Most people think the best house is the Dauntlesses'."

"Which one is that? This Georgian chappie?"

Mark nods.

"Most people are right, for once. That'd certainly do me. Course, I'd never dream of turfing the Dauntless clan out. You don't in Peveril, do you? It isn't that sort of place. But maybe they'd take me in as a paying guest. I could help around the house. Do a bit of work in the garden. Give Patty and Paul a hand getting the *Pintail* onto hard standing and slapping on a lick of varnish."

Mark crouches down and squints along the high street, visualizing a miniature Hillyard swaggering past all those rigid people on their plastic pedestals. He starts to laugh.

"No joke, old chap," says Hillyard. "I'm serious. Suit me down to the ground. No louts. No busybody farmers. No snoops poking their damned noses in where they're not wanted."

"No Brain," says Mark.

Hillyard snorts. "Yes, that's right. No Brain. Apart from the fine specimen" — tapping his temple — "in here."

Mark hesitates. "We posted the letter you gave us."

"Did you? That's good." He raises an eyebrow. "Perhaps I should have enquired. I'm afraid I rather took it for granted that you would."

"I saw who it was to."

Hillyard shrugs. "Well, that's understandable. You couldn't very well avoid it. It was there in black and white."

"Is Mrs Aubrey Hillyard your wife?"

"That would seem a reasonable deduction, wouldn't it?"

"And is she one of the people in high places?"

Hillyard rolls his eyes comically. "My God, you haven't lost the knack, have you?"

Mark flinches, but forces himself to hold Hillyard's gaze.

"You could say that," says Hillyard finally, looking away.

"What does 'people in high places' mean, exactly? Is it the same as the powers that be?"

Hillyard breathes out noisily, then nods. "Not far off. This country . . ." He pauses. "Ever heard of the old-boy network?"

Mark shakes his head.

"Fellows who've all been to the same schools. Then on to the same universities. Oxford and Cambridge. And then give each other jobs. You scratch my back, and I'll scratch yours."

"What sort of jobs?"

"Government posts. Captains of industry. High-court judges." He spreads his big fingers and jabs them at the world beyond the shed. "Imagine you're a Martian. By some damnable fluke, your spaceship touches down in Oatley. You shoot out your eyes on stalks, then slither off to take a peek at the people in the High Street. Nothing wrong here, you think. A lot of free agents, all going about their business."

"What's a free agent?"

Hillyard frowns and chews his overgrown moustache. "A free agent," he says, "is someone who's able to make up his own mind what he's going to do, and then does it. You're one. So am I. So's Lou. Most of that lot, on the other hand" — nodding at the door — "aren't. And that's where our Martian friend makes his mistake. He sees PC What's-his-name, for instance —"

"Pointer."

"He sees PC Pointer giving a kid a clip round the lughole, or helping an old lady across the road, and doesn't realize that he's really a puppet. Controlled by someone he'll never meet, sitting in an office in Whitehall."

"A person in high places?"

Hillyard nods. "A person in high places. And of course, the cunning of the thing is, PC Pointer doesn't realize he's a puppet either."

"Is that what your wife does, then? Control people?"

Hillyard laughs. "Well, in a manner of speaking. Though in Molly's case, it's not so much what she *does*: it's who she *knows*. Look through her address book, and there's a Lady this and an Honourable that on every other page." He notices Mark's startled expression and smiles. "You probably think I oughtn't to be talking about her like this, hm? It's not the sort of thing a chap does. Bad form and all that."

Mark shrugs.

"But that's how they get away with it, of course. No one dares say anything. So they're free to go on . . ." He holds his hands out and waggles them, twitching invisible strings.

"So that's why the Brain goes for them!" says Mark. "If it can get the people in high places, they'll get everyone else!"

Hillyard nods. "Very perceptive, Mark," he says slowly. "Very perceptive indeed. They're like a lot of dominoes. You line them all up like this, then knock the first one over, *ping*. And the others all follow, one after another, *bang bang bang*."

"So is she working for them? Your wife?"

"I don't know, Mark. And that's the truth."

"Why did you write to her, then?"

Hillyard sighs. "It's the last throw of the dice for me. Wouldn't have done it if there'd been any alternative. I'm just hoping she's still on the side of the angels. If she is, then she'll be able to get them to call off the hounds."

"Sammy?"

Hillyard nods. "If she isn't . . ." He starts to shrug, then stiffens, his neck still shrunk into his shoulders.

"What?"

"Ssh."

Mark turns. Now he can hear it himself: a muffled fumbling sound from inside the house. A second later, the back door latch clicks.

"Mark?"

Mum. He holds his breath. Out of the corner of his eye he sees Hillyard casting about for somewhere to hide. It's hopeless: the only place big enough is under the table, and he'd have to clear a clutter of boxes out of the way first.

"Mark?" The door opens. "Oh, you are here. Why didn't you answer when I —" She jumps and shrinks back. "Oh!"

"Good evening," says Hillyard.

She stares at him, blinking. Her hand goes to her unruly hair, then drops again.

"I hope you don't mind," he says. "Railways are a passion of mine. There's a small nine-year-old bit of me that will never be reconciled to not being the driver of the Mallard, thundering through the night in a cloud of sparks. And Mark was kind enough to offer to show me his set-up."

Her mouth moves, but she says nothing.

"I'm sorry, I can see I've startled you." He gathers up his knapsack and buckles the strap. "Inexcusable to turn up unannounced like this. I shall remove myself at once."

She glances back at the house. "It's just that it is rather late."

"I know. A thousand pardons."

He starts towards the door. For a few seconds, as if she doesn't understand what he's doing, she stays where she is, blocking the entrance. Then, with an embarrassed "Sorry", she steps clumsily aside. As he's passing her, she murmurs, without looking at him: "Thank you. It's nice for Mark. To have someone to take an interest."

He gazes down at her, then reaches out and gently tucks a stray curl behind her ear.

"Goodnight."

After he's gone, she and Mark stare at each other. Her face is hot, and she keeps touching the twist of hair Hillyard moved, as if to make sure it's still there.

"We won't tell Dad, will we?" he says.

She shakes her head. "Anyway. Do come in and watch the rest of the programme, poppet. It's so exciting. I'm sure you'd enjoy it." The dazed look in her eyes is fading. Behind it, Mum is beginning to reappear. "And then it's straight off to bed with you."

He doesn't usually remember his dreams. This one, though, is so vivid that the details stay with him long after he's woken up, bleeding into the edge of his vision. When he draws the curtains and looks out over the garden at Church End, he can sense the aliens from Mars Colony everywhere: under bushes, behind doors and windows, spreading beneath the ground like tree roots, upending gravestones, cracking foundations, rippling roads and lawns and flower beds. And immediately he turns away, he has to fight the urge to spin round again and check that he hasn't missed the terrifying moment when they start to break out and swarm across the landscape, burying cars and houses beneath their seething bodies, reducing Oatley to a mindless anthill.

His mother's in the kitchen, straining on tiptoe to peer into a cupboard.

"Morning, Mum."

"Oh, hullo, sweetie." She takes down a packet of cornflakes and hands it to him. As he puts it on the table, he notices that she's only laid two places.

"Where's Dad?"

"He's not feeling very well. So I gave him his breakfast in bed." She smiles. "Which means there's just the two of us this morning. So," she adds, taking the milk bottle from the fridge. “What did he think? Mr Hillyard? About Peveril on the Swift?”

“He thought it was terrific.”

“Yes, well, it is.” She settles herself next to him, drawing her chair close to the table. “Anything in particular?”

“All of it. He said he’d like to live there.”

She laughs. “That could be a bit difficult, couldn’t it?”

“Not if he drank a shrinking potion.”

“Well, no, I suppose if he did that . . .” Her voice trails off. She shunts the cornflakes towards him. “Here.”

Mark fills his bowl and hands the packet back to her. She puts it down, then seems to forget about it.

“Did he say *why* he’d like to live there?”

“No Mr Montgomery,” he says, splashing milk onto his cereal. “No Mr Barron.”

She laughs again. “No Stan Green.”

“No Harry Doggett.”

“No Ernie.”

“No Brai —”

He stops himself too late. She’s still laughing, but she’s puzzled.

“No ‘bray’, did you say? What do you mean? Has he got a donkey for a neighbour, or something?” She pauses. “I wouldn’t put it past Mr Montgomery doing something like that. Sticking a bad-tempered old Eeyore in the field next door. Just to annoy him.”

He shoves an overflowing spoonful of cornflakes into his mouth and shakes his head.

"What *did* you say, then?"

"Nothing."

"Don't speak with your mouth full. 'Brain', was it?" He points to his bulging cheek.

"All right," she says. "Anyway, Peveril appeals to him, that's the main thing. Perhaps it reminds him of a real place. You know, where he's from or somewhere."

She pauses. Mark busies himself with his bowl, scraping his spoon against the rim with a sound that sets his teeth on edge.

"Where *did* he grow up?" she says. "Has he ever told you?"

"No."

"What about where he was living before?"

Mark shakes his head.

"Well, he's quite a man of mystery, isn't he?" She hesitates. "You're really quite sure, are you? That you can't let me in on his secret?"

He nods.

"I wouldn't breathe a word to anyone. Honestly."

"Mum, I told you. I promised!"

She half-shuts her eyes and presses a palm to her forehead. "No, of course, sorry, you're quite right. I . . ."

She stops and looks towards the door. Dad is calling. His voice is so weak that Mark can only tell from the intonation that he's saying Mum's name.

"Oh dear," she says under her breath. She slides her chair back abruptly and slips out into the hall. But then, instead of going up to him as Mark expected, she stands at the bottom of the stairs and calls:

"Yes? What is it?"

Mark can't hear the response.

"All right," shouts Mum. He's surprised how abrupt she sounds.

"Cigarettes," she says, coming back in. "He's only got one left, apparently."

"Do you want me to go and get some?"

"Oh, would you mind, sweetie? It's just I . . ." She sits down, smoothing her hair with both hands.

"No, that's OK," he says, standing up.

"Finish your breakfast. It won't kill him to wait half an hour, will it?"

"I *have* finished." He notices the empty bowl in front of her. "Aren't you going to have anything?"

She shakes her head. "I'm not hungry. Maybe in a minute."

He lingers. What's the right thing to say? *Are you feeling OK? Can I get you anything?*

"Don't worry about me," she says. "I'm fine."

"All right." He clicks his tongue. "Come on, Barney."

He sidles down the path and out into Church End. Mr Robinson straightens up from his digging and flaps a hand full of spring onions at him as he passes. Batty Mrs Slater, watching from her porch, gives him a toothless smile and tick-tocks a finger at him. Even the churchyard, he thinks, as he approaches the entrance, seems quite benign this morning: butterflies throng the hedge, and from the thick grass beyond he can hear a chorus of bees. If he had to go in there now, it wouldn't bother him . . .

Barney stops suddenly. Ears pricked, he stares at the lychgate, a deep growl shaking his throat.

A man unfolds himself from the shadows. His eyes are hidden by the brim of a white hat, but Mark knows him at once by his linen suit and the black bag in his hand.

"Hullo, chum."

Barney lunges forward. Mark tugs his lead so violently that he half falls, his claws skittering on the tarmac.

"You're Mark, aren't you?" says the man. "I'm — well, you can call me Mr Sammy."

"What do you want?"

"I'd like a quick chat. If you've got a moment."

"What about?"

The man reaches inside his jacket, pulls a photograph from the breast pocket.

"This gentleman," he says, handing it to Mark.

It's a picture of Aubrey Hillyard. It must have been taken some time ago, because it shows him with short hair and a well-kept beard, and wearing a sports coat and a collar and tie. But the bearing of the head, the shape of the mouth and the bird-of-prey eyes are unmistakable.

"What about him?" says Mark.

"Friend of yours, is he?"

Mark shrugs.

"I spotted you slipping in to see him."

"Yes. I saw you."

He raises his eyebrows. "Where was that?"

"Willetts Lane. You were taking pictures. I ran after you. Don't you remember? You must have seen."

The man smiles, not admitting or denying it. "Who's that chap?" he says, pointing across the road.

Mark turns. "Mr Robinson."

"What colour's his fingers?"

"What do you mean?"

"You're a bit slow this morning. That place of his is a marvel. Never seen a garden like it. So last night I thought I'd treat myself to an evening stroll and a sniff of his roses. And what do you think I saw? Our friend here" — nodding at the picture in Mark's hand — "sneaking out of *your* house. At least, oh, I don't know, a good hour after my bedtime when I was your age."

"How do you know it was my house?"

The man chuckles. "Easy enough to find out where you lived. A fellow in my line who couldn't do that should hang up his deerstalker, shouldn't he?"

"What is your line?"

"I thought you knew who I was. That's what you told me yesterday."

"You said you didn't see me yesterday!"

"No, I didn't." The humour's gone. He tilts his head back and stares down his long parrot-beak nose, daring Mark to challenge him. Mark bites his lip. Barney jerks forward again, growling.

"Not very friendly, your dog, is it?"

"He is with some people."

"What, like Mr Hillyard? Obviously a popular fellow, Mr Hillyard, in your neck of the woods. You. The dog. Your parents. Or *one* of your parents, anyway. What is he, old school pal of Dad's? Someone he knew in the war? Or —"

"It's none of your business."

He shrugs. "Suit yourself." He leans forward, plucks the picture from Mark's hand. "If you don't want to tell me, I can always pop down the street and ask him in person, can't I?"

Mark shivers. Without realizing it, he's allowed himself to be backed into a corner.

"He's not a friend of my dad's." His mouth's dry. "My dad's never met him."

The man nods. "Ah."

"All right?" says Mark.

"We've made a start. But we're not there yet." He clears his throat. "How about Mum, then?"

"*She* knows him. A bit."

"How much is a bit?"

Mark shrugs.

The man starts to edge past him. "At home now, is she?"

"All right," says Mark. "She met him just a few days ago. In the High Street."

The man leans forward. "I've got X-ray eyes, sonny," he says, peering at him. "I can tell when people are lying. You ask anyone: I'm known for it. Never wrong."

"I'm not lying! That was the first time! She'd never seen him before in her life!"

"Scouts' honour?"

"Cross my heart and hope to die. I was there!"

The man studies him for a moment more, then nods.

"Well, I always knew he was a fast worker. But this must be a record, even for him. Meets her out walking. And abracadabra, couple of days later, he's paying her a late-night call. Without seeing your dad."

"He wasn't calling on her," he says. "He was looking at my model railway."

"Model railway, eh?" says the man, as if he doesn't believe him.

Mark starts to blush. "Yes."

"Well, that's a new one."

"A new what?"

Sammy shakes his head. "Is that what your mum told you to say?"

"Course not!"

"Come on, sonny. A chap like our friend there? Going to see a model railway? At nine in the evening? Not very likely. Not given *his* history."

"What history?"

The man licks his lips. "Well, let's put it like this: if I carried on the way he seems to have done, my wife wouldn't let me back in the house."

"You shouldn't believe what people say about him!"

The man smiles. "Lies, *mein Kapitän!* All lies!" he says, in a Goon Show voice.

"Well, they are! And I don't care what you do, you'll never brainwash us! So you might as well just give up now and go home!"

Barney picks up the anger in his tone and hurls himself forward again. Mark pulls him back, but the effort of holding him is making his arm tired.

"You want to keep that dog under better control," says the man. "If it bites me, one word with your policeman chappie, and I could have it put down" — snapping his fingers — "just like that."

*The policeman chappie*. Of course: the man's in league with PC Pointer, isn't he — and everybody else. They've all been brainwashed They're all enemies. There's no point arguing with any of them.

"All right," he says. "Come on, Barney."

"Oi, hang on a minute. I haven't finished. Where are you off to?"

Mark doesn't reply. But when he's twenty yards away and safely out of reach, he looks over his shoulder and calls:

"You won't win!"

Then he turns back and hotfoots it towards the High Street.

# CHAPTER THIRTEEN

Time's an old fraud. It telescopes. The unimportant things compact, smaller and smaller, until they vanish into an imperceptible black hole. Only the important ones resist the gravitational pull, stand their ground — grow even larger, in fact, in contrast.

So, from this remove, the two weeks after Mark's encounter with Sammy seem shrunk to a more or less undifferentiated blur of dewy mornings and sluggish afternoons. As if by a miracle, the powers that be appear, at a stroke, to have given up. First, Sammy himself vanishes, melting away as quickly as he came; then, as if they're taking their lead from him, the other conspirators — Montgomery, Barron, Harry Doggett — seem to lose interest as well. When Mark meets one of them, they no longer ask where he's going, or warn him that something is afoot: in fact, they scarcely appear to notice he's there at all. Something — he can only guess what it is — seems to have sent them into wholesale retreat.

As the pressure starts to ease, life returns more and more to a game: an old door found in the wood becomes transformed into the *Kon-Tiki*; the trunk in the attic is raided for funny clothes, yielding a plumed hat for Lou and a mysterious eyepatch for Mark. Against this backdrop, only a few distinct episodes stand out — lumpy old fossils thrown into sharper relief by the erosion of everything around them.

Fossil one: Murky and the Jains. It's a few days after his encounter with Sammy, and Mum and Dad have gone to RAF Feltwell, where Dad's giving a lecture to the airmen. Mark is stretched out under the apple tree, reading *Knight's Fee*. Barney lies next to him, twitching and whimpering in his sleep. From somewhere in the distance there's a faint knocking sound. It registers at the edge of Mark's consciousness, like a finger dimpling the surface of a balloon without breaking it. Then it stops, and someone is calling:

"Hullo!"

Instantly, Barney's on his feet, bristling.

"Hullo!"

Barney starts to bark. Mark hooks a finger through his collar.

"Sssh, boy!"

They go back into the house. He shuts Barney in the hall, then opens the front door.

"Oh, Murky!"

"Ah, there you are."

"Sorry. I was in the garden."

She nods, snorting. She seems older: grey and stooped and out of breath. She sags towards him, both hands clamped on the knob of a twisty briar stick.

"My parents are out, I'm afraid," he says. "They should be back soon."

She shakes her head. It's a moment before she can speak. "Not your parents I'm after," she says, gulping air between the words. "Hoping for a chat with you."

"Oh. Right. Well . . . Come in."

"Thank you."

He shows her into the sitting room, grabbing Barney before he has a chance to ambush her and penning him against the wall with his leg.

"Ah," she says, stopping just inside the door. "A television. That's new, isn't it?"

"Yes."

"I'm rather surprised. I thought your father was dead against them."

"He was."

"Did *you* talk him into getting it?"

He shakes his head.

"What made him change his mind?"

He hesitates. "I don't know."

She stares at him. He drops his gaze, trying to deflect another question.

"Well, my mother would be appalled," she says, after a moment. "But I'm going to be thoroughly impolite and sit down without waiting to be asked."

She subsides onto the sofa. Mark releases Barney, who stalks over to her and sniffs the cat-smell on her stockings.

"At this rate, I shall be the last person in the village with*out* a television," she says. "Apart from poor Mrs Pledger. Wouldn't be much use to her, would it? Just a blur in the corner."

"No." He perches on the edge of Dad's chair. Barney flops at his feet.

"I'm simply too old, I suppose," she says. "Even the wireless still seems like magic to me. I've never quite got used to switching the thing on and having someone I haven't met talking to me. A television must be even worse. You can *see* whoever it is too. It'd be like having a house full of uninvited visitors. Do *you* find it like that?"

"I don't mind." He studies her closely, monitoring her reaction. "Long as they don't try to brainwash me."

She laughs. "Oh, I'm not bothered about that. My brain could probably do with a jolly good scrub. I just don't want to be trapped in my own sitting room by someone like — who's that chap? You know, Professor Joad — who knows for a certainty that he's right and everyone else is wrong about absolutely everything."

"You just switch off."

"I know, but . . . It sounds silly, doesn't it, but I can't help feeling that would be a bit rude? Switching off a guest in mid-flow. Even an uninvited one." She pauses a moment. "Anyway, I didn't come to talk about televisions. I came to apologize."

"To me? What for?"

"For being such a poor friend."

"You're not —"

"I have been, and that's an end of it. Not knowingly, of course. But that's no excuse. We all know what the road to hell is paved with, don't we?'

He shakes his head.

"Have you ever heard of the Jains?" she says.

"*Jane's Fighting Ships*?"

She smiles. "J-A-I-N-S. Chaps in India who go round pushing brooms in front of them."

"Why?"

"So they don't accidentally step on an insect. They're so frightened of doing something wrong, they hardly dare do anything at all. Or so my Indian uncle Arthur said."

"That's silly," says Mark.

"Exactly what I thought, when he told us. But now I'm beginning to think perhaps the Jains had a point after all." She shifts uncomfortably. "Honestly, I could kick myself. Why would a grown-up man suddenly find himself without somewhere to live? And why, if he did, couldn't he simply go and stay with a relation? Isn't there a brother or a sister or a cousin somewhere who'd take him in? If not, wiser heads than mine would see that as a sign that I should have thought about it twice before helping him myself."

"Aubrey Hillyard?"

She nods. "But what bothers me most is you, Mark. I know you took pity on the man and tried to befriend him. And that's very much to your credit. But it's got you into an awful pickle with people in the village, I'm afraid. Mr Montgomery and so on. And I feel dreadful about that."

"I don't mind."

"Well, I do. If I made a mistake, it's unfair that *you* should be penalized for it."

"You didn't make a mistake. You're helping him to do something really important."

"Is that what he told you?"

"And Mr Barron and Mr Montgomery and Mr Pointer don't want him to. That's why they've been so nasty to him. But they won't win. You'll see. They won't."

She stares at him. Her eyes seem smaller, as if the surrounding skin has started to grow over them.

"Well, he tells a good story, evidently," she says finally. "But one of these days, very soon, I'm afraid he's going to get his comeuppance. And when he does . . ." She shakes her head. "You have a heart of oak, young Aurelius. So does that girl you like to play with. But honestly, he's not worthy of either of you. You should both stop letting him twist you round his little finger. No one'll think the worse of you for it if you do."

"He's not twisting us round his little finger. He's —"

Barney jumps up suddenly and rushes to the door, whimpering. A second later they hear the click of the latch. Mark barges Barney aside and peers out into the hall.

"Hullo," says Mum. She gently lowers a bag of shopping onto the table, then turns towards him and smiles. "Oh, you're still here, are you?"

He nods.

"I thought you'd have been out and about on a day like this."

"Murky came."

"Oh, did she?"

He nods again. Behind him, Murky says: "But she's just leaving."

"Really?" says Mum. She pushes past him and looks into the sitting room. Murky is bent forward, levering herself up with the stick.

She grimaces and says: "Hullo, Jenny."

"Well, this is a nice surprise," says Mum. She glances back along the hall.

"We've got a visitor," says Mum.

"No, you haven't. Pretend you haven't seen me," says Murky, lumbering towards the door just as Dad is walking into the house, clutching a buff wallet of lecture notes.

"Would you like to have a bite of lunch with us?" says Mum.

"That's very kind, but no, thank you. I just popped in for a word with Mark, who looked after me very well." She hobbles past her into the hall. "He's an excellent host, your son. Not to mention jolly good at reading *Old Possum's Book of Practical Cats*." She looks at Mark. "On which subject: tea, young Aurelius? On Thursday?"

"All right."

She nods and lifts her stick. "Well, goodbye."

After she's gone, Dad stares at Mark for a moment, then disappears into the study. Mum waits for the click of the door, before beckoning Mark into the kitchen.

"So, you've been here all morning then, have you?"

"Yes."

She nods.

"Why?" he says. "Did you want me to do something?"

She shakes her head, tugging at a curl of hair. "Oh, no, it wasn't that."

"I'll take Barney for a walk this afternoon, if that's what's worrying you," he says.

"Yes, I'm sure you will, poppet." She hesitates. "No, I only thought maybe you'd seen your friend Mr Hillyard, that's all."

"Aubrey."

She flushes. "Aubrey. I was just wondering how he was. But it doesn't matter."

She turns away and starts unpacking her bag.

Fossil two: the hideout. The sun's already high over the hedge above the chalk pit, but the ground's wet underfoot. Nine, then. Nine-thirty, at the latest. On the face of it, that seems a bit odd. Why have they arranged to meet there rather than at the railway carriage? Probably just because they assume it's safer. Even though there's been no sign of Sammy or Mr Montgomery or Mr Barron for a week or more, it's possible someone might still be keeping a watch on Twenty Acre Wood.

"Yes, I approve," says Hillyard, leaning down to squint inside. "Very commodious and well appointed, as our eighteenth-century friends would have said."

"What does that mean?" says Lou.

"Elegant ballroom. Grand staircase."

Lou laughs.

"Extensive kitchen gardens, producing the choicest *fruits et legumes*." He straightens up, hands on his hips. "You go in. I'm going to lurk out here for a minute. Just take a quick shufti, as our eighteenth-century friends would *not* have said. To make sure no one's spotted us."

Mark and Lou crawl in and settle themselves on opposite sides. After a moment, they hear a hose-pipe sluice of liquid spraying the leaves of the hedge. They catch each other's eye and giggle. A few seconds later, Hillyard thrusts his head into the opening again.

"Seems to be all right," he says. "Nary a soul to be seen." He surveys the narrow space, then waves his hand. "Scoot over, one of you. Let a chap squeeze in."

He unlatches the strap on his bag and takes out a packet of chocolate digestives. "Lou, you're in charge of these. We've had enough of crumbs and broken bits. From now on, only the best will do. So open with care, if you please." He rummages in the knapsack again and produces three bottles of Stones ginger beer. "I, meanwhile" — extracting Mark's knife from his pocket and flicking open the bottle-opener — "will attend to the drinks. Here. And here. Cheers."

They clink bottles. "Cheers."

"So," says Hillyard. "What's the consensus?"

"What's the what?" says Lou.

"Consensus?"

She shakes her head.

"It means the agreed opinion about something."

"Well, I think this is super," says Mark.

"And so do I," says Hillyard. "But I wasn't referring to the pleasures of a day out with friends, delightful though they are. More to the general situation, as of oh-whatever-it-is hours this morning."

"About the Brain, you mean?" says Lou.

He nods. "The Brain, and all its devilish legions. Why have they decided to leave us alone all of a sudden?"

"Cos they know they've lost!" says Mark.

Hillyard grimaces. "We should beware hubris."

"What's hubris?" says Lou.

"Pride before a fall."

"But they *have* lost!" says Mark. "It's obvious, isn't it?"

"You think they've admitted defeat?"

Mark nods.

"And what do you suppose would have made them do that?"

"Must have been your letter," says Lou. "Cos that's when everything stopped, wasn't it? The day after we posted it. Or the day after that, anyway."

Hillyard nods. "That was the idea, of course. But this, frankly, exceeds my most fevered imaginings."

"It doesn't matter what it was, does it?" says Lou. "The main thing is, you can get on with your book now."

"It's just I can't help feeling perhaps it's a little bit too good to be true."

"Well, what else could it be?" says Lou. "If it isn't that?"

"What indeed?" He glances at Mark, eyebrows raised.

"I don't know," mumbles Mark. If they're not going to acknowledge *his* role in tackling Sammy, he can't mention it himself.

Hillyard hesitates, tapping out a steady rhythm on his biscuit with his fingertips. "They never mentioned any names, did they?" he says finally. "Barron and Montgomery and Co.? When they were talking?"

"What sort of names?" says Lou.

"Names you weren't familiar with?"

She ponders a moment, then shakes her head. "Don't think so."

"You, Mark?"

"Can't remember."

"Try. Starts with an 'S'."

"Sammy!" says Lou.

"No, not Sammy. Ends in an 'N'. Ring any bells?"

"No," Mark says. "Can't you tell us the whole name? That might help."

Hillyard shakes his head again. "Better not."

"Is this S blank blank N after you, then?"

"Might be."

"Does he work for the Brain too?" says Lou.

Hillyard hesitates, then waves his hand. "Oh, don't worry about it. Let sleeping dogs lie. Least said, soonest mended."

"But —" begins Mark.

"*Least said, soonest mended*. A veritable treasury of folk wisdom today, old Aubrey, isn't he? A cliché for every occasion. No job too small. Parties catered for."

Lou laughs.

"Anyway, perhaps you're right, Mark, and the trick's really worked. Stranger things have happened. And every day that goes by makes it a bit more likely. That doesn't mean we should stop being careful, of course.

You know." He clamps his ginger beer bottle between his knees, sticks his half-eaten biscuit between his teeth, then holds his eyes wide open with his fingers. "Peeled at all times," he says, retrieving the digestive. "That's the ticket. But no need to meet trouble halfway. All right?"

Mark and Lou nod.

"See, there I go again. *Meet trouble halfway*. And while you're at it, don't waste your time crying while the sun shines. Never got anyone anywhere."

Lou laughs. "You mean —"

"I know what I mean. Or making hay over spilt milk. Or searching for a needle in a silver lining."

"How about cutting your coat to suit your haystack?" says Mark.

Hillyard nods. "Yes, that's very sound advice. Always followed it myself." He tugs the collar of his smock. "And above all, two's company, and three's an awful lot of people to fit under a bush. I move that the meeting be adjourned. And — providing the coast's clear — reconvened at number one, the Railway Carriage."

All the way down the hill, Lou and Hillyard walk together, talking and laughing. Mark follows a few paces behind, telling himself a story. One day, when it's all over, and the Brain has been roundly defeated, they'll arrest Sammy. They won't hurt him, of course: just put him in a room with a square window high up in the wall and ask him questions.

*What was it?* they'll say, *that finally made you realize it was pointless going on? The letter Mr Hillyard sent to his wife?*

And Sammy will shake his head sadly and say: *No, it was that plucky young chap Mark Davenant. The way he stood firm and said we could never win. Reminded me of nothing so much as London in the Blitz. When I saw the set of his jaw and the look in his eye, I knew it was all up for us.*

# CHAPTER FOURTEEN

Mr Montgomery's Humber is parked in front of the shop. That's unusual: he normally uses his Land Rover when he's driving round the village. As Mark gets nearer, he can see Mr Montgomery himself, feet and arms crossed, leaning against the big shiny wing. He's talking to PC Pointer, who stands frowning with concentration, clutching his helmet to his chest. Two weeks ago, Mark would have turned back and gone to Hillfield the long way round to avoid their seeing him. Now, though he's still nervous, he keeps going. He isn't doing anything wrong. And he's got as much right to be in High Street as they have.

"Morning," says Mr Montgomery.

"Hello," mumbles Mark. As he passes the shop, he glances inside. There's no sign of Lou — but her father is there behind the counter, nodding at someone half-dissolved in the reflection in the glass. Mark tacks closer, shading his eyes to see who it is: Mr Barron.

His stomach tingles. His legs feel achy. But he forces himself to hurry on to Hillfield without looking back.

"Well, we're making progress, young Aurelius," says Murky, as she opens the door. "I didn't forget this time.

Everything ready and waiting. And nobody else here to disturb us."

He follows her into the sitting room. The book's on the arm of the sofa, and a tray on the table.

"Sit down," says Murky. "And tell me how you are."

"I'm fine."

She settles herself opposite him. "Really?"

He nods.

"Good. And did you take my advice? About Mr Hillyard? You didn't, did you?"

He shakes his head. "But it's all right. Nothing's happened. I just saw Mr Montgomery and Mr Pointer on my way here. And . . ."

"Where?"

"Outside the shop. And they were OK. They didn't tell me off or anything. So . . ."

"That's something, I suppose. But when the moment comes, you really should make sure you're nowhere in the vicinity. It's not the sort of thing a boy ought to be mixed up in."

She still thinks they're going to get Hillyard. He longs to say, *It's all right. They're not going to do anything. The Brain's lost*. But he knows he mustn't, not yet. So he shrugs and looks down at his bare knees, squeezing them together with his hands.

"Well, just promise me one thing, will you?" she says. "If anything *does* happen and people start asking you questions or accusing you of things, tell them to come and see me, all right?"

He hesitates. "All right."

She nods. "Good. Now, what are you going to have?" She leans towards the tray. Two bottles stand shoulder to shoulder. "Here's old faithful, the elderberry. Or else, if you feel like it, I thought you might try the gooseberry. Made with last year's crop. And big fat chaps they were, if you remember."

"Elderberry, please."

She pours a trickle into his glass, then opens the other bottle and fills her own. As she levers the scuffed lid off the biscuit tin, Mark notices her fingers are trembling.

"A special request today, if you don't mind. Macavity. Can we start with him?"

"All right. I like Macavity." He opens the book, flicks to the right page and begins to read. But he's barely finished the first verse when Murky exclaims:

"Oh, dash it!"

Mark looks up. "What?"

She shakes her head and points to the front of the house.

"I didn't hear anything."

"Car."

Mark cocks his head. Yes, the slam of a door, then footsteps on the gravel.

"I'd better go and see," she says. But it takes her several seconds to get out of her chair. As she limps into the hall, the bell rings. She clears her throat noisily. Mark hears the rattle of the loose handle, the peep of the hinges.

"Yes. Oh, hello."

"Afternoon." It's Mr Montgomery's voice.

"Heavens," says Murky.

"Hope you don't mind. We thought it better if we all came. You know Mr Bennett, don't you? From the shop?"

"Yes, of course."

"And these other gentlemen" — chuckling — "need no introduction."

"No. No."

Mark tiptoes to the sitting-room door and peers through the crack into the hall. All he can see is Murky's back.

"Would it be all right if we? . . ." Montgomery again. "Just for a couple of minutes?"

"I've got a visitor," says Murky.

"We won't keep you long. It is quite urgent."

She sighs. "All right, then. Come in."

"Thank you."

Mark presses himself into the corner.

"We'll go into the dining room," says Murky.

He looks through the crack again. Murky first, then — in a slow, clumping procession — Mr Montgomery, Mr Barron, PC Pointer and Lou's father. They file through the door opposite and half-close it behind them. But he can still hear quite clearly as Murky says:

"Please. Sit down."

There's a scraping of chairs.

"So, what can I do for you?"

"There's been a bit of a development," says Mr Montgomery. "Mr Pointer had a letter this morning. From that detective chappie."

"Oh, what, you mean —"

"The man who calls himself Sammy, yes. He's found something. He thinks he's got him."

"Really? What does he say?"

"Why don't you show Miss Murkett, Dick?"

There's a long pause. Mark holds his breath till he can hold it no more, then has to put a hand over his mouth to stifle his gasps. Finally Murky says:

"John Slindon?"

"That's what he says." PC Pointer.

"Well, he certainly thinks the evidence points in that direction," says Mr Barron. "It's only circumstantial at this stage, of course. But —"

"Does that seem likely?" says Murky.

"You'd be surprised," says Mr Montgomery. "Happened a good deal, apparently. That's why we asked Mr Bennett to join us. He was in Intelligence. Knows all about it."

"And you think, do you, Mr Bennett? . . ."

"I'd say it's quite possible." A strange voice: so careful that the words seem to be released one at a time, like a speak-your-weight machine. "But before we go on, do you think it might be a good idea to —"

"Oh, yes, of course," says Murky. "Mr Pointer, would you mind, since you're there?"

"Right."

The door shuts, the latch springing home with a decisive click.

Blast blast blast. He can still hear them, but they're muffled now. He cranes his head into the hall. That's better — but he can still only pick out the occasional phrase: *V2 — Regent's Park — on the train*. He creeps across the hall and leans his ear against the wood. Murky is saying:

". . . To talk to Mr Crossman about it, rather than me? He's the JP."

"Well, needless to say, we did discuss it." Mr Barron. "But Constable Pointer thought he'd be unlikely to issue a warrant just on the basis of a letter. And once a warrant has been refused, of course, it all becomes more difficult."

"Well, *I* can't issue one."

"No, but you're the landowner. You gave the man permission to live there in the first place. Constable Pointer feels he can't act without your agreement. Some people might consider that over-nice, under the circumstances, but —"

"Agreement to what?"

"The idea" — Mr Bennett, the words ratcheting out like the links on a bike chain — "is that Mr Pointer turns up out of the blue, tells him he has reason to believe, etc. etc., and tries to surprise him into making a confession. Thereby saving everyone a lot of time and trouble. Not to mention expense."

Murky sighs. "Well, yes, I can see it might spare that poor woman . . ."

"It would, no question," says Montgomery. "Otherwise we have to leave it to that Sammy fellow. See what more he's able to dig up."

"And it wouldn't do the village any harm, would it?" says Mr Barron. "If we — well, Constable Pointer — could claim the credit? Show that we can sort this kind of thing out for ourselves? It might make quite a splash in the papers."

There's a pause. "When?" says Murky. She sounds suddenly different: tired and old and cornered.

"No time like the present," says Montgomery. "When we're finished here, if you're agreeable. Before he can get wind of it."

Another pause. "All right."

"We have your approval, then?"

"Yes, if you want to put it like that. I'd rather we weren't in this situation at all. But I've only myself to blame. So —"

"Thank you."

"Right, then," says Mr Barron. "We won't take up any more of your time."

There's a clatter of chair legs. Mark bolts into the sitting room and half-closes the door, angling it just as Murky left it.

*No time like the present*. That means that if he's going to warn Hillyard, he has to do it now. He looks quickly round the room. On Murky's writing desk are a pad of paper and a pen. He tears off a sheet and scrawls:

*I'll finish reading another time*.

Then he folds it inside *Old Possum*, puts the book on her chair and ducks out through the window.

He sprints along Willetts Lane and crawls under the fence at the corner of the wood. At the edge of the trees he pauses. The door of the railway carriage is cracked open, but the warning tea towel is hanging in the window. Too bad: he'll just have to chance it.

He hurries across the clearing and up the steps, and raps on the rattly glass. There's no response.

"Aubrey!" he calls. "It's me! I've got to tell you something. It's really important."

Still nothing. He pushes the door wider and yells into the fug:

"Can I come in?"

"What the devil is it?" Hillyard is there, a bent fag resting in his fingers and a halo of tobacco smoke rising slowly from his hair.

"What's going on?"

"I've just seen them! They're coming to get you!"

He clicks his tongue. "Who is?"

"PC Pointer."

He blinks. "What do you mean, *get* me?"

"They were all at Murky's. Him, and Mr Montgomery, and Mr Barron, and Lou's dad."

"*Lou's* dad?"

Mark nods. Hillyard glances behind him, then leans so close that Mark can smell his ashtray breath.

"Go on."

"He'd had a letter."

"Who had?"

"PC Pointer. From that man — you know — Sammy. And Lou's dad said it'd trick you into making a confession."

"Wait, wait, you're going too fast for me. Lou's Dad said *what* would trick me into making a confession?"

"The letter."

"A confession of what?"

"I don't know."

Hillyard frowns, pinching his lips. "So what does it say, this letter?"

"I didn't hear all of it. But it was about someone called John Slindon."

Hillyard shuts his eyes, then opens them again. "Right," he says. "We must be about our business. You'd better come in."

He unblocks the doorway and turns towards the clutter of furniture and suitcases and boxes. "OK, Lou. You can show yourself. It's only Mark."

A blanket covering two chairs erupts into a conical tent, then falls away. Lou steps out, clutching her knapsack. Mark glowers at her. She flushes.

"You were going to see Miss Murkett," she says, shrugging. "So I came on my own for once."

"No arguing, you two," says Hillyard. "There isn't time. Mark, you get out there and keep watch. Soon as you hear or see anything, knock on the window three times, like this" — he raps the glass with his knuckles. "Then make yourself scarce, if you can. Lou, you help me get the place ready."

"What do you want me to do?"

"I'll show you. Off you go, Mark. Chop-chop."

Mark backs out, shuts the door, and stations himself on the top of the steps. From inside, he can hear Hillyard and Lou muttering, and the thump of something heavy as they shift it. He tries to concentrate on scanning the paths into the clearing and listening for the crack of twigs, but an image keeps interposing itself: Hillyard's face when he heard the name John Slindon.

What made him react like that? Fear? No, not exactly: he wasn't trembling. Anger?

There's a noise. At first he thinks it might just be a bird, but then he hears the rhythm of it: *thud thud thud*. He knocks hurriedly on the window. Hillyard emerges and stands next to him, listening. After a moment he says:

"OK! Go!"

Mark jumps down the steps. As he reaches the bottom, he hears Hillyard calling:

"Lou! Come on! Get out of there!"

A moment later she flies past him, clutching her knapsack. He pelts after her towards the woods. But as he reaches the edge of the clearing, he trips on a strand of bramble hidden in the grass and goes sprawling. He struggles up again, brushing the dirt from his grazed knees, but when he tries to stand a violent pain in his ankle makes him cry out.

"What are you up to?"

He recognizes the voice, feels the weight of a hand on his shoulder.

"Nothing."

"I saw you," says PC Pointer. "You and the girl." He grabs the lobe of Mark's ear and pinches it. "Come on! Tell me!"

"We're not up to anything! Mr Hillyard lets us play here, that's all!"

"Why were you trying to run away, then?"

Mark shrugs. PC Pointer yanks his ear. Mark sobs, then bites his lip. Something is moving at the edge of his vision. If he can just hold out another second . . .

"I haven't the slightest idea what you're doing here . . ." Yes: Aubrey, bustling to the rescue. "But I won't stand bullying. So you'd better let him go."

Pointer straightens up, releasing his ear. "I saw him and another kid acting suspiciously. I thought maybe they'd been making a nuisance of themselves."

"Not to me, Constable, I assure you."

Pointer stares at him. Hillyard stares back. Mark edges away, rubbing his sore ear.

"Will you explain yourself, please?" says Hillyard.

"I'd like a word with you, sir, if you don't mind."

"About what?"

Pointer glances at Mark. "Maybe we could go inside, sir?"

Hillyard nods. "All right."

"And as for you, sonny, you'd better get along home. I'll be speaking to your parents about this. And the girl's. See what *they've* got to say about it, shall we?"

"Look at the boy's knees," says Hillyard. "And the way he's limping. He's in no fit state to get along anywhere. The least I can do is offer him my hospitality. The run of my extensive collection of plasters, except that I haven't got any. But somewhere to sit, anyway, and a biscuit to keep his strength up . . ."

"I think it would be better if he wasn't there during our . . . discussion, sir."

"And I think it would be better if he was."

They stare at each other again. Finally, Pointer looks away.

"Very well, sir. As you wish."

Mark and Pointer follow Hillyard into the carriage. In the doorway, Pointer removes his helmet and stands looking at the chaos, wrinkling his nose. Hillyard grabs two chairs and slams them down next to the tea chest.

"Take a seat, if you want."

"Thank you, Mr Slindon, I will."

Hillyard peers round, then turns to Pointer and says:

"Are we expecting someone else?"

"No, sir, not as far as I know."

"Only, unless my ears deceived me, you said Mr *Slindon*. My name's Hillyard."

"Can you prove that, sir?"

"That's who I am. Why the devil should I have to prove it?" He looks at Mark. "Can you prove that you're called Mark Davenant?"

Mark shakes his head.

"The boy's name is not in question, sir. But we have reason to believe that you are really Mr John Slindon. Who deserted from the army in 1945."

"Have you, now? And I have reason to believe that you're a prize booby."

"I'll just make a note of that, sir, if you don't mind," says Pointer.

"Help yourself. But if you're going to write it down, let me just rephrase it. Using the correct legal term. I have reason to believe that you're a complete arse."

Mark has to cover his mouth to keep himself from giggling. Pointer takes a notebook and a stub of pencil from his pocket. As he's writing, Hillyard rummages in his smock for his pouch of Golden Virginia and rolls himself a cigarette. He lights it and blows a stream of smoke in Pointer's face.

"That's A-R-S-E," he says.

Pointer tucks the pencil behind his ear, then looks up.

"Have you by any chance got an identity card, sir? Confirming that you're Aubrey Hillyard?"

"It may have escaped your notice, Constable," says Hillyard. "But we are no longer obliged to carry identity cards."

"Even so, a lot of people have kept them."

"I am not among their number. On the day the damned things were abolished, I got drunk. Drunk and disorderly." He leans forward and whisks the helmet from Pointer's knee. "To my considerable credit, I even managed to snaffle one of these."

"You realize, sir, that's a serious offence?"

"I do, Constable," says Hillyard, holding the helmet a few inches out of Pointer's reach, daring him to try to snatch it back.

"How about a passport, sir?" says Pointer, flushing. "Or a driving licence?"

"Would you care to tell me by what authority you're asking all these questions?"

"As I say, sir, we have reason to be believe —"

"*What* reason?"

"Confidential information. That's all I can say at present."

"Well, you and your confidential information be damned. If you have grounds for believing I'm not Aubrey Hillyard, tell me what they are. Otherwise, you can go and —"

“One thing, sir, I don’t mind saying. From what we’ve been able to establish, it seems that a Mr Aubrey Hillyard was killed in a V2 raid in Regent’s Park. Just a few months before the end of the war.”

“Poor chap. I’m sorry.”

“His identity papers were never found.”

Hillyard shrugs. “Must’ve been a common enough occurrence, I’d have thought.”

“Possibly. But Aubrey Hillyard is a rather unusual name.”

“Ah, so that’s an offence now, is it? Having an unusual name?”

“No, sir.”

“And soon it won’t just be the unusual ones, will it?” He rams his cigarette in his mouth and pushes back the sleeve of his smock. “36841,” he says, making the figures on his bare arm with his finger. “That’s what you and your masters would *really* like, isn’t it? Then you’d be able to dispense with names altogether.”

Pointer’s lips move, but he says nothing.

“Well, you’re just going to have to wait,” says Hillyard. “It’s coming. But thank something or other, we’re not there yet. And in the meantime” — pointing at the door — “the way out’s over there.”

Pointer sits gawping at him. Then, very slowly, he gets up. Hillyard holds out his helmet in both hands, as if it were made of porcelain.

“Before I go,” says Pointer, taking it and nestling it against his stomach, “would it be all right if I just had a quick look round?”

“Have you got a search warrant?”

"No. But if you've —"

"All right." He gets up. "In that case, help yourself. Come on, Mark."

He pushes the door open with his foot and struts out onto the steps. Mark limps after him. They cross the clearing and stretch out in the shade of the first line of trees. Hillyard props himself on his elbow and gazes off into the distance, tapping his lip with a grass stem. The afternoon sun turns his shaggy head into a black silhouette fringed with gold. Lou's right: he's just like Aslan. He *is* Aslan, preparing to fight the forces of the White Witch.

"Damn," Hillyard says softly. "I thought we had them on the run."

"I know," says Mark. "But we can still win. We *will* still win."

Hillyard twists round, raising an eyebrow. "You think?"

"Course! You really showed him just now."

Hillyard shakes his head. "A holding action, I'm afraid. King Canute trying to keep back the tide. Pointless, probably. We'll all just be numbers in twenty years, whatever we do."

"No we won't! Don't forget your book. When people read that, they'll realize, won't they? What the Brain's doing to them?"

"Possibly." He folds the grass stem over his thick finger and snaps it in two. "If it ever sees the light of day."

"It will!" says Mark. "I promise!"

There's a long silence. From inside the railway carriage they hear the thud of furniture, the rattle and clang of saucepans. Finally, Hillyard says:

"I think PC Booby must have more or less finished by now." He pushes himself to his feet. "Needless to say, he won't have found anything, thanks to you. So I'm going to go and reclaim my kingdom."

"Shall I come with you?"

Hillyard shakes his head. "I suspect he won't be in the best of tempers. So my advice is to clear off pretty sharpish, before he has a chance to take his frustration out on you." He points at Mark's legs. "And get those war wounds attended to, or they could turn nasty."

"All right."

He hobbles into the wood and starts towards Willetts Lane. He's only gone twenty paces or so when Hillyard yells:

"Wait! I forgot something!"

He stops and turns. "What?"

Instead of shouting, Hillyard hurries after him. Even then, he glances over his shoulder before he speaks, to make sure there's no one else listening.

"A map," he says. "Could you get me a map?"

"What kind of a map?"

"A map of this area."

# CHAPTER FIFTEEN

He can't sleep. As the church clock strikes four, he turns his light on and picks up *Tom's Midnight Garden*. He's already finished it, but suddenly longs to start again, to lose himself again in Tom and Hatty's world. Another sleepless boy. Another girl. Another mystery. Only theirs, of course — eventually — has an answer.

He opens it. There, on the inside cover, he reads:

Mark Davenant
Perry Cottage
Church End
Oatley
England
Europe
The World
The Solar System
The Universe

When did he write that? Not that long ago: his birthday. But he can't even remember why he did it, or what it felt like. If he were doing it now, he'd just put: *Mark Davenant, Perry Cottage, The Universe*. The only things he feels he understands are here, in this room: the pile of books on the table, the dark sentry box of the cupboard, the heap of clothes on the chair, Barney panting at the foot of the bed. He's living in a spaceship. Beyond the safety of its four walls, there's nothing but an endless sweep of stars, cold and unknowable.

He tries to read, but it's no good: he can't concentrate. He turns off the light again, then kicks away the blankets and lies under the sheet, watching the dawn seep round the edges of the curtains. In the dissolving darkness, he picks his way through what happened yesterday. Something about it troubles him. PC Pointer had been sent packing. So why did Aubrey seem defeated afterwards, rather than elated?

A map. That much is clear, at least: Aubrey wanted a map. Mark gets out of bed and tiptoes over sleeping Barney to the door. There's no sound from the rest of the house. Pinching his baggy pyjamas to his waist, he creeps down to the study. He shuts himself in, then switches on the light. He scans the shelf of guides and photography books above Dad's desk. That's where it ought to be. The only question is: did Dad put it back?

Yes, thank goodness: it's there. Mark knows it by the tear in the spine even before he sees the title: *Cobwell and Surrounding Area*. He slips it inside his pyjama top and sneaks back into the hall.

Halfway up the stairs, he hears noises from his parents' room: the squeak of a bed spring followed by a muffled thud, like a slipper dropped on the carpet. He hurries into his own room and scrambles back into bed. A moment later, someone pads into the bathroom and locks the door.

Dad, probably, getting ready for another early-morning expedition. Mark lies there rigid, listening to the slow sequence of noises: flush, splash, click, footsteps — not loud, but not stealthy, either. He holds his breath. *Please please please, don't let him go looking for the map* . . .

It's OK: he hears the sound of the back-door latch — and then, a few seconds later, the gate. Mark pushes the map under his pillow, then turns over, drawing up his knees. He finally has a plan. He rehearses it in his head: go to the hideout — see if there's a message from Lou — then take Hillyard the map, and ask him to explain about yesterday. As — in his imagination — he reaches Twenty Acre Wood, the trees start to grow thicker and thicker, rolling towards him like a dark wave, reducing everything to the shrinking pinprick of a television screen . . .

It's almost eight when he wakes. He pulls on his clothes, doesn't bother to wash or comb his hair and rushes downstairs. The table's laid for breakfast. Mum's sitting reading a letter, but there's no sign of Dad at all. He went out hours ago. Surely he must be back by now?

"Hullo, Mum."

She looks up, flushed, pressing the paper flat against her chest. "Hullo, poppet."

"Where's Dad? I thought you'd have started."

"Oh, he just went into the darkroom. He finished a film this morning and wanted to see what he'd got on it. Are you hungry?"

"Not specially. I think I'm just going to go out, if it's OK."

"All right."

He goes back into his bedroom, puts the map in his knapsack, then hides it under his notebook, camera and telescope. As he emerges on to the landing, Dad appears from the darkroom, wiping his hands on a scrap of towel.

"Oh, there you are, old thing. Come here a minute. Something I want to show you."

Mark follows him in, and Dad shuts the door. The only light comes from the enlarger. The white square at its foot is covered by a murky negative image, so big that it spills over the sides onto the work surface.

"Look at this. See anything?"

Mark squints, trying to decipher it. The dark area at the top is sky, and the dappled billows of light underneath are obviously trees. Twenty Acre Wood again, presumably. But what's the subject? He searches for a fox or a deer shape in the foliage. Nothing: not so much as the blob of a pigeon or the white cutout of a crow.

"What?" he says.

"There."

Dad points to the bottom right-hand corner. At first Mark can't see anything distinctive at all: just a jumble of pale leaves and branches streaked with dark patches of sunshine. Then he notices that one of the patches has a sharp angle in it, like an elbow. He scans down, and finds a greyish foot and the lower part of a trousered leg. Then up, to where the head should be. Yes, he's got it now: the rim of a hat, and under it the line of the forehead, and a long parrot-like nose.

"The Lesser Crested Snooper," says Dad. "What on earth's he doing there? And why's he gone to so much trouble to disguise himself? Who does he think's going to see him, at six o'clock in the morning?"

He glances at Mark. Mark tries to laugh, but can't.

"Well, I think it's pretty comical," says Dad. "I set out to look for badgers. And I end up with this chap instead, skulking in the bushes, perfectly camouflaged. I'm going to do a print. To show Mummy. You want to stay and help me?"

Mark shakes his head. "I've got something to do."

Without waiting for a reply he slips out, shuts the door behind him, and runs downstairs. Mum's still sitting at the table.

"I'll be back later," he shouts, and hurries outside before she has a chance to stop him.

It takes him fifteen minutes to reach the edge of the clearing. The whole place feels deserted. The trestle table's gone — and on the door of the railway carriage, covering most of the window, is a notice. He looks round: no, he's quite alone. He tiptoes across the grass and up the steps to read it:

Private Property.

No Trespassing.

Keep out.

Underneath the handle, someone's fixed a black hasp and staple, and secured it with a padlock.

*There'll be a knock on the door at dawn. And no more Aubrey Hillyard*. Aubrey was right, then. He could be miles away by now — locked up in a police station, or in some top-secret underground bunker, where the powers that be take people for questioning. And of course, they won't just have arrested him: they'll have got his book as well. The war is over. After all that he and Hillyard and Lou have been through together, the Brain has finally beaten them.

He retreats into the trees and starts back towards the village. He has no plan, no thought — just an unbearable tender fluttering on his arms and legs, which he knows will only be eased if he can see Lou. He stays in the wood as long as he can, pausing every few seconds to listen, in case someone is still keeping watch. As he reaches the corner, he hears voices and stops to peer into the lane. Two figures are coming slowly towards him, slashing at the high grass along the verge. He squidges up his eyes to see them more clearly. Not the powers that be: it's Stan Green and Ernie, laughing and play-fighting. He shrinks back behind a tree, waiting for them to pass. They're obviously excited about something, though the regular *thwack* of their sticks makes it impossible to hear what they're saying. When they're almost alongside him, one of them slices the heads off a clump of cow parsley, whipping a shower of tiny white flowers into the air. Then their footsteps start to grow fainter, and he slips out into the lane and makes a dash for the village.

When he reaches Hillfield he stops, and — leaning against the gatepost — unhitches his bag, takes out his notebook and writes:

*They've got him. We need to make a plan. Meet me at the hideout at eleven.*

Then he tears out the sheet, folds it into a small square, and starts up the High Street.

The shop's empty. He walks in, wincing at the loudness of the bell. Lou's mother emerges from the back.

"Hullo." He holds out the message. "Could you give Lou this for me, please?"

"Lou's not —" She stops and takes the square of paper. "Just hang on a second."

She disappears back into the room behind the counter. There's a flurry of whispered talk. Lou's dad comes out, holding the note.

"You're Mark Davenant, aren't you?"

"Yes, sir."

"I've just been talking to your father. On the phone." He readjusts his glasses on the bridge of his nose. "Did he send you here?"

"No. I —"

"Hm," says Mr Bennett. "And you'd like us to give this" — waving the note — "to Lou, would you?"

"Yes, please."

"Lou's gone away," Mr Bennett says.

"Where?"

"And when she comes back, we've told her she's not to have anything more to do with you. So —"

"That's not fair!"

"So" — holding the note out — "you'd better have this back, hadn't you?"

Mark hesitates. After a moment, Mr Bennett withdraws his hand and — still watching him — starts to unfold the paper.

"Stop! It's private!"

Mr Bennett raises his glasses with his finger and squints at the note.

"'They've got him.'" He reads on for a moment, then glances up at Mark. "Who do you mean? John Slindon?"

"His name's Hillyard."

"It isn't. And you know it isn't." He lifts his hand, waving the note. "The proof is here. *They've got him*. What does that mean? *How* have they got him? Hm?"

Mark bites his lip.

"By finding evidence that he's a liar. That he isn't who he said he was. That's what any reasonable person is going to assume, isn't it?"

"That's not what I meant," blurts Mark. "I meant they'd *taken* him."

"*Taken* him? Who has?" When Mark doesn't answer, he goes on: "Has Lou ever told you what I did in the war?"

"No."

"I was in Intelligence. You know what that means?"

"Not really."

"It means I interrogated people. Prisoners. Enemy agents. Hundreds of them. All trying to save their skins by saying *That isn't what I meant*. After a while, you develop a feel for it. You can tell when someone's lying."

"I'm *not* lying."

Mr Bennett's thin lips bend, like an opened-out paper clip. It's the first time Mark has ever seen him smile.

"How old are you?" he says.

"Ten."

Mr Bennett nods. "Accessory to a crime. Conspiring to pervert the course of justice. I'll be interested to see if PC Pointer agrees with me, but my view is that there isn't a court in the land that wouldn't convict" — flourishing the note again — "on the strength of this. They can't send you to prison, of course. But there's always Approved School."

Mark lunges forward, snatches the note and runs out of the shop. By the time he hears the ping of the shop doorbell behind him, he's already past the post office.

He can't go home — not with angry Dad waiting for him and Mr Bennett in furious pursuit. So at the top of the High Street he turns right, onto the Burdon Road. When he's opposite the old Wool Pack, he stops and looks back. Mr Bennett hasn't reached the corner yet. He scrambles over the stile onto the footpath, then slithers into the ditch where he met Lou a few weeks ago, and crawls under the canopy of stinging nettles. He'll be safe there, at least for a bit. Long enough to decide what to do.

Run away: that's his first idea. Take to the road, like Hugh in *Brother Dusty-Feet*, and hope to fall in with a band of strolling actors. Maybe one day they'd be travelling past a sinister tower with barred windows, and he'd hear a voice he recognized calling out to him, and he'd realize that's where they were holding Hillyard, and find a way to rescue him . . . But no: there aren't any bands of strolling actors these days. And he hasn't got any money, apart from the ten-and-sixpenny postal order. And the only person he can think of who might take him in is Murky — and she seems to be on *their* side now.

He'll just have to go back and face the music. He tears the paper into tiny scraps and buries them under a root a few feet away.

He trudges homeward, watching the junction by the war memorial, braced for a quick *volte-face* if anyone appears.

Dad's been cutting the lawn. Mark smells it as he turns in at the gate. When he opens the back door, he finds him sitting at the table. His short-sleeved shirt is dark with sweat, and he's dabbing his forehead with a handkerchief.

"Hullo, Dad."

Dad nods. "Where have you been?"

"Just out."

Dad stares at him, then nods again.

"I was about to wash the car. Do you want to give me a hand?"

It's so unexpected, so out of place, that Mark feels he must have taken a wrong turning somewhere, and sidestepped into a dream.

"I can do it by myself if you want," says Mark.

"No, let's do it together. You pop out and get the things."

"OK." As he opens the shed and walks in, he blinkers his eyes with his hands. He doesn't want to see Peveril: it's become too bound up with Hillyard. He gropes around in the dark until he finds the two buckets, one nested inside the other. He checks that the chamois leather is still draped over the rim, then carries them back inside. Dad clanks them into the sink and starts filling them, one at a time.

"Wash or polish?" he says.

"I don't mind."

"No, you choose."

"All right, then. Polish."

Lugging a bucket apiece, they hobble down to the road. Dad unstraps his watch, slips it into his pocket, and plunges both hands deep into the water. Mark watches as he pulls out the sponge, like a cormorant grabbing a fish, and starts attacking the dusty haze on the car roof. There's something odd about him — as if Mark is looking at him, simultaneously, with his own eye and a stranger's. The scar on his bare arm, the hint of sunburn on the neck, the frown of concentration are all familiar. But his lightness on his feet, and the lithe way he moves, seem to belong to someone entirely different: a dashing man of action, like Lawrence of Arabia. Mark shuts his eyes for a moment, wondering if Dad will still be the same when he opens them again. He is. *That's him*. Mark shakes his head in wonder. *That's my dad*.

"Come on," says Dad. "Before it gets dry."

Mark wrings out the leather, and starts following behind, reducing the smears of water to tiny pearls.

"You ought to be able to see yourself in it," says Dad.

"I can. Look."

"So," says Dad. "Tell me about the girl from the shop."

"We didn't do anything bad, Dad. Honestly."

"What exactly *did* you do?"

"What did Mr Bennett say?"

Dad shakes his head. "I want to hear it from you. Hm?"

"I don't know, Dad."

"Of course you know. You just don't want to tell me. Because you're worried what I might think."

Mark says nothing.

"Mummies and Daddies? You're the husband and she's your wife?"

Mark shakes his head. After a moment, Dad plunges the sponge into the bucket, retrieves it and sets to work on the windscreen.

"It's nothing to be ashamed of, old thing," he says. "You're going to be a man one day. She's going to be a woman. Of course you're both curious. That's only natural."

"It wasn't that, Dad. Honestly!"

"Well, all I'm saying is, you shouldn't feel bad about it if it was. And nor should she. Whatever her parents say."

"It was that man living in the woods. We thought it was unfair. The way everyone picked on him."

"Ah, yes, the man in the woods. Mr Bennett told me about him. An affront to all decent, right-thinking citizens. They're a couple of Mrs Grundys, the Bennetts. Typical tradespeople. Narrow-minded. Stuffy. They ought to be living in the *Eighteen* Fifties."

"Well, they don't need to worry about the man in the woods any more."

Dad glances at him.

"He's gone," says Mark. "I was there this morning. The carriage is all shut up."

"Is it?" He hesitates a second. "Ah" — raising a finger — "the snooper. The chap in the picture. That's probably what he was doing. Sneaking up on the poor man. Ferreting him out. He looked a bit like a ferret, didn't he?"

"Yes."

Dad nods, then turns and starts trying to dislodge a splattered insect. After a few seconds, he stops again abruptly, shaking his head.

"What is it, Dad?"

"They're just the sort of people who voted for Hitler. Get rid of the gypsies. Get rid of the Jews. Anyone who doesn't belong." He pauses. "Do you know what he said?"

"Who?"

"The girl's father. He said you were a delinquent. And that I should tell you, if you didn't behave, we'd wash our hands of you."

"And what did you say?"

Dad shakes his head again. "What do you think? I told him . . ." He takes a deep breath. "I told him I wasn't going to be lectured to by him. And that he should mind his own bloody business."

"Thanks, Dad."

Dad nods and touches his shoulder. "So let's get this done, shall we?"

"All right."

"I want it to be the cleanest car in the village."

# CHAPTER SIXTEEN

Once, when he was being Robin Hood, he fell out of a tree and bashed his knee. For a moment he was just shocked. Then the pain came, fiercer and fiercer. In the midst of it, only one thought penetrated his mind: *I can't bear it*.

This is like that. Not just Hillyard, but Lou too. It's not simply that she's gone — he could cope with that for a few weeks; no, it's that her parents have told her she can't be friends with him any more when she gets back. The future stretches away to the horizon, blank as a moonscape. There's no one he can talk to about what's happened, no one to help him decide what to do next. He'll be locked away inside an invisible cell.

After lunch, he goes out with Barney. The village is dead. That's what it feels like: not just empty, but senseless, as if someone's snipped the whole network of nerves connecting church and pub, fields and cottages. Perhaps it was only Hillyard's presence that had been keeping the place alive. And now they've got him, and the Brain has taken over . . .

At Willetts Lane, he leans down and unsnaps the lead. Barney runs ahead, then swerves into Twenty Acre.

"Barn!" he yells. "Come here, boy!"

As Mark reaches the end of the Lane and turns towards the hideout, Barney emerges from the trees and bounds past him up the hill. Mark jog-trots after him, and — at the top — scrambles up the chalk pit. He whistles Barney, then stands for a few seconds in front of the entrance, wiping the sweat from his forehead.

"Gallion!"

It's pointless, of course. He crawls into the hideout, flips over onto his back and gazes up at the black lattice of branches pricked with blue. The light is so dazzling that it makes his eyes ache. He shields them with his arm and lies there in the darkness, listening to Barney snuffling about in the wheat. After a few minutes, the noise outside stops, and he's aware of Barney coming in and flopping down next to him. Sleep nibbles the edge of his consciousness. He's simultaneously by himself and with Lou. She's gone away and she's lying beside him, saying his name in his ear. He's in the hideout, and he's somewhere else . . .

It's Barney that wakes him. Mark can feel him stiffening, pressing himself against his thigh.

"What is it, boy?"

Barney's ears are pricked, and a low growl vibrates in his throat. Holding his collar with one hand, Mark manoeuvres himself to the entrance and peers out.

"Are you the Mackeson type?" A man, no more than three feet away. He's in silhouette, so for a moment Mark can't tell who he is. Then he squats down, and the sun catches the side of his face.

"Nice place you've got here," he says.

Mark blinks. Darkness still hovers at the edge of his vision.

"Not talking to me?" says Sammy. "I was still hoping we could be friends." He catches Mark's eye and smiles. "I know we got off to a bad start. My fault, probably. How about we shake and make up? Would that help?"

He holds his hand out. Mark ignores it.

Sammy nods, then rocks back, so that his bum hits the ground with a thud. He crosses his ankles, and bends over to pinch one of his narrow shoes. "Phew. You led me quite a dance there. I'm not used to all this cross-country stuff. Haven't done it for years. Not since training in the war. What's the dog's name?"

"Barney."

"Hullo, Barney. Good boy."

Barney's ears drop, and his tail softly thuds the earth.

"There we go. Pals now, eh?" Gingerly, he starts scratching Barney's head. Barney lays his muzzle on his paws.

"Look," says Sammy, sitting up again. "All right, I've put my foot in it, and you don't want anything to do with me. Fair enough. I understand. I wasn't as tactful as I might have been, was I?" He taps his knuckles. "But still, I've a feeling you've have got the wrong end of the stick about me. Who exactly do you think I am?"

Mark shrugs. "You work for the Brain," he says.

Sammy chuckles. "The *what*?"

"The Brain. The powers that be."

Sammy raises his eyebrows, pulls a comical face. "Well, that's one way of putting it, I suppose. The powers that have a healthy bank balance, more like. I'm a private detective. You know what that is?"

Mark nods.

"People hire me to find things out. Mostly what their wives are up to. Or their husbands. You ask any chap in my line of business and he'll tell you the same. You may get a bit of jam from missing kids and whatnot, but divorce is your bread and butter. So when Mrs Hillyard rang me up to say *Mr* Hillyard had disappeared, I naturally assumed . . . you get my drift?"

"Yes."

"Only turned out it was bit more complicated than that. As I expect you very well know."

He looks quizzically at Mark. Mark says nothing.

"All right." He settles himself comfortably, wrapping his arms round his knees. "Let me tell you a story. Once upon a time there was a chap called Aubrey Hillyard. Pleasant, mild-mannered sort of a bloke, by all accounts. Tried for the army at the start of the war, but they wouldn't have him. Too short-sighted. So he ended up being a schoolmaster. Cushy number, you'd have thought. Nice quiet life, while the rest of us are off fighting the Jerries. Except, as luck would have it, his house gets hit by a V2." He sniffs. "And evi*dent*ly, it's a bit of a mess. When the firemen get to him they find the head over here, and the rest of him over there. His wallet's in his pocket, but there's nothing in it except a few receipts. No Identity Card, no ration book. The only way they can identify him is from what's left of his teeth, poor old chap." He exhales noisily. "Anyway, this is where it gets interesting. Because a year or two later, out of the blue, another man turns up, saying *he's* Aubrey Hillyard. With me so far, are you?"

Mark nods.

"Right. So now we need to introduce another character. John Slindon. This chap *was* a soldier. D-Day, Battle of Normandy, over the Rhine, VE Day. Sees the whole thing through to the end — then suddenly, *boom*, disappears, just like that." He studies Mark's face. "You're thinking *he* must have been killed, too, in Germany. But he wasn't. He'd just come back on leave. Got off the boat, and that was that. Didn't go home. Failed to report back for duty. Never seen again." He pauses. "It happened more than you'd think. Me, I couldn't wait to get back to civvy street. But there were blokes who were perfectly all right in the war, but couldn't stick going home at any price. The missus, the kids, the job. The same faces on the train every morning."

From another time, from the ash-scented dimness of the sitting room at Hillfield, Mark hears Murky saying, *It was too much for him. He just couldn't cope with rents, and taxes, and hire purchase agreements*.

"Slindon didn't have kids. But he did have a missus. Imagine what she must have gone through. Not knowing what had happened to him. Just sitting there, waiting and waiting and waiting. How long's she going to give it, do you think? Before she finally gives up and accepts he's never coming back? A year? Two years? Three?"

A solid wall suddenly gives. Mark can feel it, like a rearrangement of his internal organs. He frantically tries to repair the damage — *it's a mistake; Aubrey would never behave like that* — but it's as useless as daubing paint over a crack.

"The law says seven," says Sammy. "After that, he's presumed dead, and she's free to re-marry, if she wants to. But she never did. Didn't have the heart for it, I suppose." He sighs, as if the grief is his. "Only then — here's the big moment — a few months ago, her brother sees a man on the train he's ninety-nine per cent certain is Slindon. He's a good bit older now, of course, and wearing a beard; but he's the right build, and the eyes are the same. But he's the other side of a packed carriage, so the brother can't say anything. When they get to Marylebone, the fellow sets off like a bat out of hell and disappears in the crowd. So the brother goes to the Transport Police and says he thinks he's just seen a deserter. They make a note of it, but tell him that, unless they know the name he goes by now or where he lives, there's nothing more they can do."

"Are you the brother?" says Mark.

He's never seen Sammy laugh before — not like this, mouth wide, showing a livery tongue and a chaos of yellow teeth.

"How do you know, then? That that's what he did?"

"Oh, I only found out later. I'd been hired by someone called Mrs Hillyard, remember? Her husband had walked out on her, and she wanted me to find out why. That day, apparently, he'd gone to London to meet a literary agent. He was fine when he left in the morning, she said. But when he came back in the evening, he was a changed man. Told her he was leaving, wouldn't say where, threw a few things in a suitcase, and off he went. So I said, must be something to do with this literary agent, then. What's his name? And she said, it's a woman. A Miss Saunders. And of course, I thought, *ba-boom*."

He searches Mark's face for a reaction. Mark bites his lip.

"But turns out I was wrong," Sammy goes on, his voice flatter, as if he'd been depending on Mark's response to give him energy. "Miss Saunders had only met him for the first time that day. The minute he walked in, though, she could see he'd got the wind up about something. Kept looking out of the window, as if he reckoned he was being followed. And seemed less interested in getting her to take him on than in finding somewhere to hide. Did she know some out of the way place where he'd be left in peace to get on with his book? If she did, would she *please* use her good offices with the owner? Ring any bells?"

Mark stares at his feet.

"So I thought, all right, something else must have happened that day, mustn't it? Maybe when he was on the train. So I made enquiries at the station. And when they told me someone had reported seeing a deserter, of course, I immediately put two and two together." There's a long pause. "It's a serious offence, desertion. And so is being a bigamist. You know what that is?"

Mark nods.

"So you'll understand why it's so important we get hold of the fellow. Which is why I wanted a word with you. Where is he?"

"I don't know." Mark can't seem to fill his lungs, so the words trickle out in a half-whisper. "I thought you'd taken him."

"Me!"

"Or the police."

"The police aren't that clever." He pauses. "Come on. You and he are pals, aren't you? He must have said something about where he was going."

"He didn't!"

Sammy half-closes his eyes and twitches his nose. "The question is, do I believe you?"

"It's the truth. Honestly. Promise."

He nibbles his lip. "All right. All right. But if it turns out you're fibbing, you'll be in it up to here." He pushes himself to his feet. "And what about the girl?"

"She's gone too."

Sammy's eyes widen.

"Not with him," adds Mark. "Her parents sent her away."

Sammy nods. He reaches inside his linen jacket, takes out a notebook and a pen. "Here," he says, scribbling. "This is my number. You hear anything, you ring that, all right? Reverse charges. You lead me to him — well, let's just say, you won't find us ungrateful. There'll be a reward. More than enough to buy you a whole new train set."

He tears off a sheet. Mark takes it, saying nothing. Sammy leans down and touches Barney's head, then quickly withdraws his hand.

"Bye, Barney. Friends now, right?"

He turns and starts walking slowly away. As he reaches the gap in the hedge, he stops and looks back over his shoulder.

"Don't forget," he calls.

Then he continues onto the track and disappears behind a screen of bramble.

*Bigamist*. When Mark gets home, he waits till he hears Dad going up to the bathroom, then slips into the study and pulls out the dictionary. He looks up the word: *A man or woman living in bigamy*. He drops his eye to the next entry. *Bigamy. The crime of having two wives or husbands at once*.

Two wives: Mrs Hillyard and Mrs Slindon. And one husband.

# CHAPTER SEVENTEEN

Where are we now? The second half of August, probably. Summer's starting to fade. The days are still hot, but the evenings are getting shorter, mornings cooler and dewier. And school is beginning to assume a solid form — the lines of tables in the class room, the chemical smell of the lavs and the sickly, meaty reek of glue bubbling on the black stove — which casts a darkening shadow over the last weeks of the holidays. Time is running out. And, maddeningly, Mark doesn't know how to use what's left. There's nothing he can do to help Hillyard: he's not even sure he *wants* to help Hillyard after what Sammy told him. He needs to recalibrate his compass, recover his sense of direction — but that's something he could only do by talking to Lou. He starts writing a letter — *Dear Lou, Lots of things have been happening. Aubrey's gone and that Sammy chap* — then realizes that he's no idea where she is, and that he'll only make her parents angrier if he asks them.

He reads, he takes Barney for walks — though going to Willetts Lane and the chalk pit is like chafing the scab off a wound now, so he heads in the other direction, up towards out-of-the-way Cockenhoe, which has never recovered from the Black Death and consists of no more than a church, a farm and one row of starved-looking cottages. He's always found the wood above it a bit eerie, but now he likes the feeling it gives him of mingling with the dead. Their world at least seems understandable. If he turned a corner and saw one of them standing there — belted tunic, turned-up pointy shoes, carrying a scythe or a bow — he thinks he'd know how to talk to him.

One morning, as he's sitting by himself after breakfast, staring at his empty cereal bowl, Mum comes in from the hall, jingling the car keys.

"Hullo, mopey," she says. "You still here? At a bit of a loose end, are you?"

He shrugs.

"It's such a shame they've sent your friend away," she says. "It would have been nice if you could have played with her. Still . . ." She moves towards the door, lifts the latch, looks back. "How's Peveril these days?"

He shrugs again.

"Why don't you give Patty and Paul an adventure?"

"Maybe." But he knows he won't. Peveril on the Swift feels almost as unbearable this morning as Twenty Acre Wood. Perhaps, though — the thought is flashed into his head by the glint of the ignition key — there might be a chance, if he went with Mum, to raise the subject of Hillyard with her. "Where are you going?"

"Just into town. I need to get a few things for the garden."

"You want me to come along and help?"

She shakes her head. "I'd love you to, sweetie. But there won't be room, I'm afraid. There'll be canes. Bags of compost." She hunches her shoulders, presses her hands to her sides. "I'm going to be driving like this as it is."

"All right."

She leans down and touches his chin. "Oh, do try to cheer up. Dad's in the study, so don't disturb him, will you?"

He shakes his head.

"But otherwise, you've got the place to yourself. Use your imagination. There must be *something* fun you could do."

If he can't speak to Lou, he thinks, after Mum's gone, that only leaves Murky. He'd ruled her out before because he wasn't sure which side she was on. But now he's no longer certain which side *he's* on. And at least she'd be able to tell him about Identity Cards and ration books.

He gets up and carries his bowl into the kitchen. As he's rinsing it, Barney nudges the back of his thigh.

"No, boy, you stay here. Stay! Stay!"

Barney cringes. Mark grabs his collar and drags him towards the hall, then stops. The study door is half open, and through it he can hear the clatter of the typewriter. If he shuts him in the hall, he'll pester Dad. And if he leaves him here, he'll whine and scrabble till Dad has to go and let him out.

"All right. Come on, then."

He doesn't have to worry about people seeing him any more. But still, he doesn't want to have to venture past the shop and risk feeling the blast of the Bennetts' disapproval. So he goes the other way, across the Plaistow, where Barney can run free, and then along a narrow path behind the council houses. As he comes out at the far end, by the bottom of the High Street, he sees Ernie's mother Winnie walking up the other side of the road, rumpling a dirty apron between her hands. She moves with an odd jitteriness, as if — rather than a warm late summer's day — it's the depth of winter and she can't wait to get back to her own fireside. When she catches sight of him, she stops, points in his direction, mumbles something he can't hear, then hurries on again before he has time to cross and ask her to repeat it.

"You wait here, boy." He ties Barney to the gatepost and starts along the drive. He can see cats in the laundry yard, but the house itself has a strangely sealed-up look, like an unopened parcel. The windows are all closed — even the one in Murky's bedroom — and show nothing but a mucusy grey-green reflection. He advances over the threadbare gravel, frightened of making a noise. When he rings the doorbell, the far-off tinkle seems too loud.

There's no reply. He tries again. This time, he thinks he can tell from the lonely quality of the sound that the house is empty. He turns the handle and pushes. The door is locked.

He walks round to the back. She isn't sitting at the table where he saw her with Miss Saunders, or fighting the overgrown shrubs with her trug and secateurs. She's obviously shut the place up and gone into town.

He's surprised: he can't really visualize her anywhere but here.

He slowly retraces his steps, kicking sulkily at the tussocks in the Plaistow, giving Barney plenty of time to race from one side of the field to the other, wearing himself out.

As they come out onto Church End, Mark can see that the car still isn't back. He lets himself in, clutching Barney, and peers into the hall. The study door is still ajar, but the sound of the typewriter's stopped, and he can see Dad standing in front of the window, fag in hand, gazing out into the garden. He backs away, and — leaving Barney spreadeagled on the kitchen floor — creeps outside again. He still doesn't really want to play with Peveril on the Swift. But the shed, he knows, is the one place where Dad won't disturb him.

It's the stink that hits him first: a rich sweet rottenness, like blue cheese, tinged with the faint bonfire smell of smoke. Maybe there's a dead rat under the pile of clutter? The thought of finding it makes him feel sick, but — if that *is* the cause of the pong — he knows the longer he leaves it the worse it will get. He'll just have to heave the thing out and then mop over the floor. He switches on the light, looking for the two car-washing buckets. They've gone, for some reason. He advances on the first row of boxes. There's something different about them too. It takes him a moment to identify it: his tent is missing. Someone must have sneaked in and stolen it, along with the buckets. Who would do something like that? The only people he can think of are Stan and Ernie. Maybe, after all, they saw him hiding in the trees the other day, and thought he was spying on them, and decided to punish him.

*Peveril on the Swift*. He turns quickly, his neck cold with sweat. Everything's in one piece, as far as he can see — the buildings, the vehicles in the High Street, the 4-6-0 and its three coaches standing in the station. But still there's something amiss. He leans closer. Yes, it's the figures. All the people have been gathered up and crowded together on the platform. Mr Makepeace stands slightly apart from the rest, with the dog from Abbey Farm crouched next to him. He's gesturing towards the train, like a shepherd herding sheep. It's as if the whole town has decided — or been *ordered* — to leave at the same time . . .

Barney is barking. Mark opens the door and sees Mum coming up the path. Her hair's wilder than usual, her face blotchy from the heat of the car. She's carrying nothing but her handbag.

"Hullo, poppet."

"Where's all the stuff?"

She smiles, rolls her eyes. "Do you know, they didn't have it, after all that? Such a nuisance. But a case of great minds thinking alike, probably. Everybody else wanting canes and compost for *their* gardens." She nods at the shed. "Anyway, you found something to do, I see. How's Peveril on the Swift?"

He shakes his head. "Someone's been messing around with it."

She frowns. "With *Peveril*?"

"Yes."

"Who?"

"I don't know. But somebody's been in there. There's a horrible smell, for one thing."

He leads her inside. She wrinkles her nose.

"Yes, it's not very nice, is it?"

"And they've taken my tent. Look."

She surveys the pile. "Oh, dear, yes, so they have."

"And the buckets. And" — pointing at Peveril — "look at this."

She runs her eye over it. "It seems all right to me. What's the matter with it?"

With his finger, he draws a lasso round the figures on the platform. "The people. They're not all meant to be squashed together like that. Someone's moved them."

She nods. "Well, yes, I agree, that is a bit funny. But you can put them all back where they were, can't you?"

"Mum, it's my layout! No one else is meant to touch it!"

"I know, sweetie. It's annoying. But it's not the end of the world, is it?"

She's nibbling her lip, and pulling nervously at her hair.

"Did *you* do it?" he says.

"*Me*?" She flushes, shaking her head. "No, of course not! I wouldn't dream of it!"

"Well, somebody must have. I'll bet it was Stan Green. Or Ernie."

She sighs, raises her eyebrows. "Well, yes, I wouldn't put it past them."

"Should we tell the police?"

"Oh, I don't think we need to do that. It was only an old tent, wasn't it?" She laughs. "You can't really count the nasty smell. Or putting everyone in Peveril on the platform."

"But they might come back."

"They're not likely to, are they? I mean, if there was anything else they wanted, they'd have taken it, wouldn't they?"

"Well, can we at least put a lock on the door, just in case?"

She hesitates. "Well, maybe," she says, with a sigh. "But not yet. My guess is it won't happen again. If it does, well, let's see then."

"But it wouldn't cost much, would it?"

She shakes her head. "It's not that. I'm just worried about Dad. You know he's a — well, that he imagines everyone in the village is against us. So if we tell him we've had a break-in, he won't see it as just one of those things that happen sometimes. He'll think it's a conspiracy. That they're trying to drive us out."

"Like Aubrey Hillyard."

She looks surprised. "Yes, I suppose. A bit like that. So let's just leave it for the moment, shall we? I promise you, if they *do* come back and take an engine or what have you, I'll buy you another one. Only I'm pretty sure they won't. And Dad needn't know anything about it at all." She smiles, trying to coax a response from him. "Is that a deal?"

He meets her gaze, scowling, for a moment, then looks away. "OK."

She nods and moves towards the door, then stops again.

"By the way, do you happen to know what's happened to the map?"

He flushes. "What map?"

"The local one. I can't seem to find it. I wondered if you'd borrowed it for some reason?" She hesitates. When he doesn't answer, she goes on, "I'm not angry about it. I'd just like it back, please. OK?"

He can't look at her. Staring at the floor, he mumbles, "OK."

"Thank you, sweetie."

She's right: there's no repeat of the break-in. Over the next few days, the smell fades, and Mark starts to reassert his dominion over Peveril on the Swift. After a week or so, he's able to go into the shed without steeling himself for an unpleasant discovery. Soon, it's almost regained its old place in his life, as the one dependable refuge in an ever-shifting landscape.

And the landscape *is* becoming more puzzling by the day. Dad's shut in the study, working on something. Nothing strange about that, but more and more there seems to be no rhyme or reason to Mum's movements. Some days, she's always exactly where he'd expect to find her: in the garden or in the kitchen, or sitting at the table, going through bills; other times, she's nowhere to be seen. One lunchtime, he and Dad converge at the same moment, both assuming that they'd somehow missed her calling them to come and eat. The table's bare; the kitchen deserted. Five minutes later they hear the car, and Mum comes in hot and flustered, twisting a strand of hair.

"Sorry," she says. "You must both be starving. I got caught at the shop by Murky. She's a dear old thing, but she does talk a lot sometimes." She stares round, as if she's not sure where she is, then nods. "Right: let's see what I can rustle up."

For a few days, things return to normal. But then, one morning after breakfast, Mark's about to go up to his room when she calls from the kitchen.

"Come in here a second."

From the study they can hear the sound of the typewriter: a faint *clack clack clack*, as if Dad's crossing out something he wrote yesterday.

"Why?" says Mark.

"I've a favour to ask."

He slouches in and stands next to her.

"Elevenses," she says.

He glances at the clock: 8.45.

"Yes, I know," she says. "But I have to go out. And I probably won't be back in time. So I want *you* to do it this morning, all right?"

"Where are you going?"

"Oh, just into town. I'll be home for lunch. Thank you, poppet. You're an angel."

After she's gone, he fills the kettle and lays the tray. Then, Barney in tow, he creeps past the closed door of the study and up to his room, where he curls up on the bed and retreats into the world of *Under the Hollies*. But it's hard to stay there this morning. Normally, when he's reading, the church clock takes him by surprise, but now he finds himself constantly listening for it, and hearing — hidden beneath its bland announcement of the time — other, secret, meanings: *If I've finished this page before it strikes, Lou and I will be friends again, and everything will be all right*. And sometimes, too, he's hit by an overwhelming need to get up and look out of the window. But every time he goes, he just sees the usual front garden and a grey square of road, and — beyond it — the Robinsons' weed-clogged crazy paving.

*Ting ting ting*. Quarter to eleven. He rolls off the bed, tiptoes down to the kitchen and makes the tea. Then he carries the tray out into the hall, and — balancing it on one knee — knocks on the study door.

"Dad?"

"Yes?"

Dad's sitting at the desk, staring at a half-covered sheet of paper in the typewriter. As Mark goes in, he looks up, the hardness melting from his face.

"Oh, hullo, old thing." He nods at the table. "Just stick it there, will you?"

"All right." He tries to be careful, but can't stop the cup and saucer jingling as he sets the tray down.

"Thank you," says Dad. "Are you going to join me?"

Mark shakes his head, puzzled. "I don't drink tea."

"Well, get something else, then. Something you'd like."

Mark goes to the kitchen. What he'd *really* like is some orange drink, but Mum keeps that for treats, so he runs a glass of water. When he returns, Dad's settled himself in the arm chair. He nods at the other side of the table.

"Sit down. Is that all you're having? Very abstemious."

Mark perches on the Windsor chair. Dad leans forwards, fills his cup, dribbles in a few spots of milk. He picks up a biscuit, then slides the plate towards Mark.

"You'll have one of these, at least, won't you?"

Mark takes one.

Dad sips his tea, closes his eyes. "Aaaaaah."

"Is it OK?"

"Perfect. Best cup of tea I've had in ages." He opens his eyes again and smiles. "Do you know what I've been doing?"

Mark shakes his head.

"Mummy hasn't said anything to you?"

"No."

Dad nods. "I've been writing letters to people. About a plan I've got." He pauses, studies Mark's face. "This has been a bit of a funny summer, hasn't it, what with one thing and another?"

"It's been all right."

"Has it? Well, that's good." He snaps his digestive in two. "But you've had a few adventures, haven't you, poor old chap? First, the Akers girl. Then that fellow living in the wood. And, to top it all, *Sturmscharführer* what's-his-name at the shop.

Mark laughs. "Bennett."

"*Sturmscharführer* Bennett. *So ist's recht*." He nibbles at a corner of biscuit, sprinkling crumbs.

"Anyway, I want *next* summer to be a bit different. You're going to be going away to school in a couple of years, aren't you?"

*Away*. Are they planning to send him to boarding school, then, like Mr Crossman's son Robin?

"Am I?" he says. "Where?"

"Well, that's something we need to have a chat about. But before that, I thought we should all go somewhere together. *En famille*."

"A holiday, you mean?"

Dad nods. "I'm seeing if we can get someone to give us a caravan. Or *lend* us a caravan. And then what we'd do is go down to Folkestone, get on a boat, drive all the way across Europe: France, Italy, Yugoslavia, Greece."

Mark frowns. "Why would someone give us a caravan?"

"It's free advertising for them." He reaches over to the bookcase, runs his finger along the frayed spines of the old magazines. "Lots of pictures of their Eccles Enterprise or their Argosy Twelve or whatever it is standing in front of the Matterhorn or Lake Como. And an article saying how easy it was to handle, and how well it stood up to the roads."

Mark visualizes the photos: him and Mum and Dad — the shirt-sleeved, man-of-action Dad he saw when they were washing the car — smiling into the camera, with the caravan and a couple of locals in *lederhosen* and felt hats behind them. He could sneak the magazine into school, leave it lying where Nigel and Ben — no, not Nigel and Ben, *Lou* — would find it . . .

"So what do you think?"

Mark's stomach is fluttery. He nods.

"Good. I hoped you'd like the idea." He smiles. "So all we've got to do now is persuade Mummy."

"Doesn't she want to do it, then?"

Dad nods. "Women are a changeable lot. She'll come round, I expect. Once she sees that we chaps are sticking together."

The flutteriness in his belly deepens into a throb. Those two words — *we chaps* — have overturned the natural order of things. For as long as he can remember, Mum has been at the centre: the mid-way point between him and Dad. Now, suddenly she's been pushed out, and he feels Dad's magnetic force pulling him closer and closer, *too* close . . .

"Anyway," says Dad, "I suppose I'd better get on with writing to Eccles and Argosy, hadn't I?"

Relieved, Mark stands up.

"But see you at lunch."

*Yes, if she's back in time*. He peers into Dad's eyes, wondering if he's thinking the same thing. But there's no hesitation there, no uncertainty.

"OK." Mark stands up and heads for the door.

"Where do you keep going?" Mark asks, a day or two later.

"Oh, just out and about. When Dad's busy like this, it's a good opportunity to catch up with things. And I've got two hungry chaps to provide for, haven't I?" She smiles. "Speaking of which: I have to nip into town this morning, and I was wondering if you'd mind doing me a favour and picking up some sausages from the shop?"

"Can't you get them in town?"

"I could. But if we do it at the shop, they can go on the account, can't they?"

He hesitates. "All right."

She kisses him on the forehead, then scoops up the car keys.

If he goes straight away, that'll still leave him a couple of hours before lunch to walk up to Cockenhoe. He clips on Barney's lead and hurries out. As he turns into the High Street, he notices a woman standing in front of the shop. She has her back to him, but from her height and the baggy drape of her skirt, he knows it's Murky. She's talking to someone in the Bennetts' narrow front garden, though the jut of the entrance prevents him seeing who it is.

"Hullo!" he calls.

She half turns. "Ah, young Aurelius!" she says, beckoning to him. "Come and join us!"

Standing in the angle of the porch and the house, one plimsolled foot pressed against the wall, is Lou. She's had a haircut, and her skin is brown and freckly from the sun. Her shirt and shorts seem too big for her, as if she's shrunk in the last two weeks.

"You know Mark, don't you?" says Murky, as he approaches.

"You're back!" he says.

It sounds silly, even to him. He expects her to laugh, and say, *Of course I am, stupid!* Instead she just gives him a sharp nod.

"Lou and I have been comparing notes," says Murky. "She's been at the seaside. And I've just —"

Lou pushes off from the wall. "I've got to go in now."

"Really?"

"Yes."

She starts towards the front door of the house. Mark calls:

"Lou!"

She stops and faces him, saying nothing. He folds his thumb and forefinger, making their secret sign. She doesn't respond.

"I've lots to tell you. He's gone. And —"

"I know."

"And that Sammy chap —"

"I can't talk to you."

She turns and goes inside. Murky watches until the door closes, then looks at Mark.

"I'm sorry," she says. "I didn't realize. I thought —"

"It doesn't matter."

She plants her stick in front of her and leans forward, clutching the top with both hands.

"Yes, it does. Aubrey Hillyard?"

He nods.

"Oh dear, oh dear," she says, shaking her head. "That man. The trouble he's caused." She hesitates. "They think you're responsible, do they? Her parents? For her getting mixed up with him?"

He nods. "It's not your fault, Murky."

"Yes, it is. But gosh, you're a staunch chap, aren't you?" She reaches out and touches his hand. "I've just been away with Jane — with my niece — for ten days.

And do you know what she said? She said, *You're lucky to have a friend like that boy, Mark Davenant, Aunt.* And she's right. I am."

He blushes. His throat tightens. He doesn't trust himself to reply, so changes the subject.

"Is that why the house was shut up?"

"I beg your pardon?"

"Hillfield."

She frowns, drubbing her forehead with the heel of her hand. "Oh, no! I didn't forget again, did I? You didn't turn up, expecting —"

"No, it's not that. I just . . ." He racks his brains for the right phrase. What is it that grown-ups say? "I just looked in, on the off-chance."

"Oh, that's a relief. No, out of the blue, dear Jane said, 'When was the last time you had a holiday, Aunt? Why don't you come to Scotland with me?' So I asked Winnie Ostler to look after the cats, and off we went. And very jolly it was, too." She smiles. "Anyway, you and I must arrange something soon. Tea and cats. Before you go back to school."

"All right."

"How about Friday?"

"OK."

"Splendid." She reaches two fingers inside her sleeve and pulls out a handkerchief. "I'll make a knot. To be sure to remember."

He smiles and goes inside the shop. Mrs Bennett is behind the counter. She acknowledges him only with a tiny nod, but when he asks for the sausages, she gets them without a fuss and meekly adds them to the account.

"Anything else?" she says, looking up.

"No." He forces himself to add: "Thank you."

Two things nag at him as he walks back. The first is like an animal in its burrow: he knows it's there, can hear it scuffling about, but can't coax it out into the open where he could see what it is. The second is quite clear-cut: what Lou said to him. He replays it, again and again, in his head, trying to hear the missing word at the end: *I can't talk to you* now; or *I can't talk to you* ever? He's blown backwards and forwards, from one side to the other — but, in the end, it's impossible to decide between them.

When he gets home, he puts the sausages in the fridge, then calls Barney again and walks up to Cockenhoe, sloughing off the pretences of the present, getting ready to appear as his true self with medieval ghosts.

It's not till the following afternoon that it hits him. When she's finished clearing out the lunch things, Mum says:

"I just need to pop down to the post office." She wipes her fingers on her apron, then slips her hands behind her and unties it with a fidgety movement. "I'll wash up when I get back. Unless you feel like doing it?"

He shakes his head. "I'm taking Barney out. But I can go to the post office for you, if you want."

"That's all right." It's not the way she says it: it's the frightened expression in her eyes. And suddenly he remembers: that's exactly how she looked when she got back late for lunch, and said she'd been held up by Murky.

The rat's out of its hole. She *couldn't* have been held up by Murky: that was when Murky was on holiday with Miss Saunders.

"OK," he says, turning away, in case his face betrays that he knows she's been lying. "Are you going in the car?"

"To the post office? No, of course not."

He nods. "Come on, then, Barns."

He clips on the lead and hurries out. When he reaches the church, he glances back. Still no sign of Mum. He darts through the lychgate, then slips round and crouches behind the low flint side wall, pressing Barney to the ground beside him. They're there for only a couple of minutes before he hears the familiar groan of hinges and sees Mum emerging into Church End.

He ducks his head and holds Barney's muzzle shut, to stop him whimpering as she goes by. When her footsteps start to recede again, he counts to fifty, then sneaks back out, still grasping Barney's nose. She's almost at the pub. He tiptoes after her — ready, at any moment, if she looks back, to walk normally and pretend he was going that way anyhow. When she turns into the High Street and disappears from view, he breaks into a run. He arrives at the corner just in time to see her going into the post office.

He's pretty certain she didn't know she was being followed, but he can't be sure. In case she did and is deliberately trying to put him off the scent, he decides to hide in the thick clump of grass and dead-nettles alongside the war memorial and see what she does next. A few moments later she reappears, pauses outside the door and drops something into her handbag. She looks both ways, then crosses the street and starts back towards Church End.

As Mark hunches lower, something sharp jabs his knee. He stops himself crying out, but, without thinking, lets go of the lead. Barney bounds into the road and leaps up at Mum, nearly sending her flying. She looks round, her face changing into a startled scowl.

"What on earth do you think you're you doing?" she says, as Mark emerges from his hiding place. "Ambushing me? You're a bit old for that, aren't you?"

He shakes his head, clasping his knee with both hands.

"Oh, you've hurt your leg. Yet again. Let me see." She prises apart his fingers. "Ouch. That looks nasty. You really must be more careful. Better come back and let me disinfect it. And then put a plaster on it."

He hesitates.

"Come on, wounded soldier. Lean on my arm. I'll take Barney."

Grimacing, unable to think of anything but the pain, he lets her lead him home.

# CHAPTER EIGHTEEN

Only a week to go before school now. The world is shrinking by the hour. Even the house is closing in, intruding on his privacy, demanding to be listened to. He lies on his bed, trying to untangle the knot in his head, but every footstep (Mum or Dad?), every door shutting (coming in or going out?), distracts him. When he hears voices in the hall or the clang of a saucepan in the kitchen he knows that the machinery of life is running normally, but then he finds himself straining to catch the next sound — the click of the latch, the slam of the car door — that suggests it's about to plough off the rails again. And always there's the danger that the creak of the loose tread on the stairs means that one of them is coming to see him: either baffling Dad (will he be sweet or sour this time?) or deceitful, no-longer-dependable Mum.

More and more, as the cut in his knee begins to heal and he's able to walk normally again, he finds himself escaping back to Cockenhoe. The woods there are larger, wilder, more deserted than Twenty Acre, and the trees press closer together — so that in some places there's no space even for broken branches to fall to the ground, and they end up snared in the arms of their neighbours. On the far side is a gnat-infested pond, where — even this late in the year — you can still sometimes see dragonflies. The khaki surface, slick with algae, is so smooth that Mark half expects it to be broken by the sudden eruption of a hand clasping Excalibur.

His favourite spot is the hole left by an uprooted beech. The trunk lies at an angle, its torn roots, caked with earth, forming a kind of canopy. The hole underneath is overgrown with vines and brambles, and the only way in is through a shallow channel in the soil that, bit by bit, Mark manages to scrape out with his own hands, with puzzled Barney looking on. It's like the hideout, only better: when he's inside, no one, even if they walked right past, would have a clue that he was there. But no one ever does walk past: the whole wood seems to belong only to him, Barney and the dead. Stretched out along the floor of the crater, his head cradled by the sloping side, he's at last free to think.

*Mum — Lou — Hillyard — Sammy — Brain — Desertion — Bigamy — Dad*. They're all snarled up: start with any one of them, and it can lead to any of the others. But slowly he begins to unpick them and lay the strands out side by side. When, finally, he's able to look at them clearly, he can see that — despite everything that's happened over the last couple of weeks — the most important question is still Hillyard. Was he telling the truth, or was Sammy? Everything really hangs on that: not just who he can and can't trust, but whether the world he's living in is as — until the start of the summer — he'd always imagined it, or is in the grip of sinister forces that only he and Lou and Hillyard see.

Lou. Perhaps he could sneak out at night, and get her attention by throwing stones at her window. But he doesn't know which is her room, so he'd be just as likely to wake her parents. What about writing another note, asking her to meet him at the hideout? No, they'd see him slipping it through the door — and, even if they didn't, they'd probably guess who it was from and refuse to give it to her.

It's useless: she's back in the village, but there's no way of reaching her. He'll just have to wait till Friday. At least then — finally — he'll be able to speak to Murky.

He gets to Hillfield just as the church clock strikes four. The sitting-room window's open, and a gangly marmalade cat is stretched out on the sill, snoozing in a lozenge of afternoon sun. As he goes up the steps, Mark catches the sound of Murky's voice from inside. She must be on the phone.

He eases out the bell pull. There's a half-hearted tinkle, then — almost instantly — approaching footsteps. The door cracks open.

"Hullo, Mur —" he starts, and then her head appears, craning round the edge, one finger to her lips.

"What? . . ." he mouths.

"Ssh."

She holds the door wide, beckons him inside, then shuts it behind him. He follows her through into the sitting room. There, on the sofa, hunched forward over her knees, clutching a glass of lemonade, is Lou. When she sees him, she gasps and sits up broomstick-straight. She stares at him for a second, then glances at Murky, looking for an explanation.

"I don't like to be underhand," says Murky. "But I can't stand unfairness, either — and this is jolly unfair. If your parents are cross with anyone, it should be with me, for letting that man Hillyard come and —"

"Slindon," says Lou.

"All right, letting that man Slindon come and live here. They certainly shouldn't be angry with poor Mark and veto your being friends with him. I've known the boy all his life, and never met a more sterling character. Whatever he's done, I'm quite sure he was only trying to do the right thing. Sit down, Mark."

He squeezes himself onto the other end of the sofa. In front of him is a tray cluttered with plates and knives, bread and jam, the lemonade jug, the battered biscuit tin.

"And nobody should be punished for trying to do the right thing, should they? So I thought this would be the chance for you to have a proper chat, without worrying about interfering grown-ups." She moves towards the door. "What would you like to drink, Mark? It's starting to feel autumnal, so I'm going to have my usual berry."

Mark nods at Lou's glass. "What she's having, please."

"Right. I'll be back in a tick." She waves at the tray. "Do help yourselves, won't you?"

Lou watches Murky go, then turns towards Mark, pushing herself back into her corner of the sofa. Her bare legs, brown from the sun and hazy with tiny golden hairs, seem longer and more muscular than he remembers. As if she's suddenly conscious that he's looking at them, she crosses them and folds them back, so that her feet are under her bum. For a second or two she and Mark look at each other shyly, without speaking. Then Lou says:

"This is a bit funny, isn't it?"

He nods.

"What do you want to talk about?"

"Tons of things."

She drops her gaze. "How's Barney?"

"Oh, he's all right."

"Just the same?"

He nods.

"Still chasing after rabbits?"

Mark hesitates. "Gallion."

She colours, but doesn't say anything.

"Come on." He pauses, waiting for her to reply. When she doesn't, he says: "You can't have forgotten."

"Gallion," she murmurs.

"OK." He glances at the doorway, to make sure Murky isn't listening. "Well, what *I* want to talk about is . . . You know . . ."

She shakes her head.

"Yes! I've got to give you all the latest gen. Last time we were all together in Twenty Acre, PC Pointer had just turned up, hadn't he? Well, after you'd gone, he searched the railway carriage. Only, he didn't find anything. But then the next day —"

"Yes, I know all that," she says.

"What, about Aubrey? How —"

"John Slindon."

"You shouldn't call him that."

"It's his real name."

"You don't know it is. Not for sure. It's just something —"

"Yes, I do."

"How?"

She shrugs. "Anyway, I know he ran away. And nobody knows where he is now."

"He might not have run away. He might have been *arrested*, mightn't he?"

She shakes her head again. How can she be so certain? He started out thinking *he* would be filling *her* in on all that's happened over the last couple of weeks. Now he's beginning to wonder if, somehow, she knows more about it than he does.

"Have you been talking to Sammy?" he asks.

She looks down quickly. "Everyone knows," she says. "His name's John Slindon. And he deserted from the army. And he's a bigamist. You know what that means?"

"Course."

"And now he's gone and done a bunk."

It's not what she's saying that upsets him so much as her tone: no-nonsense and completely sure of herself, like a not very imaginative grown-up.

"Where have you been staying?" he says. "At the Brain's headquarters?"

She clicks her tongue. "That's a silly thing to say. There isn't a Brain. He made it all up. And you believed him."

I *believed it? What about you?* But to say that is to admit she's right, and the Brain isn't real.

"Here we are," says Murky. She's carrying a glass of elderberry wine in one shaky hand and an empty tumbler in the other. She looks at them both for a moment, then gives the tumbler to Mark. "Can I leave you to help yourself? I've just got a bit of cat duty to attend to. Then I'll be with you."

He waits till he can hear the clump of her shoes on the kitchen flags.

"So you think it's all *my* fault, do you?"

She shakes her head, tracing something on her knee with one finger.

"Well, your dad does, doesn't he?"

She nods. "Miss Murkett's right, it *is* unfair. I did say, but . . ." She reaches out and touches the back of his hand. "Daddy's like a firework." She mimes an explosion. "*Bang!* But he always calms down in the end. I'll probably be allowed to talk to you again in a few weeks. We'll just have to play something else — another game, not the Brain, I mean. Peveril on the Swift or something. I like Peveril. And then it'll be OK, I expect."

Tears sting his eyes. It *wasn't* just a game. Or, if it was, she can't simply decide that on her own: it's something they would need to *agree*, after they've been over everything together. And how could she imagine they'd be able to play Peveril now, without thinking about Hillyard? Maybe the people she was staying with actually *did* brainwash her. Maybe he really is now entirely on his own . . .

"When I was away I did birdwatching," she says. "That was fun. You have a pair of binoculars. And a bird book. And you write down all the different sorts you've seen. Divers. Yellowhammers. Goldfinches . . ."

Here, at least, is his chance to find out who she was with. "Where were you?"

"At my aunt's. A place called Emsworth. It's by the sea. There's not much of a beach, so you can't paddle or anything. But they have boats. I went out in one."

"Your uncle's?"

She shakes her head. "My uncle was killed in the war. He was in the navy. He got a medal. My aunt showed me."

*In the navy. Got a medal.* Would that make him a person in high places?

"Did you tell her? About Aubrey?"

"Slindon."

"All right, Slindon, then."

She shrugs. "A bit."

"Did you mention the Brain?"

She hesitates. "I wasn't going to, not to start with. But then —"

"What, she wheedled it out of you, did she?"

She shakes her head. "It was . . ."

*What?* He jiggles his legs with impatience.

"Oh, let's not talk about it."

"Why not?"

"I just don't want to . . ."

She breaks off as Murky comes back into the room.

"So," says Murky. "How are you getting on?"

"All right," says Mark.

"Friends again?"

Lou shrugs.

"Oh, dear," says Murky. "Not that man still, I hope?"

Lou nods. Murky shakes her head, sighing, and sits down heavily in her chair. "And you still haven't eaten a thing," she says, noticing the tray. "Too busy arguing, I suppose. Come on, tuck in."

They each dutifully take a plate and a slice of bread.

"That's it. Now, do you think this might be a good moment for some entertainment?"

She looks from one to the other, eyebrows raised. Neither of them speaks.

"Have you told Lou, young Aurelius?" She picks up *Old Possum* and flourishes it. "About our little tradition?"

Mark glances at Lou. She nods.

"He's jolly good, I can tell you. Would you like to hear?"

"All right," says Lou.

Murky leans forward stiffly and gives Mark the book. "You choose this time. Whatever you feel like."

He puts down his plate and flips through the pages. He doesn't want to bore Lou or embarrass her. Which one would she like best? Finally, for no particular reason, except its jaunty tempo, he settles on "Skimbleshanks, the Railway Cat".

He's only read three or four lines when he notices, out of the corner of his eye, that Lou is smiling and moving from side to side in time with the rhythm. When he reaches the end of the first verse, she gets up and starts dancing, hopping from one foot to the other.

Murky laughs and accompanies her with a noiseless handclap. As Mark finishes, the clapping becomes audible.

"Well, I must say," she says, her voice trilling with delight, "I didn't expect that! Not just poetry, but ballet too! Who needs television, when they can have Mark and Lou to tea?"

*We'll just have to play something else*. Before she went away, she seemed — if anything — even more loyal than he was, saying they must both be steadfast, promising to stand by Hillyard, come what may. Why, then, has she changed so much? All the way home — bypassing the shop, in case the Bennetts see him and guess that he was at Murky's too — he dissects their conversation, looking for clues. But, try as he may, he can't find an answer.

He's started to feel superstitious about Mum: if she's not there when he gets back, something terrible is going to happen. So it's a relief, as he opens the back door, to see her sitting at the dining table, staring intently at a half-empty cup of tea.

"Hullo, Mum."

She looks up. She's wearing make-up, and he can smell scent on her skin, but her face powder is streaked with tears. She tries to smile. "Hullo, poppet. Did you have a nice time?"

"It was all right."

She nods, but there's a blankness in her eyes that makes him think she didn't take it in.

"Are you OK?" he says.

She doesn't reply.

"What's the matter?"

She shakes her head. He glances into the hall. The study door is open, and he can't hear the typewriter.

"Where's Dad?"

"He's upstairs. He's got a bit of a migraine."

"Oh. Is he upset about something?"

"There was a letter. In the afternoon post. From Argosy Caravans."

"And they won't . . ."

"No, they will."

"They're going to give us one?"

"Well, it's not definite yet. But they say they're interested."

"Well, that's *good*, isn't it? It means we'll be going abroad next summer. If they *do* give us one, I mean?"

She says nothing. He sits down.

"Aren't you pleased?"

She sniffs and turns her head towards the kitchen, so that he can't see her face.

"Isn't *Dad?* . . ." he begins — then remembers how Dad reacted when he won the *Amateur Photographer* competition.

Without looking back at him, she reaches out a hand and gropes around until she finds his.

"You know I love you, don't you?" she says.

"Course. Mum . . ."

She turns towards him again. "Hm?"

It's her eyes that stop him. They make him think of a rickety old building, the roof caved in, the walls leaning at an impossible angle. Remove one brick, and the whole thing will come tumbling to the ground.

"Nothing," he says, withdrawing his hand. "I'm going to go and play with Peveril on the Swift."

# CHAPTER NINETEEN

The next day, he's at Cockenhoe again. As he turns onto the path, through the little stand of conifers bordering the road, he feels the strain in his shoulders and the flutter in his stomach start to ease. This has become his redoubt: the last place left that still makes sense to him. When he's here, it's like not merely playing with Peveril, but being in Peveril itself, safe in his own dominion — without the constant fear that, at any moment, the door might open, and a grown-up walk in and break the spell.

After they've gone a couple of hundred yards and there's no danger of Barney running back onto the road, he leans down and unclips his lead. Barney looks up, tail wagging gratefully, then sets off ahead of him. There's a cool blustery breeze, making it feel more like autumn than summer, and, through the gaps in the treetops, he can see grey-tinged clouds starting to close in, massing for an assault. He's got a sweater tied round his waist, but no raincoat. He just has to hope that, if it comes to it, the tree-root camp will be watertight . . .

A shot: some way off, but loud enough to make his ears ring. Barney stops dead, cringing.

"Here, boy!"

But it's too late: with a yelp, Barney bolts into the trees. Mark ploughs after him, furious with himself for being so stupid. Why did it never occur to him there'd be gamekeepers here? For the simple reason he's never seen one. But of course there must be, particularly at his time of year: the place is loud with pheasants, after all, and the shooting season will be starting any day now.

"Barney!" But he has to say it softly, in case the gamekeeper hears. There's no response. He takes a chance, claps his hands and whistles.

"Come on, boy!"

All he can hear is the dying echo of his own voice.

Blast and damnation. Maybe the gamekeeper's got him. But in that case, surely, there'd have been shouting, barking, even, perhaps — the sweat on his neck turns cold — another shot? Barney must have gone deeper into the wood.

Mark trudges up the hill. He's only come this far once or twice: it's so overgrown that it's impossible to walk more than a few paces without having to climb round or over or under something, so he normally sticks to the area near the pond and his camp. He moves forward slowly, listening for the tell-tale sound of rustling in the bushes, stopping every couple of minutes to whistle. When he gets to the ridge at the top, he sees that the slope on the far side is clearer. Aware that Barney might be miles away by now, he breaks into a jog-trot.

Something slices his shin like a knife. He falls, thrusting out his hands. They smack the ground violently, wrenching one wrist, grating his palms. In the distance, he can hear a dull clunking sound, like a stick hitting an empty tin.

He rolls over, clutching his leg. But more than hurt, he's shocked and angry. This is someone's fault. They deliberately tricked him. He wants to know who it is. He wants to get his own back.

"Ah, I suspected as much."

He looks round. There's no one there. He must be concussed.

"This is becoming something of a habit. First, Barney. And then, as night follows day, Mark."

A bush ten feet away suddenly moves. A hand, a filthy sleeve, the fringe of a red-grey beard.

"What the hell are you doing here?"

Mark is too dazed to reply.

"Did someone send you?"

Mark shakes his head.

"Promise?"

Mark nods. "Where's Barney?"

"Barney is quite safe. And quite happy — apart from the muzzle I had to improvise for him, which he finds irksome. You, on the other hand —"

Hillyard moves forward, squats down next to Mark and pulls open his clenched fists. "And this" — clicking his tongue — "is starting to be rather predictable too, isn't it? Every time I see you, you've got some ghastly injury, even more lurid than the last one. Those are nasty grazes."

"I fell over something."

"You fell over a tripwire."

"Did you put it there?"
"I did."
"Why?"
"Why do you imagine?" He leans closer to Mark's hands, frowning. "Yes, we'd better get those cleaned up. I haven't got much water left, but needs must. First, though" — looking up again sharply — "I want to know why you're here."
"I was having a walk, that's all."
"Why here?"
"I like it. I come here a lot. I can't go to Twenty Acre any more, can I?"
Hillyard stares at him, then nods.
"And — did you hear that shot? It frightened Barney. He ran away. So I was just trying to find him. I didn't know you were here."
"Nobody told you? Gave you even the slightest hint?"
He shakes his head. "I'd no idea *where* you were. You just disappeared. At first I thought you'd been arrested. Then I didn't know what to think."
"Good. Even so, it leaves us with something of a conundrum. But first things first. Let's get you to the field hospital."
He stands up, takes Mark's hand and helps him to his feet.
"All right?"
Mark nods.
"Not far."
He leads him a short way down the hill, then right towards a clump of vines and bramble. Mingled with

the sneezy sharpness of the leaves is a smell of wood-smoke.

"Sorry," says Hillyard. "This is going to hurt a bit. But it's the only way in, I'm afraid. Pretend you're a baboon, and put your weight on your knuckles."

He kneels down and ducks into a space below the lowest branch. It's like the tree-root camp: no one who didn't know would guess it was there. Mark bunches his fists and creeps after him, wincing with pain. The first thing he sees, as he comes out the other side, is Barney, tied to a stake, with a rough rope halter holding his mouth closed. Beyond him is a small white tent, its roof speckled with an instantly recognizable pattern of rust-coloured stains.

"What are you doing with that?" he says.

Barney lunges towards him, then lets out a strangled whine as he reaches the end of his tether.

"Ssh. Keep your voice down," says Hillyard, crawling into the tent. "And shut that bloody dog up."

Mark puts his arms round Barney's neck and rubs his cheek against his head. Again, he feels as if he's slipped into a dream: one that he's had before, this time, in which he half knows what will happen. He puts a finger in his mouth and bites till he can't stand it any more.

"Right," says Hillyard, emerging from the tent, carrying a flannel, a towel and a bottle. "Come on. Hands out."

"I said, what are you doing with my tent?"

"All in good time. Hands."

Mark opens his palms and holds them out. Hillyard cleans them with the flannel and dabs them dry with the towel. Then he uncorks the bottle and tilts it towards him.

"Right. This is going to sting a bit. Soon be over, though."

"What is it?"

"Brandy." He starts to pour. The raw skin feels as if someone's set light to it.

"Ow!"

"*Shoosh shoosh shoosh*. Come on. Brave soldier. Now the leg." He washes Mark's shin and dribbles brandy onto the wound. Mark grits his teeth.

"That's it," says Hillyard. "Count to ten. Slowly."

Mark counts. By the time he's finished, the searing has dulled to a tingly throb.

"All better?" says Hillyard.

Mark nods.

"Good." He looks at the bottle. "How about a noggin yourself, Aubrey? Steady the nerves? That's a kind thought. Think I will."

He takes a swig and wipes his lips with the back of his hand.

"What I'm doing with your tent is living in it. Though only *pro tem*. You'll get it back in due course."

"Did you steal it?"

Hillyard shrugs. "Didn't seem to be doing anyone much good where it was. You leave a tent in a place like that — rats, damp, no light — it'll start to rot. Better for it to have some use. Chance to air out." He glances at the tent. "It's grateful for it, believe me. Last thing at night, it always says thank you to Uncle Aubrey for getting it out of that bloody dungeon and giving it a bit of a holiday."

Mark just manages not to laugh. "Why didn't you ask? I'd have let you borrow it. You know I would."

"Wasn't time. That's the long and the short of it. After our little *contretemps* with Constable What's-his-name, I sat down and put my thinking cap on. I realized he'd probably be back the next day — *they'd* probably be back the next day, if not before. I had a few hours at most. So I packed up and did a midnight flit. Only place I could think of going was your shed. I knew the way, I knew I'd be safe there till morning. And I knew — all right, point taken, that's a bit impertinent — I *hoped*, let's say, you wouldn't mind."

Mark remembers the dead-rat smell, the figures crowded together on the platform at Peveril on the Swift.

"And there," Hillyard goes on, "I found the wherewithal to make myself reasonably at home up here. So I'm afraid I helped —" He pauses, and squints up at the sky. "Did you feel that?"

"What?"

"A spot of rain."

"No." But it is colder, all of a sudden, and darker too, as if someone had just turned off a light. "You could at least have left me a note."

Hillyard is still tracking the progress of the clouds. "Too risky," he mutters.

"Why, didn't you trust me any more?"

"There, you must have felt it that time! Come on, let's get inside. It's a leaky devil, this tent of yours. But better than being *en plein air*."

Mark *can* feel it now. He gets up and follows Hillyard to the tent.

"Don't forget Barney," says Hillyard.

"He'll be all right."

"No, he won't. Poor brute will be soaked. Go on. Quick! Get him."

Mark unties him. But instead of going into the tent, Barney suddenly lunges round the side, towards a conical pile covered with a ragged scrap of tarpaulin, and starts scrabbling at it. As the edge lifts, Mark sees the bloodied nose of a rabbit and one staring eye, smoky and dull as an old marble. Next to it, just visible, are the twin mouths of a shotgun.

"Here, boy!" He jerks the rope and drags Barney back to the entrance.

"Was that you?" he asks Hillyard.

"What?"

"The gun just now. Were you shooting rabbits?"

Hillyard shrugs. He reaches into a corner and picks up a tin. "Man cannot live by baked beans alone."

Mark crawls in, bending his body to fit Hillyard's bear-like bulk, then hauls Barney after him.

"Lie down, boy!"

The tent smells of mildew and sweat and smoke. But there's something else too — something so completely out of place that Mark suddenly blurts:

"My mother!"

Hillyard looks sharply at him. "What about her?"

"*She's* been here, hasn't she?"

"What makes you say that?"

Mark sniffs, twitching his nose. Hillyard frowns, puzzled.

"Her scent."

Hillyard is still for a moment, then nods slowly. "Ah, yes, I should have thought of that. Bit of a give-away, I suppose, to anyone in the know. Not that I was *expecting* anyone in the know. Or anyone else, for that matter." He nibbles the fringe of his moustache. "Are you proposing to tell her?"

"What?"

"That you've been here? That you know?"

Mark says nothing.

"She's a good woman, your mother," says Hillyard. "Truth be told, I more or less owe her my life."

*Truth be told*. Mark shakes his head.

"OK," says Hillyard. "I can see the story I gave you needs some small revision. Everything up to my hiding in the shed was just as I said. After that, well . . ." He pauses. "The fact is, I should have been off the premises at dawn the next day. I wasn't. It was so dark, I lost track of the time and overslept. Your mother came in to get a bucket. And there I was, in all my glory. Unwashed. In dire need of a change of clothes. But instead of screaming her head off and summoning the constabulary, as anyone else would have done, she asked me what I was doing there. And when I explained, told her the powers that be were on my tail, with a view to shutting me away for God knows how long, she said she'd help me. All right?"

A sudden gust of wind outside sends the tent door flapping. Rain starts pattering on the roof.

"That's the truth, this time," says Hillyard. "Scouts' honour."

Mark looks away. In the corner of the tent, sticking out from under Hillyard's sleeping bag, he sees a familiar torn spine. *Do you happen to know where the map is, Mark? I can't seem to find it*.

"So here's what you're thinking," says Hillyard. "You're thinking: why did we go behind your back? You and I were meant to be pals, weren't we? So why didn't we take you into our confidence?"

Mark's eyes are stinging. He bites his lip.

"I'll tell you why: it would have been too dangerous, that's why," says Hillyard. "You're a marked man. They knew we were friends, didn't they? So you might have been followed coming here, and led them to me without meaning to."

"I'd have been careful."

"I'm sure you would. But it isn't just that. They're not an especially scrupulous lot, these gentry. I don't think they'd be too particular how they found out where I was. So if you *knew* where I was, you'd be at risk. Of interrogation. Maybe something worse. And I thought you'd been through enough on my account already. So you see the quandary I was in? *We* were in? Your mother and me?"

"I suppose." Mark hesitates. "So . . . is it true?"

"What?"

"That you're a man called John Slindon. And that you're a deserter — and a bigamist."

Hillyard says nothing.

"So all that stuff you told us about the Brain," Mark continues, "and how they think you're a big threat, and that's why they're after you — you made it all up?"

"Well, that rather depends."

"No it doesn't! Either it's true or it isn't!"

Hillyard pats the pocket of his smock, then seems to forget what he's feeling for and lets his hand flop on his thigh.

"Truth's a funny thing," he says. "Not always to be confused with the facts."

Mark shakes his head, exasperated.

Hillyard nods. "All right. I know." He pauses. "You in a hurry?"

"Not specially."

"Then I'm going to talk to you, Mark. Man to man. After that, you'll just have to make up your own mind." He reaches for the brandy bottle, unstoppers it and takes a swig. "So, yes, I am John Slindon. That's the *fact*. The kind of fact Sammy and PC Booby would recognize. They've got a birth certificate and a marriage certificate to prove it, and that's the end of the matter, far as they're concerned. But it's not the truth. The *truth* is that I'm Aubrey Hillyard."

"That's not possible."

"I don't mean I'm the poor devil who got his head blown off by a V2. And I should point out, incidentally, that I didn't *steal* his papers: they cost me a fortune on the black market. What I mean is, the man I am now is me, and John Slindon isn't. Couple of weeks after VE Day, Corporal John Slindon got in a car with a couple of clever chaps from T-Force and drove them to a place called Mittelbau." His eyes narrow. "What, surprised to hear I was just a corporal, are you?"

Mark shakes head.

"Yes," says Hillyard. "Not officer material, they said. Too bloody bolshie. Anyway, when they all got back in the car that evening, John Slindon wasn't John Slindon any more."

The downpour is so heavy now that the tent is shaking. Spits of water make their way through gaps in the fabric.

"Damned thing," says Hillyard. "Might as well be sheltering in a sieve." He wipes a sleeve across his forehead, then turns back to Mark. "You've no idea what I'm talking about, have you?"

Mark shakes his head.

"OK." He takes another drink from the bottle. "Ever heard of Mittelbau?"

"No."

"It's where the Jerries built the V2 rockets. Or rather, where they forced the unfortunate *Zwangsarbeiter* to build them. Yes, I know. Can't say I find it a particularly pleasing one, but definitely an irony. The Yanks had stumbled on the place just a couple of months before. April '45. They'd been told to expect something a bit unusual. What they found was hell. An overused word, of course. *What the hell's going on? It was hell in there*. I mean the real thing. Someone had pinched the blueprint from Old Nick and followed it to the last detail." He clears his throat. "I wish I didn't have to tell you this, Mark. If it was a half-decent world, the whole thing ought to be flat-out inconceivable. You want me to stop?"

Mark shakes his head.

"It was built next to a concentration camp. Offshoot of Buchenwald, called Nordhausen. So the prisoners could be used as slave labour. Poles, Russians and French, mostly, the poor so-and-sos. They'd all gone by the time I got there, of course, but you could see what it'd been like for them. Miles and miles of subterranean tunnels. Dark, airless, unbearably hot. Thousands of half-starved souls staggering under loads *I* couldn't have carried. If they fell, they were kicked or beaten with rifle butts. If they tried to escape, they were tortured and hanged. They died at the rate of 250 a day. Can you believe it? 250 a *day*. Which means more people died in a week *making* the V2s than were *killed* by the V2s. Whatever the Jerries thought they were doing, all they'd really created was a huge death factory. A ruthlessly efficient process for transforming human beings into expendable objects." He pauses. His face is flushed. A blue vein stands out on his temple. "Didn't do them any good, of course. They were in the grip of something they didn't understand — something that had turned them into calculating machines. So many units in, so much production out. Everything else is bunk, as Henry Ford would have said. If you can't enter it into an account book, it doesn't exist." His eyes are wet. He squeezes them shut, presses the lids with his thumb and forefinger. "That's the impossibility. My being Aubrey Hillyard is nothing, simply a kid's magic trick. But *that*: that's just —" He shakes his head.

Is he acting? Did he make all this up too? Mark can't decide. He remembers Dad telling him in a sombre undertone about Belsen: the piles of skeletal bodies, the commandant apologizing for the state of his records when he surrendered; the photographs that Mark isn't allowed to see. Is this the same thing?

"And do you know why the clever chaps from T-Force and I were sent there? You think it was because the powers that be wanted to understand how human beings could do that to one another, so they could prevent it ever happening again? Not a bit of it. No, it was because that's where the rockets were, and the Yanks had promised us half the booty, and our job was to try to persuade them to keep their side of the bargain. If we could just get our hands on our share, you see, we'd be able to learn how to build the things for ourselves. But the Yanks, of course, didn't *want* us to get our share. They wanted to keep the whole caboodle. So there we were, us and them, prowling round like a couple of dogs after the same bone. Needless to say, the Yanks won: snaffled the lot and told us we could go hang. Pretty soon, our side realized they'd been outwitted and started hunting elsewhere. But I couldn't get Mittelbau out of my mind. Never will."

"Is all this true?"

"Give you my word."

"Honestly?"

Hillyard touches the corner of one eye and holds up his finger. A pearl-like tear glitters on the tip. "Can't you tell?"

Mark hesitates, then nods.

"I'd glimpsed the future, you see," says Hillyard. "The way the world was going."

"Why?" says Mark.

"What?"

"Why was that the future?"

Hillyard doesn't answer at once. He lets out a slow unsteady sigh, then looks out of the tent door, as if drawing strength from something he can see there.

"Because," he says finally, "we're in the grip of — I don't know what you want to call it. A force? A malign power?"

"The Brain?" He whispers it, frightened of rousing something to anger.

Hillyard seems not to hear him. "All over the world, you've got boffins beavering away night and day, discovering things, building things. We think they're doing it for us, to make us quicker, safer, more powerful. *They* think they're doing it for us, too. But they're not. That's what I saw at Mittelbau. People reduced to nothing more than ciphers, existing only to serve their master. Stripped of their names. Stripped of the power to say 'I': 'I want, I think, I am.' Stamped with a number, so that the master can neatly enter them in his book. He who has eyes to see, let him see."

"But that's not us. It was the Germans, wasn't it? And we beat them!"

Hillyard nods. "And what was the first thing we did then? Even before they'd surrendered? Jostle to get our mitts on what *they* had, so we could sign up for service under the same master. Now we've got *bigger* rockets. Warheads that can kill *more* people."

"But we need them. Because of the Russians."

"Yes, that's what we're told. And the Russians are told the same thing, because of us. And the Germans were told they needed the V2s to win the war." He hesitates. "And we're all in such a funk, we're prepared to go on submitting ourselves to greater and greater control. Which is just what *it* wants."

Mark is dizzy. He can't argue — doesn't even know any more if he *wants* to argue.

"Nothing too much *here* yet, I grant you: just more and more forms, more and more rules, more and more hoops to jump through. But it's on its way. Creeping up, bit by bit, on all the things that made us what we are. 'You shall not be an *I*. You shall be 11479. The only designation that matters is the one the Master gives you.' " He takes another slug of brandy, then sits there, frowning with concentration. "It's all around us," he says. " 'You shall not be Aubrey Hillyard. You shall be John Slindon, until such time as the Master sees fit to allocate you a number, by which you shall thereafter be known.' And the worst of it is, the damned thing's getting cleverer. Now we're going along with it because we're frightened. Soon it'll be because it's persuaded us it's what we want."

"Are you talking about the Brain?" Mark says, louder this time.

Hillyard hesitates, then slowly smiles. "The Brain's a warning: what the future will look like if we don't wake up. It hasn't happened yet. The nearest television comes to brainwashing at the moment is telling us which soap powder to buy. But once everyone's got one, it will, if we're not on our guard. It'll start watching us — whether we're watching *it*, or not. Moulding us to its own needs, under the guise of giving us something. You mark my words. When you're my age, you'll look back and say, *Aubrey was right*."

Rain starts to puddle in a slack patch of canvas. Hillyard bats it off with the back of his hand.

"Anyway," he says. "That day in '45, that was when the scales fell from my eyes. I'd seen some horrors, but —" He shakes his head. "I was due to be demobbed a few months later, but I knew I couldn't go back. Not to the old life, John Slindon's life. You know: the wife. The house in Raynes Park. The job in advertising. The 8.05 train in the morning, the 6.27 at night." He catches Mark's expression. "All right: I know, in the eyes of the world, I don't cut a very admirable figure. But to live like that, like John Slindon, you have to take certain things for granted. And I couldn't take them for granted, not any more. It was like telling a chap that he's got to go back to his room on the first floor of a bombed house — and there *isn't* a first floor. It's gone. Nothing to stand on at all. Just empty space."

"But you've still got a wife, haven't you? Another wife, I mean?" says Mark.

"What, Molly, you mean? That's a different kettle of fish entirely. No 8.05 with Molly. No job in advertising. No house in Raynes Park. Whatever else you say about her, she has the means to keep a man from that." He ducks his head to look through the tent door, then lifts the sleeping bag and pulls out an almost full pouch of Golden Virginia and a packet of Rizlas. "Have to be a bit careful with these," he says, starting to make a roll-up. "Case someone catches a whiff and comes snooping. But this wind ought to do the job, oughtn't it?"

"You can't go on staying here, can you?" says Mark. "Sooner or later, someone'll find you."

Hillyard smiles. "Someone *else*, you mean?"

Mark nods.

"No, I am planning to move on. I'd have gone sooner, if I could. Trouble was, I didn't even have enough for a railway ticket. But I should be able to in a couple of days, *Deo volente*."

"How?"

Hillyard holds up his unsealed roll your own, as if he's proposing a toast. "Your mother, God bless her," he says, then licks the rim and closes it. "Another ten bob now. That's all I need."

"Where will you go?"

Hillyard shrugs his eyebrows. "You ever heard of the Auxiliary Units?"

"No."

"Not surprised. They were as hush-hush as you could get. I had a chum in one." He lights his cigarette and slowly fills his lungs. "If the Germans invaded, they were to take to the hills. Live off the land. Fight to the death. Well, what I've decided is, that's what I'm going to be. A one-man Auxiliary Unit." He blows a pencil of smoke towards the entrance. "Stay free. Do whatever I have to to survive. Never give in."

"I've got ten bob you can have," Mark blurts.

Hillyard's eyes flood with tears. He doesn't try to blink them away, but lets them snake down into his beard.

"You really are the best pal in the world," he says. He puts his big hand on Mark's shoulder. "I shan't give you the 'No, I couldn't possibly'. I shall gratefully accept. On the understanding that I'll pay you back as soon as circumstances permit." He sniffs and catches a dribble from his nose with his finger. "Just one thing, though. Would you mind giving it to your mother, and then she can bring it along with the rest? Simply as a precaution. In case they're still keeping an eye on you. All right?"

"All right."

"Thank you." He nods and swallows. "And then I may have just one last job for you."

# CHAPTER TWENTY

Something that was broken has been mended. That's his first thought when he wakes in the morning: all the scattered fragments have suddenly been gathered up and miraculously reassembled into the familiar pattern. He feels the sense of completeness in his whole body: head, fingers, arms, feet, all finally working in harmony again. Life has regained its shape. The battle lines are clearer than ever. After weeks of confusion, he at last knows where he stands.

The one piece still missing is Lou. He's certain that if he could only talk to her, tell her everything Hillyard had told *him*, he'd be able to convince her. Then they could be *real* friends again — not just politely playing at bird-watching, but joined like Siamese twins by the secret knowledge that, after all, they had fought together on the right side, and their adventures had not been in vain. But the trouble is, of course, he *can't* talk to her. He could ask Murky to invite them both to tea again — but then he'd have to explain why. And — remembering her apologies, the harrumphing way she talked about "that man" — he knows that changing her mind about Hillyard would be beyond him.

At breakfast, it's hard not to let slip what happened yesterday. When Dad retreats behind *The Times*, and Mum — as if she's been waiting for the moment — says off-handedly, "By the way, I shall be popping out for a bit this morning," Mark catches her eye and smiles. Puzzled, she frowns and mouths, "What?"

He wants to say, "It's OK, I know where you're going." But he daren't, not with Dad there — even though, for all he knows now, Dad might approve of her helping Hillyard as much as he does. Instead, he asks:

"What time are you leaving?"

Mum glances at the clock. "Oh, I don't know, about ten, probably." She hesitates. Then, more loudly, she says to the wall of newspaper, "Will you be all right, Jeremy? I've got a bit of shopping to do."

There's no reply.

"Well, I'm just going to nip down to the post office," says Mark. "But I'll be back before you go, OK?"

"All right, sweetie. But honestly, you don't have to. Just as long as you're here for lunch. No need to bolt your breakfast."

"I've finished." He gets up, fingering the postal order in his hip pocket. "Stay, Barney!"

He slips out into Church End and half-runs as far as the Fox and Hounds. Then, instead of crossing the High Street, he ambles down the bank in front of the council houses, keeping his eye on the shop. *Come on, Lou. Come on, please*. When he's directly opposite, he stops. From here, he's high enough to see into the bedroom windows, and — while pretending to examine something on the ground — he sneaks a glance at them, willing her face to appear. But it doesn't. After a couple of minutes, he realizes that, if he stays any longer, people may start to get suspicious — so, reluctantly, he descends the bank, crosses the road and makes his way up to the Post Office.

"Morning, Mrs Pledger."

"Morning." She looks up, smiling, her gaze directed at a point three inches to his left. "Mark, is it?"

"Yes."

"Let me feel that smooth skin."

He bends forward, submitting himself to her. She shivers as her fingers run over his cheeks. Her beaming face is barred with a stripe of dusty light from the window. On the wall behind her is a sombre brown-and-beige poster: *The Post Office Guide Supplies All the Answers*.

"Yes, lovely," she says, withdrawing her hands and holding them together as if she's praying. "How are you, dear?"

"All right, thanks. Can I cash a postal order, please?"

"How much for?"

He takes it out and slides it across the counter. "Ten and six."

She picks it up and angles it towards the light, squinting through her thick glasses, then nods and puts it down again, pinioning it with her thumb, as if she's worried it might try to escape. "Buying something nice with it, are you?" she says, opening the till. "Something for that railway of yours?"

"No, this is for something else."

She pauses, her hand poised over the drawer. "Hm?"

"It's a secret."

"Oh, I see. A present for Mum, is it?"

He hesitates. She laughs.

"Oh, you don't have to tell me," she says, waving away her own nosiness with a flick of the wrist. "You just enjoy it, whatever it is."

It's only when he's on his way home — the bright new tanner clinking with the remains of last week's pocket money, the ten-bob note folded tightly in his hand — that he starts to wonder how exactly he's going to do this. He can't just say, "Please give this to Aubrey for me." First he has to find a way of letting her know, without startling her, that *he* knows what she's been doing for the last few weeks. That means being able to talk to her alone somewhere, without the risk of Dad walking in on them.

As he passes the church, he sees her with her back to him, loading something into the rear of the car. That's lucky: he can catch her now, before she has time to go inside again. He calls:

"Hullo, Mum!"

She straightens up abruptly, bashing her head on the lid of the boot.

"Ooh, are you all right?"

She turns, rubbing her scalp with one hand and slamming the boot shut with the other. "You made me jump."

"Sorry. Can I have a word with you?"

"What, now?" She looks at her watch.

He nods.

"What about?"

He points at the car. "Let's get in."

Her brow creases. She clicks her tongue. "Why?"

"We can talk there."

"Does it really have to be this instant?"

"Yes."

She opens the driver's door and gets in. Mark goes round to the other side and slips in next to her. The Turkish bath heat and the reek of upholstery are so powerful that they take his breath away for a moment. Then another smell lays itself over the fug: Mum's scent.

"What is it?" she says.

"Yesterday I was up at Cockenhoe."

Her frown deepens. She looks not just baffled, but frightened too. One sudden movement, one loud noise, he feels, and she'd be off, like Barney in the wood.

"I found something up there."

Her hand goes automatically to her head. But her hair's unusually neat this morning: there are no strands to tug at.

"You can guess what it was, can't you? Aubrey's camp."

"Aubrey *Hillyard?*"

He nods.

"What on earth is *he* doing there?"

He can't bear it. It's like being on a frozen pond and feeling the ice give. How can he make her stop pretending without actually calling her a liar?

"You *know* what he's doing there, Mum. And it's all right. He told me all about it. I think it's good you're helping him."

Her door's still open. She grabs the armrest and pulls it shut. "*What* did he tell you?"

"Everything. Don't worry. Honestly. You could have said before. I wouldn't have sneaked."

She turns away from him and stares straight ahead through the windscreen. The tip of her tongue appears like a tiny paintbrush, varnishing her lipsticked lips.

"What *exactly* did he say?"

What *did* he say? Not a lot, really, about her. Mark pulls together the few phrases he can remember. "He said you're a good woman. And that you saved his life."

"Nothing else?"

"Well, that's pretty good, isn't it? I mean, saving his life?"

"Yes." Her voice is flat. "That was nice of him."

He seems to have made her unhappier. Why? Surely she ought to be glad that he thinks she's done the right thing, and that Hillyard is so grateful?

"Why are you being such an old misery guts about it, then?" Mark says.

He hopes that'll make her laugh, but she just shakes her head.

"You're absolutely sure?" she says. "That's all he said about me?"

He shrugs. "Yes. More or less."

"OK. I'm sorry. It's all just been a bit of a strain. Trying to make sure no one saw me."

"Well, nobody did, did they?"

She shakes her head again.

"And he's going to be leaving soon, isn't he? Then you won't have to —"

"Is he?"

"That's what he said. He said he only needed another ten bob, and then he'll have enough. So that's why I went to the post office just now. To get this." He unfolds the note and holds it out to her. "He asked me to give it to you."

She stares at it, as if she's never seen anything like it before, and has no idea what it's for.

"So can you pass it on to him, please?" he says. "Or" — Is this what she wants? What she's waiting for? — "shall I come with you?"

"No." She takes the note, snaps open her bag and pulls out her purse. "But he'll be happy to get it, I know. I'd have given it to him myself, only I still haven't got quite enough. I'm having to be careful, just taking out a few bob a time. But I should be able to pay you back in a couple of weeks."

"He's going to do that."

She slips the note into her purse, saying nothing.

"Are you going there now?"

She nods, then glances towards the house. "I ought to be on my way."

"OK." He lifts the handle and pushes open the door. He's already half out when she leans across and grabs his wrist.

"You won't mention any of this to Dad, will you?"

"I don't think he'd mind, Mum. He'd have done the same thing himself, I expect. He says the people in the village are a lot of Nazis. For driving Aubrey out like that."

She shakes her head violently. "He wouldn't understand. He'd think the whole place knew about it, and they'd be coming to get *us* next."

He visualizes Dad's wounded sulky face. Yes, it's not hard to imagine him reacting like that.

"All right."

"Promise?"

"OK. Promise."

He shuts his door. Before he's reached the gate, he hears the engine starting and sees the car moving off. He waits till it's out of earshot, then slips into the house, easing the latch into place with his finger to prevent it clicking. It's better if Dad doesn't know that Mum's gone yet. The change in his behaviour recently — the way that, when they're alone in the house together, he's started taking Mark into his confidence — makes Mark feel queasy. And it would be even worse now, because he knows Mum's secret, and would have to pretend he didn't.

He quiets Barney, then hooks a finger through his collar and opens the door into the hall. They're already halfway up the stairs when he hears Dad calling,

"Is that you, old thing?"

He goes back down and cranes his head into the study. "Yes?"

"Come here a sec. I want to show you something."

There's a half-unfolded map on the table. As Mark approaches, he recognizes the bulge of East Anglia, the coast of Germany and Holland and northern France, the Pinocchio nose of Brittany.

"I'm planning our route," says Dad.

"What, for next summer?"

Dad nods. Still looking at the map, he takes a packet of Players from his pocket, absently taps one out and sticks the end in his mouth.

"Have they said they'll definitely do it, then?"

"Give us a caravan? No." He lights his cigarette. "But it's a good idea to be prepared. They may want to know exactly where we're going. Have a look at this."

He opens the map wider. The Dolomites appear — the Italian lakes — a blue corner of the Mediterranean.

"There are two choices," he says. "Either we can do this: across France, into Switzerland, then through Italy to Trieste. Or" — moving the hand with the fag in it northwards, over the Alps, leaving a trail of smoke, as if he were dropping marker flares along the route — "this: France, Germany, Austria — and into Italy that way. What do you think?"

Mark shrugs.

"No preference?"

Mark peers closer.

"Where's Mittelbau?" he says.

"What?"

"Mittelbau. Or Nordhausen?"

"Why do you want to know that?"

"I was just wondering."

Dad hesitates. "It's up here," he says finally, pointing to a spot just inside the East German border. "Nowhere near where we'd be going. It's where they built the V2s."

"I know."

Dad frowns at him. "*How* do you know? Who've you been talking to?"

He feels himself starting to colour. "No one."

"What, you mean you *read* about it somewhere?"

*In the Eagle*. But he keeps all his old *Eagles*. If Dad asked him to show it to him, he'd be sunk.

"No."

Dad stares at him, saying nothing.

"Murky said something about it," blurts Mark.

"Murky told you about Mittelbau? The concentration camp? The slave labour?"

"Yes."

"Well, I'm surprised. I wouldn't have thought even she would do that, not to a ten-year-old boy. I shall have a word with her about it."

"No . . . Sorry, Dad, I'm being silly. I forgot. It wasn't her. It was Aubrey Hillyard."

Dad narrows his eyes, squints at him through a gauze of smoke.

"You know, the chap in Twenty Acre Wood."

"How could it have been? He's gone, hasn't he?"

"Yes. I mean before."

Dad takes another slow pull on his cigarette. He looks like the German interrogator in a war story. "Why did he tell you about it?"

"He went there. In 1945."

Dad shakes his head. "It was liberated by the Americans."

"Yes, but afterwards." How has he got in this muddle? He tries to extricate himself. "Anyway, it doesn't matter. Let's go the Switzerland way. That's what *I'd* like. We might see a St Bernard." He ruffles Barney's head. "What do you think of that, boy? We could bring back a little barrel, couldn't we" — catching Dad's eye and smiling — "and make you wear that?"

He's angling for a laugh. Instead, Dad scowls and leans toward him. Smoke fills the space between them, making Mark's eyes smart.

"He was just trying to impress you. 'How I captured the V2 factory single-handed.' "

*That's not fair*. But if he says so, it'll only get him into even deeper trouble. He bites his lip. Dad stares at him in silence, then twitches suddenly, as if someone's pricked him with a pin.

"Always assuming, that is . . ." he says slowly.

He stops. But the rest of the sentence is obvious: "That *you* are telling the truth." Mark prays that the smoke is thick enough to hide his burning cheeks.

"Something's going on, isn't it?" says Dad. "Have you *seen* him? Hillyard, or whatever his real name is — Slindon? Is that it? Since he disappeared? Do you know where he is?"

Mark shakes his head.

"You promise me?"

Mark stares down at his knees.

"You *do* know, don't you?" says Dad.

Mark grips his chair with both hands to keep himself from squirming. "I think I know where he might have gone."

"Where?"

He shakes his head again. Dad holds his cigarette over the ashtray and knocks off a tube of ash.

"You do realize," he says, "that he's wanted by the police now? If you know something, and you don't tell them, then you're —"

"I don't know! I'm just guessing, that's all! All right?"

Dad frowns at him for a moment, then turns and looks out into the hall. Mum, that's what he's thinking about: Mum's behaviour over the past few weeks.

"You'd better leave me to get on now," says Dad abruptly, glancing back at him.

"But we haven't decided yet, have we?" says Mark, desperate not to go until he's managed to deflect Dad's mind from Mum and Hillyard.

"Decided what?"

"You know. About next summer. The route we're going to take."

Dad folds the map. "I very much doubt if we're going to be going anywhere next summer."

"Oh, don't say that, Dad! I'm looking forward to it!"

"Get out!" He slaps the map on the table. "Go on! Out!"

Tears are burning his eyes, but he turns away so that Dad can't see them. Only when he's upstairs and safe in his room does he surrender to his misery — a shivery pang that seizes his whole body, then forces itself out again in wave after wave of strangled howls. The worst of it is that he knows it's his fault: somehow, without even thinking about it, he pressed the switch that turned kind Dad into angry Dad. And in the process he's broken his promises to all of them: Mum, D Hillyard.

What's he going to tell Mum? He needs to see her before she gets into the house, explain what's happened, warn her about Dad. He creeps downstairs again, collects Barney, then sneaks out and waits on the mossy patch of path next to the kitchen, where he can see the gate but Dad can't see him. Just as the church clock is striking one, he hears the far-off whine of an engine dropping into second gear, and feels Barney stiffen beside him. Half a minute later, the Vauxhall noses into view.

He runs down and opens the driver's door while she's still fiddling with the keys. She looks up at him, sees his expression.

"What is it?"

"Dad. He's in an awful mood."

Her eyes widen. "You haven't told him, have you?"

He shakes his head. "But I think he may have guessed."

"Why? What did he say?"

"Nothing. It's just . . . Well, I told him something Aubrey said. I didn't mean to. It just slipped out."

"Something about *me?*"

"No, but I got in a muddle . . . And that made him a bit suspicious. I think he realized something's going on. And that you're tied up in it."

She nods slowly. She's very pale, despite the heat of the car. She looks sad, but strangely calm — like someone who's just received bad news that she's been expecting for a long time.

'I'm sorry, Mum."

She shakes her head and gets awkwardly out the car, moving as stiffly as Murky.

"All right," she says. "I'll go in and see him. I'll probably be some time. If you want something to eat, you'd better help yourself. There's bread. And some cheese in the fridge."

She retrieves her bag and locks the car. She greets Barney mechanically, then starts up the path. She's almost at the house when she stops and looks back.

"Oh, I almost forgot." She opens her bag and takes out an envelope. "He asked me to give you this."

Mark hurries after her and collects it. It's addressed in Hillyard's handwriting: "Mark Davenant Esq." He tears it open and takes out a single sheet of paper. As he starts to read, he hears the click of the back door latch.

Dear Mark,

Such generosity! That ten bob must surely represent at least the 6 and the 0 of a brand new 4-6-0 for Peveril on the Swift. I am deeply touched. You really are the best pal in the world.

As I hinted when we met, I have one last kindness to ask. Now that, thanks to you, I can afford the fare, I am planning finally to make my escape tomorrow. Who knows where I shall end up? Another wood? An abandoned boat? A hole in the ground? Wherever it is, though, rest assured: the resistance will go on.

Before I leave, I shall need to collect a few things from the railway carriage — a risky undertaking, given that the powers that be may still be keeping a watchful eye on the place. Would you be willing to act as our lookout? H-hou is 6.00p.m. Once the deed is done, I give you my word, I shall trouble you no more — except, of course, to return the ten bob.

Yours ever,

A.H.

PS. Needless to say, this is all *strictly* 'twixt ourselves. Please destroy this note when you've read it.

He goes through it a second time, then a third. It's like standing by a fire when you're cold. You linger as long as you can — because, the instant you move away, you know you'll start shivering again. *Such generosity. You really are the best pal in the world. Would you be willing to act as our lookout?*

Yes, he would. It'll be a last chance to prove himself — to salvage something from the summer by seeing the adventure through to the end. It won't be victory, but it won't be total defeat, either: it'll be a sort of Dunkirk, snatching our forces from the jaws of the enemy, so that they live to fight another day. And perhaps, once Hillyard's safely out of the way, things will get better at home. If Mum doesn't have to pretend any more, maybe life can return to normal.

Lou, though, he thinks, as he tears the paper into tiny pieces — what to do about Lou? If he could just explain, let her know what Hillyard told *him*, she'd understand, finally — or at least be prepared to give him the benefit of the doubt. But he needs to do it now, before Hillyard leaves, so that she has a chance to see him again.

A go-between. Someone to deliver a note for him.

He doesn't want to go into the house again: even upstairs in his room, it'd be impossible to ignore the skin-searing radiation pulsing out from the study. He stuffs the bits of note into his pocket, then opens the back door and shoves Barney inside, screwing up his face to make a hum in his ears, so that he doesn't have to hear what he dreads: sobs, raised voices — worse still, a louring silence, like the prelude to a thunderstorm.

He sees Murky even before he reaches the bottom of the High Street. She's halfway up the drive, wearing her moth-eaten hat and two mismatched gloves, butchering ivy with an old pair of secateurs. When she hears the crunch of gravel she turns, shading her eyes with her hand.

"Ah, young Aurelius." She blinks, perplexed. "We hadn't —"

"No, don't worry. I just wanted to ask you to do me a favour."

"Anything, unto half my kingdom." She nods at the patch of wall she's just cleared. The bricks are half worn away and sandy with disintegrating mortar. "Not that my kingdom is a particularly desirable prize, in its current state."

"I want you to deliver a note for me."

She wipes her forehead with the back of a glove. "Where?"

"At the shop. For Lou."

"Why can't you deliver it yourself?"

"Cos she wouldn't get it. If her parents knew it wa from me, they wouldn't give it to her."

"Really? As bad as that?"

"Yes."

She hesitates, then holds out a hand. "All right."

"I haven't written it yet. Can you lend me some paper? And an envelope?"

She nods, opens her arms and looks down at her earth-streaked gardening clothes. "I don't want to traipse dirt everywhere. Go in and help yourself. The writing desk in the sitting room. Top left-hand drawer."

There are cats everywhere: lying on the front step, patrolling the hall with raised tails, perched at the top of the stairs. They study him as he walks through the front door, then lose interest when he goes into the sitting room rather than the kitchen.

In the drawer, he finds an almost new pad of Basildon Bond and a packet of envelopes. But the pen lying next to them is dry, and there doesn't seem to be a bottle of ink anywhere. In the end, he has to make do with a stub of pencil.

Dear Lou,
I've seen him. He's been hiding. His real name *is* John Slindon, but he only pretended because they really are after him. Everything else is true. Promise. I'll tell you about it when I see you. Anyway he's leaving tomorrow at six. I'm going to keep watch for him in Twenty Acre Wood. You can come too. Meet me at the hideout at five.

Honestly he was telling the truth.

Mark

He folds it, slips it into an envelope and licks the flap. When he goes outside again, he finds Murky waiting by the front door.

"Leave it there," she says, pointing to the hall table. "So I don't forget."

"Will you write the name on, please?"

She raises her eyebrows.

"Otherwise they'll guess who it's from."

She hesitates. "Yes, all right."

He gives her the envelope and the pencil. She takes off her gloves, writes "Miss Lou Bennett", and then, in the top left corner, "By hand".

"If I didn't know you were the soul of honour," she says, flapping it against her palm, "I'd want to know what's inside. But —"

"Thanks, Murky," he says, and hurries down the drive before she can see the heat rising to his face.

# CHAPTER TWENTY-ONE

*Peveril on the Swift! This is Peveril on the Swift!*

*Goodness, Patty, you're cutting it a bit fine, aren't you?*

*Morning, Mrs Dauntless. Yes, I overslept, I'm afraid.*

*Well, you're only young once. I was just the same when I was your age.*

Mark picks the figures up, reaches for the Oxo tin, then puts them down on the platform again. He isn't ready yet. It's like one of those dark winter mornings when he has to get up to go to school but can't bear to leave the warmth and safety of bed. Peveril *is* safety: the one tiny corner of the world that still runs with clockwork regularity, and where raised voices and sulky silences are unknown.

*Looks as if we're in for another lovely day.*

"Mark?"

The door opens, throwing a searchlight beam across the layout, picking out the Dauntlesses' house, the hermitage, Sheepfold Hill. He turns. A powerful waft of scent hits him.

"I'm off now," she says. "To collect him."

"What time is it?"

A bit after four." She's almost in silhouette, but the curve of one cheek is in the light, pale as a crescent moon. "But he's going to need a hand with the tent and things."

She pauses. He's worried she's going to ask him to go with her and he'll have to explain why he can't: he hasn't mentioned Lou, and wants her appearance to be a surprise. But in the end she says:

"So you'll make your own way there, will you?"

He nods.

"How will you know when it's six?"

"I'll guess."

She shakes her head. "Take this." She unbuckles her watch and hands it to him.

"How are *you* going to manage?"

"*He*'ll tell me. We'll see you at the railway carriage, then?"

"OK."

She turns, jangling the car keys.

"Where's Dad?"

"Upstairs."

"Migraine?"

She nods. "Don't worry." All the force has gone from her voice. "I'll deal with him when we get back."

He can't play any more, and he doesn't want to go back in the house and risk being tugged into the orbit of Dad's misery. He eases the train out of the station and into the Abbey Tunnel. Then he switches off the controller, and — taking care not to alert Barney — creeps out, latches the door behind him and tiptoes down the path.

Church End is empty. He dodges into the Plaistc and heads towards the bottom of the High Street. It's only when he reaches Willetts Lane that he realizes how long it is since he's been there. The grass is still thick, but it's starting to lose its colour, and the leaves on the trees are becoming lustreless and parched.

He turns up the track to the chalk pit, then cuts through the gap in the hedge. The corn's been harvested, the field reduced to a waste of stubble. The hideout's still there, but ragged and overgrown, and naked without its screen of wheat.

"Gallion."

No reply. But he said five o'clock, so it's still early.

He wriggles inside and pokes his fingers into the message hole. It's empty. He brushes the floor free of twigs and spiders, and lies down. As he sits up, he thinks he catches the hum of a distant engine; but the instant he turns his head, trying to work out where it's coming from, it's gone. He must have imagined it.

*Come on, Lou, or there won't be time to tell you everything*.

He goes to the entrance and peers out. The field's empty, apart from a flock of pigeons scavenging for grain. He retreats inside again, scrapes a little grave in the soil and buries the fragments of Hillyard's message. Where on earth *is* she? If her parents had told her she couldn't come out this evening, surely she'd have had a chance to nip up and leave him a note? Maybe she never got his message in the first place? Yes, that's the likeliest answer. Chances are it's still lying on the hall table at Hillfield . . .

The sound of a motor: a long way off, but unmistakable this time. Not a tractor or a Land Rover: a car. Mum and Hillyard arriving at the edge of the wood, presumably. He can't wait any more: he has to get to the railway carriage.

He crawls out of the hideout and starts down the hill. When he reaches the gap in the hedge he pauses and listens. The engine he heard before has stopped, but there's a second one now, further away. Shading his eyes with his hand, he squints across to the other side of the valley. At the entrance to the farmyard he can just make out the black beetle back of a car roof. It could be Mr Montgomery's Humber: it's too far away to tell. But why would anyone leave it there?

He breaks into a jog-trot, skipping and dodging over the rough chalk. The further he goes, the less like the Humber it seems. When he gets to the bottom, he stops and looks again. As he does so, a brilliant dazzle of light from the farm hurts his eye — as if someone there is watching *him*.

He turns into Willetts Lane. Fifty yards along, the Vauxhall has been pulled off to the side. It's lying at an odd angle, listing like a grounded boat and almost touching the trunks of the nearest trees. He glances through the window. There's no one inside.

He plunges into the wood, taking the same path he followed when he first stumbled on Aubrey Hillyard almost three months ago. As he approaches the clearing, he can hear murmured voices, a metallic groan, surreptitious bumps and squeaks. He pauses at the edge of the trees, keeping himself hidden until he's quite sure that it's Mum and Hillyard making the noise, not Mr Montgomery and Mr Barron. The door's open, and piled outside it are a scuffed leather suitcase and couple of bags. After a few seconds, Mum comes out onto the top of the steps, carrying a cardboard box.

"Mum!"

She looks up, startled. He runs towards her.

"There's someone up at the farm!"

"What, Horseshoe Farm, you mean?"

He nods.

"Who?"

"I don't know. But they were watching me. At least, I think they were."

She hesitates, then looks inside and calls:

"Aubrey?"

"What?" He appears in the doorway, enormous, bulked out by a roll of bedding in his arms. "Oh, there you are," he says, nodding at Mark. "Welcome to —"

"Mark thinks he's seen someone," says Mum.

Hillyard looks at him, raising an eyebrow.

"There's a car up at the farm. I think it might be a police car."

"Why?"

"Well, it's black."

"So are most cars. Good old Henry Ford again. 'You can have any colour you want. As long as it's black.' So —"

"Even so," says Mum, touching his sleeve. "I think perhaps we should go, don't you?"

"What, now?"

She nods. "Just in case."

Hillyard shakes his head. "I'm sure it doesn't mean anything."

"But what if it does?" says Mum.

"Then it'd be a whopping coincidence, wouldn't it?" says Hillyard. "There are three people in the world who know about this. And they're all here. For the rozzers to have tumbled to it on their own would require a deductive skill far beyond the capacity of your average Special Branch officer. It's not the police we have to worry about, it's that damned farmer and his cronies."

Mum stares at him, saying nothing.

He sighs. "All right. Let's get a move on, then." He beckons Mark. "Want to give a hand?"

Mark follows him into the carriage. It's dark and smells of rotten food. The corners are hung with cobwebs. Next to the stove stands an unwashed plate covered in mould. On the underside of one of the piled-up chairs lies the model boat Hillyard was making. It's still unfinished — but on the prow, in rough-edged black letters, Mark can see *Pintail*.

"Tugs the heart strings a bit, doesn't it, seeing the old place again?" says Hillyard. "Happy days. Tea and biscuits. Swapping yarns about Peveril on the Swift and my starry-eyed young honeymooners."

"Mr and Mrs X?"

Hillyard nods.

"Haven't you given them names yet?"

"It may have escaped your notice, but I've had one or two other things on my mind." He picks up his Remington Portable, snaps on the top and gives it to

Mark. "Run this out to the car, would you? And th come back for episode two."

It's heavier than Mark expected. Holding it in both hands, he wobbles down the steps, then retraces his route as fast as he can to the Vauxhall. He opens the boot and heaves the typewriter inside. As he slams the lid shut again, he's suddenly worried that the people at the farm might have heard it. Sticking to the grass to muffle his footsteps, he sneaks to the end of the lane, then cranes his head out just enough to peer up the hill. The car's still there. But now he can see figures standing in front of it, too: three of them, all in dark clothing. Something heaves in his stomach, as if it's trapped there, and trying to fight its way out.

He ducks back into the wood and sprints to the railway carriage. Mum and Hillyard are both inside.

"Quick!" he yells. "It *is* the police! I'm sure of it!"

Hillyard rockets through the door. He's already at the bottom of the steps before Mum shimmers into view behind him, uneasy and insubstantial as a ghost.

"Why?" says Hillyard. "What did you see?"

"Men in uniform."

"At the farm?"

"Yes."

"Right. Out." He turns back to the carriage. "Out!"

Mum stumbles down the steps, almost trips, then steadies herself.

"One bag each," says Hillyard. "Go! Go! I'll follow you."

"Have you got the book?" says Mark.

Hillyard seems not to hear him. "Move!"

Mum and Mark pick up a bag apiece and start unning towards the lane. Behind them they hear the click of a padlock, then the thump of his feet as he races after them. By the time they reach the Vauxhall, he's swerved past them and pulled up the boot.

"Chuck it in. Anyhow. Doesn't matter. Mark, you get in front with your mother."

Mark slides in. Behind him, Hillyard stretches out across the back seat, yanks the door shut with his foot, then works himself as far down onto the floor as he can.

"Is that a good idea?" says Mum, looking over her shoulder as she gets in.

"If they stop us, I'm done for anyway," says Hillyard. "The only hope is that they don't see me and wave you through."

She doesn't reply. Her hand is shaking so much that it takes her a couple of seconds to line up the key with the ignition. Finally she slips it in, switches on and presses the starter. As she lets in the clutch, the rear wheels start to spin, but the car doesn't move. She revs the engine. The tyres scream, the Vauxhall shakes, then suddenly lurches forward.

"Gently, gently," mumbles Hillyard. "You're taking the vicar for a Sunday afternoon drive."

Mum says nothing, but grits her teeth and clutches the steering wheel with both hands. The car edges towards the High Street, jolting over ruts, swooshing against the ridge of grass that runs down the middle of the lane. Mark looks at the speedometer: nine miles an hour. It's nightmarishly slow, but he knows she can't go any faster. He glances behind him, out of the back window. No sign of anyone following them. Almost there now. In another minute or two they'll be on the open road. He can see the sagging gateposts at Hillfield, feel the track starting to get smoother, hear the spit of stray bits of gravel . . .

Two policemen appear from Murky's drive, barring the way. Mum stops. One of the men walks round to her door, making a winding motion with his hand. She lowers the window.

"Good evening, madam."

"Evening."

"Would you mind telling us where you've just been?"

She points behind her.

He nods. "And why would that be?" He leans down, peers inside. "Not a lot of traffic along there, as a —" He falters as he spots Hillyard. "Ah, I see. Engine off, please."

"What?"

He twists his wrist. Mum switches off. He catches his colleague's eye and nods at the car. The second man walks past Mark and stops.

"Right," says the first man.

They open the two rear doors simultaneously. Neither of them says anything. Slowly, heavily, Hillyard hauls himself up onto the seat. He stares at Mark, frowning. His beard is tinged red by the sun. There's a slackness, a defencelessness in his eyes that Mark has never seen before. After so much ducking and dodging, the U-Boats have finally got him: he's fatally holed, powerless to keep the sea from surging in.

"Get out of the car, please, sir."

Mark starts to cry. "The resistance . . ." he starts, then can't go on.

Hillyard touches his shoulder, then reaches into his pocket and takes out Mark's knife. He holds it up by the ring and studies it closely. Then, like an officer surrendering his sword, he offers it to Mark.

"Here."

"You can keep it if you want."

"No."

Mark takes it. Hillyard turns to Mum. She's hunched forward over the wheel, eyes closed, sobbing. Hillyard reaches forward and brushes a stray curl with his fingertips.

"All right," he says, looking up at the first policeman.

The man moves out of the way. Hillyard levers himself out and stands looking down at him, flexing his shoulders.

"She hasn't got a clue," he says. "Give you my word. She was just doing me a kindness. Taking me to the station. So you can let her go." He positions himself where Mum can see him in the wing mirror and flicks his hand. "Go on. Go on."

The policeman leans on the roof and puts his head in at the window again.

"Are you local, madam?"

"Yes."

"I'll need your name and address." He takes a notebook from his tunic. "Mrs —"

"Davenant. Perry Cottage. Church End."

He copies it down slowly, like a small child learning how to form letters. "Thank you." He nods: *You can go now*. "But please don't leave the area without letting u know."

The two men lead Hillyard past the Vauxhall and into the drive. Mum doesn't move. She's weeping, almost silently, her fists clenched tight. Mark hears doors slamming, the throat-clearing grind of a starter. A black police Wolseley noses past the gatepost and stops at the road. Mark peers into the back. All he can see of Hillyard is a wild fringe of uncombed hair. Blocking the rest of him is a small man in a linen suit, who answers Mark's gaze with a blank expression. Then the car eases out, turns left towards Cobwell and in a moment is eclipsed by Murky's wall.

Mum hasn't even looked up. Mark puts a hand on her shoulder.

"It's not your fault, Mum. You did your best."

She says nothing. He can feel her stiffen.

"It's all right."

She shakes her head. "It isn't all right. It's all ghastly."

"No, it isn't." *Yes it is*. They have to go home. Face Dad. Eat a meal together. He takes her watch from his wrist and drops it in her lap. Without opening her eyes she fiddles it on and fastens the strap.

She sniffs. "Has Dad said anything to you?"

"What about?"

"Plans."

"What, next summer, you mean?"

"No, not next summer." She pauses, trying to get the rhythm of her breathing back. "We've decided it would be better if you went away to school."

Why on earth is she talking about that now? "I know," he says. "Dad said."

She half lifts her head, looks at him with one eye. "Oh, so he has spoken to you about it, has he? When?"

"I don't know. A few days ago. What's it matter, anyway? It won't be for a couple of years, will it?"

She shakes her head. "I'm not talking about in a couple of years. I'm talking about now. Immediately."

He looks out of the window. The brick wall, the wheat field, the grey strip of the High Street have lost their solidity. They start to buckle, as the world used to when he saw Roman soldiers or knights riding by. But there are no knights or soldiers now.

"Why?" he says.

"We just think that would be best."

"But I'm still going to The Hoops!" *Please. That's the only place where I can see Lou.*

She doesn't reply. He shuts his eyes. The blackness is crowded with maggoty figures. Hovering behind them, over them, penetrating them, is Hillyard's face, huge, unbearably sad, lit by a thin golden glow. Mark tries to think, to find an argument. Only one thing comes into his mind: *money*.

"It'll cost too much," he says.

"I've spoken to Grandma. She's going to help." She lets out a sigh that makes her shoulders shake. "Anyway" — pushing herself upright, fumbling for the key — "I suppose . . ."

She starts the engine and jerks the car into gear. All the way up the High Street and along Church End, neither of them says another word.

* * *

He spends the whole of the rest of the evening in his room. Mum doesn't call him down to supper. That, at least, is a relief: he's not hungry, and he dreads having to see Mum and Dad together. He's not even sure that there *is* any supper: there's no sound coming from the kitchen.

He doesn't want to think. Nowhere that thought can take him offers any refuge, any scrap of shelter from the storm. He's aware of something forming at the edge of his mind: not an idea so much as a *shape* — a giant iceberg looming against the horizon. But every time it starts drifting towards the centre of his consciousness, he pushes it away again.

To numb himself, he takes out his old *Eagles* and doggedly goes through all the stories he's never really liked: "Storm Nelson", "Harris Tweed, Special Agent", "The Three Js". It takes hours, but gradually he finds he's having to read sentences three or four times before he understands them. He starts to yawn. His eyelids sag. He forces them open, but a few seconds later they're at it again, more insistent now, painting over his eyes with darkness, blacking them out against the Blitz . . .

*There are three people in the world who know about this. And they're all here*. He hears it so clearly that for a moment he thinks Hillyard's in the room with him. Then he's awake and knows that's impossible. But in the same instant he's aware that the iceberg has broken free while he slept, and it's too late to banish it again.

He contemplates it, aghast at its size, the way it blots out everything else. Now he *has* to think, darting back and forth, trying to find an alternative explanation. He can't: it's inescapable. He's conscious of a vein of lava starting to run through him, fiercer and fiercer, hotter and hotter. If he can't find a way to direct it outside himself, soon it will rupture . . .

What to do? Bash on her door? Smash the windows? No, he'd be caught. There must be another way of doing it.

Chalk: that's what he needs. He gets out of bed and rummages in the table drawer. Yes, there at the back: just one piece, in the middle of a clutter of broken crayons and old pens.

He pulls on his clothes and slips the chalk into his pocket. Barney's still asleep, but he daren't leave him. He prods him awake, then — on tiptoe — leads him downstairs, grasping his muzzle.

He doesn't know what time it is, but it's still dark, apart from a fingernail moon that keeps slipping behind clouds and then reappearing. Even Stan Green's dad won't be up yet. Every door is shut, every window curtained. The coaches at the garage are locked away, the petrol pumps abandoned. The only hint of life is at the Fox and Hounds, which leaks a faint smell of last night's beer and cigarettes.

When he gets to the shop, he quickly checks the houses opposite, to make sure he's not being watched. They're as blank and sealed up as everywhere else. As he turns back again, he feels a patter of rain on his neck. He takes a deep breath. No point hanging about.

Holding Barney with one hand, he pulls the chalk from his pocket, creeps up to the Bennetts' door and writes:

TRAITOR.

# CHAPTER TWENTY-TWO

He just wants to hide. But Cockenhoe is as bad as Twenty Acre Wood now, blighted by an unbearable sense of loss. And it's the same with the village. When he looks at the High Street, it's impossible to see it with the innocent eyes of three months ago: every building — pub, garage, Hillfield — has succumbed to an unbreakable spell. Even the enchantment of the post office has soured, turning Mrs Pledger's kindness into something to be feared. *Did you get something nice with that ten and six? Looking forward to going back to school, are you?*

Worst of all, of course, is the shop. Why did she do it? What could have made her betray Hillyard? He can't imagine. But a world in which such treachery is possible is a world where no one and nothing can ever be trusted again.

At home, at least, he's able to shut himself in his room. But a flimsy door with a loose handle isn't enough to insulate him from the poisonous chill spreading through the house. There's one final, dreadful attempt to pretend that nothing's changed: on the morning after Hillyard's arrest, they all have breakfast together. From the moment he arrives to the moment he leaves, Dad says nothing. He doesn't eve glance at his newspaper: he just sits at his end of the table, looking fixedly past both of them, as if he were entirely on his own, contemplating some unpleasant memory. At first, Mum tries brightly to make conversation, but the weight of the silence forces the breath out of her, and for the last ten minutes nobody speaks at all. After that, Mark eats by himself. But, even then, there's always the fear that either Mum or Dad will walk in and try to win him to their side, and he'll end up crushed between them.

He spends most of the time out of doors. So much of the landscape is enemy territory now that he sticks mainly to the roads, keeping Barney on a short lead, pressing himself into the side whenever a car or a tractor goes by, searching for a scrap of hedge or a fallen tree where he can take shelter. It's useless: everything's too muddy, or too narrow, or means running the risk of being caught for trespassing. One afternoon he goes further than usual, up to the old wartime pillbox on the ridge between Oatley and Burdon. It's damp and reeks of pee. People have scratched names and messages into the concrete walls. "Wot me worry." "Stan Green wos ere." As they go inside, Barney hangs back, whining. Maybe it's haunted, he thinks: dogs are meant to be sensitive to ghosts — *real* ghosts, that is, not imaginary ones. He turns and hurries down the hill, sweat prickling in the small of his back.

He's homeless: a fox without a hole, at the mercy of the hounds. He's so tired he finds himself drifting off as he walks, then jolting awake again a few seconds later. He's aware that people are starting to look at him oddly: Mr Robinson, glancing up surreptitiously from his digging; Betty Doggett, watching him with her thumb in her mouth like a wondering child. When Mark limps into the house, even Mum — who, it seems, is being carried further and further out of reach by some invisible current — stirs herself to say:

"Are you all right?"

"Yes." Because to admit that he isn't would open the door to a conversation that he has to avoid at all costs.

The next evening, he's startled when he walks in to find Murky sitting at the table.

"Ah, young Aurelius." She leans forward, both hands clasped on her stick.

"Oh, hullo."

"You don't really mean that, do you? What you *really* mean is, 'What on earth are doing here, Murky?' But you're too well brought up to say it."

Mum, hovering in the kitchen behind her, gives a tiny smile, the first Mark has seen in days.

"And the answer is, I've got something to give you." She wiggles her stick. "And I was wondering if I could entice you to come to the house and get it?"

"What, now?"

"Yes, if you'd do me the honour."

He glances at Mum. She nods.

"All right."

It's only after they've started along Church End that Mark wonders if he's been stupid. Maybe Mum knows that he doesn't want to talk to her about school, and has asked Murky to broach the subject instead. H braces himself for the opening salvo. But she unusually quiet — and, when she does speak, it's only about how chilly the weather is getting. He can't guess what she's got for him, but whatever it is, she seems to be delaying saying anything more until he's actually holding it in his hand.

As they approach the shop, he switches sides, so that he's walking next to the road and she's between him and the red-eyed, fire-breathing Mr Bennett he half-imagines to be lying in wait for him. Even so, he feels cold, and his mouth is dry. *He can't know*, he tells himself. *He can't possibly know it was you*. He glances furtively at the house as they pass. There's no trace of chalk on the door. It suddenly occurs to him that perhaps no one even saw it. It could just have been washed away by the rain in the night. Now he thinks about it, that probably is what happened. He's relieved — but disappointed too. He'll have to find another way to reach Lou in her bunker, let her know he knows her secret, and she isn't safe from him.

"Are you eating?" asks Murky, as they walk up the drive. "You look like a hungry young dog. Bit of cheese or something?"

"No, thanks."

"Sure?"

He nods. She opens the door and leads him through the hall and into the sitting room, cats swarming at her heels.

"Sit down."

He perches on the sofa. Immediately, a wave of tiredness breaks over him, pressing on his eyes.

"Oh, poor young Aurelius."

He opens his eyes again. She's watching him the way Mum used to when he was ill in bed. She leans over and touches his forehead.

"No temperature. But you're not well." She stands up again. "Did you know I was a nurse?"

He shakes his head.

"Yes, in the Great War. We saw a lot of chaps like you. Shell shock, they used to call it. All we could do was make sure they got plenty of rest. And regular meals." She hesitates. "Do you want to go and put your feet up now for a bit?"

"No, thanks."

She goes on looking at him, then nods and lowers herself stiffly into her chair.

"This awful business," she says. "It just seems to drag on and on, doesn't it? And I'm afraid you're not the only one who's been having a bad time of it. This morning I had a visit from a very unhappy young woman. She asked me to give you something." She reaches across and takes an envelope from the writing desk. He recognizes Lou's careful, squeezed-together handwriting. "If we continue like this, there won't be anything left for the unfortunate postman to do, will there?"

He holds his hand out. She ignores it.

"I don't know exactly what it says, of course," she goes on. "But I gather there's been some sort of a — what, a misunderstanding?"

"Not a misunderstanding. She did something."

"All right: she did something. I think I might be able to guess what, but I'm not expecting you to tell me. I don't *want* you to tell me. All I know is, she's quite frantic about it, poor girl. Desperate to explain herself. But she's worried that you won't meet her."

He thrusts his hand out again. "Let me see."

She shakes her head. "So that's the question? *Will* you meet her?"

"How do I know? Till I see what she says?"

Murky waves the envelope. "Don't be hard on her, Mark. You remember, when they had gold coins, they'd check if they were forged or not by biting them? If you could see teeth-marks afterwards, you'd know they were genuine. I've always thought that was a good test for people too. And there are tooth-marks all over poor Lou. I've known you much longer than I've known her, of course, but there, anyway, I'd say the two of you are very much alike. Both absolutely the real thing."

Mark shakes his head.

"Really, I can't ever imagine her deliberately doing anything underhand."

"She did."

"Well, *if* she did, she must have had a reason for it. Perhaps she was trying to protect you."

"No, she wasn't! She stabbed me in the back!"

"I'm sure she didn't mean to. She wouldn't. One of the reasons I like her is that she shares my high opinion of you. You couldn't have a loyaller friend. And no one should be condemned before they've had a chance to defend themselves. Isn't that a sound principle?" She flinches, as the ginger cat jumps onto the back of her chair and rubs itself against her neck. "Isn't it what we were fighting for, among other things?"

Mark says nothing. In the silence, the cat launches itself noiselessly into her lap and stands there, back arched, sinking its claws into her thick skirt.

"Please," says Murky, scratching its head. "And if it turns out I'm wrong, you have my full permission to come back and tell me I'm a silly old woman."

He hesitates. "All right."

"Thank you." She hands him the envelope. He opens it and pulls out a sheet of lined paper:

> I can't put it all in a letter. Meet me at the hideout at ten tomorrow. Then you'll see. PS. Please come.

The next morning is cold and flinty. He hunts about in his drawer and finds a pair of long trousers and a sweater smelling of mothballs. Then he collects his mac from the hall, picks up the lead and calls Barney.

It's starting to rain: big hard drops that chill his cheeks and sting his eyes. He turns up the collar of his coat, loops the lead round his wrist and puts his hands in his pockets. Even so, he can't stop shivering.

He doesn't want to go any nearer to the railway carriage than he has to, so he cuts straight across the middle of the bristly wheat field. The hideout looks as exposed and desolate as ever. He pauses a few yards short of it. Should he say *Gallion*, or would that be using a spell that has lost its power? The next moment, Barney settles the question for him: tail windmilling, he surges ahead, scrabbles excitedly at the entrance and wriggles inside.

Mark drops to his knees and peers in. Lou has her arms round Barney's neck, her face pressed against his slathery muzzle. Her eyes are wet and red-rimmed. Her cheeks are still freckly, but all the ruddiness has gone, leaving her sickly pale. Next to her is her knapsack, pushed by something inside into a lopsided pointy shape.

"Hullo," she says.

"Hullo."

"Are you coming in?"

"There isn't enough room. I'll stay here."

She shakes her head. "You'll get wet. Come on, Barney. Lie down. Get out of the way."

She shoves Barney to one side and pushes him to the ground, making a small gap. Mark crawls in and manoeuvres himself into a sitting position. She makes no attempt to move her outstretched leg, but he manages to avoid touching it.

"You didn't say *Gallion*," she says.

He shrugs. "That was when we were friends, wasn't it?"

She bites her lip. "I saw what you wrote on the door."

"Good."

She sniffs. She's trying not to cry. Barney nuzzles her, whimpering. Mark looks away. It would be easier if she was angry, and they could have an all-out shouting match.

"I'm not a traitor," she says. "Whatever you think."

"Yes, you are. We said we'd always help him, didn't we? We promised."

"He's the traitor," she says.

"*Aubrey?*"

"Slindon."

"No, he isn't."

"Yes, he is."

"Why, just because he pretended his name was Aubrey Hillyard?"

"That. And —"

"There was a reason for that! I could have told you, if only you'd trusted me."

"What reason? That place, you mean? Where they built the rockets?"

For a moment he's floored. Then he mumbles, "Partly."

"Yes, he told me about that," she says.

"When?"

"That last day at the railway carriage. Just before you came to warn us about PC Pointer. Aubrey told me he'd lied to us: he wasn't really Aubrey Hillyard at all, he'd borrowed someone else's name, because he'd seen something so awful that he couldn't go back to his old life. The life he'd had before the war." She unfastens her knapsack and pulls out a book. "He asked me to take this for him. Said if PC Pointer found it, and saw the name, he'd get into trouble."

She hands it to Mark: *Our Young Aeroplane Scouts in Turkey*. It's old and worn, with a faded picture on the cover of a biplane under fire. He opens it. Inside, in childish blue crayon, is written:

John Arthur Slindon
33 Parson Street
Coulsdon
Surrey
England
Great Britain
The Empire
The World
The Solar System
The Universe

Mark shrugs. "That doesn't prove anything. Well, not anything he didn't tell us, anyway."

"Eventually. When he had to."

"Well, he couldn't tell us before, could he? Not until he was sure we wouldn't give him away?"

She winces. "He didn't tell us cos he knew we'd realize then. What a bad man he was. I bet you that's the *real* reason."

"He's not a bad man."

"Treating his wife like that," she says. "That was wrong."

"I know. But he didn't have any choice."

She appears not to hear him. From her bag, she produces a Picnic and a Bounty bar.

"You want one of these?" she says, holding them out.

He hesitates, pride battling hunger.

"Come on. You choose."

"All right."

He takes the Picnic and rips it open. She slits the seam of the Bounty, as delicately as if she were undressing a doll, and breaks off a small mouthful.

"We might be married one day, mightn't we?" she says. "And if we were, you wouldn't do that to me. I know you wouldn't. Just disappear, and not tell me anything. Not even if you were still alive or not."

An earthquake passes through him. He clutches his mac closer, hoping she hasn't noticed.

"He didn't care about her, or us, or anyone," she says. "Just himself. He's a liar and a cheat. *And* a thief." She pauses, watching him closely. Then she picks up *Our Aeroplane Scouts in Turkey*. "I didn't just take this. I took something else as well. He didn't ask me to, but I decided to anyway. Cos I still believed all that stuff about the Brain then. And I thought, if PC Pointer saw what he'd been writing, he'd tell the powers that be. So —"

She collects a torn brown envelope from her knapsack.

"Do you want to see it?"

"What, his book, you mean? Is that it?"

She nods.

"All right."

"I wasn't going to show you. But I think I'd better. Or you won't understand."

He takes it and pulls out a thick sheaf of paper. It's a carbon copy, the letters slightly smudged, the margins dirty. There's no title. He starts to read the first page:

Night was beginning to fall as we turned off the main road. Ahead of us rose a gentle hill thrown into silhouette by the last of the sun. Along its base lights were starting to appear in cottage windows. The air was misty with wood smoke.

"There you are," said my companion. "Pretty, isn't it?"

"Yes," I agreed.

"You don't sound very sure," she said. "Not still worried, are you?"

"Well, it's always a bit nerve-racking when a young woman invites you home to meet her parents for the first time."

"Oh, that's happened to you a lot, has it?"

"Once or twice. And it's *especially* nerve-racking when her father's a doctor. You keep imagining he's going to take one look at you and say, 'Don't think much of this specimen. Fallen arches, I shouldn't wonder.' "

"Idiot!" she said, laughing. "Daddy's not like that at all. Ah, here's the crossroads."

All I could see were two tiny openings to left and right, each no wider than a footpath.

"That's a bit of an exaggeration, isn't it?" I said. "Cross*lanes*, more like."

"Well, that's what you may call them, my fine Lunnon gentleman. But to a simple country girl like me they're cross*roads*. And whenever I see *that*, I know it means I'm home again."

She pointed to an old-fashioned signpost on the corner. I glanced at it and read:

Peveril on the Swift ¼.

Mark looks up at Lou. She nods. He starts riffling through the pages. The names fly up at him: *Dauntless, Makepeace, Hoskins, Gallion, Hermitage, Waggon, Pintail, Patty, Paul, Patty, Paul, Patty, Paul, Patty . . .*

"I don't . . ." he says. "I mean, is it? . . . You know, *my* stories?"

She shakes her head. "Look at the end," she says, leaning forward and lifting the pages. "Well, it isn't finished, so it's not quite the end. But as far as he got with it."

I parked in front of the Waggon and got out. Everything seemed pretty much as I remembered it. Except for one thing: the whole place was quiet as the grave. I could still hear the rush of the weir in the valley, which meant that at least the Swift was still going about its business, but apart from that there was nothing. No voices, no footsteps, no traffic noise. For the first time in my life, I knew what it must have been like for the chaps who boarded the *Mary Celeste*.

I started slowly down the High Street. The first thing that struck me was that all the curtains were closed. As a general rule, people only draw their curtains in broad daylight if they've something to hide. By the law of averages, you'd expect a couple of shady customers in a place the size of Peveril on the Swift. But an entire street full of them? What the devil could they all be up to?

When I was almost at the bottom, I saw a chance to find out. Someone had left a tiny gap, through which I could just make a faint blue glow. In slow motion, so as not to alert whoever was inside to my presence, I crept up and put my eye to the glass.

I soon realized I needn't have worried. There was only one person there: a young woman, kneeling in front of her television like a worshipper at a shrine. Her eyes were glazed, her mouth set in a beatific smile. After half a minute or so she got up and turned towards the window. I've no idea what she was seeing, but it wasn't me. I could have broken into a dervish dance and she wouldn't have noticed. Slowly, as if it were part of a ritual, she raised a hand to her ear and left the room. A moment later the front door opened and she emerged into the street.

Instinctively I drew back, but again she looked straight through me. She shut the door without locking it and set off down the hill. I followed her. A moment later I saw where everyone had gone. They were thronged in front of the railway station, as still and silent as a pen full of cattle waiting outside the slaughterhouse. In the sea of faces I recognized Dr and Mrs Dauntless, Hoskins, Makepeace, Mr and Mrs Gallion, Patty. Like everyone else, they each had a hand cupped over one ear. Neither increasing or slackening her pace, the woman I was following meekly took her place among them. No one paid her the slightest attention. I elbowed my way to Mrs Dauntless and shook her by the shoulder.

"For God's sake!" I said. "What's happening here?"

It was as if I'd knocked into a piece of machinery and accidentally set it in motion. The hand over her ear twitched. Then she said — or *something* said, using her vocal cords:

"Seven-four-three-two goes where it is needed."

I looked frantically round. There was just one face missing: Paul Gallion. They still hadn't got Paul.

Like a madman, I dashed back up the hill and down Mill Street. Paul was the only hope now. I was almost at the Old Mill when the door opened.

"Paul!" I yelled.

He stopped, his eyes staring blankly at me, his hand to his ear.

"Eight-nine-two-zero goes where it is needed."

Mark looks up again. Lou is watching him, her eyes wide with concern.

"See?"

He nods. "Why? . . ."

She shakes her head. "He couldn't make up his own place, I suppose. So he took yours. And all the people living in it. Without telling you." She hesitates. "Now you see, do you? Why I told them? Because he stole Peveril. Peveril on the Swift! And did *that* to it. And I'm your friend."

He's only ten. He still doesn't have the full measure yet of what's happened to him, the scale of the catastrophe. But he knows enough to cry — abandoning himself to his grief more violently than he has ever done in his life. The tears are so fierce that he can barely see her. He shuts his eyes and drops his head into his hands.

After a moment, he feels her arms snake round him.

Right. That's it. Journey's end. The earth turns clockwise again. The Mallard resumes its sprint to Edinburgh, lurching obliviously over the points that might — for one split second, before that old fraud Time foreclosed the possibility for ever — have taken it in a different direction. In a reverse earthquake, rubble is resurrected as houses, Barratt homes erupt in fields and meadows. Clumsy Amstrads, quick as a card trick, riffle their way into PCs, PowerBooks, tablets. Outside in the street, butchered snippets of pop music summon people to their mobile phones.

Welcome back.

And just to complete the homecoming, this morning, another run-in with the powers that be.

Nothing new about a burglary, of course. *That* could have happened anywhere, any time. No, it's the aftermath that drives the point home.

*Please note: for quality and training purposes, this call may be recorded. If you would like to request a quote, please press one. If you are calling about an existing policy, please press two . . .*

I negotiate my way through the numerized labyrinth, 2, 1, 3, 2, 4.

*We are sorry for the delay. Your call is important to us. Please wait for the next available agent. Alternatively* — here the voice suddenly bursts like a ripe melon, as full of glee as if it were telling you you'd won the lottery — *why not visit our website, www . . .*

I shudder. How to translate, to reduce the whole mess of particularities and loose ends into the language of PINS and passwords and FAQs?

*Or to speak to one of our agents, please continue to hold*.

I hold. A seventeen-bar snatch of music — the kind of goopy, violin-rich confection they play to battery-hens to increase the yield of eggs — starts washing into my ear. When it's over, it begins again.

"You're through to Janice. How may I help you?"

"There's been a break-in. They've taken —"

"Let me stop you right there. What is your policy number?"

I tell her. I give her my full name. My postcode. My date of birth. The first and third digits of my security code.

"So what's the problem?"

I explain. I *try* to explain. They've got my wallet. And the car keys. And the car's still outside, so I need to have it towed to safety, and the locks changed.

"We'll send out a recovery vehicle. Can I take your credit or debit card number for the excess?"

"I haven't got a card number."

"I need a card number."

"I told you, I was burgled. My cards were in my wallet. Can't I give the guy cash, or a cheque or something?

"The computer needs a card number, before it'll authorize a call-out."

"So what am I supposed to do?"

"I need a number."

And the picture? The pastoral scene?

Time to tiptoe in and take a final gander.

Yes, it seems pretty much the same. Still a long-dead dog and a girl (not dead, thank God) and a boy on the threshold of his first — his terminal — experience of betrayal. Still a bearded rogue in a smock, about to piss on a pair of kids.

But there *is* a difference. There, in his Glacier Mint eyes. For years, when I looked into them, all I could see was a Judas: the practised assurance, the conscienceless instinct for self-preservation of a lifelong liar and cheat.

I still see that now. But mixed with it, I also, unmistakably, glimpse something else: the unwanted but inescapable burden of a prophet.

**Other titles published by Ulverscroft:**

## NOT FORGETTING THE WHALE

**John Ironmonger**

When a young man washes up on the sands of St Piran in Cornwall, he is quickly rescued by the villagers. From the retired village doctor and the beachcomber, to the priest's flirtatious wife and the romantic novelist, they take this lost soul into their midst. What the villagers don't know, though, is that Joe Haak is a city analyst who has fled London, fearing he may — inadvertently — have caused a global financial collapse. But is the end of the world really nigh? And what of the whale that lurks in the bay?

# SLEEPING ON JUPITER

## Anuradha Roy

A train stops at a railway station, and a young woman jumps off. She has wild hair, sloppy clothes, a distracted air. The sudden violence of what happens next leaves the other passengers gasping . . . The train terminates at Jarmuli, a temple town by the sea. Here, among pilgrims, priests and ashrams, three old women disembark — only to encounter the girl once again. What is someone like her doing in this remote place? Over the next five days, the old women live out their long-planned dream of a holiday together; their temple guide finds ecstasy in forbidden love; and the girl is joined by a photographer battling his own demons. As the lives of these disparate people overlap and collide, Jarmuli is revealed as a place with a long, dark past that transforms all who encounter it . . .

# THE PAST

## Tessa Hadley

Three adult sisters and their brother meet up at their grandparents' old cottage during one long, hot summer. The house is in need of expensive renovation, and the siblings must decide whether to commit the funds or sell up. But under the idyllic surface, tensions are growing. Alice has brought with her Kasim, the twenty-year-old son of her ex-boyfriend — who makes plans to seduce the quiet Molly, Roland's sixteen-year-old daughter. Meanwhile, Fran's young children uncover an ugly secret in a ruined cottage in the woods. Passion erupts where it's least expected, blasting the self-possession of Harriet, the eldest sister. And Roland has come with his new (third) wife, whom his sisters don't like. A way of life — bourgeois, literate, ritualised, Anglican — winds down to its inevitable end: both a loss and a release . . .

# THE SUMMER OF SECRETS

## Sarah Jasmon

The summer the Dovers move in next door, sixteen-year-old Helen's lonely world is at once a more thrilling place. She is infatuated with the bohemian family, especially the petulant and charming daughter Victoria. As the long, hot days stretch out in front of them, Helen and Victoria grow inseparable. But when a stranger appears, Helen begins to question whether the secretive Dover family are really what they seem. It's the kind of summer when anything seems possible — and then something goes terribly wrong . . .